Patricia Lawson was born in Buckinghamshire. The daughter of a factory worker, she left school at sixteen to work. She has been writing since the 1960s, and *A Price Above Rubies* is her second novel. She lives with her husband in Wiltshire.

Also by Patricia Lawson

The Tangled Garden

A Price
Above Rubies

Patricia Lawson

KNIGHT

Copyright © 1991 Patricia Lawson

The right of Patricia Lawson to be identified as the Author of
the Work has been asserted by her in accordance with the
Copyright, Designs and Patents Act 1988.

First published in 1991
by HEADLINE BOOK PUBLISHING PLC

First published in paperback in 1992
by HEADLINE BOOK PUBLISHING PLC

This edition published 2003 by Knight,
an imprint of Caxton Publishing Group

10 9 8 7 6 5 4 3 2 1

ISBN 1 84067 371 0

Phototypeset by Medcalf Type Ltd, Bicester, Oxon

Printed and bound in Great Britain by
Cox & Wyman Ltd, Reading, Berkshire

Caxton Publishing Group
20 Bloomsbury Street
London
WC1B 3JH

**For Heather,
with my love**

ACKNOWLEDGEMENTS

I am not an historian. In writing this novel I relied upon the expertise of many people and have read many books. In particular I am indebted to the following authors – John Adair for the information gained from his *Founding Fathers*, Antonia Fraser whose book *The Weaker Vessel* taught me so much concerning the role of women in the seventeenth century, and Brian Dobbs for his *Drury Lane*.

I would also like to thank the American Indian Department at Hay Castle, Hay-on-Wye who assisted me in my research, and to extend a very special word of thanks to Nanepashemet, research associate and curator of the Wampanoag Indian Program, Plimoth Plantation, Massachusetts, who so kindly supplied the names of my Native American characters.

Patricia Lawson
Wiltshire

'Who can find a virtuous woman? For her price is far above rubies.'

Proverbs 31:10

A Price
Above Rubies

CHAPTER 1

June 1641
The Cotswolds

There were no bells at the wedding: bells were the music of the Devil. But there was joy in abundance.

The path to the church had been strewn with rushes and with flowers gathered early that morning from gardens, from hedgerows, and from the meadow. The congregation was dressed in Sunday best and there was laughter and gaiety as Lucy was led in by her bride-men. Bridesmaids, carrying bouquets of rosemary, accompanied the groom. Now the couple stood together, about to take their vows.

Margaret sat and watched her brother with his bride. At seventeen, soon it would be her turn to wed. The prospect made her nervous but she did not question the necessity of it, nor the inevitability.

'Wilt thou, Tobias Hawkins, take this woman to be thy lawful wedded wife?'

Tobias' reply was quiet and almost inaudible. 'I will.'

'And wilt thou, Lucy Cobb, take this man to be thy husband?'

'I will.'

The preacher asked for the ring — a small enamelled band — to be placed upon her finger. Tobias fumbled, nervous, and jumped visibly when the Reverend William Dillington raised his voice as if it were from the Almighty Himself. 'Those whom God hath joined together, let no man put asunder.'

Tobias smiled sheepishly; he did not like to be the centre of attention.

The congregation intoned a psalm, unaccompanied by

musical instruments. Music was a pleasure so sensual that even the most devout of minds could be swayed from worship.

'The Lord is my shepherd. I shall not want.'

It was Margaret's favourite.

'He maketh me to lie down in green pastures. He leadeth me beside the still waters.'

It was comfortable and familiar. Beyond the churchyard wall sheep cropped the grass. The lives of all who stood here were governed in some way by the flocks which roamed the hills.

Margaret blushed and bowed her head. Already, even without music, her mind had taken flight across the hillside. And she must prepare herself for the sermon – a sermon which would last for at least an hour, or maybe nearer two. Today she was determined that she would pay attention. Later the family would discuss and analyse its content. She would be expected to have retained all that she had heard.

Beside her, her mother, Anne, sat listening intently, turning every now and then to flip through the pages of her Bible, locating the relevant text with practised ease, and marking the page with a thread. Others, too, were searching their Bibles, but most were content just to sit and listen: they were ill-taught to read their names, let alone their Bibles.

Her father, Nehemiah, sat stiff-backed in concentration. Margaret loved her father. Usually she sat beside him but today they were separated by the three younger sisters of whom she had been given charge. It was not an arduous task; all had been trained from an early age to sit in silence. Even now, baby Rachael, who was barely two, sat on the other side of her mother, sucking her fingers and drifting luxuriously into a doze. Soon Rachael would be the baby no more. Anne was again pregnant. A new infant would take Rachael's place come autumn.

Beyond Nehemiah sat her brother Samuel, younger than Margaret by less than a year. She blushed again when she saw him listening intently. Once more her mind had wandered. She closed her eyes, determined to pay attention.

An hour later they poured from the church, youngsters giving vent to high spirits which had been kept in check.

'The favour's mine.' A young man playfully snatched one of the ribbons from Lucy's sleeve.

'And mine.'

'And mine.'

Lucy laughed as young hands tugged at the brightly coloured ribbons sewn, for the purpose, upon her russet dress. Within moments all were gone, and fluttered instead from the hats of the young men.

Tobias gently took her hand. 'Are you all right?'

'Yes, thank you.' She smiled, straightening her hair and smoothing down the fabric of her dress.

But even as she did so she squealed and laughed anew — this time because they were subjected to a hail of corngrains and pieces of oatcake. Tobias raised his arm to shield her.

She was a pretty girl of much the same age as Margaret, but she was fair-skinned where Margaret was dark. Today, as befitted a bride, her hair was hanging loose about her shoulders, with a circlet of wheat and myrtle upon her brow.

'The gloves,' someone said. 'Where are the gloves?'

Several of the young men carried gloves, richly embroidered and worked with beads. They were a gift from the groom. Now Lucy took off her own gloves and gave them to the bride-men who had led her into church.

'Come,' called Nehemiah, 'there's food and ale in Dunscombe.' He led the party out of the churchyard, across the hills towards their own home village.

It was a long walk: Dunscombe lay some four miles away. As they reached the crest of the first hill they could see the spire of its own parish church in the distance. It was a fine enough building, but inside were practised the rituals of an Anglican faith, so polluted by the influence of the hated Archbishop Laud that it smacked of little less than Popery. To worship there was anathema to the family, who chose to walk the four miles each Sunday to a church where the preacher preached of true religion, and never failed to deliver a good and lengthy sermon.

They walked easily, with the steady pace of those used to walking long distances, laughing and chatting as they went. The older children ran on ahead, while those too small to walk were carried by their parents.

Two women, heavily pregnant, were seated upon the

3

backs of ponies which shambled lazily at the pace of the walkers. Anne was only six months into her time; she walked with ease among her family.

Margaret loved these hills. She loved the vast expanse of open grassland, sheep starting to attention and scattering in all directions as the party forged its way across their midst. She loved the spring of short turf, and the smell of it — that certain scent of grass bruised by passing feet, combined with all the other scents of open grassland; the scent of fresh clear air, of herbs and flowers and of sheep; the musky combination of oily wool and dung.

She had travelled more widely than most who lived in the village. With her father she had journeyed to towns where they had bought wool or sold their cloth. Even so, she had never ventured beyond a radius of some thirty miles. Most had gone no further than the market town some eight miles to the south.

Here and there, as they walked, they passed a tiny hamlet sheltering within a fold of the hill — a few houses huddled together, protected from the wind which roared across these parts in winter, a farm or two situated where time and countless generations had located pockets of fertile soil. Some were prosperous by the standards of the time, with crops growing in their fields; others barely scratched a living. Hovels hardly fit to be called a home were shelter for the families of labourers who broke their backs in endless toil.

They had almost reached Dunscombe when a horseman rode up behind them.

'It's Rupert,' cried Tobias. 'He's arrived in time to join the celebration.'

They stood and waited as he cantered the last few hundred yards towards them. A striking youth, he had a dash and style about him which contrasted with the homely cut of others among the party.

'You've chosen a good moment to return home,' greeted Nehemiah. 'It's the day of the wedding.'

'It's more than timely, Uncle, I'm here to help with the hay harvest. But I knew of the wedding — I wouldn't have missed it for the world.'

He reached down from the saddle to shake the hand of his cousin Tobias. 'You're to be congratulated, my friend.

There's many a man would pay dearly for such a prize.'

Lucy lowered her head and blushed.

'And how are you, my dear Aunt Anne?' He reached out his arm about Anne's shoulders and kissed her, full and hard, upon the cheek.

'I'm well,' she laughed, and pushed him away. 'And you're mighty forward since you went to Oxford.'

'But you like it well enough,' he laughed, and kissed her again.

Margaret had kept her distance on the edge of the crowd. 'Margaret, don't you welcome your cousin Rupert?'

'It's good to see you,' she said; but she held back when he reached out his hand towards her. 'You've been gone a long time.'

'Too long, it seems. You grow in my absences.'

She turned and walked away, feeling uncomfortable.

Her father glanced after her, then turned to Rupert. 'There's celebrating to be done,' he said.

'Then let's away and get it started.' He turned his horse and they all began once more to make their way across the final hill.

Rupert waited until the party was well strung out, then he spurred his horse in the direction of Margaret who was walking alone.

'Methinks I'm not welcome.' He swung himself down to walk beside her.

'You're always welcome. You're part of our family.'

'You don't seem too pleased.'

She looked at him. 'What am I supposed to say?'

'Have I done something to offend you?'

She hesitated. 'No, of course not.'

'Then why are you behaving so coolly?'

'I'm not,' she said. 'You're imagining it. I'm no different to the way I've always been.'

He studied her for a moment, then said lightly, 'How do you like my new doublet and breeches?'

'Very grand. You've become a fine gentleman since you went to Oxford.'

The doublet was of green velvet, unbuttoned to reveal a shirt of white linen. His falling band was edged with lace, and his breeches, of matching green velvet, were trimmed

5

with ribbon loops and braid. Above his bucket-top boots showed a froth of lace boot hose; his spurs jangled as he walked beside her.

'You're mixing in fine company at the university.'

'Fine enough,' he said. 'But it's good to be home.'

A transition had occurred within their relationship. 'We're no longer children,' she said aloud.

'Indeed we're not, but I much prefer you as you are today.'

'I'm the same as I've always been.'

He smiled at her. 'Do you remember how we used to play?'

'It was a long time ago.'

'It's a different game we'd play today,' he said.

She turned from him abruptly.

He was sorry that he had said it. 'I've stayed too long at the university,' he said. 'I must hurry home sooner next time.'

She was not sure how to respond but a sudden buzz of activity turned their attention towards a nearby thicket of scrub and trees. The children had gone on ahead, playing in the undergrowth. Now they came running out, babbling and tripping over themselves in their haste to retreat. An older boy, more foolhardy than the rest, turned and threw a stone.

'Foolish boy!' His mother caught him and slapped him soundly about the ear. 'Now look what you've done.'

An old woman hobbled out of the thicket, a bundle of kindling twigs clutched beneath her arm.

An air of tension had arisen within the group. 'The stone must have hit her,' someone whispered. 'There's blood on her.'

'He's made himself immune by drawing blood.'

'And put the rest of us in danger.'

'Walk on,' said Nehemiah calmly. 'She won't trouble us.'

They fell silent but the old woman hobbled towards them, gabbling something unintelligible.

'Just walk on,' said Nehemiah again.

They quickened their pace, walking stiffly, with quick furtive glances in her direction.

Rupert swung back upon his horse. 'Don't,' cautioned

someone, but he headed towards her at a steady pace, so that she was forced to turn back into the thicket. He followed a few steps.

'. . . curse on her,' he heard her mutter. 'And make her barren.'

He shivered and spurred his horse to re-join the group.

'Her head was bleeding,' said Margaret.

'It was only a small wound.'

'What did she say?'

'Nothing that I could understand.' He determined to tell no one lest it should come to the ears of the bride.

'She's to be pitied.'

'She's to be cursed,' he said. 'Curse her with her own curses.'

The incident had brought a change of atmosphere. An air of subdued tension did not dissipate until they reached the village. They came down to it from off the hilltop, past the parish church with its bell tower and hated aroma of incense, down towards the clusters of houses dotted about the central green and along the course of a small, fast-flowing river.

Nehemiah's house stood in the main street. It was modest in size, though larger than many others. Half-timbered, it had a jettied first storey which housed the weaving loom.

A table had been set out in the street before it, piled high with roast meats and hams, a large carp, several capons and pies, tarts, cheeses and loaves of bread, and several bowls of wild berries.

They were hungry from the exertion of their walk. They fell upon the food, helping themselves to thick slices of meat, with hunks of bread, washing it down with quantities of ale and beer.

A wagon arrived from the other end of the street and beside it, on horseback, Anne's sister Elizabeth rode pillion with her husband.

'A cask of my finest wine to help along the celebration,' announced Sir Henry as he dismounted. 'And wishes of good health to all who drink it.'

He gave Tobias a hearty slap of congratulation across the back and set about organizing the removal of the cask from the wagon.

Elizabeth, too, greeted the couple; but her eyes were upon Rupert. 'You look well, my son.' She embraced him with warm affection. 'It's good to have you home.'

'Home for the hay harvest,' he smiled. 'And to greet my dear mother.'

She held him at arm's length. 'Such fine clothes,' she chided. 'And such extravagance.'

'It's only the fashion. Don't you like it?'

'I like it well enough,' she smiled. 'But my son's too much a man.'

'All sons become men,' he laughed. 'It's the way of things.'

'Come,' she led him away from the main body of the party, 'tell me all about yourself and about the goings-on at Oxford.'

Later, their appetites satisfied, the younger members of the wedding party made for the green. Sounds of wild horseplay began to echo through the village. Two young men wrestled, while another group kicked a sheep's bladder in a rough, undisciplined game of football. An itinerant fiddler, hearing of the wedding, had turned up to play and groups were dancing, interrupted every now and then when invaded by the footballers.

Anne sat with Elizabeth, watching the dancing. 'It was a fine ceremony,' she commented. 'The Reverend Dillington gave a stirring sermon.'

'I don't understand why it couldn't have been at our own parish church,' said her sister. 'It makes no sense to walk four miles to distant churches.'

'It makes sense to all who believe in what is right.'

'And it lays them open to the abuse of "Puritan".'

Anne was unmoved by the comment. 'They may call us any name they choose,' she said. 'Those who walk openly in the name of God will be called many harsh names.'

'You could serve Him just as well in our own parish church.'

'And bow at altar rails, with a priest in robes and a prayer book in his hand?' she retorted. 'It's little effort to walk where we can find a proper preacher.'

8

Elizabeth sighed and turned to other matters. 'I hear you met with the hag Agnes Bennett on your return.'

'We did. And she was bruised by a child who ought to be whipped for his behaviour.'

'There are those who foresee danger.'

Anne shook her head. 'I really don't believe her to be in league with the Devil.'

'There are plenty who do.'

'There's enough ill-fortune abounding, without accusing an old woman who has no husband or family.'

Elizabeth raised an eyebrow. 'She is given to cursing. And there are those who'd swear she bears the mark.'

'There are those who'd swear to anything to bring ill fortune upon others,' said Anne. 'I'd rather offer a little charity to one who's suffered enough.'

Elizabeth shrugged. 'Perhaps you're right. We've more than enough trouble in our lives, without concerning ourselves with Agnes Bennett.' She glanced across at the bride and groom. 'Lucy's a pretty girl,' she said. 'Tobias deserves to be happy.'

Anne nodded. 'She'll make him a good wife.'

'She's a little tender in stature, but no doubt she'll fill out with time.'

'She's sturdier than she appears. And she brought a good dowry. She was by far the best of the girls available.'

Elizabeth conceded the point. 'And you'll be needing her help.' She inclined her head towards Margaret who was dancing a short distance away in the company of Rupert. 'Margaret will be leaving to take marriage vows of her own quite soon.'

'Aye, if her father stops dallying,' sighed Anne. 'There's no one he considers fit to take her.'

Elizabeth laughed. 'A belief of many fathers, I hear.'

'But not one which will settle her future. There's no end to the young men he has in mind for her, but he's no nearer to making a choice.'

'I hear there are a number of young men who'd be more than eager to take her.'

'But none whom Nehemiah considers good enough.'

Elizabeth laughed again. 'He always has shown favour towards her. No man ever loved a daughter more.'

'But he treats her as a son. Takes her with him wherever he goes. Swears he's come to depend on her.' Anne sighed and threw up her hands in exasperation. 'I ask you, is it a maid's place to be bargaining over the price of wool or discussing the sale of cloth?'

'I'm sure you exaggerate. He enjoys her company, but he loves her far too much to jeopardize her position.'

'Perhaps. But I shall be glad when he's found her a husband. It's time she gave herself to the more seemly pursuit of raising children.'

Nehemiah and Sir Henry were also watching Margaret and Rupert as they danced. 'That young pup of yours pays a mite too much heed to Margaret,' observed Nehemiah. 'He hasn't left her side since he arrived home.'

'They've been friends since childhood.'

'But I don't care for the way he looks at her now.'

Sir Henry roared with laughter. 'The boy's learned the pleasures of a man.'

'But not with Margaret.'

'I'm sure he means nothing by it,' said Sir Henry. 'He merely recognizes a comely maid when he happens upon one.' He looked towards Margaret with a nod of approval. 'She'll make a welcome catch for some young man.'

'I've plans for her,' said Nehemiah. 'She's got a fine mind.'

Sir Henry turned to him with a look of astonishment. 'A woman with a fine mind is not a catch,' he said. 'She's a liability.'

'There'll be some man who'll appreciate her. But I've yet to find him.'

Sir Henry looked at him sideways but decided to reserve further comment.

'What of Rupert?' enquired Nehemiah.

'Arrangements are well in hand. He's to be betrothed to the eldest daughter of Sir John Butler. He's got spice in his veins. It'll be as well for him to marry.'

'He has, indeed,' said Nehemiah, looking again at the two dancing on the green.

'Sir John's without sons. In due course Rupert should do well from it.'

'A merchant, I hear, like yourself. Well established in London.'

'My warehouses could hardly compare with Sir John's. He deals in the very best of silks and spices.'

Nehemiah hesitated to ask why Rupert had been accepted for such honour.

'She's not the most beautiful of women,' conceded Sir Henry, 'but she's a good catch.'

The footballers came careering across the green towards them. The two men moved amiably to one side in order to let them pass.

'How did you find the city last time you were there?' asked Nehemiah as they resumed their seats.

'In turmoil. There's trouble brewing. It's going to affect us all.'

'But surely there's a need to clear the air, with Lord Strafford gone to the block? And now, at last, thank God, Parliament's rid us of that cur, Archbishop Laud.'

'It's a sad day when an Archbishop is confined to the Tower.'

'Aye, maybe, but it's worse still that he tried to lead us all back towards the stench of Popery.'

'It won't end with Laud and Strafford,' commented Sir Henry. 'Parliament's pressing the King too far. They've even had the audacity to pass a bill forbidding its dissolution without the members' own consent.'

'There's a need for strength,' said Nehemiah. 'He'd rule without Parliament forever, given the chance.'

'But it'll do no good to harass him. There's enough danger to the country from the Scots. And now it seems the Irish are about to rise.'

'It's little wonder that the Scots are in revolt. There's not a godly man alive who wouldn't rise up in protest when the King insists on imposing the prayer book upon him.'

Sir Henry shrugged his shoulders. 'I really don't see why the prayer book service should cause so much dissension.'

'Then you know nothing of true religion,' retorted Nehemiah.

Sir Henry had no wish to dispute with his brother-in-law. 'The King needs to raise an army in readiness against the Irish, but it's causing great difference of opinion.'

11

'And no wonder. Who's to say that he won't turn the army upon his own people?'

Sir Henry stiffened visibly. 'I know it's been said, but who could seriously charge the King with such an intention?'

'Anyone who recognizes a tyrant when he sees one! This King of ours would do anything to impose his will against the wishes of the people.'

Sir Henry drew the line at such comment. 'That's little less than treason, sir.'

Both men realized they had gone too far. They let a moment or two lapse while they gazed out across the revelry of the wedding celebrations. Eventually Sir Henry said quietly, 'I fear a time will come when every man will have to choose whether he's for King or for Parliament. It'll be a sad day.'

'Aye,' said Nehemiah, equally quietly. 'But there's no doubt which path the man of God will have to choose.'

Margaret and Rupert were unaware of the seriousness of their fathers' conversation, or even of the fact that their parents were watching them.

'Come,' said Rupert. He led her away from a particularly vigorous jig. 'I'm quite tired out by all this boisterous merriment.' Already they had danced to 'Sellingers Round', 'Hunting the Fox', 'Tom Tyler', and 'John Come Kiss Me'.

Margaret laughed and walked over to the still-laden table where she helped herself to a piece of marchpane.

'Will you walk with me?'

She pretended not to hear.

'It's a warm evening. You could show me the hiding places of our youth.'

'You know them well enough without my showing you.' She turned away and began smoothing the ruffled tablecloth.

'But I need to walk with you again in the places where we played.'

She cast him an indecisive glance.

He smiled at her gently. 'There really isn't anything to fear, you know.'

She blushed. 'I think we'd best return to the dancing.'

'Please.' He took her arm and led her gently in the

opposite direction. 'I'm only asking you to walk. Where's the harm in that?'

She half wished to apologize. 'It's a pity that we need to grow,' she voiced again.

'There's nothing for you to fear. I've loved you too long to cause you harm.'

She nodded and returned his smile. 'You've always been like a brother, and I thank you for it.'

They walked down the dusty, rutted street, skirted the fairy ring and the huge old oak tree which had stood for centuries upon the village green, then made their way out into the hills.

It was a fine clear evening with hardly a stirring of a breeze. The scents of June came to them as they disturbed the vegetation. It was the time of midsummer magic, a time when fairies danced and all kinds of secrets unknown to man were almost revealed. The feel of it hung heavy in the air.

'How do you like Oxford?' she asked. 'Do you have to work hard?'

'Aye, and play. There's no work without play.'

'What kind of play?'

'Oh, hunting — all kinds of revelry. We drink rather more than is good for us; play a mite too much at the cards and dice.'

'You've changed,' she said. 'I don't know if I like the person you've become.'

He smiled. 'I'm still the same old Rupert. I'm not debauched.'

'I didn't mean . . . '

'It's all part of my education, learning about life in all its facets.'

They came to a small hollow within a fold of the hill. 'Shall we sit down?' He indicated a fallen tree trunk and brushed a few dead leaves from it with the side of his hand.

She nodded and sat down beside him.

'Why do you fear the coming of womanhood?' he asked after a few moments had elapsed.

'I don't fear it,' she said truthfully. 'It's just that things have changed between us.'

'Don't you like it that I find you beautiful?'

'It's unseemly.'

He threw back his head and laughed. 'There are many things which are unseemly,' he said, 'but which are mighty enjoyable.'

'But not between us,' she said seriously. 'We're friends; we've always been so.'

'Yes,' he said quietly. He turned and looked at her, no longer laughing. 'We've always been friends.' He reached out his hand and touched her arm. 'What plans have they for your future?'

'Father's spoken about a number of young men. He hasn't decided yet which one to choose.'

'And which one of them would you prefer?'

She shrugged. 'I don't know. It's not for me to say.'

'Come on, you can tell me.'

'I don't know,' she said again. 'I'll do whatever Father thinks is best for me.'

'But you must have some preference.'

'I'm sure he knows much better than I do who's best for me.'

He was silent for a long time, then said, 'Don't you ever think of love?'

She looked at him sharply. 'Of course I do. I'll learn to love the man who marries me.'

'But there's the other kind.'

She moved uncomfortably. 'Yes,' she said. 'It's called amorousness. And you promised . . . '

'They say it's a wonderful feeling.'

'Maybe, but those who fall into its clutches soon envy those whose marriages are built on firmer foundations.'

He said nothing again for a while.

'There are more serious considerations,' she said to break the silence. 'There's much more to think about when arranging a marriage.'

'I've heard that your own father and mother married for amorous love.'

'What nonsense you do talk! My father would never act so irresponsibly.'

'Then why didn't your mother marry into a better family? She could have married as my mother did.'

'She did well enough,' Margaret retorted, rising to the defence of her father. 'I can assure you that you're mistaken.'

'Perhaps.' He got up and walked a few steps, idly kicking at the loose gravel on the hillside.

'It couldn't have been,' she mused. 'Everyone knows that children of passion are weakened by it. You've only got to look at us to see that we're all strong and healthy.'

'Perhaps,' he said again, 'it's best forgotten.'

'Yes, I think it is.'

He continued to stand a short distance away kicking at the gravel.

'What of your own future?' she asked more kindly.

He held her eyes for a long time. 'I'm about to be betrothed.'

'Oh?'

'To Isobel Butler.'

'I hadn't heard.'

'We're to be married in the spring.'

'Oh,' she said again. 'Are you happy?'

'You know I'm not happy.'

'Oh, Rupert.'

'She's got the body of a cornsack, and a face which could frighten an ox.'

Despite herself, she giggled. 'You're exaggerating.'

'Maybe. But she could hardly be called attractive.'

'She'll grow more beautiful as you learn to love her.'

'I doubt it.'

'Does she try to please you?'

He looked at her. 'Yes, I must admit she tries.'

'Then what are you complaining about? That's the very best foundation for marriage.'

'I know, but . . .'

'But what?'

He came and knelt before her, holding both her hands in his own. 'Oh, Margaret, why can't we marry as our hearts dictate?'

She pulled away from him and rose quickly to her feet. 'Rupert, you promised . . .'

'I need to speak of it.'

'You said last time . . . you promised you'd never speak of it again.'

'I know. I've tried but I can't help it. Margaret — I've just got to have you.'

15

'Rupert!' She was shocked.

'You know it as well as I do. You've known it for a long time. You've always known it. Ever since we were children.'

'I know no such thing.'

'And now I'm about to be betrothed to someone else.'

She looked at him. 'Well, you must have agreed to it.'

'I tried. After what you said, I tried to forget. But I can't. Oh, Margaret, I can't go through with it.'

'Then you must ask to be excused from the contract and find someone else.'

'I don't want anyone else,' he said. 'I want you.'

'You can't have me,' she said. 'I'm your cousin.'

'Cousins are free to marry.'

She raised her voice. 'Rupert, you deliberately misunderstand me. I'm your cousin not a suitable bride for you.'

'Let me be the judge of that.'

'You're like a brother. And even if it weren't so, Sir Henry would never allow it. He'd laugh at the very idea.'

Rupert lowered his eyes. He knew it to be true as much as Margaret.

'His son marrying the daughter of a master weaver! I can just imagine what he'd say.'

'Then we'll have to find some way to convince him.'

'I don't want to convince him, Rupert. Whatever strange notion you keep in your head, it's yours alone. It's nothing to do with me.'

'It's everything to do with you.'

'It's nothing to do with me,' she repeated. 'I want no part in it.' She stormed off and sat on a log with her back towards him.

'Why don't you admit it?' He left her alone for a time then came up behind her. 'You know it as well as I do.'

'I know no such thing.'

'You love me too.'

'I do not.'

He took her gently by the shoulders and turned her round. 'Look me in the eye and tell me that you have no feeling for me.'

She let out an exasperated sigh. 'I'll always love you, but as a brother. This notion you have is sheer foolishness.'

'I want to marry you.'

'Well, you can't. And the sooner you accept that fact the more comfortable it will be for you.' She looked at him. 'And for me.'

'I could make you so happy.'

'Oh, Rupert, it's very sweet of you but my father could never put up the kind of dowry which would be expected, and . . .'

'To hell with the dowry.'

She shook her head at him. 'Don't be silly, dear, of course it matters. You can't go against all convention, just because of some foolish notion which has taken over your head. You're heir to Oakbourne.'

'But if you love me . . .'

'I don't love you,' she almost shouted. 'I keep telling you I don't love you.'

He was hurt by that. He turned his head and a look of pain crossed his face. 'You do,' he said. 'You just won't admit it for fear of upsetting our parents.'

She was sorry to have hurt him. She put out a hand and touched his sleeve. 'You'd most certainly upset Sir Henry,' she said gently. 'There's no doubt about that.'

'But I'm prepared to face his anger if only you'll have me.'

'I won't,' she said. 'I don't know how many times I have to tell you.'

His shoulders had slumped. He turned his back on her. For a moment she suspected that he was crying.

'I've got to be going,' she said gently. 'It's getting late. They'll have missed me.'

He shrugged without turning round. 'Then you'd better go. There's not much point in your staying.'

'I'm sorry.' She hovered behind him. 'I didn't mean to hurt you.'

'It's all right,' he said but he still did not look at her.

'Well, goodbye then.' She kissed him lightly on the back of his head and walked away.

As she walked back to the village she glanced up at the sinking sun and realized it to be even later than she had thought.

'Why, Margaret, where have you been?' Anne came up behind her as she hurried across the green. 'You've almost missed the bedding.'

17

'Sorry, Mother.' She was quite breathless. 'I've been walking with Rupert and forgot the time.'

'Then hurry now. Lucy needs you.'

'Yes, Mother, I'm sorry.'

She made her way back along the street, still turning over in her mind the conversation she had just had with Rupert. As she opened the door she could hear the sound of girls' voices and laughter from upstairs.

Lucy was standing surrounded by the bridesmaids who were giggling and chattering as they removed her clothing. Her gown lay across the bed and she stood in her bodice and her petticoat.

'Oh, Margaret, you're here. I'm so glad you've come.'

The girls were removing the narrow ribbon sash from her waist and untying the lacing of her bodice.

'Are you afraid?' Margaret stooped and began to unfasten the skirt.

'A little . . . apprehensive.'

'There's nothing to fear. Tobias is the gentlest of men.'

'I know. It's not Tobias; it's my . . . my duty.'

'You'll manage easily.' She said it lightly, though she was not sure that she would have been so confident had she been standing in the other girl's shoes. 'Tobias won't ask more of you than you'll readily give.'

'But I give him everything,' said Lucy earnestly. 'He's my husband: I want to serve him.'

'There's nothing to worry about.'

Lucy nodded, but she still looked apprehensive.

'Here.' Margaret turned and reached out for a small pillow which she had placed beside the bed. 'I've made you a gift to bring you pleasant dreams.'

Her mind was still centred upon the conversation with Rupert. She wondered what would happen if he spoke openly of it within the family.

The pillow was of linen embroidered in her finest hand and stuffed with feathers, painstakingly plucked and cleaned. Aromatic herbs and lavender gave off a delicate perfume.

'You're all so kind to me.' Lucy leant forward and kissed her on the cheek. 'You've welcomed me so readily into the family.'

Margaret returned the kiss, her mind still distracted. 'We're happy to have so sweet a bride for our brother.'

'Are you quite well?' Lucy became aware of her distraction.

'Yes, of course.' She attempted to bring her mind back to the matter in hand.

They had disrobed Lucy to her undergarments and knitted stockings. 'Throw the stocking, Lucy,' cried the girls. Laughing, she untied the garters from above and below her knee.

She distributed them among the girls. Then, removing a stocking and holding it above her head, she whirled it once or twice before letting it fly across the room. The girls leapt and grabbed.

'Margaret – catch!'

But Margaret made no attempt to reach out for it.

'You were dancing with Rupert,' said Lucy as they resumed the undressing.

'Yes.' She almost blushed.

'He's become so grand since he went to Oxford.'

'Yes.'

'And handsome.'

'Yes, I suppose he is.' She wished that Lucy would find some other topic of conversation.

'And soon to be married, so Tobias tells me. He heard it from Sir Henry.'

'Yes, so I hear. To someone named Isobel Butler.'

'How exciting.'

'Some time in the spring.'

'We're all to be wed.'

'It comes to us all,' said Margaret wryly. Lucy looked at her.

'Tobias and I; next it will be Rupert; soon it will be your turn.'

Margaret felt a pang of embarrassment and discomfort.

'I wonder who you'll . . . '

'I've no idea,' she said. 'But you'd better get into your nightgown. Tobias is coming up the stairs.'

He was accompanied by his party of young men, pale-faced and nervous for he, too, had been undressed by his companions. The girls kept them waiting outside the door until Lucy was safely tucked into the bed.

There was insufficient room in the small chamber for all the wedding guests who pushed and jostled beyond the door. Others thronged the stairs or stood beneath the window calling out loud – and often coarse – advice and salutations. The young men bade Tobias to climb into the bed.

The ribald humour continued for some time until, eventually, Nehemiah called out to them, 'Away, my friends, or they'll never get the opportunity to carry out your instructions.'

In the midst of the confusion, Agnes Bennett hobbled down the street towards her hovel at the far end of the village. The crowd opened up to let her pass. She looked neither to left nor to right, but muttered to herself as she hobbled on arthritic legs, misshapen long ago by rickets.

As she crossed the green, she stooped painfully to retrieve a loaf of bread which lay discarded upon the grass. She tucked it beneath her skirts, and made her way home to the first supper she had eaten in a week.

Alone now, Tobias and Lucy lay silent and far apart, each aware of every movement which the other made but neither knowing how to bridge the gap which lay between them.

'You've eaten well? Have you enjoyed the celebration?'

'Oh, yes. I've never enjoyed myself more.'

'I'm glad.'

There was silence.

'Margaret has made me this pillow,' said Lucy shyly. 'Everyone has made me so welcome.'

'They're pleased to have you with us.' He paused and almost looked at her but without quite catching her eye. He coughed. 'So am I.'

She smiled and coloured but did not reply.

'I almost feel that I know you well already.'

'Me, too.'

'We've sat in church so many times since we were children. I remember, too, how we played . . . '

'And once . . . ' She hesitated and blushed. 'I expect you've forgotten.'

'No, I haven't forgotten. And I remember how many times I looked at you as you grew to be a maid.'

She lowered her eyes and flushed scarlet.

'But we've never talked much,' he said.

'We've conversed in plenty since we've been betrothed. Why, I do believe you could take me to task for prattling, the way we've conversed these last few months.'

'But never quite so close . . .' He swallowed hard. 'Never quite so close as here . . . in bed.'

He felt her involuntary movement beyond the space which separated them. 'I'd imagine,' she said timorously, 'that conversation is conversation, no matter where one happens to hold it.'

'Yes, I expect you're right.'

Once again the silence engulfed them.

The sound of dancing and of merriment drifted up to them from the green. Below, in the street, the crowd was roaring on a pair of wrestlers writhing on the hard-baked soil.

'I'm afraid,' said Lucy at last, 'that I don't please you.'

He turned quickly towards her. 'Why do you say that?'

'You don't want . . .'

'I don't want to force myself upon you,' he said quickly. He reached out tentatively and laid his hand gently upon the soft flesh of her upper arm. He felt her tremble. 'I don't want to cause you distress.'

'You're my husband.'

'And a stranger in your bed.'

It was her turn to reach out for him. She lifted one finger and laid it against his cheek. 'Never a stranger,' she said softly.

His voice, in response, was slightly hoarse. 'I'll do my best to carry out my duty,' he said. 'I'll care for you and give you the very best that I can afford.'

'I only want to please you, and to be allowed to love you.'

'I'll do everything I can to give you reason to love me.'

'I've begun already.'

He moved more closely so that he lay beside her and laid his hand more firmly upon her arm. 'It's a good foundation.'

She looked up into his eyes, now but a few inches from her own. 'I'm strong,' she said. 'I'll bear you many children.'

He swallowed hard. 'Do you think . . . ' He hesitated. 'Do you think that we might begin?'

He sensed that he caught a gleam — almost a twinkle — in her eye. 'I'd been wondering if you were ever about to do so.'

Her brashness shocked him, but it brought a surge of feeling which thundered through him. He wrapped his arms about a body which responded instantly, moulding itself against his.

The roar of the crowd swelled from the street below. Somewhere, someone let out a great raucous, bellowing laugh which brought others in its wake. Within the bed, the young couple heard nothing of it.

CHAPTER 2

The air was warm and clear, retaining still the softness of summer but now with that certain clarity which comes for a short time in early autumn.

It was three months since the wedding. On several occasions before returning to the university Rupert had tried to seek out Margaret alone but she had studiously evaded him, making certain that she was always in the company of others. He had seemed unhappy and withdrawn but she knew that no good could come of allowing him to speak again of his feelings towards her. After a time he had cut short his visit and had returned to Oxford.

She sat and thought of him as she rode with Nehemiah in the warm autumn sunshine. As they brought the string of pack ponies to the crest of the hill they could see for miles — vast expanses of green stretching out before them, white dots of sheep, farmstead chimneys sending smoke in a straight upward haze of grey, for there was hardly a breath of wind. High above, a sparrow hawk hovered, sharp eyes riveted upon its prey, while closer at hand a grouse took off in lumbering flight.

They had been out since dawn. Already they had called at more than a dozen cottages and farmsteads. The packs when they had started out had been crammed with wool, gradually now being replaced by yarn.

At each cottage door Nehemiah collected the yarn, weighing it and paying the spinster at the rate of some fourpence ha'penny per pound. Then they stood for a moment or two, exchanging news, sharing a mug of ale, before leaving her with a further supply of carded wool and fixing the day upon which they would come by again.

The women worked long hours to spin the yarn but, even so, it took fifteen of them to keep the loom supplied. And there were others, too, who had first to card the wool and young men to willey it by beating it with sticks.

Margaret made a conscious effort to turn her mind away from Rupert. 'Father, there's talk in the village concerning Agnes Bennett.'

'Aye, so I hear. It won't cease 'til they see a noose about her neck.'

'They're afraid of her jibbering.'

'There's many a rich old widow who jibbers in her feather bed,' commented Nehemiah. 'Yet no one calls them "witch".'

'I've listened to her, Father. It's true she jibbers, but she talks to her family. She talks to them as though they were still close by.'

'It's a sign of lunacy.'

'But is it evil? She talks to her husband, Father, not the Devil.'

'Maybe so. But there aren't many who'd tarry long enough to listen.'

'She must have loved him.'

'Aye, she was a fine woman in her time. Before she grew old.'

'She can't still the passage of time, Father, no more than you nor I.'

'But age brings ugliness, Margaret. People fear such ugliness.'

'I'm sorry, Father. It grieves me to hear people accuse her. She's nothing but a poor old woman in need of our charity.'

He looked at her and shrugged. 'I've no doubt you're right, but once the people have caught hint of commune with the Devil there's little chance of persuading them otherwise.'

'But couldn't we offer her our charity, Father? Couldn't I take her a little extra comfort, just now and then?'

'I wouldn't want you to be seen offering sustenance against the will of the village. It wouldn't be wise.'

'I could go unobserved.'

He smiled at her. 'You're a godly child,' he said. 'Take

her a basket; but take care to leave it on the doorstep, and don't venture inside.'

'I'm sure she wouldn't harm me.'

'It's safest to be sure,' he said.

They were skirting Wychwood Forest — a strange place inhabited by a wild unruly assortment of squatters, fugitives and others who took no note of law. It was a royal forest where, like all royal forests, poaching was on pain of death. Yet still the poachers hammered in their stakes to spear the deer at their jumping places, then contrived a myriad ways of hiding tracks and carcasses.

'Do you think we shall ever see the King?'

'I doubt it. Even if he were to choose to hunt round here, we'd be chased away.'

'It must be strange to live a life of hunting, and to wear fine clothes and sit on a throne all day.'

Nehemiah sighed. 'I vow he's got other matters upon his mind this day.'

'Is the news really bad?'

'Worse than I thought. But change can't come soon enough to teach this King of ours the fear of God.'

'But he is the King.'

'And he must learn that he answers to the One on High, the same as other mortal men.'

'Surely there's no one who would dare to teach a King.'

'Already Parliament's raising an army.'

'An army!'

'There must be men prepared to take a stand when a monarch turns on his own people.' Nehemiah shook his head and shifted his weight on the pony's back. 'At this very moment he's in Scotland, and who's to doubt that he's setting up some deal to use their troops against us?'

The prospect disturbed Margaret who sat in thought on it for some time as the string of pack ponies wended its way steadily onwards.

'There's terrible unrest in London,' went on Nehemiah.

'Will you take me to London one day, Father? You've often promised.'

'Some day, perhaps, but not now. There's rioting in the streets, and no knowing what sorcery those Irish Papist devils may be up to.'

'It frightens me, Father, to hear of such things.'

'Why, child,' Nehemiah turned and smiled at her, 'there's no way that we shall see trouble. There's little which will affect us in these quiet hills.'

'Can you be sure?'

'Yes of course. Men have fought for centuries over the good and evil of this land, yet life goes on. There's little which changes here in these parts.'

'I do hope so, Father, but it gives me a feeling of dreadful foreboding.'

'It's your imagination.' He smiled. 'We'll continue to live as we've always done.'

They were approaching a ford. Conversation stopped as they led the ponies down towards it, splashing into the centre where they allowed them to rest and to drink.

'Sir Henry often goes into London,' she said as they sat waiting.

'Aye, on business. So will Rupert once his betrothal's settled.'

She became uncomfortable at the mention of her cousin.

'If it ever does get settled,' her father went on. 'It seems he dallies to the point of lunacy.'

She turned her head, pretending to slacken the rope of a drinking pony.

'Anyone would think he didn't want the marriage, the way he's carrying on. He's got the dowry of the eldest daughter of Sir John Butler and the promise of all his wealth, yet it seems he's still not satisfied.'

'I can't imagine why,' she said uncomfortably.

'Nor I. Sir John will call an end to it if something isn't settled soon.'

Margaret bit her lip. 'That's a lot to lose if her father calls it off.'

'Indeed it is. But it seems that the girl's set her mind to Rupert, and Sir John's too tender of her to end negotiations lightly.' He turned to look at her. 'Has Rupert spoken of the matter to you?'

She gulped, forcing it quickly into a cough. 'Why should he mention such things to me?'

'I thought maybe he'd spoken.'

'He'd hardly speak to me of such weighty matters.'

'No, I suppose not.' He tugged on the rope of the lead pony and set them moving again.

She was not happy to be less than truthful with her father. 'Father,' she said at last, 'what if Rupert wished to marry someone else?'

'Who?'

'Me.'

'You, child?' He laughed outright at that. 'I think it hardly likely.'

'But just suppose.'

He looked at her and smiled indulgently. 'Child, he's got the dowry of the daughter of Sir John Butler. He's hardly likely to look to you.'

She was acutely uncomfortable. 'He's developed many strange ideas since he went to Oxford.'

'Strange, maybe, but not that strange. Rupert is heir to Oakbourne. He'll be looking for a dowry far in excess of anything we could offer him.'

'Perhaps he doesn't care for wealth.'

'He cares for wealth, all right,' smiled Nehemiah. 'He's always enjoyed the comforts of his father's fortune. He's not going to turn down the opportunity of advancing it. Besides,' he said, 'Sir Henry would have some comment to make upon the matter. I can just imagine what he'd have to say if Rupert began to look to the daughter of a master weaver.'

'That's what I said.'

'When?'

'When he spoke of it.'

'When he spoke of what?'

'He said he wanted to marry me.'

'He said what!' Nehemiah stopped stock-still and turned to look at her. 'When was this, child?' But then he remembered the day of the wedding. 'It was at the wedding, wasn't it?'

She nodded. 'And at other times before that.'

'And what did you say?'

'I told him it was a foolish notion.'

'Sensible child. I can't imagine what has got into the boy.'

'Nor I.'

'And what else did he say?'

'He tells me that he loves me.'

Nehemiah sighed and shook his head. 'You know what this would mean?' he said. 'It would bring dissension into our family. Sir Henry would never agree to such a match and I could never . . .'

'I know,' she said. 'That's what I told him.'

'Yes, I see.' He sat and looked at her for a long time, rocking gently backwards and forwards in rhythm with the pony beneath him. 'And tell me, Margaret,' he said, 'what do you think of all this?'

'I told you.'

'But what do you really think?'

'I told you, Father, it's a foolish notion.'

'So you did.' He rode on for a further time before he said, 'But do you wish that it were not so?'

'No, Father.' She said it with conviction.

'You're sure?'

'Yes, Father.'

'You know that I'd go to great lengths to secure your happiness?'

'But it's not necessary, Father. I've no wish to marry Rupert.'

'Your own mother and I . . .'

She looked at him, waiting for some family secret to be revealed, but he thought better of it.

'You've always been close friends,' he said. 'Even as children.'

'But friends, Father. I love him as a brother. I've no wish to be his wife.'

'That's just as well,' said Nehemiah. 'I can't imagine Sir Henry would have allowed it to be brought about.'

'I'm sorry, Father. I only told you because you spoke of Rupert's reluctance to go through with his betrothal. And you asked if I knew.'

'Yes, I'm glad you told me.'

They rode a short while without speaking, then Nehemiah said, 'Margaret?'

'Yes, Father?'

'Would you look at me and tell me plain that you nurse no thoughts for Rupert.'

'I nurse no thoughts, Father. Rupert is like my brother.'

'Good. Then I think it's best that we say no more of it. I think nothing but dissension would come of it if the matter were known within the family.'

'Yes, Father.'

'And in the unlikely event that Rupert should come to me, then I shall refuse him.'

'Yes, Father.'

'You're sure you speak to me true?'

She bit her lip. 'Yes, Father.'

'Good.' He looked at her and smiled. 'You know I shall never promise you to someone who doesn't please you.'

'I'll do whatever you think is best for me, Father.'

'You're very special to me, child. I'll never commit you to a marriage in which you'll be less than happy.' He reached out a hand and touched her lightly as the ponies plodded steadily side by side.

It was five o'clock by the time they arrived home. It was time for supper and Lucy was laying the table, the inner glow about her of one who has recently discovered herself with child.

Tobias walked through the parlour on his way back to the loom. He touched her gently on the shoulder as he passed.

Margaret and Nehemiah led the pack ponies through the stone-flagged horse passage into the yard at the rear of the house where the apprentice, Matthew Crawshaw, took charge, removing the heavy panniers and attending to the needs of the animals.

Behind the stables was a pig pen and vegetable garden, an orchard with hives of bees. Hens scratched in the dry soil beneath the trees, and a cow chewed languorously on the cud. Three ewes, separated from their lambs the previous May and kept for milk, were destined for slaughter in November, lack of winter feed denying them survival into another year.

Supper was a bowl of broth with vegetables, thickened with barley, a loaf of freshly baked rye bread, still warm from the oven, and home-made cheese. It was a happy family meal shared by all, including Matthew Crawshaw, sitting round the heavy oak table which stood down the centre of the room.

But work had not ceased: there was still daylight beyond the tiny latticed windows.

Nehemiah pushed back his chair at the head of the table and issued instructions. 'Samuel and Matthew, you can carry up the newly spun yarn into the attic. Tobias, you and I will stack the cloth ready to be taken to the fulling mill tomorrow. I want an early start in the morning.'

Mary and Sarah rubbed their eyes and went back to their quilling — winding bobbins ready for the loom. They were aged eight and ten. Like everyone else, they had been at work since dawn. They slowed their pace at this, the final hour of the working day.

Margaret went out into the yard to tend the livestock, shutting away the fowl from the night-time predatory eyes of foxes, looking in on the ponies to ensure that Matthew had secured them properly. The pigs grunted in recognition as she shooed them into the pen and she gave them a scratch upon the tough flaky skin of their backs.

By the time the family gathered once more in the parlour there was barely enough light by which to see. Tobias made room for Lucy near the fire and sat close beside her, his hand lightly touching the small of her back.

'You look tired, Mother.' Margaret lit the tallow candles placed about the room and stirred the fire into a blaze.

Anne sat, one hand on her forehead, the other resting upon her tightly stretched belly. 'I'm near my time. The day fatigues me.'

'Go to your bed,' said Nehemiah.

But Anne smiled. 'Not until after the reading.'

All had been taught to read, including the girls and Matthew Crawshaw. Each took their turn. Tonight it was Samuel. He lifted the book from the table in the corner and opened it at the title page:

'Acts and Monuments of these latter and perilous days, wherein are comprehended and described the great persecutions and horrible troubles that have been wrought and practised by the Romish prelates, specially in this realm of England and Scotland, from the year of our Lord 1000 unto the time now present.'

It was Foxe's *Book of Martyrs*.

'Read of John Hooper,' said Nehemiah.

Samuel turned to the page on which was described the burning of Bishop John Hooper on a wet and windy market day in Gloucester. He read of how seven thousand people had gathered to witness the burning, had swarmed up trees or gathered on rooftops to see him chained to a stake, with faggots of wood and straw piled about his feet.

But the straw was wet. It took three attempts to set the fire ablaze. Repeatedly, the flames rose and scorched him, only to die away and to be lit again. For almost an hour he stood choking in the smoke, unable to die.

The younger children chewed their fingers.

'Now read of the good people of Islington,' said Nehemiah.

Samuel read of a group of people who had met to pray in a field at Islington, only to find themselves arrested. Seven were burned at Smithfield, six at Brentford, while two more died in prison.

On page after page were listed the details of men, women and children burned, imprisoned, persecuted or buried in dunghills.

Samuel closed the book and they sat in silence as though each had witnessed the suffering of their own kin.

'It's good to remember those who went before us,' said Nehemiah quietly. 'They mustn't vanish from memory.'

'Can we hear about the children of John Scrivener?' asked a hushed young voice. 'Of how they were made to light their father's fire?'

But Nehemiah said no, it was time for bed.

'Then can we see the pictures?'

'Just one,' said Nehemiah indulgently and ordered Samuel to turn to the final woodcut in the book.

The figure of Justice was blindfolded, holding in one hand an uplifted sword, while in the other was a pair of scales. On one of the scales was the Bible. On the other, an assortment of chalices, church bells, a monk, and even the Devil himself, all endeavoured to weigh it down.

'There's nothing that can outweigh the Word of God,' said Nehemiah, and sent them all to bed.

* * *

Next morning, when they rose at dawn, Anne remained in her bed. 'The pains are upon me,' she said. 'My time has come.'

'I'll stay with you, Mother.'

'Go with your father. He says he needs you. Though why he can't take Samuel or Tobias I can't imagine.'

'There's work for them to do at the loom.'

Anne shook her head. 'It's not seemly for a maid.'

'I'll stay with you, if you want me to, Mother. Father wouldn't ask me to leave you, if I'm needed here.'

Anne shook her head, more gently this time. 'Off you go. I've Lucy nearby if I need her.'

Margaret kissed her on the cheek. 'I'll be home at dinner time. I'll come straight to you.'

'You're a godly child,' smiled Anne. 'Though your father would employ you otherwise.'

Matthew had re-loaded the pack ponies with cloth. They stood quietly swaying, stamping their hooves as they adjusted to the load. Margaret and Nehemiah took them two miles downstream to the fulling mill which served the community, not only for cloth but for the grinding of flour. The cloth would be soaked and soaped, stretched with force on great notched timbers, then set out to dry on racks across the field.

In her bed, Anne lay waiting for the contractions to intensify. She was thirty-six and, like most women, had spent the years of her marriage almost continuously pregnant. Out of nineteen pregnancies, five had not come to term, three children had died at birth, another two had not survived the first hazardous year of life. Her firstborn son had lived to the age of four; and little Hannah had broken all their hearts by fading slowly into death less than a year ago.

She thanked God that she had been left with seven who were sound in body and in spirit. She was grateful, too, that she need no longer fear that she would die in childbirth and leave behind a motherless family. She had grown daughters now, and a daughter-in-law, who could fill her role.

On her way back from the fulling mill Margaret stopped off at the hovel inhabited by Agnes Bennett. She cast a glance in all directions to make sure that she was unobserved,

32

then quickly placed a basket before the door. The old woman had been squatting in the undergrowth behind the shack: she came hobbling out, waving her fist and shouting abuse.

'It's all right,' said Margaret, pointing towards the basket. 'I've brought food.'

'Poison! I'm to be poisoned in me own bed.'

'It's not poison,' she said, hurt. 'It's fresh-baked bread, with bacon and a piece of cheese.'

'Poison,' the old woman spat out again.

Margaret stepped forward and took the bread from the basket. She took a bite from it and offered the remainder to Agnes Bennett; but she shied away, increasing the volume of her abuse.

'I'll leave it here beside the door. But I'll take the basket,' she said, 'in case it's noticed.' She began removing the contents and laying them upon the soil.

Agnes Bennett hovered, mistrustful. She was sixty-three and had long ago learned to put no reliance on her neighbours. Long ago, too, she had learned that the most effective means of defence was to induce fear: and nothing induced fear like a swiftly aimed curse.

'I'll come again. I'll bring more food.'

But the old woman ignored her, turning painfully on her heel to hobble away.

Dinner was at eleven o'clock. It was the main meal of the day and everywhere people stopped to take their time about it. In fields and cottages workers put down their tools and settled down to eat and to take a nap.

The family gathered in the parlour but there was an air of subdued tension as they listened for sounds from the room where Anne lay.

'I've brought you something to eat, Mother.' Margaret held out a bowl of oatmeal and peas into which she had cut some sops of bread. 'It will give you strength.'

Anne turned her head. 'Thank you, but I've no stomach for food.'

'Shall I call the midwife?'

'No, not yet. I'll tell you when the time's right.'

A contraction caught her so that she gasped and arched

her back. Margaret stood and watched her, powerless to help.

'Oh, Mother, I hate to see you in this pain.'

'Hush, child. Your own time will come and you'll bear it like everyone else.'

Margaret wiped the sweat from Anne's brow with a piece of cloth.

'It's only a woman's torment: and little enough for the joy of bringing forth a child.'

'I don't think I want to bear children.'

Anne was shocked. 'Hush, child, I won't hear such blasphemy.'

'I'm sorry, Mother.'

'It's our inheritance, from Grandmother Eve.' She softened her expression and reached out a hand. 'Go, read your Scriptures and remind yourself once more.'

Margaret had read them more times than she could remember.

'She was deceived,' went on Anne. 'And as a result of that sin we all must suffer. It was God's decree. "And unto woman He said, I will greatly multiply thy sorrow and thy conception . . ." '

'And,' took up Margaret, ' "in sorrow thou shalt bring forth children." '

'You see, you do know it. And don't you rejoice in the blessing by which we're able to redeem ourselves?'

Margaret sighed. 'It's so difficult to keep faith.'

Her mother smiled. 'Your own time will come, then you'll understand.'

Margaret sighed again and turned to other matters. 'Is there anything I can get for you, Mother?'

'A little water, just to moisten my lips.'

As she held the water to her mother's lips the pain came again.

'Oh, Mother, I wish there was something I could do.'

Anne pushed her away. 'Go, child. You'd best not tarry here if it upsets you so. You're of little help to me with such an attitude.'

'I'd rather stay.'

'I'm sure there's work for you to do. Go, and send Lucy to me. You can come back when I've got a baby in my arms.'

Margaret left reluctantly. She walked into the yard and squatted to relieve herself into the hole which had been dug behind the pig pen.

'God hear me,' she said aloud, 'this day I vow that I shall never bring forth children.'

Then she fell to her knees and prayed. She knew that she had sinned.

At one o'clock Lucy called Midwife Taylor, who came into the room wiping her hands upon her apron: she had been tending a sick cow in a nearby byre. Labour was well advanced but by two o'clock Anne still lay sweating and gasping.

'There's something wrong.' The midwife opened Anne's legs and pushed in a hand. 'I can feel a leg. The child's caught the wrong way round.'

'Is that bad?' asked Lucy.

'It's more than bad. It's stuck fast. I can't move it.'

'What can we do?'

'There's a chance sometimes of turning it.' She pushed with brute force so that Anne writhed and gasped. But it was no good. 'It won't move,' she said. 'It's tangled up.'

'Then what . . . ?'

Midwife Taylor thought for a moment, then wiped her hand on her apron and walked out of the room. She was gone for some time.

Lucy hovered, uncertain, panic rising at being left alone with the groaning, semi-conscious woman. She did not know what to do.

When she returned, Midwife Taylor had in her hand an iron hook, of the type used by thatchers.

'What are you going to do?'

She stood for a moment beside the bed, testing the weight and thickness of it in her hands. Then, with determined action, she turned and thrust the hook into the womb.

With one last cry, Anne lost consciousness and left a body limp and motionless for the midwife to manipulate as she chose.

'It's done,' she said at last. A slippery, bloody mass slid into view.

'May God be praised,' gasped Lucy. But, even as she said

it, she could see that the child's leg lay broken and misshapen, and it had a wound on its thigh where the hook had gouged it.

'Is it alive?'

'Aye, just. But it's puny and weak.' She washed the baby and wrapped it tightly in swaddling bands.

'But what of the leg?'

'It's a pity about the leg. It won't be of much use, if the child survives at all.'

Anne groaned, recovering consciousness. 'Is it over?' she gasped. 'What of the baby?'

'A daughter,' said Midwife Taylor. 'Safely tucked into her cradle.'

'May the Lord be praised,' Anne whispered and sank again into oblivion.

Nehemiah stopped work and went to see his wife and newborn daughter. He stood beside the bed looking down at Anne's face, pale and drawn after hours of pain.

'I pray you'll forgive me,' she begged, 'for producing yet another girl.'

Nehemiah smiled at her. 'I've two fine sons. I'm more than content.'

'But it's another burden on your purse.'

'And another joy in my heart.'

'She's a sickly child,' she said. 'And with a lifeless leg.'

'It's enough that she lives.' He took her in his arms and kissed her. 'We shall call her Anne. We've not had an Anne since we lost our firstborn girl.'

So the child was named. But for a reason closely related to the baby-talk of her sister Rachael, she was known always as Bibby-Anne.

News spread round the village that action was about to be taken against Agnes Bennett. It seemed that someone had recalled the incident upon the day of the wedding and had linked it to the misfortune of Anne's delivery. 'The child was cursed,' word went round. 'Cursed in the womb.'

Anne was distressed. 'There's no curse on my child. The disfigurement was caused at birth.'

But Midwife Taylor did nothing to help. She related in

the fullest detail the way in which the child had been entangled and incapable of entry into the world.

Hysteria heightened when, one day, Agnes Bennett was chased into the wood. Shortly afterwards a hare came coursing across the grass, making a bolt for it back in the direction of her hovel. 'It's her familiar,' someone cried. 'Gone to summon the Devil to her aid.'

Before she was fully fit, Anne took her baby and set out one afternoon for Oakbourne House. She wanted to speak with her sister Elizabeth. It was late October and, although still mild, the air held the sharpness of advancing autumn. She walked down the main street and out along the rutted track towards the wood.

There were people in the wood for, although the land belonged to Sir Henry, he conceded to the villagers the right to forage for kindling, nuts, wild fruits, and the eggs of birds. They greeted Anne as she passed, enquiring after her health; but she gave none the satisfaction of discussing with them the rumours concerning Agnes Bennett.

Hogs were rooting in the undergrowth where they had been turned to ferret for fallen acorns. On the farthest edge of the wood, labourers were gathering bracken for winter bedding. Piles of logs had been cut, waiting for a wagon to transport them to the house.

On more open land, a field had been ploughed ready for barley; in another, wheat was being sown. She raised her hand in greeting to the women who walked along the furrows, broadcasting the seed.

She was tired by the time she reached the house — a fine stone building with large latticed windows and a roof of moss-grown slate. She found Elizabeth in the pantry.

'You're well? Come, sit down here and rest. Surely it's early to be leaving your bed.'

'I'm well enough, but mighty glad of a stool to perch on.' She sank down gratefully.

'You've caught me at a busy time,' said Elizabeth. She turned to issue instructions to the young girl who was working beside her.

'I've got a lot to do in my own kitchen,' said Anne. 'But this year I've relied on Lucy and Margaret.'

'And Lucy's well with the coming child?'

37

'Radiant. Tobias has done well for himself.'

'Good. He deserves to be happy.'

She did not stop work: Anne did not expect her to. There was no time to waste at this time of the year. Fruit recently gathered from orchard and hedgerow needed to be stored; there was wine to be made and ale brewed; vegetables had to be pickled for the long months when none would grow; conserves and jellies to be made, and salves, cordials and pot pourri for doctoring the sick; there were extra candles to be made for long winter evenings. Livestock would be slaughtered before November: meat would need to be salted and dried, hams to be smoked in the chimney.

'Why do you bring the babe?' There was a note of disguised disapproval in Elizabeth's voice. 'Surely she'd be best left in her cradle?'

'She's warmly wrapped, and I want to keep her with me. She's a sickly child and I want to keep watch over her. I've decided, too, to feed her with my own milk.'

'You can't be serious?' Elizabeth momentarily stopped what she was doing. 'A woman of good family choosing to nurse her own child?'

'She's weak. I don't want to give her over into the charge of a wet-nurse.'

'She'll grow weaker still if you persist in such foolishness. Give her to Moll Simmonds. She's strong and healthy, and full of milk.'

'She's a slattern.'

'And raised two healthy youngsters of her own.'

'And overlaid another.'

'Ah, well, yes. That was unfortunate. I hear she fell asleep while she was feeding it in the night.'

'A mistake I'm not likely to make if I feed my own.'

'I think you forget sometimes,' said Elizabeth, 'that you come of good family.'

Anne hitched the baby more securely into the crook of her arm. 'I've lost too many and this one's very weak.'

'You're not alone in losing children.'

'I know . . . I didn't mean . . . ' Ann reached out swiftly towards her sister.

'You must do as you please. But I believe it's a positive

38

danger to your health, not to mention the unpleasantness of it.'

Anne smiled. 'I didn't come to speak of myself but of Agnes Bennett.'

'Agnes Bennett?'

'There's rumour that she's about to be charged.'

'So I hear.'

'And your husband will be asked to sit in judgement.'

'She'll be fairly tried. Henry doesn't take lightly his duties as Justice of the Peace.'

'I know. But there are others who'll sit with him: others who'll be less fair and who'll be caught up in the fear of the people.'

'You do them an injustice,' said Elizabeth. 'They're good men and they'll listen to the facts.'

Anne shook her head. 'They're naming my child. I don't want my Bibby-Anne to be the cause of her downfall.'

Elizabeth stopped her work. 'I think you're worrying unnecessarily,' she said. 'She'll be given a fair trial and she will be freed if the charge isn't proved.'

'I only hope you're right. I don't like the mood of the people.'

'Well, I'll speak to Henry. But I'm sure he knows what's going on.'

'Thank you. I couldn't rest until I'd come and spoken of it.' Anne got up and began to move towards the door. 'But I must be getting home now. There's so much to be done.'

'I'll walk with you. I've got to go down to the dairy to see about the cheeses.'

They walked out of the pantry and into the vegetable garden, past the fish ponds and the dove-cote — both extra sources of food during the coming winter months — on towards the dairy.

Oakbourne had been their family home as children: Anne knew it well. For generations, their ancestors had been content to eke out a reasonable living as yeomen farmers. But their father had been gifted with a talent for increasing his lot. He had acquired additional land and had farmed it with skill, increasing his flocks and using the fertile soil to grow more crops.

39

It had placed the family in a position where Elizabeth, as the oldest daughter, had caught the eye of Henry Mainwaring. A younger son of good family, he was without land of his own but he had an astute mind which he had put to good use as a merchant in the city of London.

Elizabeth had been heiress to Oakbourne. An epidemic of smallpox had taken the sons. Even today, both Anne and Elizabeth still bore witness to their own ordeal in the disfigurement of their pock-marked faces.

Elizabeth had accompanied her husband to live in London. But in '26, when their father had gone to his grave, she and Henry Mainwaring had returned to Dunscombe to take their place in the family home.

During their stay in London, Henry Mainwaring had found himself in a position to be of service to the Duke of Buckingham. Nothing was ever mentioned of the exact nature of the service which had been performed, but it had been sufficient to cause him to kneel before the King and to rise dubbed Sir Henry Mainwaring.

Sir Henry had used the title to increase his business interests in the city and to further enhance the grandeur of Oakbourne. He had enlarged the property, building on extra rooms with large windows. He had acquired still more land and now employed additional men to farm it for him.

As the two women walked across the orchard towards the dairy both happened to glance up into the tree ahead of them: both saw the sprigs of apple blossom growing in amongst the ripe fruit still waiting to be plucked.

'That's an omen of death,' said Anne. 'I don't like to see blossom growing with the fruit.'

Elizabeth shivered. 'There's been a feeling in the air for months. I feel it on Henry each time he returns from London. I don't understand the ways of government but there's unrest and fear.'

'My only concern is for my household,' said Anne. 'I only pray that our own dear family may be allowed to live in peace and health.'

'Amen to that.' Elizabeth gave her sister a kiss on the cheek and they parted, each to their own duties.

* * *

When Anne arrived home she found Lucy lying on her bed, weeping. She was bleeding heavily.

'You've lost the child,' Anne said without hesitation.

Lucy turned her face into the pillow.

'It's not unusual with the first.' Anne sat down and took her hand. 'You've a lifetime in which to bear many more.'

'But I've failed.'

She stroked her thumb across the back of Lucy's hand. 'It's God's way of bringing us to an understanding; so that we may be humbled and purified of our sins.'

'But I don't know how I've sinned.'

'We're all prey to the Evil One, we're all daughters of Eve. Search your heart and pray for enlightenment.'

'May God forgive me: I know I'm prone to vanity and to covetousness.'

'The Lord is merciful. He finds it easy to forgive a repenting heart. You're a godly child, my daughter. I'm glad you've come to live here under my husband's roof.'

'Do I serve you well?'

'Very well,' Anne said. 'Now, rest and don't leave your bed until you're fully recovered.'

An hour later, Tobias came to Lucy. He bent and kissed her tenderly on the cheek. 'Are you in pain?'

'Only in my heart. I've dishonoured you.'

'You've done no such thing.' He lifted her from the pillows and hugged her. 'I'll not have you say such things.'

'But I wanted so much to bear you a son.'

'And so you will.' He kissed her hair. 'Just wait and see — we'll have twenty sons.'

She half smiled at that. 'I'll pray hard for repentance, but there are so many sins to overcome.'

'I'll pray with you, in gratitude for your coming to me.'

She laid her head against his neck. 'You're good to me, husband. You overlook my weaknesses.'

He tilted her chin so that he could look into her face. 'You're the fairest, most sweet and tender wife that any man could ever have. And I thank God for sending you to me.' He kissed the tears from her eyes. 'Now go to sleep. I'll come to you again at suppertime; and I want to be greeted with a smile.'

41

She closed her eyes and sighed, sinking down into the pillow. 'You shouldn't have left the loom.'

'Father told me to come. But I must get back.' He turned at the door. 'I love you,' he said softly. 'Sleep now and grow strong.'

Accusations were duly made against Agnes Bennett. She was brought before Sir Henry and two others, who listened to the evidence before them. The old woman had earlier been stripped and examined by Midwife Taylor but the Justices were unimpressed by the account of warts and blemishes found upon her person.

'These are nothing but the fleshy imperfections of old age,' stated Sir Henry.

'Or the teat on which the Devil sucks,' countered Midwife Taylor.

'There's no evidence of sucking.'

'Those who slake His lustful thirst find devious ways of disguising it.'

'Was she pricked?'

'Aye, and didn't feel the pain.'

'Show me again.'

A needle was produced and pierced into the brown mole-like blemish on the old woman's neck. She jumped and squealed.

'How can you say she feels no pain?'

'I'll try another,' offered Midwife Taylor but Sir Henry shook his head.

'Dismiss the marks,' he said. 'Now, tell me, what evidence of this familiar?'

A number of witnesses came forward describing the witnessing of a hare running in the vicinity of the old woman's hovel.

'But has this animal been seen to enter the door?'

'No, sir, but running full pelt in that direction.'

'But never close enough to claim it goes inside?'

'No, sir,' said the witness reluctantly.

The Justices then turned to evidence of actual harm and called a number of other witnesses who testified to the death of a horse, a tree which no longer bore fruit, and a young woman who had been convulsed with sudden raging pain.

The three men listened, then called Anne to speak. She had been sitting at the back of the room.

'My child was damaged at birth,' she said. 'It was necessary to use brute force in order to deliver her. Her leg was injured in the process.' She looked across at the midwife. 'Midwife Taylor must vouch for this.'

'I vouch only that the child was entangled in such a way that no earthly hand had bound it.'

'But she lived.'

'Aye, and with a useless limb.'

'It's enough that she lived,' said Anne. 'The Lord is with her.'

The Justices continued to sit patiently until all had spoken. Then Sir Henry turned to Agnes Bennett. 'Old woman,' he said, 'repeat for me the Lord's prayer.'

A hush fell across the assembled crowd as she began. 'Our Father . . . which art in heaven . . . '

They waited for her to stumble, knowing that if she did, it would be as a result of evil influence.

'Hallowed be Thy name . . . '

Senility and failing memory were coupled with an illiterate mind.

'Thy kingdom come . . . Thy will be done . . . on earth as it is in heaven . . . ' She dragged it out, phrase by phrase, as if summoning some deep inner source of strength.

At last it was done. The inheld breath of the crowd was let go in disappointment.

The Justices conferred for a further time. 'We find,' said Sir Henry at last, 'that the woman Agnes Bennett is found guilty of scolding. She'll be set in the stocks for a period of half a day, and afterwards she will be confined in a brank for a further week.'

'There's need of a noose,' protested someone.

'This is no hanging matter,' said Sir Henry. 'There's insufficient evidence of witchcraft.'

'We shall see,' whispered Midwife Taylor. 'There are others we can find to try her who'll prove less squeamish.'

Anne returned home to her family with a sense of deep relief. The sentence was justified in the light of the old woman's persistent scolding, but her life had been spared.

Agnes Bennett was confined for twelve hours in the

stocks, while the villagers hurled abuse and quantities of putrefied refuse. Afterwards she was padlocked into an iron bridle which would hold fast her tongue for a further week. She submitted to it all in a state of confused detachment, cursing all beneath her breath.

Margaret took a bowl of broth to her door, knowing that the old woman would be unable to chew on more solid food. She took particular care that she went unobserved but, as usual, the offering was taken from her without acknowledgment or thanks.

Agnes Bennett supped the broth, spluttering and clanking on the bridle, then threw the wooden bowl down upon the ground.

Margaret bent to retrieve it. 'I'll come tomorrow,' she said. 'As usual.'

The old woman made no response but turned away, hobbling back into the filth and darkness of the hovel.

Margaret went home and attended to her chores. It was almost dark when she went into the yard to secure the livestock for the night. She was in the stable when a voice attracted her attention. She jumped in fright.

'I'm over here.'

She turned and saw Rupert beckoning her. 'Rupert! What on earth are you doing here?'

'I came to see you.'

'Whatever for?'

'You know full well.'

'Why aren't you at Oxford?'

'For God's sake, Margaret, I must speak with you.' He caught her arm and drew her close beside him. 'It's vitally important.'

'Come into the house,' she said, agitated. 'If you want to speak to me, you can do it in company of my parents.'

He held her fast and made her listen. 'On Sunday, I'm to be betrothed to Isobel Butler.'

'Sunday?'

'There's no way I can avoid it any longer.'

'From what I hear, you've dallied long enough already.'

'You know why I've dallied.'

She turned her face.

'This is our last chance, Margaret. Next Sunday I shall be betrothed.'

'I wish you well.'

'For God's sake, Margaret,' he said fiercely. 'After Sunday it will be too late. There'll be no going back.'

'What do you want me to say?'

'Say you'll reconsider. Just tell me that you love me and you'll be my wife.'

'You know I can't.'

'Why?'

'It wouldn't be right.'

'To hell with what's right. I want you as my wife.'

She sighed and turned away. 'You know I can never be your wife, Rupert. You need someone of good breeding; someone of status; someone who can bring a dowry . . . '

'How many times must I tell you . . . '

'And how many times must I tell you I'm not the person for you? Go and marry your Isobel. She'd suit you so much better than I.'

'I don't want Isobel,' he said vehemently. 'I want you.'

'But I don't love you,' she said. 'Not the way you want me to.'

He sagged, deflated. 'When will you ever admit it?' he said dejectedly. 'I suppose when it's too late.'

'I'm sorry,' she said. 'It always pains me to know that I've hurt you.'

He looked up. 'I've got horses tethered at the end of the lane.'

'What for?'

'We could run away.'

'What!'

'We could be married before anyone could stop us. That way my father would have to accept it. There'd be nothing he could do about it.'

'Have you spoken to him of me?'

'No, I haven't mentioned it.'

'Then . . . '

'It's best this way. If I spoke of you, I know he'd forbid it. That's why I've kept quiet. By the time it's put before him it'll be too late. He'll have to agree or cause a scandal for all to hear.'

'But that's a dreadful thing to do, Rupert. It's terribly wrong.'

'I know,' he said. 'But desperate situations call for desperate actions. I know he'll never agree to my marrying you, and Uncle Nehemiah won't feel able to consider my proposal without my father's goodwill. If we're married, it will be too late.'

'But it's wrong.'

'I know it's wrong, my sweet, but I love you. I love you enough to risk everything.'

She did not know what to say.

'I've waited and waited for you to come to admit your real feelings towards me. I wanted you to come joyously, acknowledging the love that we have for one another. But now I've no alternative but to beg you. Please, Margaret, I'm being pressed daily into this betrothal. I can't delay it any longer.' He looked at her hopelessly. 'If I speak of my love openly, we shall be forced apart. They'll use every means to make it quite impossible for us to marry. If I continue to keep quiet, I shall be forced to marry Isobel. There's no way I can win.' He took her hand and said tenderly, 'Except to run away. By the time we come back it will be resolved.'

Margaret was moved by his appeal. There was no mistaking the true sincerity of his love for her.

'I spoke to my father of your feelings,' she said.

'Oh?' he exclaimed. 'What did he say?'

'He said that if it were my wish he would go to great lengths to secure my happiness.'

His face lit up. 'Oh, the dear man. I should have known. He is most good and generous. Then all's not lost.' He grabbed her hand. 'We've an ally. We'll find a way.'

She gently loosened his grip. 'I told him,' she said, 'that it's not my wish.'

'But it is.'

'No, Rupert,' she said. 'I'm most touched by this love which you have for me, but it's not returned.'

He closed his eyes and swallowed.

'If it were our parents' wish that we should marry, then of course I'd gladly do so. And I'd learn to love you in the way you desire. But it's not their wish. It would cause dissension throughout our entire family. Things would never be the same again. My father would make sacrifice but it would be at the cost of his own personal pain. The strength of the family is most precious to him . . . ' she looked at her cousin. ' . . . And to me. I won't do anything which would disrupt the family. My mother and her sister would be torn apart. My father would be pained to see such a thing happen, and be burdened beyond endurance on his purse.'

'I wouldn't ask for . . . '

'It's not just the dowry. It's so many things. Sir Henry has great hopes for you. You're heir to his fortune and he expects you to make a good marriage.'

'I only want you.'

'But you can't have me, my dear. I'm so sorry. If it were right, I'd marry you gladly and would do all that I could to be a good wife to you. But it's not, and I can't go along with it.'

'Say you don't love me.'

'I don't love you,' she said. 'Not in the way you wish me to love you. I love you dearly as a brother and will always love you, but not in the way you require.'

He sighed defeatedly. 'Then there's not much more to be said. I might as well go and marry Isobel.'

'If she's not to your liking, perhaps you could ask to step down and find someone else who would suit you better.'

'What the hell does it matter,' he retorted, 'who I decide to choose?'

'Then perhaps you should wait. Let time ease your pain.'

But his disappointment took the form of truculence. 'No,' he said. 'If that's how you feel about it, I'll marry her. Then perhaps they'll leave me in peace.'

'Take care . . . ' she began.

But he rounded on her as he turned away. 'What do you care? What does it matter to you who I marry? I'll marry anyone I choose. It makes no difference to you. You don't love me.'

She heard him sob as he walked off, disappearing into the darkness.

She went back into the house to listen to the reading before preparing for bed. She sat quiet and subdued, telling no one of the conversation.

CHAPTER 3

On the following Sunday Rupert Mainwaring was betrothed to Isobel Butler. In the spring of 1642 they were married. Isobel remained at the home of her parents in the village of Chiswick, awaiting the time when Rupert would complete his studies at Oxford and transfer to one of the Inns of Court in the city of London.

Margaret had seen nothing of him but thought of him frequently and wondered if he would ever be happy.

He came to Dunscombe on May Day Eve, less than a month after his wedding. He had come on the pretext of needing to speak urgently with his father but found an excuse first to call upon Margaret.

He found her in the orchard behind the house, where she was collecting the cow to be milked. He made a detour, off the main street and along the course of the river, until he was close enough to call out to her. He reined in his horse.

'Margaret?'

She looked up and felt a moment's apprehension. 'Rupert, how nice to see you.'

He smiled at her. 'Is it?'

'Of course.' She tethered the cow and walked towards him while he, in turn, dismounted from the horse. 'How are you?'

'Well. And you?'

'I'm very well,' she said, then lowered her eyes, not sure what to say next.

'I'm here on business for the King.'

She looked at him sharply. 'What business could you possibly have for the King?'

'On his behalf,' he corrected. 'The people of Oxford are doing all they can.'

'In what way?'

'He's in need of support. It's up to us all to rally to the Cause.'

'Are matters really that bad?'

'Worse,' he said. 'And getting more serious by the day.'

'Oh, Rupert.' She was genuinely concerned. 'It's not wise to become involved in such things.'

'I must. We need to help raise cash for an army.'

She shook her head, knowing well her father's view upon the conflict. 'It's not for me to speak of such things but you'd be well advised to steer clear of trouble.'

'I'll not be in trouble, but I must go urgently to see Father. He'll be certain to help.'

It was a sudden illustration to her of that which she already knew: Nehemiah and Sir Henry had differing political opinions.

'Father wouldn't agree,' she said. 'I just hope this dreadful conflict won't bring problems between them.'

'They're family,' he said. 'They won't allow it to cause dissension.'

There was a silence between them. She bit her lip and looked away from him. Neither knew what to say. She could feel his discomfort.

'How's Isobel?' she asked at last, forcing some kind of false normality into her voice.

'She's well.'

'I'm glad.'

'Margaret?'

'Yes?'

'You know what I want to say.'

'What?' she asked kindly.

'I was a fool.'

'Oh Rupert.'

'In a fit of pique I went through with it.'

'Perhaps it was my fault.'

'No,' he said. 'I was angry and upset.'

'I'm sorry.'

'I was so hurt.'

'I'm sorry,' she said again.

'Nothing else seemed to matter. But now I'm trapped.'

'Oh, Rupert,' she said, 'I wish you wouldn't look at it like that. I'm sure you could be very happy if only you'd just give it a chance.'

'I should have refused to go through with it.'

She felt pity for him but did not know what to say. 'I did warn you . . . '

'It's unfair on Isobel. I can never be the kind of husband she needs. And I shall spend the rest of my life wanting you.'

'Oh, Rupert, we've been through this so many times.'

'If only there was something I could do.'

'There's nothing you can do,' she said. 'You're married to Isobel. You must see it through.'

'I don't know if I can.'

'You must. If you didn't want her, you should have waited for someone else.'

'I didn't want someone else.'

'Don't, Rupert,' she said. 'We've been through it all before.'

He nodded. 'I know.' He raised his eyes and looked at her. 'But it doesn't make me any the less unhappy for what I've done.'

'I'm sorry.'

'And for what I've done to Isobel.'

'Yes.'

They stood for a long time, each looking at the ground before them.

'You'll have to do your best for her,' she said. 'It's not fair to her if you don't.'

'I know.'

'You'll come to love her in time.'

He looked at her sharply.

'If I'd waited long enough . . . ?'

She shook her head. 'No.'

He heaved a sigh and swung himself back upon his horse. 'I suppose I must be getting on my way.'

'And I must milk the cow,' she said.

He looked at her, clenching his lower lip between his teeth. 'Till we meet again.'

'Will you call back before you return to Oxford?'

'I doubt it,' he said.

'Mother and Father would be pleased to see you.'

'I think it's best . . . ' He gave her a sad but tender smile. 'Some other time, perhaps.'

'Yes,' she said. 'Some other time.' And waved him goodbye.

Rupert found his father in one of the large panelled rooms of Oakbourne and lost no time in telling him the purpose of his visit.

'Father, I must have the silver. It's vitally important to the Cause.'

'My son, this is a tall order you bring me. To pass over all the silver from the house. How much else does the King command?'

'He's in need, Father, in desperate need of our loyalty.'

'Where is His Majesty? Still in York?'

'He's rallying support, but he can't do so without funds. It's up to everyone to give everything they have.'

Sir Henry heaved a sigh. 'It wasn't wise to bring this situation upon himself.'

'It wasn't the King, it was Parliament.'

'It was the King who walked into the House of Commons at the head of an armed force.'

'He had no choice, Father. Parliament had gone too far. They knew he had to raise an army against the Irish; yet the Militia Bill robbed him of command.'

'They feared he'd turn the army upon his own people.'

'It was needed to quell the Irish rebellion, not the English.'

'Perhaps. But it still remains that he was ill-advised in the way he acted. He should have known he'd never succeed in walking into the House of Commons and arresting five of its members.'

Rupert shrugged his shoulders. 'They'd fled long before he arrived.'

'Of course they'd fled. The whole city knew that his coach was approaching Westminster.'

'And now they're safe in the bosom of their supporters. London's thick with people willing to hide them.'

Sir Henry shook his head. 'With feeling running the way

it is, he ought to have known he stood no chance of ferreting them out. He must have known that the crowds were hostile.'

'But to oppose him in a mob,' said Rupert. 'It's unthinkable for a King to be treated like that. Thank God he wasn't actually harmed. Even the Royal Guard couldn't protect him.'

'And what of the Queen?' asked Sir Henry. 'Is she still safe in Holland?'

'She's got the Crown Jewels, and is hoping to use them to recruit some good fighting men from Denmark.'

Sir Henry shook his head again and sighed. 'It's a sorry state of affairs: the country brought to such a plight. It could have been avoided if matters had been handled more wisely.'

'But the King is the *King*, Father. We can't have the people turning on him.'

'Nor the King on his people. But it's come about. Now, I suppose, we must stand by the consequences.'

'Then you'll give him the silver?'

'Aye,' said Sir Henry. 'I'll give the King my silver; and I'll wager we'll all be called upon to give a good deal more before much longer.'

'I doubt it. It'll all be over soon. We'll bring those damned Parliamentarians to heel if we can just raise an army.'

'I hope you're right, my son. I only wish I could share your optimism.'

Elizabeth came into the room. 'Why, Rupert, you look so grave. And at a time when you should be happy.'

'There's not much to be happy about, Mother.'

'How can you say such a thing? And less than a month since you were wed.'

'I wasn't thinking of my marriage.'

'Then perhaps you should. If you don't think of it a month after your wedding day, what hope is there for your wife in a score more years?'

'I'm sorry, Mother, I didn't mean . . . '

'I would hope not. You've made a good match and there's a great deal for you to be thankful for.'

He closed his eyes and looked away.

Elizabeth did not notice. 'And she makes you a good wife?'

'She does well enough.'

'But does she serve you?' She raised an eyebrow inquisitively.

Sir Henry put an end to it. 'Leave the questioning to some other time, my dear. Rupert's had little enough time to spend with his bride.'

'He's had time enough to make her with child had he put his mind to it.'

'Perhaps I have,' offered Rupert. 'But it's too soon yet to tell.'

She was pleased at that. 'Then no doubt we shall learn before too long. I'm looking forward to the birth of grandchildren.'

Rupert remained overnight and set out early next morning leading a pack pony on which were slung panniers containing silver plate and several pieces of Elizabeth's jewellery.

It was a clear, bright morning and the village was alive with the activities of May Day. People called out to him as he passed, urging him to join them; but he smiled and raised his hat, telling them he had to be away on urgent business.

The villagers were in high spirits, gathering boughs of birch and beech, great garlands of fresh green leaf, and the white pungent mass of May blossom. They set up their maypole in front of the alehouse, decking it with garlands, and with streamers of coloured ribbons. Great quantities of food had been set out: the feasting would go on all day.

In Nehemiah's house the family went about their business as they would have done on any other morning.

'They've been making merry since long before dawn,' said Samuel. 'I could hardly sleep for the noise.'

'Aye, enough to wake the Devil — if He weren't already about and stirring up the heart of it.'

'But they sound so happy, Father,' said Sarah.

'So did the children of Israel when they were dancing before the golden calf. And just as Satan rejoiced that day, so He rejoices now when He sees His people cavorting round that loathsome pole in honour of a whore.'

'But they say it's to greet the new life of spring.'

'Then let them praise the Lord who has brought us through the depths of winter,' said Nehemiah, 'and forget this cavorting which has no place in His scheme of things.'

54

'Yes Father.'

'Let's kneel now, and thank the Lord that we haven't been tainted by the sorcery of His enemies.'

They all knelt and prayed. Then they took their breakfast of oatcake and cheese with mugs of warm ale.

All day they went about their work, but it was difficult to ignore the festivities which continued throughout the hours of daylight and well into the following night. A troupe of Morris dancers crossed the green with their Fool, and Tom the piper, and their Hobby Horse; a play was enacted depicting Robin Hood with Maid Marian and the Merry Men; everywhere, people were dancing and consuming great quantities of food and drink.

Margaret and Nehemiah were sorting cloth in readiness for market the following day.

'You spoke with Rupert this morning.'

She stopped what she was doing and darted a glance at him. 'I didn't know you had seen.'

'Why should I not see? I was by the window. I saw him quite plainly.'

Margaret said a little unsteadily, 'I can't think why he couldn't come to speak with us all in the house.'

'What did he say?'

She blushed slightly. 'Not much, Father. It seems he's hoping to raise support for the King.'

'Is he, indeed? He'd be better occupied giving his mind to his studies.'

'Yes, Father.'

'And did he speak . . . ?'

'No, Father.' She chose to lie, as much to spare his discomfort as her own. But then she said, 'I think he may have had second thoughts about his marriage.'

Nehemiah raised an eyebrow but this time with a different expression. 'It's a little late for second thoughts.'

'He feels he should have waited.'

'I dare say. In view of his feelings at the time, he would have done better to let his emotions cool.'

'And now it's too late.'

'It is, indeed. Whatever error of judgement Rupert may have made, he's duty-bound to see it through. There's no choice for him now.'

'Yes, Father.'

'And what of you?'

'Me?'

'Have you second thoughts?'

'No, Father.'

'It doesn't pain you to see Rupert married?'

'Only to see him unhappy.'

He smiled gently. 'I wouldn't want to see you sad.'

'Perhaps, in time, he'll learn to care for Isobel.'

'Yes,' he said. 'For her sake, we can only hope he does.'

'How far from London is the village of Chiswick?'

Nehemiah stopped and thought. 'Three miles, perhaps; maybe four.'

'So she may be in danger?'

'I doubt it. No harm will come to her in Chiswick.'

'But if Rupert has chosen allegiance to the King . . . '

'Aye, that's true. He would be wise to stay well clear of London. The city's wholly in support of Parliament. They've got themselves organized, with the City Trained Bands standing ready.'

'Is it really going to come to war?'

'Yes,' he said. 'There's no alternative now. The King's made it plain that he'll respond to nothing less than force of arms.'

'But surely they should at least try to come to some agreement?'

Nehemiah shook his head and stared gravely at the pile of cloth before him. 'There's one important fact which can't be ignored,' he said. 'Unless the King is defeated — and defeated soundly — there are too many men in Parliament who could find themselves charged with high treason.'

'Couldn't some deal be struck to protect them?'

He coughed out a bitter laugh. 'There isn't any deal which this King wouldn't turn on its head at a moment's whim.'

Margaret stopped work and stood holding a hand to the small of her back to ease the strain. 'There's so much gloom,' she said. 'It's been building for months. It frightens me to think that good Englishmen are actually going to be at war with one another.'

'Why, child,' Nehemiah stopped and looked across at her, 'what am I thinking of? To bear you down with such matters when there's no reason for you to fill your head with them.'

'But it worries me, Father, and I know it troubles you. Now, Rupert's likely to become involved, too.'

'He must learn to act upon his own conscience,' said Nehemiah. 'And to curb his tongue in places where his views won't be welcome. But that's no reason for you to wear a frown.' He straightened up. 'What do you say to bringing a little jollity into our lives?'

She looked at him, not understanding.

'How about, on Whit Thursday, we take the family to Captain Dover's Games?'

'But that's miles away. It must be twelve miles at least to Chipping Campden.'

'Don't you want to go?'

'Yes, of course,' she said, warming to the idea. 'But the children have never been so far.'

'Then we'll borrow a wagon and take them on a journey they'll never forget.'

'Could we really? There are so many things we could show them along the way.

'Indeed we could. Now, let's get on with our work. There's a lot to do. But on Whit Thursday we'll take a holiday.'

On the day of the Games they started out well before dawn and made slow but steady progress towards the parish of Weston-sub-Edge, a mile or so from Chipping Campden. The roads of the Cotswolds were good compared to many in other parts of the country: the oxen plodded steadily before the wagon.

Long before they reached their destination they met up with other travellers, converging from all directions. By they time they reached Dover's Hill activities were already well under way.

Nehemiah bade them all be free to enjoy themselves. Lucy and Tobias took charge of one younger sister, Margaret another two, leading them between the rows of stalls which had been set out upon the grass.

Samuel made off towards an area where lines of men were kneeling, heads tucked down, elbows at their sides, allowing others to take their turn in leaping over them. He stood and watched, gasping as one youth leapt across the heads of nine kneeling men, inflicting no more than a kick on the ear of the final man.

All around him contestants were handling the pike, pitching the bar, playing at cudgels, or fighting with sword and buckler. He watched two men wrestling, gouging at one another among the feet of onlookers; then he went off to watch others playing leapfrog.

He saw a pedlar with a tray of books and parted with most of his money – twopence – the price of a chapbook. Behind a wagon he sought out a secluded spot and settled down for the best part of the morning to immerse himself in the adventures of Long Meg of Westminster. No one disturbed him as he turned the pages and read of the young maid who, dressed as a man, roamed the city at night, taking on all comers in fair fight, until at last she married a soldier and settled down to become a good wife.

Margaret allowed the younger girls to amuse themselves by watching a group of youths standing upside down upon their hands, but they soon grew bored and moved on to an area where a shin-kicking contest was taking place. She winced and chewed her lip as young men grasped each other by the clothing and kicked out in iron-tipped boots.

She was concentrating so hard that she did not hear the approach of footsteps behind her. She jumped in fright as a hand was placed upon her shoulder.

'Rupert! What on earth are you doing here?'

'Aren't you pleased to see me?'

'What are you doing here, so far from home?'

'On business. What of you?'

'We're here to attend the Games. It's a treat from Father.'

'I'm here on much less happy matters.'

'What sort of matters?'

'I'm visiting the great houses,' he said. 'Everyone's got to be urged to take a stand.'

'Oh, Rupert, you're becoming more and more involved. Why put yourself in such a position?'

'I've got to. It's no time to stand idly by.'

'You'll finish up by getting hurt.'

He looked at her and the expression on his face became tender. 'At least it matters to you that I might get hurt.'

'Of course it matters. You're part of the family. I've no wish to see you involved in bloodshed.'

'I suppose we're declaring again that I'm your brother.' She looked away.

'I'm sorry,' he said. 'But you've no idea how much it hurts.'

He took her arm, attempting to draw her a little distance from the two younger girls who were still watching the contest.

She pulled away. 'We'd best go find my parents,' she said. 'They'll be pleased to see you. You can join us for our dinner.'

'Stay and talk, just a little while.'

She ignored him and began collecting up the younger girls. 'It's best that you speak to me in the company of my parents.'

'Please, Margaret.' He held on to her arm again. 'I can't stop loving you, just because I'm married.'

'Don't, Rupert.'

'I'm sorry. It's just so difficult each time I see you.'

She turned to him and spoke firmly. 'Rupert, once you spoke of a foolish notion. Now you speak of sin.'

'I know. I'm sorry, Margaret, but it just gets harder and harder.'

'Then you must try,' she said gently. She took the girls, each by the arm, and led them back to their parents.

Rupert spent the remainder of the day with them, watching the races and the hare coursing. But the outing had been made uncomfortable for Margaret.

As summer progressed, news came of skirmishes in various parts of the country. Royalists met up with Parliamentarians, drew swords or muskets, spilled a little blood. But nothing was resolved. An atmosphere of tension rose as everywhere men chose their sides.

In the village, life went on as before, undisturbed, until one day when Margaret went to deliver food to the door of Agnes Bennett. There was no sign of her. Word went round that the old woman was missing. What was more, several other members of the community had quietly disappeared.

Far away, on the county boundary of Gloucestershire, the sheriff was receiving from his counterpart in the next shire the care of two circuit judges. They made their way in procession with an entourage of attendants, lawyers, and members of the gentry, towards Gloucester where the Assizes were to be held.

In a backstreet tavern Midwife Taylor had taken lodgings with the other members of the village who had accompanied her there. They went out into the street to watch the procession — the judges in robes of red velvet and ermine, wending their way to the centre of the city where they were met by the Bishop and the Mayor.

The farmer, Josiah Tucker, coughed nervously and backed away. 'I can't approach such fine gen'lemen,' he stammered. 'They'll not be listenin' to the likes o' I.'

Midwife Taylor had no sympathy with such hesitation. 'There's no going back now. Tonight you'll go to their lodgings and tell them why we came.'

'But I don't know how to speak t' the likes o' they.'

'Just tell them the facts. They'll see to it that she's dealt with.'

A large house had been set aside for the use of the judges during the week they were to be present in the city. On this first evening the senior of the two took his ease, seated before the fire in his gown and nightcap.

Josiah Tucker knocked at the heavy oak door and, to his surprise, was led into the judge's presence. The judge beckoned him to approach as Josiah stood fumbling with his clothing.

'Speak up, man, I've not got all night to sit here and watch you.'

Josiah touched his forelock and began. 'Sir, we do 'ear as you have a reputation for being fair.'

'Cease the flattery and just tell me what it is you've come about.'

Josiah coughed and began again. 'In our village we do 'ave a woman who be known for her witchcraft.'

'And is the fact known to the Justices of the Peace?'

'It is, but they be afraid to do anything.'

'And what leads you to make such an accusation?'

60

Josiah coughed again. 'If it please you, sir, they do refuse t' listen. They do say as there's no evidence when it's as plain as the very nose on your face, sir, that the woman be in league with the Devil.'

The judge turned to stir the coals. 'Is the woman here in Gloucester?'

'Yes sir.'

'Then bring her to me tomorrow. I'll listen to the facts and she'll be tried accordingly.'

'Tomorrow, sir?' Josiah hovered, uncertain.

'You may go,' said the judge. 'Bring the woman tomorrow and present her before my lawyers.'

'Yes, sir. Thank you, sir.' Josiah touched his forelock repeatedly and backed out of the room.

The following day, the evidence against Agnes Bennett was once more set out before a crowded courtroom. The old woman was subjected a second time to the tests and inquisition: but, again, the final result was not to the liking of her accusers.

'The sentence,' said the judge, 'is that she be whipped at a cart-tail through the streets of Gloucester.'

Midwife Taylor gasped. 'And we've journeyed twenty miles to seek justice.'

Her protest went unheeded. Agnes Bennett was taken away and quickly replaced by the next offender on the long list of cases to be tried that day.

They had to wait until the following morning for sentence to be carried out. Shortly after dawn, they stood beneath the gallows, waiting for Agnes Bennett to be brought out into the street.

A convicted man stood on the back of a cart, his coffin beside him and a halter round his neck. There was a minister with him who asked the man to repent his crime. The prisoner mumbled something, though it was difficult to hear above the noise of the crowd. Then the executioner himself asked for forgiveness; he attached the halter to the gallows, and unceremoniously lashed the horse upon the rump, sending the man writhing and kicking into the air.

The hangman turned away in preparation for the next victim. It was left to the relatives of the dying man to dash forward and to pull with all their might upon his legs, so that he was put beyond the throes of his agony. He was taken down and undressed, the clothes placed to one side: they were the spoils of the executioner.

Agnes Bennett was at last brought out and tied to the tail of a similar cart. The ox was set moving but the old woman did not go far. At the very first lash of the whip she fell to her knees. After being dragged along for a further distance, she cracked her head against the heavy wooden wheel.

It was immediately obvious that she had lost consciousness. After a couple of token lashes, she was untied and left to lie at the side of the street. The crowd moved away to watch some other spectacle. Midwife Taylor, with Josiah Tucker and the other villagers, went back to the tavern to prepare for the long journey home.

Later that same evening Rupert rode into Gloucester. He supped well then went out into the streets of the city. They were filthy with the debris of the crowds. People were lying in doorways − some drunk, some having nowhere else to sleep. He picked his feet high, avoiding the piles of rubbish and excreta, stepping over feet and legs which protruded across his path.

At a street corner he stepped across a body much the same as all the others, but then paused and retraced his steps to re-examine it.

'Agnes Bennett?' He reached out with a toe and moved the old woman so that he could see her more clearly.

'What in God's name . . . ?' He said it more to himself than to her but she opened her eyes and looked at him.

He stood for some time looking down at her, uncertain what to do, half expecting that at any moment she would turn on him with a curse. But she was more dead than alive. He moved her head again with his foot and could see that there was blood coming from her ear.

'Master's son?'

She took him by surprise. He stepped back.

She ran her tongue across dry lips and lay with her eyes turned towards him.

'Yes, it's Rupert.'

He felt he ought to move on but the fact that she had recognized him held him there. And he was curious.

'What are you doing here, old woman? So far from Dunscombe.'

She looked at him blankly. She had no idea where she was.

Despite his uneasiness, he went down on one knee. 'I'll find someone to take you home.'

'Master's son,' she said again.

'Yes.'

She closed her eyes.

'How did you get here?' He could not imagine that she had found her way to Gloucester alone.

'You know the maid.' She said it with her eyes still closed.

'The one who brought you here?'

'Your cousin.'

'*My* cousin?'

'Nehemiah Hawkins' eldest girl.'

'You mean Margaret!'

'That's what they call her.' She heaved a sigh as though the conversation was concluded. The effort had exhausted her.

'What about Margaret?'

She gave the impression of having drifted off into sleep.

'What about her?' He shook her, alarm replacing curiosity. 'She's here in Gloucester?'

The old woman opened her eyes, obviously not understanding.

'She's in some kind of danger?'

She shook her head.

'Then what?'

She closed her eyes again and held them closed with a hand which she lifted feebly and placed across her face. 'Just tell her . . . '

'Tell her what?' Rupert had to keep a grip of himself. He did not want to hurt the old woman but he was desperate to know if Margaret was in some kind of distress.

'Just tell her that I said . . . thank you.'

'What for?'

But it was obvious that he was not going to get any more out of her.

He got up and stood over her. 'Just wait here,' he said over her unresponsive body. 'I'll go and fetch someone with a cart.'

By the time he had made his way back to the inn and had organized some form of transport, Agnes Bennett was dead.

He stood looking down at her, feeling a strange impotent sadness. He gave instruction for her body to be taken home to be buried in Dunscombe.

The next time he saw Margaret he would pass on to her the old woman's most unlikely message. He did not understand it but he would report it true. Agnes Bennett had said thank you.

Nehemiah chose his moment and broke to Margaret news of an arrangement which he had made earlier that day. He was about to travel to London.

'Why, Father?' She was extremely concerned. 'It's much too dangerous for you to go to London.'

'Hush, child, there's no danger to one who supports Parliament.'

'But you might get caught up in matters of which you've no part.'

'I'll stay well clear of trouble. And I must buy wool. You know well that our Cotswold fleeces aren't suitable for all our needs. I must go to Smithfield and buy wool from other parts.'

'But there are other markets you could go to. I'll go with you. I'll go *anywhere* with you.' She caught hold of his sleeve. 'Just don't go to London.'

'I must,' he said. 'But I thank you for the love you bear me.'

'Then take me with you.'

'No, child, you stay with your mother. I'll take Samuel.' She made as if to argue but he stilled her by placing a finger upon her lips. 'Tobias will need you: he'll have to take charge in my absence.'

'I don't understand, Father. There are other towns you could go to. I don't understand why you insist on going into London.'

He stood for a moment, studying her face. 'You're a perceptive child,' he said at last. 'You see into my head almost as well as I see myself.'

She looked at him and waited.

'I'll have to tell you the truth. You won't be content with

64

anything less.' He drew her over and seated her upon a bench against the wall. 'I've got to go to London on behalf of Sir Henry.'

'Sir Henry?'

'He's in difficulty because he can't go into the city to attend to his affairs. It isn't safe for him, and there are urgent matters which need his attention.'

'Then it's even worse than I feared. You really are in danger.'

'There's no danger. They're simply matters of business which your uncle isn't free to perform for himself.'

'I don't like it, Father. There must be other people who could go for him.'

'No one who could move so freely about the city. There's no harm to befall me in a city held by men whose views I share.'

She shook her head, staring intently at the floor. 'There must be some way of persuading you not to go.'

'You mustn't even try. I've got to help your uncle. He's a member of our family and he'd do the same for me.' He smiled and placed an arm about her shoulders. 'I'll be gone for less than a week. I leave at dawn. I'll rest overnight at Wallingford; the following night a room will be made ready for me at the home of Sir John Butler.'

'Then you'll meet Isobel.'

'I'll convey your greetings.'

'Of course, but I'd rather you didn't have to meet in such circumstances.'

'You're not to be afraid. You're to comfort your mother and be of assistance to Tobias.' He kissed her and drew her to her feet. 'Now there's a lot to be done before I leave.'

Margaret remained awake throughout that night, unable to sleep, worrying about her father. In the early hours of the morning there was a disturbance in the house when Lucy began once more to bleed.

She went to her bedside where Anne was already standing, holding a cloth which was steeped in blood. Together, they made her comfortable and settled her down to sleep.

Later, Tobias joined her and held her in his arms. She lay for some time sobbing quietly into his shoulder.

'I'm unworthy of your love,' she sobbed at last. 'I don't know why you don't renounce me.'

He moved slightly so that he could see her in the light of the tallow candle left burning beside the bed. 'I love you,' he said simply. 'You're the centre of my whole existence.'

'But I've dishonoured you again.'

'You bring me comfort and pleasure; and you'll also bring me children.'

'I doubt I shall ever please the Lord enough to grant me fruitfulness.'

'Of course you will.'

'But I continue to sin, and He continues to withhold His blessing from me.'

He kissed her and held her close against him.

She lay for some time in silence. He thought that she had fallen asleep. Then a great sob shuddered through her. 'I don't think I could bear it if you said you couldn't love me any more.'

'Ssh.' He held her even tighter in his arms.

'And you will, in time. Just wait and see. In time you'll grow tired of my failing you.'

'What nonsense.' He pulled away slightly so that he could look down into her eyes. 'If I were to stop loving you, you'd first need to beat me off with a stick. And even then I'd still come back for more.'

She half-smiled at that. 'What have I done to deserve such a kind and generous husband?'

'You've been the best wife any man could desire. Now, go to sleep.' He drew her back to him, rocking gently back and forth.

Eventually, her breathing changed to the steady rhythm of slumber. But Tobias remained awake. He knew that shortly, long before dawn, he must be up to help see Nehemiah on his way. He was as concerned as Margaret at the thought of his father journeying into London.

Four days later Nehemiah was seated with Samuel in an inn at Holborn. He had completed his mission for Sir Henry, encountering no problems, and had bought a quantity of wool from Smithfield Market. All was prepared for their journey home the following day.

This evening they took their rest, enjoying the atmosphere and the companionship of fellow travellers at the inn. The room was hot and smoky, heavy with the aroma of roasting meat, and the air was charged with suppressed excitement as conversation turned again and again to talk of imminent confrontation with the King.

'We must meet just once,' said the man seated opposite. 'But conclusively.' He wore the buff coat of a soldier and had earlier identified himself as an officer in Colonel Holles' regiment of Redcoats.

'Aye,' confirmed Nehemiah. 'It's a sad fact but true.' He leaned back against the oak settle, a tankard of ale in his hand.

At the far end of the room the landlord's wife carved huge joints of pork and beef, while her daughter squeezed her way between the tables, endeavouring to keep pace with the demands of the many customers.

'We're setting out shortly towards the North,' said the officer. 'And we're in need of young men.' He looked pointedly towards Samuel.

'My son's only a boy,' put in Nehemiah hurriedly. 'He's seventeen.'

'We've many younger.'

'But not my son.' Nehemiah leaned forward placing himself between Samuel and the officer. 'I'd offer myself, before offering my son.'

'Then you're accepted.'

'No, Father!' Samuel shot forward.

Nehemiah's face registered shock. 'If I weren't too old,' he put in rapidly.

'We've many who are older.'

'But I'm two score and seven.'

The officer looked him over. 'You look healthy enough. And you're in favour of the Cause.'

'I'm for the Cause,' said Nehemiah. 'But I'm no soldier.'

'Few are soldiers by inclination. But there's a need to free our country of a tyrant.' He looked steadily at Nehemiah. 'We need to fight, just once, in one decisive battle. Then we'll all be free to go home to our families and to our businesses.'

'No, Father don't . . . .'

'If we don't rid ourselves of this King and his damnable Papist wife, we shall find ourselves with another fatal storm unleashed upon our heads. We'll all be made martyrs and burn again on the fires at Smithfield.'

'If you'll allow me,' broke in Samuel. 'I'd be glad . . .'

'Be quiet, my son, and don't say another word until I say so.'

Samuel made to speak but thought better of it. He sank reluctantly back against the hard oak settle.

'I'd join you, sir,' said Nehemiah. 'But I can only say again that I'm too old. How could I begin at my age to face the rigours of battle? And my family need me. Surely there must be younger men who'd be of much more use to your Colonel Holles?'

'Then you're a coward, sir.'

Nehemiah started at the accusation and Samuel tensed beside him.

'Our leaders are to be sent to the block as so-called traitors. Our church is to be plunged back into the depths from which so many martyrs have raised it. And you care only for your comfort, and that of your family.'

'Those are harsh words, sir.'

'And this is harsh reality. Our leaders need you and yet you think only of yourself.'

Nehemiah looked uncertain and the officer lowered the tone of his voice. 'Join us, my friend. Just one battle would rid us forever of the danger to our church, the danger to our homes, and to our families. Surely that's not too much to ask of someone who clearly loves his God and loves His church?'

Samuel placed a restraining hand on his father's sleeve but Nehemiah did not look at him.

'No,' he said quietly. 'It's not too much to ask. The Lord has called me; and I came close to stopping up my ears.'

'Good man.' The officer reached out to shake his hand across the table.

'No, Father, please!' Samuel was no longer able to restrain himself. 'I can't just sit here and let you do this. Let the officer take me, and you can go home to Mother.'

'Go to our room,' said Nehemiah. 'I'll come to you later and tell you of the work you'll have to do in my absence.

There are matters which I must discuss with this officer.'

'But . . .'

'Go,' said Nehemiah, firmly but gently.

Reluctantly, Samuel rose to his feet and left the room. Later that night he begged and pleaded with his father. He went down on his knees and wept, but Nehemiah would not be dissuaded.

'I've no wish to fight,' he said. 'The Lord knows I'm not a man of courage; but neither was the shepherd boy, David, until he was called upon by the Lord to smite His enemies. There's a need this day for every man to search his heart. I can only lean on the Lord in the knowledge that He'll hone the sword of righteousness.'

The tears were coursing down Samuel's cheeks. 'I can't see you go to war, Father. If someone has to fight, let it be me.'

'Stay on your knees, my son, and pray to the Lord for the courage to let me go.'

'Then I'll go with you, Father. I'll watch your back. Together, we'll see each other through.'

'No, my son.' Nehemiah placed his hand gently on Samuel's shoulder. 'There's other work I need you to do. You'll return home tomorrow and take the wool which we've bought. I'll give you instructions for Tobias; you must work with him. And you must heed Margaret: she's only a maid but she knows a great deal about my business.'

'Yes, Father.'

'And if I don't return . . .' Nehemiah looked away and his voice almost broke. 'If I don't return, you must work with Tobias to care for your mother, and for your sisters.'

'Yes, Father.'

'See that they marry well.'

Samuel was weeping uncontrollably.

'And, Margaret . . .' Nehemiah stopped again and bit his lip.

'Yes, Father?'

'See to it that she's allowed to choose a husband for herself. She knows better than anyone who's best to share her life.'

Samuel nodded, no longer able to speak.

'But I shall return. Of course I'll return. I've enough faith

69

in the Lord to know I shall survive. With God's help, I'll be home before the harvest is gathered in.'

'We'll wait for you, Father.'

Samuel rose to his feet and the two embraced.

Early next morning they parted company. Samuel set off in one direction, Nehemiah in another. It was five o'clock and the city was waking. Farm carts were trundling in with produce from surrounding villages, and dairy maids were driving cows through the streets to their grazing places.

The streets were narrow. Nehemiah picked his way, stepping over the open drains and dodging from side to side to avoid the street vendors setting about their business of the day. Apprentices were taking down the shutters from the shops.

He found the place where he was to join up with the regiment of Redcoats. A few days later he began the long march northwards which would lead eventually to the battle of Edgehill.

As they set out, the streets were thronged with people, densely packed against the walls of the houses, leaving just enough room for the soldiers to march through the centre. Spirits were high, inflated by the excitement of the crowds. Nehemiah marched with vigour.

They left along the same road by which he and Samuel had entered the city less than a week before, marching on through the villages of Kensington and Hammersmith. But soon it became apparent that the high spirits of the soldiers were bubbling beyond control. At Chiswick, the officers called a temporary halt.

Nehemiah sat on the village green and leaned back against a tree. He was used to walking long distances and was not yet tired, but the shade of the tree was welcome after the hot, dusty road. Opposite, stood the house of Sir John Butler where just a short time ago he had been made welcome. He knew it would not be so today in the company of soldiers.

To his left stood the church. He became aware of a commotion inside – loud shouts and laughter, the bangs and crashes of some heavy object being brought down. He rose to his feet, startled.

'You coming to join us soldier?' asked a sergeant who was passing.

'I don't know what's going on.'

'A bit of sport. There'll not be much left by the time we're through.'

'But it's a church.'

'Aye, a Laudian one. The altar rails'll make good wood for the cooking fires.'

'But not a church,' stammered Nehemiah.

The sergeant stopped in his tracks and came back to face the older man squarely. 'You gibber like a woman, soldier. What's your name?'

'Hawkins sir.'

'Then, Hawkins, you'd best come join us quick, before I think you're a lover of this Laudian hell-hole.'

'I loathe this church as much as any, but I don't see the purpose of destroying it.'

'Oh,' sneered the sergeant in mock concern, 'what would you have us do with it?'

'Shun it for the stench it's worth, but I wouldn't see you smash it up.'

'You wouldn't see us smash it up,' mimicked the sergeant. 'And you'd deny your comrades a bit of sport?'

'I don't call it sport sir.'

'You don't call it sport. Well, I suggest, Hawkins, that you come join us — and I suggest that you join us quick — before I take to thinking that you're in favour of other causes in conflict with our own.'

'I'm a supporter of the true fight . . . ' began Nehemiah, but he was interrupted by an officer.

'Leave this man alone, sergeant,' he said, 'and go attend to your men in the church. This is an army, not a mob.'

'Yes, sir.' The sergeant moved away, throwing a sidelong glance in Nehemiah's direction.

'I want order restored and the men back in line with the minimum of delay.'

'Yes sir.'

The officer turned to Nehemiah. 'This isn't of my choosing, soldier, but the men are in high spirits. They're not yet trained to discipline.'

71

'It's a tense time for everyone,' said Nehemiah. 'It's not easy to march towards battle.'

Over the shoulder of the officer he saw a figure moving behind the windows of the house. He recognized it immediately as Isobel. She stood watching him, her hands resting upon a belly not yet distended but which he knew to contain Rupert's child. There was a look of puzzled accusation in her eyes. He felt ashamed.

'We'll all feel better when we get closer to the action,' said the officer. 'There's a job to be done and we must all give it our best endeavours.'

They set off again but discipline was by no means restored. Nehemiah marched in line, his spirits no longer high. He spoke to no one but used the time to pray to his God.

'Lord, I know that this battle is just. I'll smite Thy enemies and bring them to their knees. I'll fight for the continued reformation of Thy church. We'll bring an end to the sorcery of these Laudian Papist devils.

'But, Lord . . .' He recalled the sound of splintering wood and the sight of the soldiers hauling out the lengths of altar rail upon their shoulders; then he remembered the look upon Isobel's face. 'But Lord, this is not the way.'

CHAPTER 4

Margaret brought the string of pack ponies back towards the village. She had been collecting yarn and had taken with her the young apprentice, Matthew Crawshaw. A recent thunderstorm had brought rain which was cascading in runnels down the steep hillside. The ponies picked their way with caution over the rutted track, towards the raised causeway which led to the pack-horse bridge across the river.

As she approached it, Sir Henry hailed her from the other side and sat waiting on horseback, his hat raised in his hand.

'Margaret, any news of your father?' He prodded his horse into step with the pack ponies, while Matthew dropped back and took up position at the rear.

'No, sir.' There was no disguising the coolness of her tone. 'Not a word.'

'Still nothing.' Sir Henry frowned and thought for a moment.

'Nothing since he sent word by the carrier, and that was weeks ago.'

'I must find a way,' he said. 'There must be some way.'

'Thank you, but . . . '

He turned his horse and brought it close beside hers. 'You blame me, Margaret, for what has happened.'

She looked at him sharply. 'What would you have me do?'

She stopped and bit her lip, realizing that she had been close to insolence. 'It's not for me to say.'

'But you blame me all the same.'

She did not reply.

73

'I pray to God that your father doesn't feel ill-will towards me. He's a good man, and went willingly to my aid.'

'And now he goes to the aid of others,' said Margaret bitterly.

'Aye, he does. And I wish it were otherwise.'

Again she said nothing but moved steadily onwards without looking at him.

'I've no stomach for this confrontation, Margaret, no more than your father. There's been poor counsel on both sides. It's led to a situation where neither can turn back.'

'The King shouldn't have turned on his people.'

'The King was ill advised and I'll not deny it: but we can't have the men of Parliament committing high treason.'

'I don't care whose fault it is,' she retorted. 'My father's gone to war.'

'He has, indeed, and I understand how you feel.'

She turned and looked at him. 'You think there's some way of getting news?'

'I'll send a messenger to track the progress of his regiment. It shouldn't be too difficult. With luck, we might even get some word direct from Nehemiah.'

'He said to wait until harvest. Yet September's almost over and it doesn't seem that the armies have even met.'

'There does seem to be a great deal of confusion,' agreed Sir Henry. 'It's difficult to keep track of what's going on. I had news that the King was in Coventry, then Nottingham. There's no knowing where he might be now.'

'And Father sent word from Warwick.'

'If Rupert was involved we'd hear more, but he's not with the King's forces. He's travelling the countryside gathering support and funds.'

'At least he's free from danger.'

'There's always danger in these matters; but at least he's not to be found on some battlefield.'

Margaret winced and Sir Henry realized the tactlessness of his remark. 'I'll do everything I can to obtain news. And I pray as fervently as you do that your father will return home safely.'

She was torn in her feelings towards him. 'Thank you, but it would have been better had he never gone to London.'

They parted company at the point where the track divided.

Margaret and Matthew made their way towards the main street, while Sir Henry turned right towards the wood and Oakbourne House.

They had not gone far before Margaret was hailed from behind by another traveller. The man was travel-stained and damp from exposure to the recent thunderstorm. He spurred his tired horse to catch up with them. An even more tired pack pony trotted behind.

'I pray you . . . ' He stopped abruptly when he realized that he was addressing a woman.

He turned instead to Matthew. 'Boy,' he said, 'do you know the way to the home of a certain Reverend William Dillington?'

He was young and handsome in a way which left Margaret disconcertingly embarrassed.

'Why, yes, sir. But 'tis hard to say . . . ' Matthew was a shy boy, not used to being confronted by strangers.

It was left to Margaret to overcome her embarrassment and to offer a reply. 'He's in the next village, sir, some four miles from here.'

The man did not look at her. He would obviously have preferred to speak to Matthew.

'He's the minister of our church,' she said.

He glanced at her for the first time. 'Then we're of like understanding.'

She made a slight movement of her head but said nothing.

'He's been recommended to me as a minister of true zeal,' he said. 'I wish to seek hospitality from him for the night.'

'He's to be found across the hills, sir. If you follow the road out of the village, and pass across the hilltop there . . .' she pointed with a finger towards the horizon '. . . you'll see the spire of his church some four miles away.'

'Thank you.' He raised his hat — a wide-brimmed copotain of black felt, its high crown wide at the base and diminishing slightly to a broad flat top. Beneath it his hair was cropped short — much shorter than the styles to which Margaret was accustomed.

He nudged his horse into a slow plodding step, keeping pace alongside the pack ponies. He could have moved on ahead but he chose not to do so, turning instead to speak again with Matthew.

'Do you also go to the church of the Reverend Dillington?'

'Yes, sir. Always, sir. I go with Master Hawkins, but he's not here at the moment. And I go with the Mistress; and with Mistress Margaret, here. Every Sunday, sir, and never fail.'

'Good boy. And do you pay heed to the sermon?'

'Why, yes, sir. Always.'

The stranger was dressed in a jacket of grey cloth, reaching to the hips, with matching grey breeches above grey wool stockings and boots of leather. A wide white linen collar, cut square, was spread over his short cloak of black serge.

'Then maybe we'll meet again. I've a mind to stay for a day or two. It's possible that I'll preach the sermon this coming Sunday.'

Both Margaret and Matthew looked at him, surprised.

'I'm the Reverend Deliverance Daniels,' he said. 'I'm on my way to take leave of an uncle in Nottingham; then I shall pass by this way again to take ship from Bristol for New England.' He noted Matthew's gasp of admiration at the mention of New England. 'My horses are lame. I need to rest a day or two before proceeding.'

'To New England,' gasped Matthew. 'I never did meet anyone as did travel so far as New England.'

'I've yet to set out on the real journey,' he conceded. 'But I allow it's likely to be a hazardous venture.'

''Tis a mighty long distance,' reiterated Matthew.

'It is, indeed, but the Lord has called me. I must face whatever perils may lie in store for me. Such a venture is not for the fainthearted, but those who have the zeal of the Lord will succeed in nurturing the plantation of the true Church of England.'

'I've heard from Master Hawkins that there be savages in the land,' said Matthew in awed respect.

'There are savages called Indians, but the Lord has summoned these heathen from the worship of the Devil and would bring them to an understanding of His true church.'

'Oh, sir,' gasped Matthew, ''tis such an adventure as I never heard of.'

'Then you must come and listen to my sermon.'

They had reached the door of Nehemiah's house.

Reverend Daniels paused for a moment before he took his leave. 'I shall keep watch for you.' As he said it he cast a glance towards Margaret which sent her pulses racing in a most alarming manner.

A second later he had turned away, tugging on the rope of his trailing pack pony. He prodded his horse into a tired trot towards the church of the Reverend William Dillington.

Word quickly spread through the village that a new preacher was passing through the neighbourhood. The following Sunday even more people than usual set out to walk across the hills to church.

From the moment that he began to preach his sermon, it became obvious that this young man was no ordinary preacher. The air was immediately charged with a fervour and excitement quite unlike anything which the Reverend Dillington had ever been able to muster. Daniels manipulated the fervour – moulding it almost as a tangible element – choosing his moment to whip it up to a point where he had the congregation about to leap to their feet, then stilling his voice to just above a whisper, which had them straining forward in their seats to catch his every word.

Margaret listened as she had never listened before, attending to every nuance of his voice, every gesture of his hand – through the first hour and into the second.

Every now and then, as he cast his eye across the congregation, she fancied that it lingered just a moment or two longer upon her than upon the other members sitting about her. She could not be sure, though, and chastised herself for even thinking that it could be so.

When it was over, the congregation fell upon him with enthusiasm. 'You must come back and preach for us again,' they begged.

But he pointed out that, next time he passed through the district, he would be pressed for time. The year was well advanced and he was anxious to take ship for New England. Already autumn gales were imminent. With each week of delay, the Atlantic crossing would become more hazardous.

'But I'm not thinking of danger alone,' he added. 'I'm thinking of the people of the community to which I'm bound. They've been without a preacher since spring.'

'Then we'll not delay you,' said Tobias. 'But we trust you'll call by on your way back to Bristol. We should like to offer the hospitality of my father's house.'

'It will take me a week to journey to Nottingham,' he said. 'Then I must spend a further week with my uncle. I should reach these parts again by mid-October.'

'We'll see you then,' said Tobias. 'You'll rest overnight and take food with us.'

It had been a brief interlude which had taken their minds, temporarily, from their concern for Nehemiah. They feared daily for his life. Yet, in fact, he had seen little of battle beyond one brief skirmish which had come to nothing.

He was not so much battle-weary, as foot-sore. They had marched for weeks. From London they had marched through Buckinghamshire, where they had met up with Colonel Hampden and his regiment of Greencoats. Together they had marched towards Northampton.

Some thirty miles to the west, Warwick Castle had lain besieged and it was near here that the skirmish had taken place. Eager for confrontation, they had marched out to the fields where the Earl of Northampton's Royalist forces were drawn up; but the Royalists had turned and fled.

Throughout the long march little had been achieved in establishing discipline. Nehemiah had witnessed the looting of houses, the indiscriminate vandalism and desecration of Laudian churches. After further plundering in Northampton, the Lord General, Earl of Essex had arrived on the scene. A code of martial law had been drawn up but still the plundering continued.

They had marched again, through torrential rain, for a further twenty-eight miles, to Worcester. Now, in late September, he was in Hereford.

On the Sunday when his family were listening enthralled to Deliverance Daniels, he was walking the streets of that distant city. He came to the doors of the cathedral. Inside, his comrades had invaded the Laudian service. He could hear the commotion as they danced in the aisles to the music of the organ and endeavoured to drown the singing of the choir.

Nehemiah had never been able to bring himself to join

78

in such activity. He knew that his reluctance made him unpopular with his fellow soldiers, but he held himself apart and prayed daily for the battle which would seal for ever the fate of these Laudian churches and put an end to his wanderings.

'You've no stomach for this soldiering, Hawkins.'

He turned, startled. He had thought he was alone. He recognized the man who stood beside him.

'I'm John Fletcher, regimental surgeon.'

'Yes, sir, I know of you.'

'And I've been watching you, Hawkins. I think you could be of use to me.'

'Me, sir?' He was taken by surprise.

'Yes, Hawkins. I'm surrounded by incompetents. I'm in need of an assistant, someone with a level head.'

'But I know nothing of the art of the surgeon, sir.'

'I'm not asking you to become a surgeon, Hawkins, merely my assistant. We're bound to engage in battle before much longer. I need a good pair of steady hands beside me.'

'I'm not sure that I'd be capable, sir.'

'You're capable. And it will keep you from the fighting. You're a man more suited to the preserving of life than the taking of it.'

'I'm not afraid, sir. I came to fight.'

'I don't doubt it. But don't tell me you relish the thought of bloodshed?'

'I'll not deny that I'd rather serve the Cause in some other way.'

'Then I'll teach you how to be of use to me. In fact, you can come with me now. Last week some fool of a musketeer shot a comrade through the leg: now the wound's so rotten with gangrene it looks as though he won't last till morning. You can assist me with the amputation.'

Nehemiah paled slightly.

The other man smiled. 'The first amputation's always the worst,' he said. 'You'll soon get used to it.'

During the second week of October news at last reached Dunscombe. Nehemiah was on the move again — this time towards Banbury. The family were relieved to learn that, even though he would be close to the scene of battle, he would not be taking part. It brought a lifting of the tension which had hung over them for months.

Margaret found herself singing as she attended to the animals at dusk. Her lightness of spirit was due also, in some measure, to the knowledge that the Reverend Deliverance Daniels would shortly be returning; but she did not allow herself to acknowledge that fact.

It was dark in the stables. She carried a lanthorn before her, casting a dim glow as she checked each pack pony.

At the far end, where it was darkest, she held the lanthorn aloft and almost squealed in fright as she tripped over a man lying warm in the pile of dried bracken at her feet.

'Rupert! You scared me nearly half to death!'

He raised his head and smiled at her but she saw he had difficulty in focusing his eyes.

'And you're foxed to a stupor!'

He apologized and endeavoured to raise himself a little further. 'I've only had a mug or two.'

'You've had more than two. You're drunk to the point of shame.' She went down on one knee in an effort to help him rise. 'You're in need of a potion to bring you to your senses.' She lifted his shoulders so that he sat propped against the wall.

'Just give me a moment and my head will clear.'

'I'll call Tobias and Samuel; we'll get you into the house. Though I daren't think what Mother will have to say to you.'

'No.' He held on to her. 'Don't go.'

'Rupert, you've got to stop seeking me out like this. You can speak to me inside the house in company of my family — if you're capable of speaking with any sense at all.'

'I had to come and say goodbye.'

'Goodbye?'

'They're sending me into battle.'

'Oh Rupert.' She looked at him gravely. 'You were willing enough to take sides. Now, I suppose, you regret it.'

'I don't regret it,' he said. 'The Cause is right. Though I admit I don't relish the thought of going into battle.'

'Yes,' she sighed. 'There's a vast difference between raising funds and standing firm on a battlefield.'

'Margaret, I think I'm afraid.'

She put a gentle hand on his shoulder. 'I'm sure you are.'

'I'm no swordsman. I've only ever fought for sport.'

'And this is hardly sport,' she sighed. The full impact of the war suddenly hit her. 'My father's on the other side.'

He nodded. 'But we're not likely to meet.'

'Oh, Rupert, I do hope not. I can't bear to think that you and my father could meet in battle.'

'And even if we did,' he went on, 'I should avoid him. There's no way that Uncle Nehemiah and I would ever shed each other's blood.'

She shuddered. 'Anyway,' she said, 'he's not taking part in the fighting. He's an assistant to the surgeon.'

'Thank God for that.' He closed his eyes. 'At least he'll be spared the fighting.'

She left him to sit quietly for a moment, her hand resting lightly on his arm.

'But I won't,' he said. 'And I don't know if I can bring myself to kill.'

She gulped. 'It all seems so terribly real now that it's so close to hand.'

He nodded and remained quiet.

'Margaret . . . '

'Yes?'

'Hold me.'

She put her arms about his shoulders.

'I'm so afraid.'

She could feel the warmth of his breath through her sleeve.

'I've never needed you more.'

'You don't *need* me, Rupert,' she said gently. 'You've got my friendship. But it's wrong to talk of need.' The thought made her slacken her hold slightly.

'I know I shouldn't ask . . . but I may never see you again.'

'What?'

'Just one kiss. I shan't ask for more.'

'No.' She let her hands fall but, when he slipped sideways, took hold of him again.

'I'm sorry.'

'It's all right. But you know it's wrong.' She kissed him lightly on the forehead. 'You've got my friendship. You know I'll always love you.'

'But as your brother.'

'As my brother,' she said softly. 'No one could have a dearer brother.'

He buried his head in the fabric of her sleeve. 'I love you, Margaret. I love you so much.'

'But you're married now. And it's wrong to speak of it.'

'I know.'

She continued to hold him, rocking him back and forth. 'Isobel's with child,' she said.

'Yes, I've done my duty.'

'You must learn to love her.'

'I can't,' he said. 'I truly can't.'

'You must, Rupert. You've got no choice.'

He sighed and continued to rest his head against her sleeve. 'I've been such a fool.'

She did not reply.

'Kiss me, Margaret.'

'No, Rupert.'

'Please.'

He lifted his head and kissed her softly on the side of the neck. She turned her face away.

'I love you so,' he whispered. 'You'll never know how much I love you.'

'Don't, Rupert . . . ' She was about to release her arms from him when he kissed her again. 'Rupert, don't!'

'I need you so.'

A combination of need, of fear, of intoxication, made him take hold of her and roll sideways.

'Rupert, no!'

She was trapped beneath him, spluttering on flakes of dry bracken as she breathed shallowly in alarm.

He kissed her again, emotion rising.

She realized with a sickening jolt that she was in real danger. 'Rupert, let me go!'

'Dearheart, please, don't make me hurt you.'

'Let me go!' She bit him on the first place she could reach, which happened to be his cheek.

'Ouch!' He almost stopped but passion drove him on to kiss her again, cupping his hand about her breast as he breathed, 'I love you, love you!'

His body had tensed to a tight urgency. She attempted to scream but he placed his forearm across her face, making

82

her gag on the thick velvet pile of his sleeve. 'Dearheart, don't struggle like that or you'll make me hurt you.'

She could not believe that anyone who had been so drunk could, in the next moment, be so strong. Her arms were free. She began flailing them about, looking for something with which to hit him. But he caught her wrists and held them pinned above her head.

'Dearheart, relax. If you'd only just let me make you feel . . . '

'Beast!'

The interjection made him pause for a moment. But his pulses were racing and the effect of the drink was to blur his finer sensibilities.

She tried to kick but his weight was upon her.

He increased the pressure upon her breast and kissed her again, forcing his tongue deep into her mouth.

She jerked her head sideways, endeavouring at the same time to contort her body in the other direction in an effort to writhe free. She succeeded only in hurting her back.

He moved, using one hand to hold both wrists above her head while the other he slid beneath her clothing.

'Dearheart, relax. That way you'll feel . . . '

She bit him again.

In the same moment she felt him force his way inside her, working himself with frenzied gasps until at last he let out a cry: 'I love you, love you, love you . . . ' and slumped exhausted beside her.

In shock, she found herself unable to scream. She lay panting and bruised, coughing on the particles of bracken in her dry mouth.

Gradually, she eased herself free from him.

He opened his eyes and looked at her. 'Oh, my God!' he gasped. 'What have I done?'

She stopped, half free of him but trapped by her clothing. She was still unable to speak.

'I'm so terribly sorry.' He could hardly get it out.

It seemed to Margaret in that instant that it had all been her fault.

'I don't know . . . I can't think what made me do it.' He put his hand to his head.

She had not fought hard enough.

'Margaret, I'm sorry.' His head was reeling. 'Can you ever forgive me?'

She had brought it upon herself.

'I don't know what to say.'

'Margaret?' As if from a great distance she heard her name being called. It was Samuel from across the yard.

She pulled her clothing free, dragging herself from beneath Rupert.

'Margaret?' Samuel called again.

'I'll never drink . . . ' Rupert held out a hand, 'as long as I . . . '

But she gave him a look of sheer hatred and walked away.

He sank his head into his hands. 'Oh my God, I'm sorry. So sorry.'

Samuel met her at the stable door. 'You've been so long, we were worried about you.' He had a freshly lit lanthorn in his hand. He took one look at her. 'Whatever's wrong? You're strewn with bracken, and your hair . . . it's all over your face.'

'I'm sorry.' How could she ever admit to having done such a shameful thing? 'The horse shied and threw me back against the wall.'

'Are you hurt?'

She could have done something to deter him. She could have screamed. She could have fought harder.

'Are you hurt?' her brother asked again.

'No.' She stood barring the door as he stepped forward as if to enter. 'It merely threw me back and took my breath.'

'I'd best go and attend to it.'

'No!' She took a firmer stance in the doorway. 'There's no need. It's tethered now.'

'Well, if you're sure.' He stepped back so that he could see her more clearly. 'You're in a dreadful state. Here, let me look at you.'

'No!' In some ridiculous way it seemed to Margaret that she must carry some outward mark of her sin. 'Leave me alone. I'll be all right.'

'Well, if you say so. But you look quite ill.'

Rupert had been about to rise and make his presence known. He hauled himself awkwardly to his knees in a state of shock and intoxication. He hesitated, not knowing what

84

to do. Margaret had denied his presence. If he revealed himself, he could make her situation worse. He waited a little longer, then heard Samuel lead her away from the door. He had violated her and had brought shame upon them both. To have done so was bad enough; but to disclose their shame for all to know . . . He decided he must keep quiet until he had a chance to speak with Margaret again.

Samuel took his sister's arm and led her back towards the house. 'We were waiting for you to begin the reading, but perhaps you'd better go straight to bed. Shall I get Mother to help you?'

'No!' she said sharply.

'Or Lucy, perhaps. She's in the parlour.'

'No,' she said again. 'I'll be all right, I tell you.'

He saw her to the door and watched with concern as she walked down the passageway towards her room.

'Perhaps you'd ask Mother to forgive me for not joining you this evening,' she said, trying to re-establish some sort of normality.

She went inside and closed the door behind her, dropping to her knees upon the floor. She went to fetch water, washing herself until she was sore. She felt that she should pray for forgiveness, but could not do so. Her sin was too great.

Next morning Deliverance Daniels returned, riding wearily down the main street.

Margaret saw him as she was returning home to the family dinner. All morning she had been in turmoil, trying to carry out her duties without disclosing her distress; yet the sickening scene of the previous evening played over and over through her mind, causing loathing and disgust to well in great tides of self-accusation. She could not forgive Rupert for what he had done; yet, at the same time, it seemed that in some perverse way she must carry the blame.

The sight of the young preacher brought new tumult within her. The naive eagerness with which she had previously awaited his return was now sullied and overlaid by a deep inner sense of her own sin and shame.

She stepped back behind cover of a large tree and watched

him pass, her eyes fixed upon his face as she attempted to conceal herself from his gaze.

But it seemed that he looked at nothing. His chin was slumped forward on his chest and his cheeks were flushed against the unhealthy grey pallor of his skin. He dismounted from his horse at the door and Matthew led it through the horse passage into the yard at the rear.

Margaret held back, not wanting to return home, not wanting to face him in the confines of the small room. Yet she knew that she had no choice: the family would be waiting for her. She slipped in through the back door.

Deliverance Daniels was seated at the table but it was obvious that he had no appetite for food.

'I trust you'll forgive my discourtesy,' he apologized to Anne, 'but it seems that my supper of last evening has turned my stomach.'

Anne glanced up at Margaret's entry but her attention was upon Deliverance Daniels.

'It worries me to see you looking ill,' she said. 'I'll fetch some physic.'

Margaret mumbled her apology and sat down at her usual place beside the children.

'Thank you, but I think I'll just go outside and take some air.' The young man rose unsteadily and pushed back his stool with a scraping noise across the floor. 'It's suddenly very hot inside the house.'

Before he had made it halfway to the pig-pen he had slumped to his knees.

Tobias had followed him into the yard. 'You're burning with fever,' he said. 'It's more than food which has turned your stomach.'

Deliverance Daniels rolled sideways so that he was lying with his head in his hands. 'I grant my head's throbbing fit to burst, but I'll feel better if I can just be allowed to lie here for a while.'

'You must go to your bed,' said Anne. The whole family was now standing looking down at him. 'You're too ill to do anything else.'

Deliverance Daniels put up feeble protest but eventually allowed himself to be helped upstairs where Samuel and

Matthew had straw mattresses set upon pallets beside the weaving loom.

'You'll forgive us, Reverend Daniels, that we don't have grander accommodation in which to house you.'

But the young man sank gratefully to rest upon the floor.

Margaret remained downstairs, covering her own discomfort by chiding the children into finishing their dinner. She cleared the table, scraping the crumbs from its surface with a further flurry of activity.

Anne called down at intervals, issuing instruction for cordial of rock samphire and for water with which to bathe his face. Margaret collected them up, leaving them on the second tread of the stair, glad that it would be considered unseemly for her to enter the presence of the young man lying sick upon the floor.

Mid-afternoon, her mother sent her out to gather a supply of fresh medicinal herbs. It was raining softly but she took a cloak and worked her way, first along the river bank, then up towards the edge of the wood.

She was concentrating hard, looking for a splash of colour, a leaf, the particular growth pattern of each herb. She did not see Rupert standing, waiting for her under cover of the trees. He stepped out as she approached, causing her to let out a stifled squeal of alarm.

He put out a hand to steady her. 'I'm sorry, Margaret. I didn't mean to startle you.'

She backed off and made to turn away but he blocked her path.

'I've been keeping watch for you all day.'

'Let me go, Rupert.'

'We've got to talk.'

'Go away!' Her heart was hammering in her chest and she felt sick.

'About what happened.' He held on to her arm.

She shook him off. 'I've no wish to speak about it.'

'There are things I need to say.'

Tears welled and overflowed. 'Haven't you said – and done – enough?'

'I'm sorry, Margaret. I've misused you.'

'You've *misused* me!'

87

'I don't know what made me do it. I got carried away and I . . . '

'Yes, Cousin. And I've no wish to discuss my sin.'

'The sin wasn't yours. It was mine.' He tried again to take hold of her. 'I'm so sorry, Margaret, but I was in my cups.'

She shook her head in bewilderment. 'To be drunk was sin enough. But to . . . ' she left the statement to trail in the air.

'I love you so much.'

'Love!'

'Yes, love.'

She felt sick again, swallowing down the nausea with a sigh as she turned her back on him. 'Just go away, Rupert. Go home to your wife and leave me to my shame.'

'I'll speak with your family. Tell them what I've done.'

'No,' she said vehemently. 'You've done enough harm. For the love of God don't make things worse by adding to my shame.'

He wanted to take hold of her, but he knew that any such action would only lead to her further rebuffing him. 'As I was keeping watch I saw a man.'

She paused. 'It was the Reverend Deliverance Daniels.'

'He went inside your house.'

She did not reply.

'You spoke to him.'

'I spoke not a word.'

'Oh, Margaret, I can't bear to think of some other man looking upon you.'

She exploded, as much in response to her own confused emotions as in response to him. 'How dare you?' she said. 'He's a man of God, and he's taken sick in his bed.'

'Then he's remaining overnight?'

'Just go away, Rupert. Just go away and leave me alone. The Reverend Daniels is taken sick in his bed.'

'How long will he stay?'

'I don't know,' she retorted. 'He's a man of God on his way about the business of the Lord.'

'Promise me that if he looks upon you, then you'll rebuff him.'

'Why should he look upon me?' she shouted. 'There's no way that he'll look upon me, I tell you. And I don't want him to look upon me. I don't want *anyone* to look upon me. And I don't want to see you, or speak to you, or set eyes on you ever again!'

'Do you hate me so?'

'Yes, I hate the very sight of you.'

He bit his lower lip. 'Then perhaps it's as well that I'm going into battle.'

She stopped short. She had forgotten that he was being sent to fight.

'You wish me dead.'

'I wish you well,' she said, but it was uttered coldly.

He stepped to one side, leaving her free to walk away. 'Oh, I almost forgot,' he said dully, 'Agnes Bennett said "thank you".'

'What?'

'She said "thank you".'

'When?'

'Just before she died. She said just to tell you: "thank you".'

Margaret began to cry. She gathered her cloak about her shoulders and made her way back towards the village, lifting a corner of the cloak to her eye.

Rupert watched her go, his own eyes swamped with tears.

He waited until she had gone inside the house then followed after her, down the main street towards Dunscombe church.

He went inside and knelt for a long time in prayer. He was not in the habit of praying, but today he searched for words.

'Lord, forgive me. I don't know how to undo this thing I've done.'

He felt the need of some answering voice but none came.

'I never meant to harm her.'

He looked up, casting his eye around the church.

'I truly didn't.'

He looked towards the east wall. Above the chancel arch, he received the answer to his plea. The Doom painting covered the entire wall. At its centre the dead were rising – rotting, mutilated flesh, sunken cheeks and empty eye sockets. He closed his eyes and squeezed them shut, but his mind was filled with the mutilation of the battle scene, the blood, the terror, the thrusting swords.

'Oh, dear God, no. Have mercy upon me.'

To the right of the painting, stood St Peter with outstretched hands. But it was the scene to the left which held Rupert's gaze. The Devil pranced, eager to receive the souls which plunged into the boiling cauldron at His feet. Faces struggled to escape the bubbling ferment, contorted with the indescribable anguish of eternal despair: arms strained upwards, clutching out for deliverance which would never come, for pity which would forever be denied.

'Oh, dear God in Heaven, extend Thy mercy.'

But the frescoes staring down at him spoke louder than any word of comfort.

He tore his eyes away and rose unsteadily to his feet. At the door, on the north wall, the painting of St Christopher looked down upon him.

'Oh, Blessed Saint,' he said, 'have mercy and watch over me. But perhaps it's best for everyone that I'm sent to die on some distant soil.'

He climbed up on to his horse and rode out of the village to join up with his regiment.

That night the condition of the Reverend Deliverance Daniels worsened. It continued to worsen with each succeeding day. Lucy and Anne took turns to sit beside him, day and night, ministering potions and cooling his brow as he thrashed in a fever. But the typhoid virus was sapping his strength.

During the second week, his skin became inflamed with a rash, his lips dry and cracked, his tongue so raw that even the swallowing down of saliva became painful to him. His mind was confused, muttering prayers which petered off into unintelligible whispers.

Margaret hovered at the base of the stairs, in a constant ambivalence of emotion, half wishing that she could be allowed to go up and to look at him as he lay upon his sickbed, yet sick at heart and filled with disgust at her own sense of sin and shame.

She went into the orchard and knelt among the rotting apples which lay fallen from the trees.

'Lord, why dost Thou choose to take this man? He's on his way to preach Thy Word to the people of New England. Who else would have such great courage to venture out on such a journey?'

A centipede emerged from beneath a curled yellowing leaf and ran across her line of vision. She watched as it scuttled from one blade of grass to the next.

'Is it because I looked upon him?'

The centipede stopped, hardly visible against the damp black soil.

'Or is it as punishment upon me for my sin?'

It occurred to her then, that if Deliverance Daniels died, she would not have opportunity to set eyes upon him again until he was carried in his shroud.

A rat, scurrying through the undergrowth, diverted her eye from the centipede. It was on its way to plunder the eggs which she had not yet gathered from the hens. She remained still, watching. It stopped to bite into the mould-spotted skin of a rotting apple.

Her mother came up behind her. 'Margaret, you're on your knees.'

She jumped. 'I'm sorry, Mother. I was praying for the Reverend Daniels.'

Anne touched her lightly on the head. 'You're a godly child,' she said, 'but hurry now. I need more herbs, else I fear he won't get through another day.'

She turned and went swiftly back into the house.

Margaret sighed. She bunched her fist and raised it above the centipede. With one quick, decisive movement she brought it down, stamping the insect into the mud. But the action did nothing to relieve her feelings.

It was 23 October. On that same day, at Edgehill, Nehemiah was about to undergo an ordeal of his own. The two armies at last faced each other.

Nehemiah stood beside John Fletcher, restraining himself from turning on his heel and taking flight. There was nothing for an assistant surgeon to do but to stand and wait until the cries of the injured signalled the commencement of his duties.

The advance was slow at first: squadrons of horse on the

wings maintained walking pace with the infantry at the centre. But when they charged, it seemed to Nehemiah as if the very doors of hell had opened. He was positioned some distance away, on the edge of a small thicket, but he could see clearly, and he could hear. First, the thundering of hooves, then the cries of the attackers, interspersed with screams. The Royalist Cavalry was sweeping all before it.

There seemed to be no stopping it. Nehemiah watched the men of his regiment falling in great numbers. And all the time there were the awful cries, and the sound of steel upon steel.

Still there was nothing he could do. There was no way of retrieving the injured.

'Stand fast, Hawkins. Soon they'll come crawling in.'

'It's the standing fast, sir, which comes so hard.'

'I know, but soon your hands will be so full there'll be no time to think of anything else.'

'We ought to go out and fetch them in.'

'We'd be of little use lying dead beside them. Soon enough they'll make their way to us. Later, when there's a lull in the battle, men will be sent out to carry them in.'

As he spoke, the first man came staggering towards them, his hands clutching at the bloody pulp of his face. His right cheek had been torn away. John Fletcher laid him beneath a thorn bush and issued instructions to Nehemiah for needle and thread.

Soon others came. Men staggered towards them on tottering legs, or crawled on hands and knees. Nehemiah had no more time for thought. He had time for nothing except coping with the increasing demands upon his energy and upon his initiative.

They were assisted by four women, wives of soldiers, who were later joined by other women from the nearby village.

'This is no place for a woman,' he said as he knelt beside a girl hardly old enough to be classed a woman. They were endeavouring to staunch the flow of blood from a gaping wound.

'I'm used to nursing the sick.' She took the man's head and placed it more comfortably upon the ground.

'But not on the battlefield.'

'I'm more use here than I'd have been if I'd stayed in my

cottage back in Aylesbury. I'd rather be here with my husband.'

Nehemiah placed his hand across the wound and immediately the thick red blood oozed up through his fingers. 'It's not right.'

'There's lots of us who come with our husbands.'

'I know,' said Nehemiah. 'But it's not right. It's not right for men to place their wives in such danger.'

The woman shrugged. 'I'm a sight better here on a soldier's pay, than I'd be starving in our cottage.'

Nehemiah thought, not for the first time that day, of Anne and the family back home at Dunscombe.

'Some dress as men. They fight beside their husbands.'

'Which is worse than tending the injured.'

The young woman smiled. 'There's not a lot of difference between using a pike and using a scythe. Not if you're used to tending the crops.'

'It's a darned sight less perilous to be handling a scythe.'

'But a sight more lonely without our men,' said the young woman. She turned to him and they exchanged a glance of mutual understanding.

'Get hold of his legs. We'll drag this one over to the surgeon.'

There was no time to watch the battle but Nehemiah did enquire of one man as he lay on the ground: 'How goes the battle, Trooper?'

The man winced as John Fletcher examined his thigh, smashed by a musket ball. 'The enemy Horse near routed us,' he gasped. 'But they've got themselves scattered across the countryside. Nothing but the Devil himself is going to regroup them.'

'God be praised. What of our men?'

'They're . . . ' The man went rigid as John Fletcher began to probe the wound.

Nehemiah let the moment pass, then wiped the man's brow with a piece of rag. 'What of our men?' he asked again.

'They're standing firm. I've never seen such courage.'

'Thank God. Then it's nearly over.'

John Fletcher gave him a look.

93

'Soon we'll all be going home.'

John Fletcher looked at him again then said to the soldier: 'I'm afraid, Trooper, that you'll likely lose this leg.'

The man blanched momentarily. 'I've still got another one to offer to the service of God. Cut it off and I'll return to the battle.'

Nehemiah was stricken with admiration for the man. 'There won't be any more fighting,' he said gently. 'After today, we can all go home to our families.'

John Fletcher glanced at him again out of the corner of his eye. 'Fetch me the saw,' he said. 'We might as well take the leg today, as leave it for the maggots tomorrow.'

By evening, activity on the battlefield had almost ceased.

'I don't understand this lull,' said Nehemiah. There was none of the jubilation which he had envisaged. 'Where's the rejoicing?'

'There'll be no rejoicing until the battle's won,' said John Fletcher.

'We haven't won?'

'No one's won — yet.'

'Then why aren't we still fighting?'

John Fletcher turned to him and Nehemiah saw again the look which he had earlier failed to interpret. 'As I hear it,' he said, 'Colonel Hampden and Sir Philip Stapleton are urging that we attack again this evening, or tomorrow morning. But My Lord Essex sees fit to listen to others.'

'But we *must* strike,' exclaimed Nehemiah. 'We must strike now and get it over.'

'Hawkins,' said John Fletcher, 'you're a good man, and a courageous one; but you know little about soldiering.'

'I only know that it's our duty to carry out the Will of God.'

'Ah, yes, the Will of God. But first you've got to take into account the fact that this army contains soldiers of fortune who see fit to prolong the battle.'

'Prolong it?' gasped Nehemiah.

'Men whose interests lie in spinning it out.'

'But that's nothing but sin!'

'It may be sin in your eyes, Hawkins, but to others it is expediency.'

It was more than Nehemiah could cope with. He sank to his knees on the spot. 'Lord, I beg of Thee, bring wisdom to Thy general and to his commanders. Have them strike again tonight so that we may vanquish Thy foes from the face of the earth; that we may live henceforth in peace and honour of Thy name.'

John Fletcher took him gently by the shoulder. 'Get to your feet, Hawkins. There'll be no action tonight beyond the tending of these injured men, and the burying of the dead. My guess is that tomorrow we'll start a race southwards to see which army can be the first to reach London.'

Unsteadily Nehemiah went back to his work. Later, when he found himself free for a time, he took a spade and went to help with the burying of the dead. He could not bear to stand inactive.

It was dusk, the light now fading fast. About him the scents and sounds of an autumn evening mingled with the reek of blood and vomit. He retched on it.

On the other side of the thicket he saw what he at first thought to be nothing but a dead horse. He took little notice of it until he noticed, beside it, a Royalist soldier with his sword raised, about to strike. Beneath the horse a man lay trapped, at the mercy of the sword.

Muscle moved faster than thought. Nehemiah ran up behind the Royalist. He raised the spade and brought it down upon the back of his head.

'May God be praised!' said the man beneath the horse. 'You're the answer to my prayer.'

Nehemiah turned first to the Royalist soldier sprawled at his feet, fearing that he had killed him; but he rose shakily and took flight.

'The cur runs like a rabbit,' said the Parliamentarian. He was attempting to make light of it, but his voice was hollow from shock and from the prolonged pain of his injuries.

'Can I be of help to you, sir?'

'Captain Mosely of the Lifeguard. And I've been trapped here since noon.' He was pinned at his legs. Nehemiah could see his feet protruding from beneath the belly of the horse.

'Are you sore injured, sir?'

'I fear so. Though I'm so numb there's no knowing.' He

95

attempted to ease himself, but the weight of the horse held him fast.

'I'll try to lift it.' Nehemiah used the handle of the spade and, when this failed, dragged a fallen branch from the thicket. He used it as a lever beneath the back of the horse. Little by little he eased the man free.

'The left leg's broken,' said Captain Mosely. 'But the rest of me appears to be as I would have it.'

'I'll take you to the surgeon, sir,' said Nehemiah. 'He'll attend to the leg.'

He hoisted the younger man across his shoulders and, with great difficulty, succeeded in carrying him, a short distance at a time, towards the wagon where John Fletcher was resting.

'What's your name, soldier?'

'Hawkins, sir.' Nehemiah laid him down again upon the ground and stretched to ease his back.

'Well, Hawkins, I'll remember this deed. If the day ever comes when I can be of service to you, I'll be glad to repay my debt.'

'There's no need, sir.'

'You think I say it lightly. Believe me, Hawkins, I'll repay you with interest.'

'I don't want anything, sir, but to be free of this soldiering. Free to go home.'

'You wish to be released?'

'I just pray for the next battle. Then we'll all see an end to it.'

Captain Mosely raised an eyebrow. 'I wish I shared your optimism.'

'It's the Will of God.'

'Ah, yes. But can we be sure that we'll win?'

'Of course we'll win!'

'Don't be shocked, Hawkins. God grants us the battle, but does He grant us the men?'

'Our men fought valiantly.'

'Some did. But there were few who could match the spirit of the Royalists.'

'God will provide.'

'If you'd watched the battle with your own eyes, perhaps you'd have seen.'

Nehemiah looked at him.

Captain Mosely shook his head sadly. 'Our men are no match for those of the King.'

'That can't be.'

'How many of your comrades enlisted for the pay and plunder?'

Nehemiah recalled only too keenly the scenes he had witnessed upon the march.

'Not all of them share our zeal, Hawkins, nor the zeal of our leaders.'

'But it's the Will of *God*,' said Nehemiah again.

'They're no match for the King's men. Gentlemen's sons, taught to handle a sword and to sit on a horse.'

It was too much for Nehemiah. 'Lord,' he offered up silently, 'what must I do to understand Thy Will? First I'm told that we're not to win with a single battle. Now I'm told that we may not win at all.'

Aloud, he said flatly: 'Take hold of me, sir. I'll get you to the surgeon.'

CHAPTER 5

As the two armies set out for London, Nehemiah passed within fifteen miles of Dunscombe. But not close enough to make a detour. A surgeon's assistant could not be spared.

Had he called at the house he would have found the Reverend Daniels a little recovered, but now Lucy lay in the throes of a similar fever. And the two youngest children, Rachael and Bibby-Anne, were fretful and with flushed cheeks which signalled to Anne that they, too, were about to become ill.

A bed was made up for Lucy in the room which Margaret shared with her sisters. It enabled her to assist in the task of nursing her without mounting the stairs.

Anne was drawn and tired. She was desperately concerned that the frail Bibby-Anne would be no match for the fever.

Margaret worked day and night. In addition to nursing Lucy, she had duties in connection with her father's business which could not be neglected. She was tired, and sick with worry. As the weeks had passed since the incident with Rupert in the stable, an even greater concern was beginning to emerge, the consequences of which were too great even to envisage.

She went in to Lucy with a bowl of broth, knowing that it was unlikely she would eat from it.

'How is Reverend Daniels?'

'Mother says he's much improved. It looks as though his life has been spared.'

'God be praised. And what of the children?'

Margaret sighed. 'She's very worried about them.'

'Oh, Margaret, I must get up and go and help her.'

'Stay where you are.' She pressed Lucy back upon the bed. 'You're in no state to go anywhere.'

Lucy began to weep, sobbing not only in her own discomfort and concern for the children, but also for yet another baby which she had aborted that morning.

'I shan't ever succeed in pleasing the Lord.'

Margaret came and knelt beside the bed, the wooden bowl cupped in her hands. 'Lucy,' she said, 'you're the most godly of women.'

'But the Lord keeps chastising me.'

'It was the fever. The babe took sick inside you.'

'I've prayed and I've prayed. I've tried so hard to repent. Yet still there's reason for Him to withhold His blessing from me.'

Margaret held the broth a little closer to Lucy's lips. 'Here, take a little sip of this. You need sustenance.'

Lucy averted her face. 'Thank you, but the very thought of it turns my stomach.'

'You've got to grow strong, for Tobias' sake.'

'Oh, Margaret, I wish I could be more like you.'

'Like me?'

'You're so godly. You're not taken up with vanity and covetousness.'

Margaret was deeply affected by the statement. 'Lucy,' she said quietly, 'if you're with sin, then mine must outweigh yours by a thousandfold.'

Lucy looked at her closely. 'What do you mean?'

'We're all tainted, since Grandmother Eve, but there are times when the burden seems to lie unbearably heavy upon us.'

Lucy looked at her, about to question her further, but Margaret rose. 'If you won't eat,' she said, 'I'll take it away.' She held a hand to Lucy's forehead. 'I'll bring more physic later to help with the fever.'

'Margaret . . .'

'I'll come back,' she repeated. 'When I've finished sorting the yarn.'

The burden of a deep but inexorably emerging fear hung heavy over Margaret. She wrestled with it whilst sorting the yarn, and again all afternoon while taking cloth to the fulling mill. On her return she was forced, beyond further evasion, to speak of it openly.

In a household where there is little privacy, certain matters do not go unnoticed. She had hoped that, with the additional demands upon her mother's attention, Anne might have overlooked it, but she had not.

'Margaret,' she said, 'there's something wrong.'

'Wrong, Mother?'

'Yes. I've noticed an absence of your terms.'

She felt her blood chill.

'You've been busy with your duties, but I've taken note on your behalf.'

'I expect they've been delayed.' Her voice wavered. 'They'll come back in a day or two.'

'It's already delayed by over a sennight.'

She tried to think of some response but failed.

'You're either sick . . . ' Even in her own mind, Anne did not complete the sentence. She did not, for one moment, consider it necessary.

Margaret felt the smarting of tears, and turned away.

'You're weeping, child.'

'Why should I weep?'

'I'm your mother, Margaret. I know when you're weeping.'

The burden, the shame, the sickening anxiety, welled up and overflowed. She broke down and cried, revealing the secret which she had kept hidden for weeks.

'Oh, Mother, I don't know how to tell you.'

'Tell me what, child?'

'I'm sick with shame.'

'Shame?' Anne began to turn pale.

'I can't bring myself to speak of it.'

Anne reached out behind her for a stool and lowered herself gingerly upon it. 'I think you'd best do so,' she said. 'It's obvious I need to know.'

Margaret poured it out, hoping for relief but finding none. Anne listened, growing paler by the moment.

'And now,' concluded Margaret, 'there's an absence of my terms.'

'Oh, may the Lord not bring down His vengeance upon us!'

'I've brought shame upon us, Mother.'

'But Rupert — the son of my own sister!'

'I'm sorry, Mother.'

'How could he do such a thing? I loved him as my own son.'

'I didn't mean to do it, Mother. He took me by surprise.'

'And with a wife big-bellied with his own child.' Anne got up and went to stare out of the window, beating her knuckles against the sill.

'And now I don't know what to do.'

'We must think of some way of securing your future.'

'Future?'

'Yes, future. There's no man now who'll take you in marriage.'

'I hadn't thought . . . I was too taken up with . . . '

'Unless . . . ' said Anne. She suddenly acquired a new animation. 'Unless we're able to work exceedingly quick.'

Margaret wondered at the sudden change.

'If we were to make some settlement,' said Anne, 'with some young man . . . A tradesman, such as young Will Powers, or even Jephro Milne. He's been talking for some time of taking a bride.'

'But, Mother . . . '

'We could get it all arranged within the month. I think it might work.

'It would be dishonest.'

Anne blanched noticeably at the accusation. 'Yes,' she said, 'but we've got no choice.'

'Surely it would come to light? My shame would be all the greater then.'

Anne turned away. 'There's no reason for it to come to light. A fruitful wife would be pleasing to her husband, and you'd go a little early into your pains. It's not unusual with the firstborn.'

'But I couldn't lie, Mother. It wouldn't be right.'

'May God forgive us,' said her mother tightly, 'it wouldn't be right. But think, child: there's no man who'll marry you once the facts are known.'

'Then I shall just have to bear it alone.'

Anne came back and stood before her, holding her at arm's length. 'Child,' she said gently, 'can't you see the foolishness of such words?'

'The shame is mine: I'll bear it alone.'

'That's rash and mindless, and you don't understand what's entailed.' She increased the pressure of her grip on Margaret's shoulders and looked earnestly into her face. 'We're not young, your father and I. I'm thirty-seven and your father is a full ten years in advance of me. How many do you know who live beyond two score years?'

'Don't, Mother.'

'And what happens to a woman without husband or father?' Margaret attempted to look away but Anne held her fast. 'To whom does she belong? To no one. And such a burden on Tobias who's got to think about raising a family of his own.'

'It's more than shame I've brought upon us.'

'Unless,' her mother began again, 'we're exceedingly quick and clever.'

She let her hands fall from Margaret's shoulders and began to pace the floor, her lips moving in rapid silent concentration. 'The dowry must be larger than your father planned . . . '

'I fought him, Mother. I did try.'

'I know that, child.'

'But there was no way of withholding myself.'

'I know,' Anne said again. 'I don't doubt it for an instant. But it makes not the slightest difference to us now. Resist or not, the deed's been done. There's no way we can reverse that fact.' She was still pacing the floor. 'We'll get Tobias to go first thing tomorrow morning.' She stopped and wrung her hands. 'Oh God, why dost Thou take our husbands when we need them most?'

Margaret took her elbow in an effort to calm her. 'Father will be home soon, when the battle's over.'

'But not in time for you. We can't sit and wait while you grow with child.'

'Maybe it won't be necessary. The terms may reappear.'

'That's a chance we can't take. The deed's been done and we're not here to gamble with the dice of fortune.'

'I'm sorry, Mother.'

'Tobias will go and speak with these young men. He can . . . ' Anne stopped again. 'I remember now,' she said. 'Young Jephro Milne – he's betrothed to the daughter of

103

Andrew Bourne. I was told only yesterday by Peg Watkins. And Will Powers is sick.'

'With consumption, I heard.'

'What we need is a young man who's readily available.' She turned to Margaret. 'Think, child, think quick. What young men do we know who are available immediately? We'll list them all and pick out the most likely among them.'

Margaret shook her head. 'I can't think, Mother; you're confusing me.'

'Perhaps we ought to be thinking of an older man. A widower, perhaps, with children of his own in need of mothering. Who do we know who's recently lost a wife and is likely looking for another match? An old man might well be more than pleased to take you.'

Margaret paled slightly. 'I can't think of anyone who'd want me.'

'Nonsense, child. You work well, and you're good with your needle. What else would a man demand?'

'I don't know, Mother.'

'It's as well I had you spend some time with your needlework when your father would have had you roaming the countryside.'

Margaret had no answer to that.

'But we've got to think of some reason for the speed. It's understandable enough that Tobias should make approaches in respect of a betrothal, but what reason ought we to give for an early marriage?'

'Oh, Mother, I'd rather not! Better to die than face the shame.'

'Nonsense, we've no choice: the shame's already upon us.'

Margaret began to weep.

'There must be some reason we can give. Yet they're certain to ask why we don't wait for your father's return.'

On the stairs, the Reverend Deliverance Daniels turned unsteadily and retraced his steps back to his bed. He had been endeavouring to go down to take a turn about the yard in order to breathe the dust of the loom from his head. Now he thought better of it.

In his weakened state he should not have attempted the

stairs alone. He fell back upon the straw mattress, fighting to catch his breath, feeling sick and dizzy. He put a hand to the throbbing pulse of his temples and rested his head back against the pillow.

He lay for a long time, turning over in his mind the conversation he had just, unintentionally, overheard.

Downstairs, in the parlour, the two women were too engrossed to hear the movement on the stair.

'We shan't tell the family of my shame?'

'Tobias must know, but I see no reason to place the burden upon anyone else.'

'Thank you.'

Anne came and knelt before Margaret, cupping her tear-drenched face between her hands. 'We must trust in the Lord. With His help we'll find a way.'

'If you think so, Mother.'

'Precious child,' she said gently, 'it's your good I'm thinking of. You know that, don't you?'

'Yes, Mother.'

'I'm only thinking to settle your future. You'll work hard in this union. With God's help, you'll find favour with your husband and be happy.'

'Yes, Mother.'

'I love you, child. Think on that always and never forget it.'

The following day, as Tobias worked alone at the loom, Deliverance Daniels engaged him in conversation.

'I'm glad you feel well enough to talk,' said Tobias. 'There were days when we feared for your life.'

'I'm much recovered. I must set out shortly on my journey.'

'Not for a while at least. You're far too weak to embark upon such a hazardous voyage.'

'I must be on my way. With every day, winter approaches. I've long overstayed the time when I should have set out.'

Tobias was full of admiration for a man who could speak so calmly about journeying into the relative unknown.

'I've been thinking,' said Deliverance Daniels. 'It occurs to me that I shall be in need of a helpmeet.'

Tobias raised an interested eyebrow.

'I'm likely to meet with many trials which are difficult for a man to face alone. The Lord is with me: but He's given us woman as helpmeet.'

'You'll doubtless find daughters of quality in New England. And more than a few widows.'

'I was thinking of your sister Margaret.'

Tobias swung round and stopped what he was doing. 'I hadn't realized you were referring to Margaret.'

'She's of marriageable age?'

'She's of age.'

'And she's strong. I fancy she'd do well in adversity.'

Anne stopped. She stood stock-still and listened to the conversation on the other side of the door. Never in all her life had she experienced so rapid, or so obvious, an answer to her prayers. She quietly retraced her steps and went to thank God for His goodness.

When Tobias told her of the proposal, she feigned surprise.

'It's a flattering offer,' he said. 'But of course I shall have to refuse.'

'Why? He's a worthy man.'

'He's going to New England, Mother. He intends to take her with him.'

'Yes,' said Anne quietly, and lowered her eyes. 'The Lord has many ways of exacting punishment for our sins.'

He looked at her, not understanding. 'There's no way that we can allow Margaret to go to New England.'

Anne no longer had need to share the burden of her secret with Tobias. If no one but she and Nehemiah knew of it, there could be absolute certainty that it would never be divulged. 'The Lord has called her,' she said. 'That's quite plain.'

'She's a maid, Mother. You speak of her as if she were a man.'

'I'm sorry,' said Anne, a little flustered. 'I'm caught with the same notion as your father.'

'There's no question of it. And he speaks of a dowry far in excess of what Father planned.'

'Your father would doubtless stretch himself. He's often said if the choice were right . . . '

'But it's not,' said Tobias. 'Father would never forgive us if we sent Margaret to a distant land.'

'Hasn't he said often enough that he's searching for a man with special attributes? This is a man of means: a preacher in the service of the Lord.'

'You speak as if you're anxious to send Margaret beyond our sight forever.'

Anne lowered her eyes and turned away. 'I only want what's best for her,' she said quietly. 'I fear you may be rejecting this man too hastily.'

'Is there more I should know, Mother?' He was becoming vaguely suspicious.

'I suggest you remember your father's instructions. He sent word by Samuel that Margaret should marry according to her choosing.'

'But not to leave this land!'

'I think it's best that you speak with her. Your father wouldn't be pleased if we were to disobey him.'

'Yes, of course. But I've no doubt that she'll refuse.'

Margaret was robbed of speech when the proposition was placed before her.

'You'll refuse of course?'

She did not begin to understand what was happening to her.

'You realize what it would mean?' said Tobias. 'You would have one week in which to marry. Then you would set out on a journey from which it's unlikely that you'd ever return.'

'Yes,' she said but in her mind she was wrestling with the most improbable turn of events she could ever have imagined. Instead of punishment, she was to receive a gift of the greatest magnitude.

'You will refuse?' said her brother again.

'No,' said Margaret. 'I should be most grateful if you'd accept on my behalf.'

'I don't understand.'

'It's the mercy of God.'

'It's a proposal of marriage.'

'It's the Will of God. I'm most beholden to His mercy.'

It was only later, as she sat at the bedside of Lucy and her two young sisters, that she began to realize what it would mean if she were to marry the Reverend Deliverance Daniels. She would have to go away, leaving them hovering between life and death, unable even to know of their fate.

When she further realized that she would never again see her father, it was almost enough to make her change her mind. She tensed and half rose, intending to go to Tobias and tell him that she could not go through with it. But she knew that she must. In His great mercy, God had given her Deliverance Daniels. For punishment, she must leave behind all that she held dear. She must go to a wild far-off place where she would be among strangers. She would never again set foot upon her beloved hills.

Tears welled and ran down her cheeks. But then she thought of the young man lying asleep beside the loom. If she must marry in haste and leave her family, there could be no one whom she would more readily choose as a husband.

The financial settlement was quickly arranged. Tobias capitulated, reluctantly, in respect of the increased dowry; but he held out for an equally inflated widow's portion. If Margaret were to be left widowed in a far-off land, he meant to ensure that she was well provided for.

The wedding was arranged for the following Sunday, which was well timed. Tobias, as part of the settlement, had insisted that they should travel to Bristol in company of the carrier. Tom Cox was due to pass through the village on Saturday and to depart again on Monday morning.

'It's not safe to travel at this time of year,' Tobias maintained. 'Many of the roads are impassable. Only those who use them constantly can find the way.'

Deliverance Daniels would have preferred some more direct route than that taken by the carrier but he accepted the wisdom of the arrangement. Even allowing for a stopover in every village, it could still prove speedier than finding himself stranded on the wrong side of marshland.

As the day approached, Margaret found herself in an increasing turmoil. She was afraid, but surely Deliverance

Daniels would take care of her? Deliverance Daniels had the courage to set out on such a journey: he would have the courage to protect her.

She feared the journey – such a great distance across vast ocean. But soon she would make her vows and must go wherever her husband commanded.

She feared the life which lay ahead. She knew nothing of New England beyond the tales she had heard – tales of hardship and danger, of loss of life in unknown wastelands, of wild animals and savages, of all the countless unknown perils which lay in the unexplored regions of the other side of the world.

She feared, also, the memory which lay uncomfortably upon the upper surface of her mind, ready always to break in upon her thoughts at moments when she was least prepared – the knowledge that she was unclean. She no longer welcomed physical contact and would jump violently at the casual touch of a hand upon her back. She closed her mind to the role which she knew she must inevitably play within the confines of her husband's bed. She feared that, in some way, her impurity lay, indelibly and unmistakably, upon her flesh.

She had spoken little to Deliverance Daniels. He seemed unsure of how to act towards her in this awkward, in-between stage. In conversation he avoided her gaze. He did not seem to know what to say.

She bumped into him one day at the door of the stable. She no longer liked going there and the embarrassment of bumping into her betrothed was thus all the greater. She blushed scarlet and dodged to one side, only to find that he, too, had moved in the same direction.

'I'm so sorry.'

'No! No, it's I – I didn't hear you approach.'

'I should have alerted you.'

She was further embarrassed to see that he, too, was blushing.

'Forgive me,' he said. 'I'm on my way to take some exercise.'

'You're feeling well?'

'I'm much recovered, but it's a long time since I sat a horse.'

'If I can be of help?'

'No,' he said curtly. 'I've no need of assistance.'

'I'm sorry,' she said. 'You've much to do.'

'I have, indeed. And so have you.'

'I hardly know where to turn,' she said. 'There's so much to prepare.'

'I'm sure that your mother will give you ample advice.'

'And with the children sick . . . '

'Yes,' he said. 'It's a most unfortunate time.'

'But at least you're recovered.'

He seized the excuse to be on his way. 'Yes,' he said. 'I have to make up for the time I've wasted on my bed of sickness.'

Margaret guessed that he would have little patience for matters of human frailty. 'I'm sorry,' she said again, and stepped to one side to let him pass. 'I mustn't delay you.'

'I shall be quite prepared by the time we leave on Monday,' he said. 'And so, I trust, will you.'

She watched him walk away from her, feeling in some way that she had been chastised.

The week raced by in frenzied activity. There was sewing to be done and linen to be gathered together. Neither Margaret nor her mother knew exactly what was to be expected of her on the journey and in the life which lay ahead.

At the same time, the work of the loom could not be abandoned. Margaret raced from one task to another with barely time to think; yet with her mind endlessly chasing the half-formed doubts and fears, hurtling her from excitement to trepidation, and back again into the deep inner knowledge of her own tarnished self-image.

In the dark hours of the night she sat beside Lucy and the children, castigating herself with the knowledge that she was about to abandon them in their hour of need. Anne could not manage alone. She had arranged for Elizabeth to come and assist her. Elizabeth would stay for as long as was needed – or until they died. Margaret wept. She could not bear the thought of leaving them to die.

Late on Saturday afternoon Tom Cox arrived. It was an event which never failed to stir the inhabitants of the village as he rode in at the head of his string of Galloways, bells ringing on the lead horse, his dog at his side. He was their link with the outside world. It was he who brought news from other parts; he who conveyed messages to distant relatives, or pocket money to youths as he passed the university; it was he who brought a few ells of fine satin for a gown, or a watch which had been repaired.

He put up at the village alehouse, where a meal and a bed of straw had been made ready for him. The horses were turned out to graze upon the green. People hovered, anxious for him to finish his supper, waiting for him to dispense the goods which he carried. There was a copper warming pan for the shoemaker's wife, a sack of seed for Josiah Tucker, some knives which had been reground, salt which was required by all who had run short at this time of year when food must be preserved.

Tobias went to see him as he sat later beside the alehouse fire, a pipe clenched between the few rotting teeth which remained in his head.

'How be things with thee, young man?' He had known Tobias since childhood.

'My wife's sick with the fever. And so are my sisters.'

Tom made a rapid mark upon himself with the tips of his fingers. 'God have mercy on they.' Then he spat out of the corner of his mouth.

'What news of the army, Tom?' Tobias had no wish to dwell upon the heavy dread which lay within him. Lucy was growing weaker.

'They's fought they battle,' said Tom, removing the pipe. 'Just t'other side, into Warwickshire.'

'God be praised!' Tobias held his hand to his mouth, not daring to hear the outcome. 'They won?'

'Now, that'd depend on thee persuasion,' said Tom, knowing well of Nehemiah's part in the conflict.

'Parliament?' said Tobias, impatient.

'Ne'er see it, m'self. Only picked up news along t'way.'

'What news, man?'

'Them's both marchin' t'wards Lon'on.'

'Then it's not over?'

'Marchin' t'wards Lon'on,' he repeated. 'T'anyone's guess which o' they'll be first t' get there.'

111

'But that can't be! It was supposed to be a single battle.'

'So them said. But they's on way t' fight ag'in.'

'You've no news of my father?' he asked, knowing well that the carrier had not.

'Didn't come by way o' Edge'ill. I 'asn't seen t' armies.'

'I trust to God he's all right. I wish it were over and he back home.'

'Them'll not be doin' much fightin' once winter sets in,' said Tom. 'P'rhaps heat'll have gone out of they by spring.'

Tobias closed his eyes. 'I can't bear to think of my father lying somewhere beneath the soil.'

'You'se no use in mournin' the soul o' a man 'less thee knows for sure he's not marchin' south. Dare say, he's suffering no more than with 'is feet.'

Tobias managed a wry smile. 'He'll get word to us if he can.'

'I's got that length o'rope thee's asked me t' bring,' said Tom, changing the subject. ''S over in corner, 'longside barrel o' oysters.'

'Thanks. And there's some other business I'd like to discuss.'

Tom Cox inclined his head and shifted the pipe from one side of his mouth to the other.

'You'll be passing through Bristol?'

'Aye, by way o' Wiltshire.'

'My sister's getting married tomorrow. They're travelling to Bristol to take ship for New England.'

'New England, eh? Them's welcome t' come along a' me. See 'em set down safe in city.'

'At what charge?'

''S usual for each o' they t' count as half a pack,' he said. 'To Bris'ol . . . ' He moved his pipe again and made the calculation in his head. 'Some't like two shillin' 'n' sixp'nce apiece oughta cover it. Then there's they baggage.'

'They haven't got much to carry. Margaret's had little time to prepare for the journey and the Reverend Daniels has got his own horse and pack pony.'

'Then seven shillin' 'll set they both down safe in Bris'ol.' The two men shook hands.

Late that night, after the family had retired to their beds,

Anne and Margaret sat beside the tiny sleeping figures of Rachael and Bibby-Anne. Lucy lay alongside them, deathly pale and barely moving. Upstairs, Matthew Crawshaw lay on his straw mattress, moaning softly in a state of delirium. He, too, had succumbed to the virus.

Both children were restless, tossing limbs weakened by fever. There was nothing for the two women to do but to re-arrange the bedclothes as they were tossed aside, and to draw back damp strands of hair from faces which were inflamed with a livid rash.

'The Lord has commanded us to be fruitful and to multiply,' said Anne suddenly, as though she had been turning the words in her mind but had not known how to begin the conversation. 'It's good and right to respond always to the appetites of your husband.'

'Yes, Mother.' The subject brought back, yet again, the deep inner sense of Margaret's own defilement.

'But not in July and August.'

'Not in July and August,' she said compliantly.

'It's too hot,' said Anne. 'It's unwise in heat.'

'Yes, Mother.'

Margaret wanted somehow to speak of her degradation, to off load it on her mother in the hope that she would receive solace and release. But these were the burdens of a woman, not a child. They were not to be assuaged by the comfort of a mother's arms. And, in any case, she could not find the words.

'And in moderation,' said Anne. 'Remember always — in moderation.'

'Yes, Mother.'

'There are some things I want you to have,' said Anne. She got up, and taking the candle with her walked from the room, leaving Margaret in darkness until a faint glow lighted her return.

'I want you to take these,' she said, sitting once more beside the bed. In her hand were two books.

'That's your Bible, Mother.'

'Yes. I want you to have it.'

'But it's precious to you.'

'It was my father's,' she said. 'Now it's yours.' She ran the palm of her hand lovingly across the deer-hide binding

113

and passed the Bible across the bed to Margaret. 'Perhaps you'll think of your family when you make your way to church each Sunday.'

'Oh, Mother, I'll treasure it.'

'And there's this.' She held up the second volume, a handbook of herbal remedies to which she had referred constantly for as long as Margaret could remember.

'But you need it, Mother.'

'I think,' said Anne, 'that your need may be greater than my own.' Her voice quivered slightly as she spoke. 'There's no knowing what pestilences may await you in a far-off land, or what miasmas may exude from the soil. I want you to know how to treat them.'

Margaret took the book and opened it, running the tip of her finger reverently across the pages.

'It will give you advice on many distempers. Remember particularly the danger of childbed fever, and the treatment of flux.'

Margaret turned the pages. ' . . . a mixture of unsalted butter and juice of red sage with walnut and ginger'; ' . . . for those stricken by the Black Death . . . a poultice of onions, garlic, and butter, with the dried root of the lily . . . a live pullet to be held against the sore . . . '

'One has to understand the humours,' went on Anne. 'It's known that the body is composed of four fluids. There's the blood, the phlegm, the yellow bile, and the black which we call melancholy. The balance must be maintained.'

'I know of the humours, Mother. It's the adjusting of the balance which will be a problem to me.'

'The book will set you right. You'll learn when it's best to purge, and when to bleed. All diseases are best treated by setting the balance right.'

'I'll keep it by me always.'

'Read it daily, child, with your Bible,' said Anne unsteadily. 'I fear you'll have need of both. Take great care if you're called upon to live in parts where the soil's waterlogged; there, you're likely to be troubled by ague.'

Rachael stirred and opened her eyes. 'Margaret?'

'Margaret's here, my sweet.' She took the tiny hand, which had grown wasted like the claws of a bird. 'I'm here beside you.'

114

'Hot.' She held out a tongue which was swollen and cracked.

Margaret reached for water which she dribbled into a mouth barely able to swallow.

'Hurts,' said Rachael feebly and turned her head back into the pillow.

Margaret wiped a cloth across the damp forehead. 'Just sleep, my sweet. The fever will pass.'

She took the hand again and sat with it between both her own. 'Oh, Mother, how can I leave? I'm needed here.'

'You must,' she said.

They looked at one another across the bed. Anne had grown haggard over the past two weeks. The smallpox scars which she had carried since youth showed up as shadows cast by the candlelight.

'I've often thought about your marriage,' she said at last. 'I dreamed of the day . . .' She stopped and shook her head. 'Oh, Margaret, what kind of wedding day is this?'

'It doesn't matter, Mother.'

'I planned such a happy day.'

'It's not important. It only matters . . .'

'If only your father . . .'

'They stopped, and each looked again at the other.

'Oh, Mother, I can't bear to think that I shall never see him again.'

'You've got his blessing, child. I've no doubt about that.'

'Will you tell him?'

'I'll tell him.'

Anne reached a hand across the bed and touched her. 'And he'll understand.'

'Will he?' Margaret sat and wept inwardly upon the fact that she would become tarnished in her father's eyes.

Eventually Anne said, 'Your Aunt Elizabeth is coming tomorrow to sit with Lucy and the children so that I can be there when you take your vows.'

'Yes,' said Margaret, wresting her thoughts away from her father.

'Elizabeth will look after them until we get back.'

'I'm glad you'll be there with me.'

'I couldn't be anywhere else.'

'But if the children need you . . .'

'Your Aunt Elizabeth will take care of them.'

'Yes.'

'Then she'll come again on Monday, after you've . . . '

'Yes,' said Margaret again.

'She'll stay until . . .'

'Until everyone gets better,' put in Margaret hurriedly.

'Until they're better,' said Anne feebly.

'I'd best wear my good gown tomorrow, Mother.'

'Yes,' said Anne. 'And we'll let your hair hang loose.'

'No,' she said falteringly. 'I don't think I want to let my hair hang loose.'

They left a further period of silence to hang between them.

'It's a pity the Reverend Daniels demands such a style of wedding,' began Anne again. 'It's true we couldn't have had a celebration, but we could have had a proper wedding.'

'It's the custom of New England, Mother.'

'But it's nothing more than an exchange of words. And without a ring.' Anne drew in a breath. 'It just doesn't seem right.'

'It's not thought proper to wear a ring in New England.' She looked down at her hand. 'And I don't suppose it matters.'

'It's a symbol. I've great difficulty in coming to terms with the view that one shouldn't wear a ring.'

'They consider marriage to be a civil matter, before a magistrate.'

'Then let's thank God,' said Anne, 'that the Reverend Daniels has agreed to it being conducted in church.'

Margaret nodded. 'It wouldn't have felt right if it hadn't been in church.'

'But without a ring,' fretted her mother.

Margaret looked down again at her hand. It seemed difficult to believe that she was actually to be married to the Reverend Daniels.

'And will you be happy with him, child? Can you give yourself to him with confidence?'

It brought such a conflict of emotion within her that she was forced to swallow on it. 'I don't know, Mother. I'm so confused.'

'But you like him well enough?'

'Oh, yes, Mother,' she said hurriedly. 'He's a most godly man.'

'And I haven't committed you to a life which is more than you can cope with?'

'I don't know, Mother. I don't know why the Reverend Daniels should even have thought to choose me for a bride.'

'Nonsense,' said Anne. 'You've the makings of an excellent wife.'

'But if he knew . . . '

'If he knew?' broke in Anne hurriedly. 'If he knew what?'

'You know, Mother. You know well what I mean.'

'You're strong and healthy, and . . . '

'And I'm unclean.'

Anne stopped and sat looking at her with gentle compassion. 'The whole incident,' she said, 'is best forgotten.'

'I can't, Mother.'

'You must forget it ever happened.'

Margaret shook her head. 'How can I? I shall remember for as long as I live.'

'You must forget,' said Anne. 'Your life depends upon it.'

Margaret looked at her and said nothing.

'And the life of your child.'

Margaret closed her eyes.

'You must go with your husband, and you must bear his child.'

Margaret swallowed.

'*His* child, Margaret, and never forget it.'

She could not speak.

'The child is his. At no time must you allow yourself to think otherwise.'

'But it's not right, Mother.'

'When I think of Tobias' wedding,' broke in Anne. 'Such gaiety! And the flowers — I remember there were so many flowers that summer, before the war.'

'Father will be home soon, Mother. The armies can't fight in winter.'

'Yes,' said Anne limply. 'He'll be home soon.'

They heard movement behind them and both turned to see Rebecca standing in the doorway.

'Mary's sick, Mother. She's burning with fever.'

117

Anne drew in her breath and rose instantly to her feet. 'I'll go to her,' she said. 'Stay here with Margaret. She'll make up a bed for you on the floor.'

Suddenly, Margaret felt overwhelmingly tired. She had not slept for days. She put out a hand to the child. Tomorrow she would walk across the hills to the church where she would wed the Reverend Deliverance Daniels. On Monday she would set out with him towards New England where, eventually, she would bear 'his' child. But she could never forget the shame which had been brought upon her.

Rebecca came and sought comfort by pressing herself close against Margaret's lap. 'We're all sick, Margaret. Am I going to be ill, too?'

'It's the fever,' said Margaret. 'It's spreading amongst us.'

'I don't want to die.'

'What nonsense you do talk.' But she ran her hand across the child's forehead. It was hot.

The following day it was a small, subdued group which walked across the hills to church. Tobias was not with them. He, too, had taken to his bed. Now there were seven lying ill.

The exchange of vows took less than five minutes; then the Reverend Deliverance Daniels went into the pulpit to preach the sermon. The congregation sat waiting in awed anticipation; but this time, although he spoke eloquently, his weakness was evident. Several times he had to reach out to steady himself as he swayed at moments of highest tension. Margaret watched him, half wondering if she should step forward to steady him, but at the same time unsure and embarrassed.

He chose as his theme 'The Place of Woman' and began by opening his Bible at the second chapter of Genesis, verse 21: ' "And the Lord God caused a deep sleep to fall upon Adam . . . and he took one of his ribs and closed up the flesh . . . And the rib which the Lord God had taken from man made he a woman and brought her unto the man."

'But the woman was no match for Satan,' he went on. 'She allowed herself to be deceived. For we read . . . ' He turned again to his Bible, this time to the book of Timothy. ' . . . "Adam was not deceived but the woman being deceived was in transgression." '

118

The congregation nodded in agreement. The women bowed their heads in modest submission.

' "But not withstanding she shall be saved in childbearing if they continue in faith and charity and holiness and sobriety." '

'May God be praised,' muttered several women seated before him.

'Wives,' he said, 'take note of Peter. He says in his First Epistle: "Be in subjection to your husbands . . . for after this manner in the old times the holy women who trusted in God were in subjection unto their own husbands. Even as Sara obeyed Abraham calling him lord." '

He cast his eye over several men seated about the congregation then went on, quoting again from the Bible before him: ' "Likewise ye husbands, dwell with them according to knowledge, giving honour unto the wife as unto the weaker vessel and as being heirs together of the grace of life that our prayers be not hindered." '

Margaret sat and watched him, waiting for him to look at her: yet, when he did so, she blushed and turned away.

She found her mind wandering to the uncertainty of her future; to the life which she must make with this young stranger who stood before her; of her mother's words . . . 'you must forget'. But she could not forget: she was unclean.

She thought of the perils of the journey, and of the strange land in which she must dwell — the land in which, eventually, she must die.

She came back to the present in time to hear him quoting ' "Who can find a virtuous woman? For her price is far above rubies" ' . . . from the Book of Proverbs. ' "A virtuous woman is a crown to her husband; but she that maketh him ashamed is as rottenness in his bones." '

He left the pulpit and took his place beside her. The congregation intoned a Psalm. As he stood next to her, she felt his arm brush past her own with a movement which sent a tingling sensation into her shoulder. She glanced up at him, expecting him to be looking down; but he had been unaware of the contact.

Back home, Anne brought out a cake which she had baked. They drank some wine. But there was little time to spend upon it. The children had been calling for Anne in her absence and Matthew Crawshaw had only a few hours remaining of his short life.

Lucy had been moved back upstairs to share the bed in which Tobias now lay. He was fighting against the rising tide of nausea, while the persistent throbbing in his head made it impossible for him to open his eyes. He put his arms about her, afraid of hurting her, yet terrified of losing her.

'Don't leave me,' he begged. 'Please don't leave me.' He knew that, if she slipped any further into weakness, she, too, would slide over the boundary into death.

That night Margaret sat and dozed once more beside the beds of her sisters, while the Reverend Daniels slept upon the straw mattress beside the loom. All were grateful that he had not insisted upon sharing a bed with Margaret. To have made such arrangements at this time of sickness would have been greatly inconvenient.

Tomorrow night they would be alone in some distant inn. Margaret bit her lip. It brought such a strange mixture of emotions that she could not cope. She dropped her head down across her arms and, in sheer exhaustion, slept until shortly before dawn.

CHAPTER 6

Two hours later Margaret was seated upon the back of one of Tom Cox's big Galloways, making her way up the hill and away from the village. Those two hours had become a blur of tears and activity. Strapping possessions across horses; hugging, for the last time, the people who had filled the centre of her life.

She had left behind a brother and his wife, lying side by side in sickness, an apprentice in his shroud. Four of her five sisters were too ill to bid her farewell, while her mother stood beside Samuel at the open door, pale and drawn by weeks of worry and exhaustion, straining her eyes to catch one last glimpse as the pack-horse train passed across the horizon.

Margaret leaned back and waved. The distant village swam out of focus behind her tears. She wanted desperately to go back for one last hug, one last farewell; but she knew that she could not. It was extremely unlikely that she would ever have an opportunity to see any of them ever again.

She was wrapped warmly in a thick cloak against the damp November air. A chill wind was blowing across the hills. Tom Cox rode ahead of her, swaying steadily to the rhythm of his horse, while she was aware of Deliverance Daniels riding a short distance behind and to her left. He had hardly spoken since they had set out.

Her mother had begged him take care of her.

'She is to accompany her husband in the service of the Lord,' he had said. 'There is no nobler duty which a woman may be called upon to do.'

121

Anne had been impressed by that. She had smiled through her tears. 'But if she gets sick . . . '

'If she gets sick, you will doubtless, Mistress Hawkins, have taught her to trust in God.'

Anne had taken hold of Margaret and had hugged her again. She had chastised herself for her own lack of faith.

In the absence of Tobias, Samuel had found himself the only man of the household. 'Till we meet again,' he had said brokenly.

Margaret had nodded, unable to answer.

He had taken hold of her hand, pumping it up and down in his efforts to subdue his emotion. 'Who knows, one of these days . . . ? You'd have a bit of a shock if I came over to New England and you found me on your doorstep.'

'Yes,' she had smiled. She had pulled away her hand and flung her arms about his neck. 'Take care of Mother and the children while Tobias is sick.'

He had nodded into her shoulder. 'Father will be home soon.'

'Yes,' she had said. 'Father will be home.'

Had it been summer, she would have been given the choice of riding in a wagon, but all wheeled vehicles were stored away from the end of October until early May. Even given the choice, she would have preferred the horse. She was comfortable on horseback and had heard the tales of travellers who had been smothered beneath loads which had shifted in jolting, unsprung wagons.

They passed through villages familiar to her, stopping at each so that Tom Cox could conduct his business.

At dinner time they took their meal at a village inn, but still Deliverance Daniels hardly spoke. The uncomfortable silence remained between them. The innkeeper's wife asked him of Margaret's preference concerning food and he was obviously embarrassed by his inability to respond. 'She will take pork,' he said at last, though she would have preferred beef.

She sat watching him beneath the cover of her lashes as they ate, uncomfortable in the silence, yet glad of the opportunity to dwell within her own thoughts. She ached with longing for the home she had left behind, feared the night which lay ahead.

Here and there, during the afternoon, they passed a solitary ploughman working in the fields. Farmers were busy slaughtering pigs and cattle for which there would be no winter feed. In barns, threshers were at work bagging grain, setting aside the straw for the few remaining livestock which were to be allowed to live into another year.

A group of women and children were gathering stones from a field, carrying them out to throw into holes along the rutted track over which the pack horses now picked their way. Their hooves made sharp clattering noises upon them, combined with the splash and squelch of mud and puddled standing water.

The air had been damp all day. As evening descended the chill seemed to seep through Margaret's clothing, settling upon her skin like a cold hand. A feeling of deep loneliness and desolation crept over her. She longed for one last glimpse of her father.

That morning, Nehemiah had woken from sleep in the village of Brentford. He was quartered in the home of a wagonmaker and had rested well. He woke with a start, knowing that something had alerted his inner sense of alarm. He listened and heard at once the sound of raised voices, and of people running in the street below.

From the window he saw scenes of confusion, Royalist soldiers hacking their way through feeble resistance. Prince Rupert had led an advance guard in an early morning attack.

By the time he had made his way to the side of John Fletcher there were casualties everywhere. The Redcoats had borne the full brunt of the attack. The two men were hard pressed to know where to start on the scene of slaughter which surrounded them.

They worked all day, as best they could — stitching, sawing, staunching blood — then gasped with relief when they heard that Colonel Hampden had led his Greencoats in a counter attack which had stemmed the tide.

There was little sleep for them that night but, by next day, the Parliamentarians had gained a commanding position. The combined forces of Lord Essex and the London Trained Bands were drawn up at Turnham Green.

'What news?' asked Nehemiah during a lull in their work.

'The enemy's turned back. Our forces are too great for them.'

'God be praised,' breathed Nehemiah. 'Then this time we really are going to win.'

'I doubt it,' said John Fletcher tartly. 'Our leaders are again beseeching My Lord Essex to attack. And, again, he's choosing to listen to other advice.'

'But we can't fail a second time.'

'They're marching away from us, towards Oxford.'

'Then we've got to follow; attack from the rear.'

'There'll be no attack, my friend. They're to be allowed to depart. My guess is that they'll put up for the winter in Oxford.'

'That's beyond belief,' sighed Nehemiah. 'We've got them at our mercy, yet we do nothing?'

'Who knows? Perhaps the King could have succeeded in breaking through and so into London. He's got supporters in Kent. Perhaps it's as well for us that he decided to turn back.'

'Such matters are known only to the Almighty,' said Nehemiah. 'What we *do* know is that the enemy is marching away from us, unhindered.'

John Fletcher smiled. 'There's also something else we can be sure of,' he said. 'There won't be any more fighting this side of winter. Cheer up, my friend. We'll tend these wounds, then I suggest that you get off home.'

'Home?'

'You might as well go back to your family. There won't be much for you to do here till spring.'

Nehemiah reeled at the thought of home. He forgot, for that moment, that the Will of the Lord had once again been thwarted.

It had been dark for a full two hours when the pack-horse train at last made its way into the village where they would spend the night. It was only Tom Cox's instinct and lifelong knowledge of the terrain which had led them across hill and dale, through fordable streams, around impassable obstacles, until at last they reached the village inn.

Margaret was tired, worn out by the journey and by the sleepless nights spent nursing Lucy and the children. She sat watching Deliverance Daniels as he sat beside the fire with a tankard of ale and the remains of the late supper which had been prepared for them. She had difficulty restraining her eyes from closing while, at the same time, her stomach churned in suppressed anxiety and excitement. Still Deliverance Daniels had not spoken beyond a few polite words.

They continued to sit for a long time as though neither knew how to break the silence.

'You may go to . . . the . . . room,' he said at last. He had avoided saying 'our'.

She rose and went upstairs. It was cold. A small fire burned in the hearth but it gave out little heat. She went to the window and stared out, shivering, half from the cold, half from apprehension. Outside it was raining, a heavy persistent rain which dripped relentlessly from the eaves and from the drab November trees almost denuded of leaves.

Eventually she undressed herself and crept into bed where she found that a warming pan had been placed between the sheets. It brought comfort to her back but did not stop the shivering. She lay and waited for the sound of his tread upon the stair.

At last, his hand upon the door, the click of the latch. He came in and stood, almost looking at her, but with his eyes slightly averted. She was paralysed by the sight of him – the outline of his head, his features shadowed in the flickering light of the candle.

He walked across the room to a chest and removed his jacket, laying it carefully across the lid. She followed him with her eyes. She had never seen him without his jacket. He stood in his breeches and shirt, causing a ripple of emotion to pass through her as she sensed the movement of his body beneath the thin layer of linen. But, at the same moment, she remembered how it had been with Rupert. She swallowed and closed her eyes, averting her face as he undressed and climbed into bed beside her.

The candle had not been extinguished: she could see the rise and fall of his breathing, the contours of his face. He made no move towards her. She began to wonder whether some initial approach was up to her. She was acutely aware that, despite all that she felt, she was lying beside her husband and had a duty to perform.

She coughed faintly by way of oblique enquiry.

He made no response, lying with his eyes wide open, staring with a fixed expression towards the ceiling.

'There are matters . . .' Her voice failed her. She cleared her throat and started again. 'There are things you require of me.'

He looked at her, as if only now aware that she had spoken.

'My duty,' she said. 'I'm aware of my duty.'

'Oh.' He said it as if with concern for her. 'There's no need. You're tired from the journey.'

'But if you . . .'

'And I'm still weak from the fever.'

'Oh, I see.'

'I must rest,' he said. 'We've to rise early in the morning.'

'Yes.'

He resumed staring at the ceiling. She lay and watched him for a long time then, with a mixture of relief and disappointment, she turned on her side and fell into the deep sleep of exhaustion.

Two days later they passed into Wiltshire. For two nights they had shared a bed together yet still they were strangers. Each covered their embarrassment and their awkwardness by keeping up a steady conversation with Tom. They crossed the infant Thames near Cricklade, then skirted Braden Forest, on towards Wootton Bassett.

'Look 'ee over there,' said Tom. 'That be tobacco. Them grows it round 'ere.'

'Yes.' Margaret had seen it growing elsewhere. 'I've seen it at Winchcombe.'

She looked over her shoulder towards Deliverance Daniels. He was riding alone, a short distance behind.

'Old King tried t' ban it. Seems them settlers out in Virginia can't be doin' with the competition.' He laughed. 'Some hope! 'Tis magistrates as owns land what grows it.'

Margaret laughed with him but she felt uncomfortable to be laughing in the presence of Deliverance Daniels.

'What part o' New England be thee goin' to?'

'I'm not sure; it's a small community called Ufferton. My husband is to be the minister there.'

'Never fancied New England,' said Tom. 'Beats me to see as why folk do feel the need t' go.'

'You're always travelling yourself.'

'On good dry sod,' he said. 'Thee'll not catch I settin' foot on they damned girt ocean.'

The reminder of the Atlantic Ocean unnerved Margaret. She sought to change the topic of conversation.

'The road's so bad in these parts,' she commented. 'It's churned beyond recognition.' They had reached a stretch where they were forced to make their way across adjoining farmland. The road had become an impassable slough.

The terrain had changed. Gone was the red-brown soil of the Cotswold hills. Here it was flat and the soil was clay. The going had become difficult with the horses' hooves sinking into soft squelching mud, slipping and sliding, occasionally stumbling into deep holes hidden beneath the surface of the puddles.

'Fault o' they damned clothiers,' complained Tom Cox. 'Cursed clothiers with they wagons.'

'It's November. Why aren't their wagons put away?'

Tom coughed out a laugh. 'Too 'igh 'n' mighty to put up they wagons. Durstn't venture they fine cloth t' back o' they 'orses.'

'My father would never do that.'

'Sight difference 'tween mas'er weaver and they damned clothiers. They clothiers own just 'bout everyone as works round 'ere. And they cottages them lives in.'

'Owns them?'

'Aye, and dustn't come near place 'alf the time. Them lives in they fine 'ouses and dustn't never get they 'ands dirty.'

'Not like my father.'

Tom inclined his head. 'Not like thy father.'

They came to yet another area where the road had disappeared beneath a slough of mud. 'They churn it up and make it impassable to everyone,' said Margaret.

'Except theyselves. Puts on extra teams and drags they wagons through on they belly. Loads'll stay dry s' long as mud dustn't come up past they axle trees.'

127

'But that can only make it worse.'

'Aye, and makes t'others follow. Else farmers' ponies 'd swim t' they necks on way t' market.'

'You still use your Galloways.'

He gave her a wink and grinned through his rotting teeth. 'Old Tom been travellin' they parts a year or two. Knows where t' slip through places 'e's got no right t' be, and ne'er a glimpse o' 'e to tell they magistrate.'

'You know all these miles?'

'Every one o' they from 'ere to Bris'ol.' He grinned again. 'Who but ol' Tom do know which o' they fields as lies fallow this year as what last year was put t' plough? And who knows where they waters rise after it be rainin', and where bog could suck 'ee under?'

Margaret shivered at the thought of it.

'And where they highwayman lurks.'

The shiver turned to a shock of alarm but he stilled it with a glance of reassurance. 'And who but ol' Tom do know they innkeeper's wife as serves best roast beef and brews best tankard o' dragon's milk?' He looked at her sideways from the corner of his eye. 'And which innkeeper's daughter do stay warmest in night?'

She lowered her eyes and blushed.

'No time in winter 'o be travellin' without likes of ol' Tom,' he said. 'Why, only last year young maid did fall over and drown in they slough yonder.' He nodded his head towards an area where the road had been churned beyond recognition.

'Drowned?'

''S 'appened more 'n once on way t' market.'

He led the way round it, across farmland, until they were safely back once more upon a reasonably stable surface.

Deliverance Daniels quickened his pace and came up to join them. Immediately both stopped their conversation and fell into a respectful silence.

He fell into step beside Margaret. She wanted him to say something but, when he did not, she lapsed into her own thoughts.

'You're somewhere deep within yourself,' he said suddenly, startling her.

'I'm sorry. I was thinking how strange this all seems,' she

128

admitted. 'I never imagined I'd ever leave my father's village.'

She wished that he would smile at her — just once.

'It troubles you that you're far from home?'

'Yes,' she said hesitantly. 'A little.'

'Then you must have faith.'

'I'll pray for strength,' she said. There was something about the way he had said it which made her flinch.

'Good. You must pray for God's pardon in numerous ways. I detect a certain lack of humility.'

'I'm sorry,' she said. 'I'll try to be aware of it, and pray for His guidance.'

He nodded. 'It's important that you bear the proper wifely attributes.'

She bowed her head and hoped that he would now move away again.

'You spoke of strangeness,' he said after a time.

'I'm sorry.' She forced herself to resume the conversation.

'Strangeness,' he repeated.

'It's all so different. One moment I was in my father's home. The next moment I was here, bound for distant parts.'

'The Lord has many surprises.'

'If you hadn't passed through our village, if you had gone some other way . . .'

'Yes,' he said and looked at her. 'I am beholden to the Lord that He led me to your father's house.'

A light lit up inside her.

'I was on my way to visit an uncle. I was to receive a settlement from him.'

'Yes. Tobias spoke of it.'

'I found him fallen upon difficult times.'

'Oh.'

'But the Lord led me, instead, to your father's house.'

He was referring to her dowry. The light went out.

'The Lord has many ways of achieving His purpose. We must pray constantly that our hearts may be opened to receive it.'

'God be praised,' she said quietly, but the tears smarted and stung behind her eyes.

*   *   *

That night she went to bed and waited again for his tread upon the stairs. She watched as he entered the room, watched as he walked towards a saddlepack lying in the corner.

He stood looking down at it for a moment. She could tell there was something different about him — a certain tautness about his posture. He bent and touched the bag then appeared to change his mind and turned away. He undressed quickly and got into bed.

Between the sheets she was even more aware of the tension in him: she knew it to be sexual. Alarm and apprehension pounded through her. The time had come.

She waited for him to touch her, her own, different kind of tension building until she was aware of her finger nails digging into the palm of her hand. Memories of Rupert came flooding in. She gulped.

He turned and looked at her, then turned away again. She continued to wait.

At last he got out of bed, walked across the room and lifted the saddlepack from the floor. He looked uncertain for a moment; then, as if with renewed determination, he opened it and withdrew from it a tightly rolled garment of heavy black cloth.

She could not begin to understand what he had in mind. She watched and waited.

He held it for a further moment then twitched the bundle towards her. 'You'll wear it.'

'What?'

'You'll wear it.'

She did not understand.

He took a step towards her and twitched it again. 'You'll kindly get out of bed and put it on.'

'Oh.'

She obediently got out of bed, mesmerized by the instruction. He took one more step across the room.

She was shy to be disclosed standing in her night attire but he moved awkwardly towards her and held out the bundle.

'You'll please put it on,' he said again. She noted that, while he half looked at her, he did not raise his eyes to meet her own.

She did not immediately reach out to take it. He twitched it again, holding it out with a growing impatience. She became wary of his mood.

As she took it from him the garment unrolled, draping itself across the floor. She stepped back and gasped, letting it fall. It was a nun's habit.

'No,' she said, shaking her head. She found herself wiping her hands upon her nightgown as though they were soiled.

'You'll wear it.'

'No.' She was still shaking her head. 'It would be a sin.'

'It's well that we repent our sins and remind ourselves of the Lord's abhorrence of popery.'

'What?'

'You will wear it.'

'No.'

'You'll disobey?'

'Yes . . . No . . . ' she said, not aware that she had.

'Within so short a time of taking your vows?'

She was totally confused. 'I don't know.'

'Then you'll obey and put it on.' He said it more kindly. 'The Lord has need of your humility.'

She bent and picked it up. He stood watching her, making no attempt to assist her, waiting for her to put it on.

'I can't.'

He gave her a look but said nothing. Still his eyes did not quite reach her own.

At first she found that she had the garment back to front. It was grossly unfamiliar to her. She manoeuvred the bulk of the cloth until she had righted it, then pulled it over her head and stood with her shoulders drooping as though the weight of it bowed her down.

'The Lord is pleased with your servitude.'

She did not know what to say.

'Now you may kneel and pray.'

The tension in him had taken a new upsurge: she could feel it across the distance between them. She stood, afraid to look at him, fearing what would happen next.

'You will kneel and pray.'

She got to her knees.

'You will pray for the Lord's forgiveness of your sins.'

'Oh, God . . . '

'With your back to me.'

She turned away. 'Oh, God . . .' she began again, afraid that he was about to approach her from behind, to touch her.

'He is needful of our . . . ' There was a tightening of his voice, as though speaking through his teeth. At the same time she heard him fumbling in his undergarments.

She prayed, silently, begging forgiveness for her reluctance to comply, waiting for the touch of his hand upon her back.

It did not come. Instead there was the sound of heavy breathing, and of vigorous movement within the confines of his clothing.

She began to pray more meaningfully, beseeching forgiveness for being here upon her knees, dressed as a nun.

He was muttering words of his own through clenched teeth, gasping and panting, with grunts almost of pain and yet with growing intensity.

At last there was a long inward gasping of breath and he let out a sound as though sinking to his knees. She almost looked round.

He remained still for a while as his breathing calmed; then he staggered to his feet and rearranged his clothing.

'You may get up now,' he said shakily. 'And take off that . . . thing.' It was almost as though he were shocked to discover her wearing it.

She scrabbled through the cloth, divesting herself of the garment, and let it drop in a heap upon the floor.

'You may go to bed.' Still he did not look at her. He picked it up and stuffed it back into the saddlepack, handling it as though it were the most disgusting filth.

She turned and crept between the sheets. She was trembling and lay with her eyes closed, trying to make sense of something which she found shocking and distasteful.

He helped himself to a mug of ale set upon the bedside table, then climbed in beside her.

She turned her head and looked at him. The contours of his face were no less handsome but something was fading inside her. And, as one emotion began to fade, another continued to grow. She feared she was pregnant and still the marriage had not been consummated.

* * *

When Nehemiah returned home he found Anne weeping over the tiny emaciated corpse of Bibby-Anne. Lucy had surprised them all by clinging to the last slender strands of life: her strength was now returning. But every member of the family, apart from Samuel and Anne, was lying sick with the fever. When he looked for Margaret he was told that she had gone away, never to return. Nehemiah knelt with his head in his hands. It seemed that, in his absence, his life had been shattered.

He went with Anne across the hills, taking the baby to her funeral. By the time they returned, Rebecca lay waiting to be buried. At midnight she was joined by Mary.

As a new day dawned, the couple knelt in numbed inconsolable grief. Of six daughters, only Sarah and Rachael remained. Margaret was many miles away.

'You must go to her,' said Anne as if reading his thoughts. 'Each day she'll travel farther away.'

'I can't,' he said, obviously torn. 'You need me here.'

'Your need is greater. You'll never be at peace until you've taken your leave of her.'

'But I can't leave you now.'

'I've Elizabeth with me, and God continues to give me strength.'

Nehemiah was consumed with the fear that he would lose her too. She read his thoughts and pushed him gently aside.

'I've not succumbed to the fever,' she said. 'It's passed me by. With God's help it will continue to do so.'

He held her against him and kissed her hair. 'I think I'd die if I lost you too.'

'I'll do all in my power to remain beside you. But at daybreak you must set out for Bristol.'

'She's been gone for more than a week.'

'You could still overtake her if you had a good horse. They were to wander the villages of Wiltshire along the way.'

'And it'll take them time to arrange a ship,' he conceded. 'I'll go and speak to Sir Henry at first light. He'll doubtless give me the use of a good horse.'

He set out next morning, riding as hard as good sense and the horse would allow. He swapped Sir Henry's horse for other, fresher, ones at various staging posts along the way, arranging to return and collect it on his way home.

The going was hard, over unknown terrain. More than once he came close to disaster when his horse slipped and fell, submerged to its shoulders in a quagmire of mud and filthy stagnant water. But each time he was able to haul free his mount and continue on his way, soaked to the waist and caked hard with a coating of thick stinking mud.

At each village he enquired of the route taken by Tom Cox. Little by little, he edged himself nearer to Margaret.

At the time when he was first setting out from Dunscombe, Margaret and Deliveranee Daniels were already approaching Bristol. They had a few more days' riding ahead of them, then a further period in the city while arrangements were made to board a ship.

At eleven o'clock they stopped at a village inn but were disturbed from their dinner of roasted fowl and turnips by a commotion outside.

'What's troubling the people?' asked Deliverance Daniels. 'There's a great deal of to-ing and fro-ing.'

'It's a group of Parliament's supporters,' said the landlord, 'hellbent on smashing the church.'

'A Laudian church?'

'Aye, all that remains of it.'

'Then it's the hand of God which directs them.' He got up from the oak settle and made towards the door.

'Where are you going?' called Margaret rashly.

The look he levelled at her brought her questions to a halt. She followed meekly down the street as he ran towards the church.

By the time she caught up with him he had an axe in his hand, crashing it down against the altar rails, crying: 'Destruction to the house of Babylon, mother of harlots, abomination of the earth.'

She stood at the door of the church, appalled by the scene before her. She swallowed on the unfamiliar smell of incense and turned to fresher air outside, returning slowly to the inn.

Much later he joined her there, his face flushed, calling for a tankard of ale to wash the dust from his throat.

'A fine day's work has been achieved,' he said. 'The hand of God is at work throughout the land.'

Margaret said nothing but he sensed her disapproval.

'Don't tell me you're already faint-hearted in the work of the Lord? There's little hope for your future if you turn your back so readily on what is right.'

She said nothing but moved to allow access to the innkeeper's wife who brought the ale.

'I'll warrant your father's been employed in much the same pursuit these past months. The troops have taken their sport in the work of the Lord.'

'My father would never . . . ' she began, but bit it back and kept the denial to herself.

'I'm told that in some parts the troops have rejoiced in smashing several hundred windows in a single day. The Lord would have them bring an end to these vile painted idols.'

She remained silent, asking herself if it were possible that her father would take part in such activity. At first she was quite certain in her denial; but, gradually, she began to tell herself that soldiers were bound to follow orders, then she began to ask herself if she would know the man her father had become.

It was late afternoon when they entered Bristol, passing through one of its twelve gates. Margaret had never seen so large a city. She was spellbound by the bustle of it — people everywhere, animals and children underfoot. Beggars scavenged with the dogs beneath the market stalls which lined the street. Housewives, with baskets of cheeses and vegetables, dodged beneath the necks of horses, picking their way over the rotting garbage at their feet.

The streets were narrow and dark, lined on either side by buildings. Colourful signs hung over shop doorways, creaking gently in the cold wind which cut from the harbour.

Everywhere was noise — cries of street pedlars selling hot pies and oysters, a herd of pigs which had been driven up from Wales making its way to the market place, the fiddle playing of an old man crouched in a doorway begging for alms.

Margaret gazed at it all. But nothing took her more by surprise than a group of men who stood chained at a street corner. Their skins were black.

'Slaves,' called Tom Cox above the din. He had seen the

135

look upon her face. 'Bound for plantations o' Virginia 'n' Carolina, God 'ave mercy on they.'

'But why are they chained?' She was unable to take her eyes from the sight of black skin and tight black curly hair.

'Doubtless for the safety of the citizens,' commented Deliverance Daniels. 'They look surly rogues.'

Over the Avon there was a bridge identical to the one in London which Nehemiah had so often described to her. Houses, built across it on either side, made it hardly possible to catch a glimpse of the water beneath them.

Wherries plied their trade, ferrying passengers from place to place, the oarsmen sinewy-armed from years of pulling against the strong tide.

At the quay it was the smell which fascinated her first. There was the usual smell of people, of rotting garbage, dunghills – which she was used to. There was also the smell of rotting fish – which she was not used to. But, more than that, there was the smell of the sea. It had been coming to her in increasing intensity for several miles as they approached the city. Now it hit her – the fresh clear smell of the sea, finding its way from the ocean, up the estuary, cutting through the stench of people and their refuse.

The harbour was full of ships, waiting for wind and tide. A large galleon had her crew aloft working in the rigging. Margaret gazed up at them and felt a sudden sharp pang of home-sickness as she thought of spiders clinging to the ceiling rafters in the parlour.

Beneath the large ships, small craft passed back and forth carrying people and cargo, rowing passengers to one ship, collecting barrels from another, transferring them to wagons lined up along the quay.

A small vessel loaded with copper had made its way round the coast from Redruth and there were many barges carrying coal.

''Tis good coal,' commented Tom Cox. He tipped his hat to one of the men off-loading it onto horses standing alongside the quay. 'Reckon he'll get some twelve pence f' each o' they two-bushel loads.'

Everywhere was bustle and confusion – the shouted oaths and blasphemies of the sailors which made Margaret turn her head, the sight of fine silk glimpsed through the wrapping of a bale, the tantalizing aroma of exotic spices which she sought to identify through the smells of fish and leather, oranges and filth.

They came at last to a quayside inn, set back behind the warehouses. An ostler came to greet them, assisting Margaret and Deliverance Daniels from their horses, joking with Tom Cox as he helped to lead the Galloways through to the yard.

They ate supper, and when Margaret went to their room she found Deliverance Daniels already there, sitting in the glimmer of a candle, writing in his large leather-bound diary. On the table beside him lay an open Bible.

'You'd best say your prayers,' he said. 'Then you may read the Bible.'

She sank to her knees, wondering what lay in store for her this night. On several occasions now Deliverance Daniels had produced the nun's habit. She had learned to put it on without comment for protest was useless. It was no less distasteful to her but she was learning to blank her mind. She would kneel and pray – pray that this time, at least, the marriage would be consummated. It never was.

'You're praying?' he asked.

'Yes,' she said, realizing that her mind had wandered. She bowed her head and communed in silence, offering thanks that she had been brought in safety to this distant city, begging forgiveness for her reluctance to step off the edge of her native shore.

He continued to write, glancing every now and then at the back of her head. When she had finished he indicated the open Bible.

'You may read,' he said. 'I've opened it for you at the First Epistle of the Apostle Paul to Timothy, chapter three. Begin at verse nine.'

She scanned the page until she found the line he required: ' "And in like manner," ' she began, ' "that women adorn themselves in modest apparel with shamefacedness and sobriety; not with braided hair, or gold, or pearls, or costly array. But (which becometh women professing godliness) with good works. Let the woman learn in silence and with all subjection . . . " '

'Tell me your thoughts upon the passage.'

She stopped and looked at him, trying to form her thoughts into some kind of comment.

'It's new to you? It appears that you've never read it.'

'Yes, I've read . . . '

'Either you've never read it, or you've ignored its counsel.'

She did not understand.

'Tell me, what's the colour of your gown?'

She looked down at her skirt. 'Lavender.' She fingered the woollen cloth woven on her father's loom. 'With blue velvet.'

'I'll take you tomorrow to a place where you can be fitted with a more modest garment.'

She looked again at her gown, now travel-stained but still a favourite. She had sat for many hours with her mother sewing it by candlelight as they listened to the reading. 'Don't you like it?' She knew immediately that she had spoken unwisely. 'I'll discard it at once,' she said.

'Good,' he said more gently. 'Now go to bed.'

She climbed into bed; and later, when he had finished writing, he went to the corner of the room for the saddlepack.

Next day he took her to the Exchange in the centre of the city where, in a small tightly stocked shop, he bought for her a dress of dove-grey wool. It had a plain white linen collar spreading to her shoulders and white turned-back cuffs on sleeves which reached to the wrists. With it went a white linen apron tied about her waist and reaching almost to the hem.

Next door he bought for her a copotain hat, similar to his own, of black felt with a wide brim and tall crown. To wear beneath it she had a white lawn cap which was to be tied beneath her chin, completely encompassing her hair.

He ordered all the gowns in her baggage to be destroyed. 'You'll have no need of them,' he said. 'I'll arrange for them to be replaced by others.'

True to his word, a young seamstress appeared a few days later carrying an armful of dresses of russet, grey and black.

'You'll look exceedingly fine,' said Deliverance Daniels.

She thought for a moment that there was a measure of admiration in his voice, but she could not be sure.

'Thank you,' she said. 'You're most generous on my behalf.'

'It's only right that I'm seen to have a wife of modesty and sobriety. It will go well for me amongst the peoples of New England.'

She was wearing the grey dress when Nehemiah first caught sight of her at the quayside, standing beside the large stone conduit which gathered water from the springs in the hills and conveyed it about the city. Her back was towards him and at first he did not recognise her. It was only when she turned that he sprang from his horse and called her, battling his way through the throngs of people crowding the quayside.

She stood and watched him, unable to believe that fate was not playing some cruel trick upon her eyesight.

'Father, is it really you?'

'It's I, child.' He gathered her up into his arms. 'And thank God I've found you.'

'But how did you know? What brings you to Bristol?'

'I learned from your mother.'

'How is Mother?' she asked quickly. 'What of Lucy, and Tobias, and of the children?'

He led her to the conduit and sat her down beside it. 'Lucy's gaining strength. She was able to wish God's blessing on your voyage.'

'Thank God!'

'And Tobias is strong. He'll overcome the fever.'

He had left news of the children until last.

'And the children?'

He turned his head. 'Only Sarah and Rachael remain.'

'Oh, Father.' She did not fight her grief but wept openly, tears welling and overflowing down her cheeks. 'They're gone, and I wasn't with them.'

He reached for her hand, seeking reassurance as much as giving it. 'I pray that the Lord will forgive my selfishness,' he said. 'I know I shouldn't mourn. They've gone to a far better place.' He increased the pressure of his hand. 'But . . . oh, Margaret, I wish they'd been allowed to stay here with me.'

'They're gone,' she said again. 'And I abandoned them.'

139

'Your mother was with them, and your Aunt Elizabeth.'

'How is Mother?'

'She's consumed with the loss, comforted in the knowledge that the Lord has taken them to a life of eternal happiness.' He said it as much to console himself as to console Margaret.

She reached out her arms about him. 'Father, I'm so glad you came.'

'I couldn't let you go without taking my leave of you.'

She lowered her head and rested it against his shoulder. 'I'm taking ship during the second week of December. We'll be on the waters for two months before we reach New England.'

He swallowed hard. ''Tis a mighty long journey you've undertaken.'

She gripped hold of him and buried her face deep within his shoulder. She would have given a great deal at this moment to have begged him to take her home.

'You always were a maid of courage,' he said. Then he stopped and held her away from him so that he could look at her. 'But you're no longer a maid. You're a woman travelling with the husband of your own choosing.'

She waited for him to comment upon the reason for her marriage.

'And you'll be happy with this man?'

She lowered her eyes.

'He's treating you well?'

She had taken her vows. She knew that she must see them through.

He looked down at her, concerned that she did not immediately reply.

She wanted to tell him of the nun's habit. But her own part in such a ritual was so distasteful, so embarrassing, that she could not bring herself to speak of it. Nehemiah sensed the sexual nature of her hesitation and experienced his own embarrassment, believing that she was having difficulty in fulfilling her new role as wife.

He blushed, adding to her embarrassment. 'Your mother spoke . . . ?' he asked hesitantly. 'She explained your duties?'

She nodded, without looking at him.

'Then doubtless it will grow easier with time.'

She doubted that she would ever find it easy to cope with the bizarre behaviour of Deliverance Daniels but could not bring herself to speak of it.

'It's often difficult in the early days. It takes time to adjust.' He wished fervently that Anne were here and he could be released from the task, as he saw it, of advising his daughter.

She nodded again. 'I'll do my best, Father. But I wasn't expecting it to be quite like this.'

He blushed again. 'It's often trying, no matter how well one's parent may seek to prepare.'

'I'm so glad you came.'

'It was a great shock to find you gone.' He was glad to be released.

'I didn't want to leave.'

'But you had to. A wife must follow her husband wherever he may lead.'

She swallowed and bit her lip. 'You know? Mother told you . . . of my . . . shame?'

He smiled gently. 'I know of no shame,' he said, though his eyes told her that he did. 'I know only that you're wed to the man of your choice.'

'Shall you ever forgive me?'

'Forgive you for marrying the man of your choice?' he asked kindly. 'I bring you nothing but my blessings.'

'But I did wrong, Father. And I'm burdened down with my shame.'

'I can't believe that, child. You were more sinned against than sinning.'

'But I should have fought . . . '

'Hush, my child.' He placed a finger to her lips. 'There's no point in dwelling upon matters which cannot be undone. You'd best forget the past and go forward in confidence with your husband.'

She sucked in a breath and felt her heart flutter. She had remembered again that she was almost certainly pregnant and her marriage had not yet been consummated.

'But I fear for you on this great voyage.'

'To be afraid would be lacking in faith,' she said shakily.

'Such great courage, my child. I will pray for your safety every day.'

'And I, Father. Not a day shall pass that I won't think of you, and pray for you, too.'

'Come,' he said. He took her by the elbow and went to fetch the horse which he had left tied to the back of a stationary wagon. 'You must take me to meet your husband. I'll sup with him this evening. Tomorrow I must start the journey back to your mother.'

After supper they sat beside a roaring fire while the serving girl brought mugs of ale. Deliverance Daniels talked with enthusiasm of the mission which lay ahead of him. Nehemiah listened intently.

'I'm beholden to the Lord for offering me such an opportunity to serve Him,' Deliverance Daniels said. 'And I thank God that I have Margaret here beside me.'

She glanced up at him.

'I was alone: now I'm given a helpmeet to travel beside me.'

Margaret was almost tempted to speak. Instead, she returned her eyes to her hands which were held loosely clasped in the lap of her dove-grey dress.

Nehemiah nodded appreciatively. When he took leave of them early the following morning he went with a lightened heart, reassured that he had left Margaret in worthy hands.

CHAPTER 7

Rupert rode down the hill towards Dunscombe, making his way towards Oakbourne House but hoping, first, to see Margaret. It was early December and a sharp frost had made the ground iron hard beneath the hooves of his horse. The air was clear and he could see for miles.

He had hoped to find Margaret going about her duties upon the hills or around the village, but there was no sign of her. He began turning over in his mind a variety of excuses for calling at Nehemiah's house before going to pay his respects to his parents. As he neared the house, he saw not a member of Nehemiah's family, but his own mother.

'Why, Mother I didn't expect to see you.' He stopped short when he saw her face. 'What's wrong? You look bowed down with fatigue.'

She almost ran to him as he sprang from his horse. 'Oh, my son, it's so good to see you safe and well.'

'I'm well but you're not. It's written all over your face.'

'It's just tiredness,' she said. 'There's been sickness here. Three of the children have been taken and Lucy came within a breath of supping with her Maker.'

'What of Margaret?'

'She's well, thank God, but married and gone with her husband to New England.'

'Husband!'

'She's wed to the Reverend Deliverance Daniels.'

He had turned pale and realized that he was still clinging to the saddle of his horse.

'You're ill, too?' She reached a hand towards his forehead.

'No, Mother, I'm well. But it's a surprise.'

'It was a surprise to us all. It happened at such short notice.'

Nehemiah came through the horse passage into the street. He stopped short when he saw Rupert and appeared to draw back.

'Greetings, Uncle. I'm sorry to hear of the sickness in your family.'

'It's been a great blow,' said Nehemiah coolly. 'But I'm glad to see you home safe and well.'

'The King's quartered at Oxford for the winter. I'm relieved of duty for a while.'

Anne, hearing their voices, came out into the street to join them. Rupert made immediately to embrace her. 'Aunt Anne . . .' But she stepped to one side, avoiding him.

'It's good to see you looking well,' she said icily.

'You've come at a good moment, Rupert,' commented Elizabeth. 'I'm just about to return home. You can keep me company and tell me all your news.'

'Forgive me, Mother. I'll catch you up but I must just first have a word with Uncle Nehemiah.'

She looked slightly put out but did not question him. 'I'm anxious to get home. I've been away for several weeks.'

'You go on; I'll catch you up.'

Anne walked over and embraced her sister. 'I couldn't have managed without you,' she said.

'It's been a dreadful time. Let's pray now you'll find some peace.'

The two women embraced again and Elizabeth made her way home. 'Don't be long, Rupert,' she called over her shoulder. 'I would like to spend time with you. I've been worried these past months.'

'Yes, Mother.'

All three watched her ride away down the street, then Anne and Nehemiah turned back to Rupert. There was a marked, but unspoken, reluctance to engage in conversation.

'Uncle?'

Nehemiah made no response and left it to Rupert to continue.

'I'm burdened down with shame.'

Still Nehemiah said nothing.

'It's burning my very soul.'

Nehemiah made an impassive gesture as though he had no idea of the matter to which Rupert referred.

'I came to speak with Margaret. I can tell by your attitude that you're aware of the reason.'

'I've no idea what you're talking about,' said Nehemiah. 'Margaret's gone to New England with her husband.'

'You *do* know. It's quite obvious that you do.' He turned instead to Anne. 'Aunt?'

She turned her face. 'I know nothing,' she said. 'And you'd best keep your conscience to yourself.'

'When I came to think of what I'd done . . . And later when I realized how easily I could have made her with child . . .'

Anne flashed him a look.

Nehemiah, in turn, shot her a quick glance of caution but it was too late.

Rupert looked from one to the other, his face blanched white. 'I'll go at once,' he said. 'How long is it since she left?'

'Her ship's already sailed,' lied Nehemiah coldly, knowing well that it had not. She was not due to embark on the *Silver Rose* for another week.

'Oh, my God, she's gone!'

'Yes,' said Nehemiah. 'And with her husband.'

'I'm sorry.' Rupert stood before them, ashen-faced. 'What can I do?'

'I've no idea what you need to do,' said Nehemiah. 'You talk in riddles.'

'You're sure she's with child?'

Nehemiah gave him a hard threatening stare which caused Rupert to lower his eyes.

'Tell me,' he said shakily, 'do my parents know?'

'There's been enough sadness in this family recently,' said Nehemiah. 'I've no idea what ails your conscience. But, whatever it is, I suggest you spare your parents knowledge of it.'

Rupert heaved a sigh and pulled himself up on to his horse. He steadied himself once he was in the saddle.

Nehemiah waited until he had kicked the horse into motion. 'And I suggest,' he called after him, 'that you don't waste your time in future calling at this house. There's little common ground in our allegiance.'

Rupert flinched. He looked round but Nehemiah had turned his back and was escorting Anne into the house. He let out a heavy sigh and urged the horse into a slow sullen trot down the main street of the village.

Samuel stepped back quickly from the window and returned to the loom. He had been working in the room above the street when he had heard the sound of Rupert's voice. He had been about to rush down and greet him when the tenor of the ensuing conversation had stopped him in his tracks. Instead, he had stood and listened, concealed from the view of those standing in the street below him.

His parents' animosity had been obvious and so, too, as he had continued to listen, had been the cause of Rupert's shame. He was in no doubt that his cousin had defiled his sister.

He cursed beneath his breath, feeling anger flare and explode into full blaze. It was Rupert's fault that Margaret had gone away; Rupert's fault that Samuel would never see her again. If his cousin had been standing before him at this moment, he would surely have attempted to hit him.

He picked up a bale of yarn and threw it against the wall. Nehemiah, entering the room, was shaken from his distraction. 'Why did you do that?'

'No reason,' spat Samuel vehemently. 'I just felt like it.'

'My son, that's no way to speak to your father.'

'I'll say what I like and I'll do what I like.'

'Go into the yard,' ordered Nehemiah, 'and stay there until your temper has cooled. I'll not have such behaviour in my house.'

Samuel stomped from the room. He had no idea why he was venting his anger upon his father. What he did know was that some day he would vent it upon Rupert. Some day he would throw *him* against a wall.

Rupert stayed on in Dunscombe for several days. He was sick with worry. He could not forgive Margaret's family for sending her to New England; for sending her into danger, on the other side of the world, when they must have known that, somehow, he would have cared for her and for the child. In one drunken moment his actions had brought disaster upon her.

He thought at first that he would go to his father and speak to him of his dilemma. But he knew that Sir Henry would be less than helpful. He would be of the opinion that Margaret must be left to the care of her husband.

Gradually, a decision was formed: he would go to New England, and he would determine to his own satisfaction that Margaret had left Dunscombe of her own volition. Somehow, he would follow her, and if she willed it he would bring her home.

He waited until he had the plan firmly established in his mind, then approached his father. He chose a moment when they were riding together through the wood, going about the business of the estate.

It was a cold morning with hoar frost coating the bare branches of the trees. The breath of the horses vaporized as they trotted over the hard soil.

'It's so good to be home,' said Rupert, trying to keep the strain from his voice.

'It's good to have you here.'

'Oakbourne's never meant more to me than it does at this moment.'

Sir Henry turned and looked at him. 'Your home's always open to you. One day it will all be yours.'

'It's the peace of the place. You'd never believe the scenes I've witnessed.'

Sir Henry looked again, this time with sympathy. 'I can imagine,' he said kindly. 'I can well understand that the taste of war isn't to your liking.'

'It's not to the liking of anyone with any sense of decency.'

'I thought you were eager for the Cause?'

'It's not the Cause, but the way it needs to be brought about.'

'I never was in favour of it,' sighed Sir Henry. 'There was poor counsel on both sides.'

'I hadn't realized . . . In the first heat of enthusiasm for the Cause, I didn't realize just how dreadful war can be.'

Sir Henry nodded. 'War never was a pleasant occupation,' he said. 'War against one's fellow countrymen is an even more bitter potion.'

'It is indeed.' Rupert decided that this was the moment to introduce his plan. 'In Oxfordshire,' he said, 'I met a man who weaves blankets.'

Sir Henry looked at him, not understanding the apparent change of topic.

'He's heard that there's demand for them in the Americas. The settlers use them as a means of trade with the savages.'

'So I believe.'

'He's got a good scheme but he's lacking finance.'

Sir Henry raised an eyebrow. 'And you're thinking of abandoning your study of the law and taking up trade?'

'No, I merely said I'd speak with you.' He turned to Sir Henry. 'It's a good scheme, Father. It would pay handsomely.'

Puzzled, Sir Henry raised an eyebrow. 'It's true there's a high demand.'

'Then you'll consider it?'

'I'd need first to know about the quality of the blankets, and about numbers.'

'I could bring the weaver to see you. He'd be pleased to discuss it with you.'

Sir Henry smiled. 'And I dare say you'd require some sort of reward for the introduction?'

'I was thinking of playing some other kind of part.'

'Oh? What kind of part did you have in mind?'

'You'll need an agent in the Americas.'

'I already have agents in the Americas.'

'I know but I thought . . .' He stopped and looked across at his father.

'You *want* to go to the Americas?'

'I'd welcome the challenge.'

'And what of your soldiering?'

'It's winter, Father. I could get permission to be absent till spring.'

'If you left tomorrow,' commented Sir Henry, 'it would be summer before you returned.'

Rupert looked across at him but said nothing.

'Oh, I see. And by summer the war may well be over.'

Rupert nodded and flashed a quick smile.

'I see,' his father said again. He sat and thought on it for a while. 'And how would you convince your superiors of the need to be away till summer?'

'I'm sure we could find a way. Especially if I could tell them that I'm urgently needed for your business.'

'Then we must make sure that the need is of the utmost urgency.'

'Thank you, Father.'

'I'll not deny,' said Sir Henry, 'that I'd rather have a son about my business in the Americas, than closer at hand on a battlefield.'

'Thank you,' said Rupert again. 'I'm most grateful to you.'

'You wouldn't rather find some other way? Here, in England, with your wife?'

Rupert drew in his breath and lowered his eyes, fearing that his discomfort showed. He waited until he had ducked beneath a low overhanging branch then checked his voice and said: 'It's not safe for me to spend time in Chiswick, Father. I've become well known for my allegiance to the King.'

'You could bring her here to Oakbourne.'

'She's happier in Chiswick, with her mother.'

Sir Henry looked at him closely. 'She'd soon get used to it. Your mother would welcome her.'

'A little later, perhaps, after the child's been born.'

Sir Henry gave him a searching look. 'You're not making the most of this marriage, Rupert.'

He bit his lip. 'It's the war. Once it's over, things will be better.'

'I do hope so. You've not had much chance to grow in love.'

The following day Rupert rode out to speak with the weaver, Edward Cook, and to bring back details of the blankets.

Sir Henry was willing to be convinced of the somewhat unreliable deal. He was unlikely to make great profit on so small a venture but profit was not, in this instance, his main concern.

'I'll arrange a ship,' he said. 'I suggest that you take your blankets to Massachusetts Bay. The Indians are peaceable there. You'll have the greatest opportunity for trade.'

Rupert was relieved: he had not known how to achieve the desired destination.

'And there's another reason,' added Sir Henry. 'Your Cousin Margaret's bound for Massachusetts Bay. You could bring back news for your Uncle Nehemiah.'

Rupert fought to hide the tightening of his voice. 'Yes, I'd be glad to. It'll be good to see her again.'

'And when you've finished in Massachusetts Bay, you can go on down into Virginia. There's other business you can do for me there. Then you can take passage home with a consignment of tobacco.'

'I'm grateful to you, Father. You could have called me coward.'

'It's not only the coward who turns his back on war,' said Sir Henry. 'It's also the man of peace.'

'Thank you,' he said, uncomfortable at being less than honest with his father. 'Some day I'll repay you.'

'You can repay me by remaining alive and in one piece. In that way we can be sure that you'll take up your inheritance and that the future of Oakbourne will be secured.'

The following day Rupert returned to kick his heels in Oxford. It would take eight weeks for the arrangements to be made and he was still sick with concern for Margaret.

When Samuel heard of the proposed voyage his rage boiled again. He expected, at first, that his parents would speak out and put a stop to it. But they did not. For weeks he waited, but nothing was said. There was obvious tension and anxiety within them, but nothing was admitted or discussed. At last he decided that, when the time was right, he would put a stop to it himself.

It was a raw, cold day when Margaret and Deliverance Daniels left the quayside inn for the last time and stood waiting their turn to board the small wherry which would row them out to the *Silver Rose*. The thick mist which had lain all morning across the estuary was giving way to a chill wind which swirled the dampness about them.

Margaret leapt warily from the quayside steps into the wherry and felt at once how it bobbed like a leaf upon the water. She had been troubled by nausea for more than a week and knew, even before she reached the *Silver Rose*, that she would be sick.

It was a small ship. Less than seventy feet long, it was to be home for fifty passengers and crew for the next two months or more. She felt the slight swaying motion of the deck beneath her feet. But it was when she went below that the full impact of combined nausea and claustrophobia hit her like a hammer blow. She was completely overcome by the feeling of confinement beneath the low deckhead, only inches above her head, and by the thick, fetid smell of the damp, airless quarters.

She stood stock-still, taking short rapid inward breaths, but was unable to restrain herself and vomited into a foul-smelling leather bucket which had been hanging from the bulkhead.

A young woman stepped beside her, placing a gentle hand upon her heaving back.

'I'm so sorry,' said Margaret, embarrassed. 'But I've been feeling ill for days. The movement of the ship upsets me.'

'You're with child?'

It was the first time that anyone, except her mother, had spoken of it. The growing unease which had been building now erupted in full panic. After four weeks, the marriage still had not been consummated.

'The sickness is only to be expected.' The young woman took the blush as confirmation. 'Have patience and it will pass.'

'Thank you, but I'm merely feeling ill.' She looked round for Deliverance Daniels, fearing that he had overheard the comment, but he was occupied in staking claim to the small area of space which was to be theirs. She made her way unsteadily towards him.

The space afforded little privacy. She rigged up a thick cloak to act as a screen, then piled their baggage around the two wooden pallets which were to be their beds. There were straw mattresses on the pallets but they were damp and stained with the urine of rats. She took out two blankets from her baggage and laid them across the beds. And all the time she constantly measured, with her eye, the distance to the nearest bucket.

The adjoining space had been taken by the same young woman, together with her husband and two small children. She smiled across at Margaret. 'You'd best go up on deck,' she said. 'You'd feel better where the air's fresher.'

Margaret nodded and turned to ask permission of Deliverance Daniels but he was already walking away. When she got up on deck he was there, watching the seamen making preparation to sail. Men, as surefooted as cats, ran aloft in the rigging breaking out the sails, whilst others heaved on the windlass hauling in the anchor.

She drew down the cold mist-laden air into her lungs. Gradually, her stomach began to settle. But, as the ship pulled out into the main flow of the estuary, she felt the full dip and sway of movement beneath her feet.

The passengers ate well that evening on fresh food newly taken aboard. Margaret remained on deck, declining the invitation to take her share.

As an early darkness fell, the heavy mist came down again. All night the ship bobbed, becalmed, having journeyed no further than Bridgewater Bay. Margaret lay on the wooden pallet, swallowing hard and trying to regulate her breathing in an effort to quell the feelings of nausea and panic which welled within her.

With dawn came a fresher, stronger wind which carried them out along the Bristol Channel and into the rise and fall of the great Atlantic.

For three days Margaret was violently sick. She lay on deck impervious to the cold rain which lashed down upon her. She moved only at night when she was gently, but firmly, cajoled into going below to her bed. All the time she was aware of the ministrations of the same young woman who had helped her when she first came aboard.

'You're a most kind and godly woman,' she said on the third day. Her good Samaritan had brought water from which to drink and to bathe Margaret's face. 'You're so good to me, yet you don't even know me.'

The woman smiled. 'If we're to be companions on this voyage, we'll all need to help one another.'

'I'd gladly help you.' She tried to raise herself up. 'If only . . .'

'Stay where you are. There's time enough for you to take your turn.'

'But your children need you.'

'Their sickness has passed. They're playing and getting under the feet of the seamen.'

Margaret made a further attempt to sit up, leaning her back against the wooden bulkhead behind her. For the first time she found that she could look at the undulating sea without feeling her stomach rising within her.

'You're feeling better, too,' observed the woman. 'It's been worse for you, being with child.'

Again panic rose. She played in her mind the scene which could occur if the pregnancy were referred to in the presence of Deliverance Daniels.

The woman mistook it for another wave of nausea. 'You're sick again?'

'No,' said Margaret, taking hold of herself. 'But I do feel as though I've been through some great ordeal. I never knew that the sea could cause such terrible discomfort.'

'Poor Margaret, it was plain to everyone that you weren't used to water.'

'You know my name.'

'I asked your husband.'

'Where is he?'

'He's at prayer with a number of the passengers.'

'He's not sick?'

'Not for a day. He strode the deck from the moment he first set foot on board, and he's supped well every day.'

'I'd best go to him.' She tried to get up and felt her head sway.

'There's no need. He's been most anxious about you, and instructed me to take the greatest care of you.'

Margaret closed her eyes and sank back against the bulkhead.

'The passengers are glad to have him aboard. He's agreed to act as our minister.'

'I've neglected my own prayers.' Margaret became

agitated, realizing that she was totally unable to account for an unknown number of days.

The young woman placed a gentle, restraining hand on her shoulder. 'You've been sick. Your husband understands your weakness.'

'Does he?'

'Of course, he's concerned about you.'

Margaret wondered if it were so. She had noted before that his comments to other people did not always tally with her own knowledge of his attitudes. 'I'll just sit here for a few more minutes,' she said, 'then I must go and find him.'

'Sit as long as you need. He won't expect you to go to him before you're well.'

Margaret smiled and changed the subject. 'I don't even know your name.'

'I'm Susannah.' The woman cleared a space and sat down beside her. 'Wife of Thomas Norton.'

'I'm most grateful for everything you've done for me.'

Susannah waved away the thanks as unnecessary. 'Thomas is a shoemaker,' she said. 'And my children are John and Eleanor.' Then pointing to her stomach, 'And I have another waiting to be born in the new land.'

'You're bound for New England?'

'Yes, though we don't know yet which part we're going to.'

Margaret sensed a note of anxiety in Susannah's voice. 'We're going to a township called Ufferton,' she said. 'My husband's to be the minister there.'

'Yes I know.' Susannah studied her hands for a moment. 'I'm not sure yet where we're going. But Thomas is a skilled craftsman, and where there are people, there's bound to be a need for shoes.'

'Of course.'

She looked across at Margaret. 'You see, our home was set to the torch so we had to make a fresh start. And Thomas had heard about others who had gone to New England.'

'You're very courageous.'

'It's not courage,' she said, 'it's necessity. Thomas has borrowed money for the venture.'

'You said your home was set to the torch?'

'Yes, the King's soldiers. There were only a few of them but they were hellbent on revenge.'

'For what?'

'For the church. It was Laudian and the Parliamentarians had taken an axe to it.'

'That's dreadful.' Margaret sucked in her breath, waiting to be told something she did not want to hear. 'What was the name of the village?'

But Susannah named an unknown village in some other part of the country.

'That's dreadful,' Margaret said again.

Susannah smiled and prepared to get up. 'It's happened many times, in many villages,' she said. 'We're no worse off than many others. Now,' she touched Margaret lightly on the shoulder, 'I'll go and fetch you some food. You haven't eaten since you came on board.'

Margaret swallowed. 'I don't think I could face the thought of food.'

'Just try. You're in need of sustenance for the sake of the coming child.'

Margaret swallowed again, her mind racing. Susannah gave her another smile and left her. She was still thinking of Deliverance Daniels when he walked up behind her.

'You're recovered?'

She jumped. 'Yes, thank you.'

'You've been sick for days.'

'I'm sorry.' She hauled herself up, feeling her legs trembling beneath her. 'I'm afraid I'm still a bit unsteady on my feet.'

'Then you must eat.'

'I'll try.'

'No doubt you'll endeavour to be present at dinner time today. The other passengers expect to see you at my side.'

'Yes,' she said again, her stomach lurching. 'I'll try.'

'That's good. There are many sick. They're in need of you.'

'I'm sorry,' she said. 'I'll come at once.'

'It's as well that Mistress Norton kept her stomach, and her head. At no time has she neglected her husband or her children.'

'I'm sorry.'

'You'd do well to learn from her,' he said. 'She's a fine example to all wives.'

'Yes,' she said, and watched him walk away.

Over the next few days Margaret found that she was coping more easily with the movement of the ship. By flexing her muscles and adjusting her stance, she could withstand the rolling motion which had previously caused her so much distress. She was still sick on occasions but it was a different kind of sickness which affected her mainly in the mornings.

As other passengers, too, started to find their sealegs, they began to strike up friendships and to pay attention to their surroundings. Their quarters, which at the start of the voyage had been fetid, now reeked of stale vomit and the accumulating smell of tightly packed bodies. They set up a rota by which they could determine a higher standard of cleanliness and take greater care of those who were still sick.

There was still plenty of fresh food remaining and they ate well, knowing that soon enough it would putrefy. Water, which had been brought aboard in wooden casks, would quickly spoil but there was no lack of rain water. The seamen stretched out lengths of canvas to catch the squalling showers.

With little privacy Margaret had hoped to be spared the ordeal of the nun's habit. But regularly, in the middle of the night when all were sleeping, Deliverance Daniels would wake her and point wordlessly to the garment which he had laid across her bed. In total silence she would put it on and obey his unspoken instruction to turn her face towards the wall. Then behind her back she would hear a faint rustling as he fumbled in his clothing until, at last, he would let out a small stifled sound and lie back on his bed. Only then would she know that she could take off the garment and, still in total silence, crawl back beneath the blanket.

There could no longer be any doubt about her pregnancy. Night after night she lay on the wooden pallet, staring up into the darkness, praying to God that the marriage might be consummated or that she might be allowed to bleed.

They had been at sea for almost two weeks when they awoke one morning to find another ship approaching, bearing down on them at speed. It was still some distance away but it could clearly be seen against the leaden grey horizon. There was an air of tension among the crew and the captain stood, feet slightly apart, staring out towards the approaching vessel.

It was not the first ship they had seen. Others had come within hailing distance, asking for news of the port from which the *Silver Rose* had recently sailed – passengers and crew, starved of human contact after weeks at sea, seeking sight and sound of others who had recently left the land. This ship was different, but Margaret did not understand why.

'Cap'n's got a nose for it,' said a seaman who had sensed her unspoken question.

She had come up on deck to breathe in the cold winter morning. She held her cloak snugly wrapped across her chest. 'A nose for what?'

'Just a feeling . . . Could be wrong, but the Cap'n's got a nose for it.'

'You mean they could intend us harm?'

'Who knows? Perhaps they just want to pass us a cask of good wine from their hold for Christmas.'

She peered nervously at the approaching ship under cover of her hand. 'She's English,' she said with some relief.

'A flag can mean everything or nothing at all. It's easy enough to run down one flag and run up another.'

Margaret's blood was running cold. Even in the depths of the Cotswolds she had heard tales of piracy on the high seas.

'It's as easy to take a flag from a captured ship as it is to plunder the cargo,' he went on. 'And flags are mighty useful for drawing to without question.'

'Oh, dear.'

'If it *is* English,' he said, more reassuringly, 'then we've probably not a lot to fear. An English cap'n's not likely to harm his own countrymen. Not like them foreign bastards.'

Margaret coloured and the seaman dipped his head slightly by way of apology for his language.

'There's few of the brigands left these days. Time was, the seas were full of 'em. Cut yer throat soon as look at yer.'

Margaret blanched and he repeated by way of reassurance:

157

'Not many of 'em left these days. Just our whore-blamed luck to meet one of 'em.'

They had been joined by other passengers as word quickly spread of the approaching ship. Women clung to their husbands, openly showing their fear.

'Best be getting below,' said the seaman. 'Cap'n won't want the sight of women on board.'

It was enough to set the husbands quickly ushering their women below.

Margaret remained where she was. 'What would they do?'

'Not wise for them to see the women,' was all he said.

The ship was closer now. She could see it clearly. It was approaching at speed yet, at the same time, it appeared to be taking an age to reach them.

'Why don't we just change course before she gets here? She won't be upon us for ages yet.'

The seaman shook his head. 'Just look at her,' he said. 'She's all o' three hundred tons, and what's the betting she's got a score or more guns at the ready?' He swished a wad of tobacco around his mouth and spat accurately over the side. 'And we're fully laden. At the rate that ship's bearing down, she's carrying no more than ballast. She'd outrun us in no time at all.'

'At least we could try.'

'There's many a cap'n as tried, and many a cap'n who's regretted it. It's the wise man who knows when he's outclassed. That way he keeps our throats attached to our heads, or saves us finding ourselves on the slave lines at Mamora.'

Margaret shivered. 'But if they're English, then we're safe?'

'If they're English then they'll probably pass us a cask of wine,' he said without conviction.

'Perhaps we should pray.'

He looked at her sideways. 'Perhaps you should just be getting below.'

She could not bear at this moment the confinement of the fetid quarters. 'I feel better up here on deck.' A lifetime spent on open hills kept her standing where she was.

'Cap'n'll order it afore long.' He measured with his eye the distance to the approaching ship.

'And there's really nothing we can do but stand and wait?'

'Not if you value your life. Either way the Cap'n can't win. If he runs he'll make it worse for all of us. If he stands to without resistance he'll be charged with collusion by the merchants whose goods we're carrying.'

'But we're not carrying goods.' Margaret saw it as a sudden ray of hope. 'With so many passengers there can't be room for any quantity of cargo.'

'But they don't know that yet. And, in any case, there's cargo what's more valuable than bulky.'

She was about to question him further when Captain Beckley turned. 'Passengers below.'

There was no questioning the authority of his command. All those remaining on deck made their way down to the dim confinement of the passenger quarters. Margaret made sure that she was the last to go. She stood just below the hatch as it was closed above their heads.

They stood for a long time, the women once again clinging to their husbands, their children gathered in clusters about their skirts. No one spoke beyond a few muted whispers. Even the children did not cry.

Margaret looked about her for Deliverance Daniels. He was in a far corner, kneeling at prayer.

At last there was a faint bump and scraping along the ship's side. Voices were raised, calling out from one vessel to the other.

'They're English, I think,' she said aloud. The comment brought some slight lessening of tension among them.

On deck, the crew of the *Silver Rose* stood facing the *Flying Swan*, counting guns and men while trying to disguise their unease.

'Cap'n Alexander Middleton at your service, sir. And you're welcome aboard to partake of a swig or two of my finest rum.'

Captain Beckley knew better than to question the invitation. The *Flying Swan* might be confirmed as English but there was no denying the stance of her crew, nor the way in which the vessel had been positioned alongside.

No sooner had he transferred to the other ship and been ushered below, than Captain Middleton invited himself on board the *Silver Rose*. As he stepped on deck the crew

159

involuntarily took two paces backwards. He was a large man with big hands and a steel-grey gaze which instantly transfixed anyone upon whom it fell. With him he brought eight of his men who stood with folded arms, each with a hand on the knife or pistol pushed into his belt. Behind him the remaining crew lined their deck, guns manned, ready to fire at a word of command.

'Good day, gentlemen. We'll not detain you for long afore we'll be on our way.'

He addressed himself to the First Mate. 'We'll just be taking a look in your storeroom, Mister. With Christmas but a couple of days away you'll no doubt be anxious to be sharing your fare with us.'

The First Mate made an involuntary movement which was brought to an abrupt halt by one look from the big man.

'We'll not be greedy. Just a few victuals to see us through the next few days.'

'We've hardly enough to feed our own number on the voyage.'

'Then I suggest, Mister, that you put back into port and replenish your supplies. You'll not let your good passengers starve on their way to New England.'

Again the First Mate made to speak and again he was silenced by Captain Middleton.

'You see, Mister, we've been idling our time these past three weeks or more waiting for the appearance of a certain *El Aguila* – and not a sight of her to be seen. I'm beginning to think that the heathen Spanish scum have sunk without trace to the bottom of the ocean. And such a waste, with all that gold stored in her hold. It's worth biding our time for a few more days, but my men don't keep watch at their best when their bellies are rumbling. A few victuals from your storeroom would set them in good humour again.' He smiled, revealing a set of surprisingly white teeth against the thick dark hair of his beard. 'If's not much to ask to allow us to enjoy the celebration of Christmas in the company of our good Spanish cousins.'

He made a movement with his hand and immediately six of his eight men moved off towards the storeroom. The remaining two, standing behind him, re-adjusted their hands upon their belts.

'And we'll just take a look at your passengers, Mister, while we're here. Invite them up on deck and we'll pay our respects to them.'

He walked over to the hatch above the passenger quarters and positioned himself to inspect the occupants as they filed past him.

Margaret, being the nearest to the hatch, was the first to emerge. She tottered slightly, adjusting her vision to the light on deck. Only gradually did she take in the huge bulk of the man before her.

He put out a hand to steady her. 'There's no need to alarm yourself. I'll not harm your pretty little Puritan head.'

She withdrew her arm from his grasp but he held on to her and kept her standing beside him while the remaining passengers filed past, spilling out across the deck.

She looked again for Deliverance Daniels who passed by, one of the last to emerge. He stood some distance away on the other side of the deck.

Captain Middleton moved among them, casting his eye over the assembled company. At one point he bent, with a smile, to chuck a small girl beneath the chin. Her mother drew her back against the folds of her skirt and the big man let her go without resistance, letting his hand glide over her cheek and across her hair.

A little further along the line a woman held her face in her hands, obviously terrified at his approach. He altered his pace, coming towards her stealthily, then shot out his hand, placing it firmly and accurately upon her left buttock. 'Rape!' he roared within two inches of her ear.

It sent the woman into a paroxysm of hysteria. Her husband hesitated, not knowing how to react. But the captain laughed through strong white teeth and moved on.

His men were transferring quantities of salt pork and biscuit.

'Limes,' he said as they passed. 'Don't forget the limes.'

They had transferred only a portion of the ship's stores when a cry went up from the other vessel which set them all looking towards the distant horizon. A large ship had appeared under full sail.

'Well, 'tis the Devil Himself in the guise of *El Aguila*. In that case, gentlemen, we'll be leaving you in peace and giving our attentions to that crew of whore-burned Spaniards. No doubt they'll have food in their own hold which will taste all the better for the smell of gold.'

He paused as he came back and stood in front of Margaret. 'I wish you God Speed,' he said. 'And may the Saints go with you into that heathen wilderness.'

With that he was gone, and the assembled company stood trembling from the shock of the encounter.

'Let us kneel and pray,' said the Reverend Deliverance Daniels, 'for our deliverance from evil.'

Captain Beckley returned while they were still on their knees. 'Is anyone harmed?' he asked and showed relief to be reassured that passengers and crew were all intact.

'We've two choices,' he announced after inspecting the storeroom. 'We can put back into port and replenish our supplies. Or we can sail on, on very lean rations.'

'The Lord will provide,' said Deliverance Daniels. 'He has sent us on this great mission and He'll sustain us upon our journey.'

'He didn't send me,' countered a swarthy man standing nearby. 'I'm not one of your Puritan sermonizers.'

'Did He not feed the children of Israel? Did He not drop down manna from the very heavens to fall at their feet?'

'You'll not find much in the way of manna falling from the skies above the ocean,' put in Captain Beckley. 'I'd lay more confidence in a few barrels stored in my hold.'

'Then we have fish. Is not the ocean stocked with the harvest of the Lord? Are we not beholden to the bounty which He bestows upon us? Oh ye of little faith . . .' He raised his arms and turned to the assembled company. 'Can you not place yourselves in the hands of the Lord? Are you so full of doubt that you care more for your bellies than for your soul? Come, kneel with me and pray that we be carried across this ocean to the land which the Lord has promised us. Why, at the Red Sea He opened up that very ocean and allowed His people to walk dry-shod across its breadth. Are we to doubt that He will see us to the other side?'

More than half the assembled company fell to their knees. 'May the Lord be praised,' said one man, 'that He should

162

purify us with this gift of abstinence that we be all the more worthy to serve Him in the chosen land.'

'Amen, my brother. To the honour of the Lord. Amen.'

'We'll take a count,' said Captain Beckley. 'All those who say heave about must now make themselves known and we'll decide by their numbers.'

'How long?' asked one man. 'How long would it take to put back and replenish our stores?'

'Best part of a month. It would be nigh on spring by the time we touched the shores of New England.'

'And I've urgent business in Boston.'

'I say we put back,' said the swarthy man who had spoken earlier. He was a farmer by the name of William Deswick. 'What good can we do landing in the depths of winter? It'll be far more than a month before we're able to set out to our chosen destinations. What good can we do holed up waiting for the snows to melt when we could put back and make sure that our women and children are fed?'

'Aye, what's the good if we're all to starve before we reach the shore?'

'We'll not starve,' said Captain Beckley. 'There's food enough to keep us alive but I dare say that some of us will be a mite thinner than we are today.'

'Then put back,' said William Deswick. 'We've enough hardship awaiting us in a foreign land without arriving half-starved.'

'I say go on,' said Deliverance Daniels. 'I've a congregation awaiting me. They've been without a preacher for the best part of a year and their spiritual hunger outweighs that of a hundred empty bellies.'

'But not mine. Nor that of my wife and children.'

'May the Lord forgive those,' said Deliverance Daniels, turning his eyes towards the heavens, 'who place their bellies before Thy mighty Will.'

'And how do you propose to get to this congregation of yours, across the snows of New England? Have reason, man, you'll be holed up like the rest of us waiting for the thaw. Or do you propose to venture out across unknown terrain in the teeth of winter?'

'The Lord will provide. It's not for me to question the timing of His hand.'

'Then I'll pray over your bones as they lie frozen on the soil.'

'There's no purpose to be served ' said Captain Beckley, 'in harsh words amongst ourselves. Let all those who wish to sail on now make their wishes known.'

Considerably more than half the assembled company signified their desire to continue.

'So be it. But let it be known that not only will rations be cut, but there's a danger of the scurvy before we make shore. The brigands have taken the best part of our pickled vegetables and all our limes.'

'Then we have a choice,' said William Deswick sarcastically. 'We're to be allowed to die from lack of food, or from the ravages of disease.'

'We'll not starve. If there were a danger of starvation, I'd put back without consultation.'

'Then let's ask the preacher to deliver us from the clutches of disease.'

'We'll allow ourselves full rations on Christmas Day,' said Captain Beckley. 'But after that there'll be no more than half.'

'But that's the very day on which we are best able to serve the Lord,' said Deliverance Daniels. 'It's the day on which we renounce gluttony and all that is evil and turn our minds to the honour of the Lord.'

He raised his arms again to those standing about him. 'Good people, let us set aside the day to fasting and to prayer as is the custom of our cousins who await us in New England, that we may make ourselves worthy to set foot upon this promised land in the service of the Lord. We shall spend the day in contemplation of our Bibles and of our inner hearts.'

'May the Lord be praised.'

'You can fast and pray to your heart's content,' put in William Deswick. 'But my family will have one good meal before they learn to live with hunger.'

Two days later, on Christmas Day, Margaret knelt at prayer and thought of her family back home in Dunscombe. It was eleven o'clock and she knew that they would be sitting at their dinner. The table in the parlour would be laden with pies and tarts; a couple of hens would have been despatched from the orchard into the cooking pot.

They would be fewer in number than last year. Only two children remained and she could only pray that Lucy and Tobias had recovered from the fever. The family would have taken a day of rest from their labours and after dinner, in the warmth of the fire, they would take down the book from the table in the corner. Someone would be chosen to read.

She lowered her head and rested it upon the open Bible which she clutched to her chest. For the first time she wept.

CHAPTER 8

Samuel waited until Tobias was fit enough to resume his duties at the loom then set out early one morning before the family were awake. He took nothing but a little food wrapped in a piece of cloth and started walking in the direction of Oxford.

For days he had wrestled with the dilemma of whether he should leave word for his parents, or whether he should allow them to worry about his disappearance. He decided to absent himself stealthily and to cover his tracks. He would explain when he returned.

It was January — bitterly cold, with a fresh fall of snow which made it all the more difficult to make headway or to distinguish landmarks in the cold grey light of approaching dawn.

Once beyond the area he knew, people were about and working. He began seeking directions which kept him on the road towards Oxford.

In parts, the snow had drifted to indeterminate depth. Several times he found himself sinking thigh deep in the cold wet mass and emerged to feel the bite of the easterly wind through his sodden clothing.

At mid-day a housewife took pity on him and warmed him with a bowl of thick broth before her parlour fire. At dusk he crept into a byre and spent the long winter night huddled for warmth among the animals.

He reached Ascott-under-Wychwood, keeping to open ground below Wychwood Forest but above the level of the flooded valley of the Evenlode. At Charlbury he found a crossing. He was tired and hungry. He had a further twenty miles to go, another river to cross. It would take him another two days before he reached Oxford.

He found shelter for the night, but no food. Next morning he went on his way thinking of the family back home in Dunscombe eating their breakfast. As he approached the river crossing at Woodstock he thought at first that he only imagined the smell of roasting meat then he realized that it came from a large well-tended fire at the side of the road. On a crudely constructed spit, two rabbits and a large duck dripped grease into the embers. Four of the King's soldiers were warming themselves in the glow.

They barely stirred themselves as Samuel approached. Then one detached himself from the fire and sauntered a few steps to meet him.

'Business?'

Samuel looked at him.

'What's your business, boy?' His attitude was bored rather than aggressive. 'Or have you lost your tongue?'

Samuel had not expected to be challenged along the road. 'I've come to seek out my cousin.'

'Business?'

Again he was uncertain how to reply.

'What's your business with him, boy?'

'I've got a message for him, from my family.'

'Harsh weather to be delivering messages.'

'It's something I need to tell him.'

'Where you from?'

'Dunscombe.'

'Never heard of it,' said the soldier.

'It's a good few miles.' Samuel pointed over his left shoulder. 'Over there.'

The soldier shrugged disinterestedly. 'Harsh weather to be delivering messages,' he said again. 'But I don't suppose the King's got much to fear from your presence.' He waved him on with a casual movement of his finger. 'And watch your step.'

He waited until Samuel had gone several paces then called after him: 'What's the name of this cousin of yours?'

'Rupert Mainwaring.'

'Oh?' Another of the soldiers took an interest. 'Rupert? I know him well.'

'Oh,' said Samuel.

'You'll probably find him at the inn near St Giles. A group of them like to throw the dice down there.'

'Thank you, sir.'

'Are you hungry, boy?'

'Yes, sir, I am.'

The soldier cut a leg from one of the rabbits. 'Here, chew on this.' He tossed it across to Samuel. 'And don't let Rupert talk you into parting with all your money at the dice.'

'No, sir. Thank you, sir.' Samuel walked on, tearing at the rabbit meat with his teeth.

Now that the moment was near, reality seemed quite different from the scenes which he had played out in his mind. He might have been tempted to turn back, had he not already walked so far.

It was growing dark again. He sought out another byre in which to settle down for the night. Next morning he made the long slow descent towards the city. At last he came down past the square stone tower of St Giles and so into the city streets.

He found the inn without difficulty. Immediately upon entering he saw Rupert at a table in the corner, one of some half dozen engaged in a noisy bantering dice session.

'Rupert.'

Rupert looked up and beamed immediate pleasure. 'Samuel! What on earth are you doing here? Come, sit down, I'll get you a pot of ale. You look as though you could do with it.' But then his expression began to change. 'There's nothing wrong, is there? You haven't come with bad news?'

'Just come outside.'

'It's not bad news? How's the family? It's not Margaret?'

'I want a word with you, outside.'

'What's wrong? Is it my mother? It's not Aunt Anne?'

Samuel turned and began to walk outside. Rupert followed him, convinced now that his cousin was the bearer of tragic news.

At the back of the inn was a courtyard with stables and a large overhanging tree.

'What is it, Samuel? For God's sake, tell me what's wrong.'

'I want your word.'

'About what?'

'That you won't go to New England.'

Rupert stopped short. 'Why?'

'You're not to follow her.'

He realized that Samuel must know about Margaret. 'You know?'

Samuel did not reply but the expression on his face was unmistakable.

'I've got to,' said Rupert. 'I've got to bring her back.'

Samuel straightened, squaring up as if to hit his cousin.

'Does everybody know?' Rupert moved position but he was in no real danger from the younger, smaller youth.

Samuel came a step closer. 'Why did you do it, Rupert? Why my sister?'

He lowered his eyes and looked away. 'I only wish to God I knew,' he said. 'I'd give anything not to have done it. I love her so.'

'Love her!'

'Yes, love her.'

Samuel was swaying back and forth on the spot, longing to hit Rupert yet knowing that he stood no chance in a fight.

'Come inside,' said Rupert. 'I'll get us some ale and we can talk about it.'

'How many others, Rupert? How many others have you forced yourself on?'

'Good God, man, I don't force myself on maids.'

'Then why Margaret? You forced yourself on her.'

Rupert swallowed and turned his head. 'Yes,' he said, 'I did. And I wish to God that I hadn't.'

'And now you're going to make it worse.'

'I'm not going to make it worse. I'm just going to fetch her home.'

'You leave her alone!'

'We can't just let her go to the other side of the world.'

'She's gone with her husband.'

Rupert winced. 'Yes, but did she go from choice?'

'Of course she went from choice. You'll leave her alone.'

'I can't believe that,' said Rupert. 'I've got to find out for myself.'

'You'll leave her alone,' said Samuel again. 'Or you'll have me to deal with.' He threw a punch with no real hope of connecting.

'I'm sorry, Samuel. I can understand how you feel, but this is between Margaret and me. I've got to follow her and bring her back.'

Samuel's frustration was exacerbated by the knowledge that he stood no chance of beating Rupert. His temper was rising and he could see no way of enforcing his will upon the larger man. A soldier rode into the yard and dismounted beside him.

'I'd be most grateful, sir,' he said, 'if I could borrow your sword.'

The soldier, taken by surprise, handed it to him.

'You'd better get one of your own,' Samuel said to Rupert.

'Are you mad?'

'Or shall I cut you down where you stand?'

'Are you mad?' asked Rupert again. 'Put it down, for God's sake, before you do someone harm.'

Samuel attempted to raise the sword but he was unaccustomed to the weight and the feel of it. 'I'll see you rot in hell before you go causing her more harm.'

'I've no intention of causing anyone harm,' said Rupert. He was at pains to moderate his voice. 'Put the sword down, Samuel, and we'll go inside and talk.'

'Get one of your own.' Samuel grasped the sword with both hands and succeeding in swinging it round above his head. 'Or I'll kill you on the spot.'

'Calm down, man. I've no intention of harming her. I love her too much.'

Samuel lunged. 'You cur! You fornicating, whore-making cur!'

Rupert stepped easily to one side.

Behind Samuel's back Rupert's comrades had been gathering. One primed a pistol and held it cocked ready, aimed at Samuel's head.

'You blaspheming pig's turd.'

'Just put that thing down and I'll try to explain.'

171

Samuel lunged again, a little more accurately this time, causing Rupert to leap.

'You can't know what it's like,' he said as he leapt. 'Some day you might. Some day you might love someone that much. Then you'll know. But, for now, it's my seed she's carrying in her belly.'

'You . . .!' Samuel lifted the sword and hurled himself towards Rupert.

At the same moment the young man with the pistol squeezed his finger on the trigger. There was a loud bang and Samuel fell down.

'You idiot! You stupid Bedlamite!' Rupert was addressing the man while dropping to his knees beside Samuel. 'What have you done?'

Samuel was bleeding from a wound just below the right shoulder blade: there was a gurgling sound coming from him.

'We must get him to the surgeon. What have you done to him? He wasn't doing any harm. He's my cousin.'

'He was going to run you through with that sword.'

'No, he wasn't. He wouldn't have hurt me. He's my cousin.'

Rupert went to pick him up but Samuel's weight was too great for him. Another man came to help him. Together they carried him back to Rupert's lodgings. It was not far but by the time they got him there both were smattered with blood. A red foam was issuing from the corner of Samuel's mouth as he lapsed in and out of consciousness. Rupert sent the other man for the regimental surgeon.

'Hang on, Samuel, please don't die.' He sat on the floor, cradling Samuel's head in his lap. 'Why did you do it? Not for one moment . . . I would never have hurt you.'

It was obvious that Samuel's life was ebbing fast. 'Just hang on until the surgeon . . .'

Samuel opened his eyes. 'Rupert?'

'Yes?'

'You'll rot in hell for what you did to her.' His eyes rolled upwards and Rupert knew that he was dead.

He laid Samuel's head gently upon the floor. 'I'm sorry, Cousin,' he said. 'Can you ever forgive me?'

* * *

Rupert strapped Samuel's body across a pack horse and took him, through the snow, back home to Dunscombe. He wanted, somehow, to find the words with which to convey his deep regret for what had happened; but he knew that they would fall upon deaf ears.

He was right. Anne and Nehemiah were in no mood for such explanations when their son was brought home strapped to the back of a pack horse.

'It was a terrible accident,' Rupert tried to explain.

'It was no accident,' said Anne, 'to shoot my son in the back.'

'He had a sword and my comrade thought . . .'

'I don't care what he thought,' said Anne. 'My son was just a boy.'

'I know. But he was trying to . . .'

'Just what was he doing?' demanded Nehemiah. 'You haven't told us yet why he went to Oxford.'

'To speak about Margaret.'

'Margaret? He knew about her?'

'He wanted to ask . . .'

'You told him about Margaret?'

'No, I thought you did. He wanted to ask . . .'

'Then who did?'

'I don't know. I thought everyone must know.'

Nehemiah realized the course which the conversation was taking. 'I don't know what else ails your conscience,' he veered it away, 'but murder is enough.'

Rupert flinched. 'It wasn't murder. And I thought everyone must know.'

'I don't know what it is that they must know. But, whatever it is, I can assure you that it's known to you alone.'

'Oh.'

'You shot my son,' began Anne again.

'My comrade shot him, by mistake.'

'No one shoots by mistake,' she said disbelievingly. 'You murdered my son.'

'I'm sorry, Aunt.' Rupert was at a loss to know how to express his own sense of hopelessness and grief. 'I don't know what to say.'

'Then I suggest you say nothing,' said Nehemiah. 'I

173

suggest you leave this place and don't come back. You're not wanted here.'

Rupert bit on the pain of the words. 'I'm sorry,' he said. 'There's been great misunderstanding.'

'There's no misunderstanding. We understand only too well the wrongs which have been done within this family.'

Rupert closed his eyes and went to turn away.

'I hear,' said Nehemiah falteringly, 'that you are intending to journey to New England.'

'Yes.'

'I would prefer it if you didn't go.'

'I've got to, Uncle. I must see her for myself.'

'You'll do great harm.'

'I mean her none, but I feel dutybound to follow.'

Nehemiah was at a loss to know what to say. He had no wish to plead with his nephew; but to seek the co-operation of Sir Henry would mean the further disclosure of Margaret's shame. 'You leave me no choice,' he decided. 'I must speak with your father.'

'I'm sorry, Uncle, but that's not possible. My father left last night for Plymouth. He'll be gone for some time.'

Nehemiah heaved a sigh of exasperation. 'And I suppose that by the time he returns you will have sailed?'

'I regret so, Uncle.' Rupert was genuinely sorry to be the cause of Nehemiah's anger but at the same time he was relieved by the timing of circumstances. 'I'm truly sorry that we can't be in agreement on this matter, but I have no choice. I feel dutybound to see Margaret and to ask her to return.'

'Then I can only hope,' sighed Nehemiah, 'that she has the good sense and the courage to rebuff you.'

Anne and Nehemiah took Samuel's body across the hills to be laid in the churchyard beside their other children. Anne cursed her nephew as she knelt beside the grave. Nehemiah, too, in that solemn moment thought that one day he might kill him.

Lucy and Tobias were puzzled as well as distressed. They could not begin to understand why Samuel had gone to Oxford.

Next day, Anne sat with Lucy at their needlework beside the fire.

'Of all the fruit of my womb,' she said bitterly, 'only Tobias and the two girls remain. Margaret is so far away.'

Outside it was snowing heavily, blocking most of the light from the window. Both women held their work angled towards the fire in order to see.

'I can't believe that Samuel has gone.'

'Such a waste,' said Anne. 'To throw down his life — and for what purpose? What has he achieved?'

'I don't understand,' said Lucy. 'He loved his cousin.'

Anne stopped for a moment on a half-drawn breath. Lucy looked up, expecting her to speak, but she did not.

'It perplexes me so to understand why he went. What reason could he have to go to Oxford? And without telling us?'

Again Anne said nothing.

'Then to quarrel with his cousin and to lose his life. It doesn't make sense.'

'No sense at all,' said Anne. 'He's achieved nothing.'

'But why quarrel? What possible reason could he have to go all that way? Perhaps Rupert . . .'

'I don't want to talk about him.'

Lucy looked up.

'He's got a lot to answer for. And now there's blood on his hands.'

'But Rupert said . . .' Lucy hesitated, measuring the wisdom of making further comment in the light of Anne's reaction. 'I thought he said it was an accident.'

'It was no accident to shoot my son in the back.'

'I'm sorry,' said Lucy quietly. 'It just perplexes me so to understand why such a dreadful thing could ever have happened.'

Anne looked at her then spent some time studying the needlework in her hands. 'There are some things,' she said at last, 'which are best left unresolved. It's not for us to question riddles for which there's no answer. Better that we don't spend our time in paining our hearts and dwelling on such matters. I think it's best that we don't speak of it again and that we banish it from our minds. Samuel has gone, and all the questions in the world won't bring him back.'

'I'm sorry.'

'And if Rupert comes back this way to Dunscombe, it's

175

best that we don't speak with him, or associate with him in any way. It would cause me great pain to know that any member of this household should disregard my wishes.'

'Whatever you say.'

'It's best,' said Anne. 'There's nothing which can undo the evil which has been done within this family.'

They returned to their needlework and sat in silence for a further time, each lost in her own thoughts. Then Anne turned full circle to her initial comment. 'With Tobias, only Sarah and Rachael remain.'

'They're fine children. They'll grow to be good daughters to you.'

'Yes,' sighed Anne. 'We must be thankful to the Lord for sparing them.'

'He'll bless you with more.'

'No.' She shook her head. 'I'm tired, and the days of my fruitfulness are gone. I don't look forward to bearing babes which issue dead from my womb.'

'I'm your daughter too.'

'Yes.' Anne smiled at her. 'And I thank God that you, too, were spared. It's up to you now to deliver the children into the household.'

Lucy bit her lip and returned to her needlework.

'You'll succeed, I know it. You're still weak from the fever but already you're gaining flesh on your bones. Very shortly you'll find yourself with child.'

'I've prayed for forgiveness but my sins are beyond number.'

'You'll succeed,' said Anne again. 'You'll have many sons.' She turned away for a moment and stifled a small sob. 'Perhaps in that way we'll all learn to forget. Our hearts and our laps will be full again.'

That night, in the warmth of their bed, Tobias and Lucy lay discussing Samuel's death.

'I shall never understand it,' said Tobias. 'I'm sure Mother and Father know more than they'll tell.'

'She said we're not even to think about it.'

'I know,' he said. 'But I can't help wondering.'

She kissed him softly on the cheek. 'All the wondering in the world won't bring him back.'

'I know. But my only brother . . .'

'I loved him too.'

He turned to her and smiled. 'We've lost so much these past months with the children gone.'

'And Margaret lost in some distant land.'

'But not you, my love.' He rolled over and took her in his arms. 'I'm so glad you were spared.'

'And you.'

'I think I'd have died if you'd been taken from me.'

They lay for a while, each drawing warmth and comfort from the other's body. He began to stroke her.

She let out a small sigh. 'You're so good to love me,' she said.

'How could I do anything else?'

'But I've caused you nothing but trouble.'

He kissed her and felt himself rising against her. 'You've given me more love and pleasure than I could ever have imagined.'

'But no children.'

'It's enough that you love me. I ask for nothing but to have you here beside me and to be able to hold you in my arms.'

'I love you,' she whispered.

'And I. Oh, Lucy, I love you.'

He began to kiss and caress, expressing his love and the relief of having her still there beside him, the pleasure of belonging to someone who loved him in return.

At the height of his passion he released his seed, beginning the life of another child within her.

On board the *Silver Rose* the main problem proved to be boredom. Storms blew up which kept them all ill and miserable below deck but, in between times, a feeling of boredom and lethargy seeped through them all.

Men and women who had been used to working from daybreak till dusk found time hanging heavily upon their hands. Day followed day, with very little to differentiate one from the other. Craftsmen took out their tools and pottered about in corners of the ship but it was not like the labour of a full working day. The women busied themselves with the care of the children and of the sick. Babies were

177

born and the women fell over themselves in their bid to be of help to the mother.

Activity heightened when an epidemic of whooping cough spread from child to child. For a while they were busy. Two children died and it seemed that grief was intensified by the attention which had been focused upon them. As the small bodies were lowered over the side of the ship a spirit of communal mourning settled upon them all.

Food was scarce and unpalatable, with half-rations further reduced when storm water seeped in and spoiled a quantity of biscuit. That which was left was weevil-riddled and infested with vermin. Most were used to experiencing hunger, particularly in winter, but now there was no work to keep their minds from their empty stomachs.

It led to feelings of frustration and short temper, exacerbated by the cramped quarters in which they were living. Minor irritations built into major conflicts, with even the occasional fight as tempers flared to the point of physical action. Youths, deprived of the opportunity to flex their muscles with a hammer or a plough, engaged in wrestling matches which frequently got out of hand.

At one point there was an organized redistribution of allotted space within the living quarters in order that certain families could be removed as far as possible from others. But Margaret and Deliverance Daniels retained their space adjacent to Susannah Norton and her husband. A friendship had grown between the two women, built upon mutual liking and respect. They spent a good deal of time together.

Both enjoyed listening to the discussions which took place among the men as they sat on dark evenings entombed within the creaking timbers below deck, the cold winds and rain of the Atlantic lashing the rigging above.

Talk centred mainly upon the land which lay ahead of them. All were apprehensive of the future, anxious to seize the challenge yet frustrated by the long weeks of inactivity as they tossed their way slowly towards the distant shore.

'It's likely we shall all die anyway,' said one man. He had lost his wife only that morning. Now he found himself alone with the responsibility of two small children. 'We shall all be dead from pestilence or savages.'

'Nonsense,' said Deliverance Daniels. 'We're bound for a thriving land which is ripe for the harvesting of the Lord.'

'It's true about the savages,' said another. 'Our lives will be in constant danger.'

'Not in all parts,' said William Deswick. 'I'm bound for an area where they're peaceful.'

'Around Massachusetts Bay, maybe. But there's danger elsewhere.'

Margaret was relieved, at least, to hear that the Natives of Massachusetts Bay were likely to be peaceable. She was seated behind Susannah's husband and saw him open his mouth as if to speak, then change his mind.

'The Lord has given us a wondrous opportunity,' said Deliverance Daniels, 'to proclaim His name among these heathen.'

Thomas Norton took a breath. 'But is it right,' he asked, 'that we should take the land from these people?'

'We're not taking the land,' said William Deswick. 'There's more than enough for all of us. And the savages are eager for trade.'

'But are these men able to understand the consequences of trading their land?'

'These are not men,' said Deliverance Daniels. 'These are heathen; in need of the Lord.'

'They're not trading in land,' said William Deswick. 'It's a vast expanse. We'll be doing no more than putting to the plough those areas they don't need.'

'In fact we're doing them a service,' said a man to the left. 'I hear they're glad to learn of our ways and to use our tools and our skills.'

'I still say it's not right to take a man's land.'

The conversation passed to other matters but it sowed a seed in Margaret's mind which exercised her reasoning for a long time to come.

'Well,' said Deliverance Daniels, 'I intend to set straight something which is closer to our immediate concern. I call upon the power of the Lord to bring an end to the blaspheming of these seamen within our midst.'

'Amen,' said someone sitting at the back.

'Three times I've spoken to the Captain and three times he's made light of it. We must all make it known, without

179

a shadow of a doubt, that we'll not abide these vile oaths and blasphemies which daily assail our ears.'

William Deswick smiled behind a derisive gesture of his hand. 'It'll take a might of power to wash the mouth of a seaman.'

'We ask you to go again to the Captain,' said the man at the back. 'It's an insult to us all and a positive danger to our women and children.'

'I'll approach him first thing tomorrow morning. I'll make it plain that the whole company are demanding it should cease.'

'You can speak for yourself and for those who ask you, but there are others who've no wish to antagonize the crew. Their language is no worse than that of the fishwife or the pedlar.'

'A comparison, sir, to a fishwife or pedlar is hardly argument for acceptance.'

'It's done me no harm to listen to the fishwife and the pedlar, and I've been doing so for the past thirty years. Leave the seamen alone, I say, and leave them to their peace.'

'You've no love of the Lord, sir, or you wouldn't talk so. To condone such blasphemy is a sin equal to the uttering of such foul obscenities from your own lips.'

'I've better things, Reverend Daniels, to put my mind to than the utterances of seamen — or of preachers.'

Deliverance Daniels rose to his feet.

'I think,' said Thomas Norton, 'it's time for prayer. The women are ready for their beds. We'd be most grateful, Reverend Daniels, if you'd lead us.'

'I'm obliged to you, Brother Thomas.' Deliverance Daniels took a deep breath. 'I got quite carried away by conversation and forgot the time. Let us, my friends, kneel and pray that we be purified of vile thoughts and deeds. That we may prove worthy of serving Him for the remainder of our days.'

'Amen to that.'

William Deswick got up and smiled to himself. He would have welcomed an opportunity to punch the Reverend Daniels on the nose.

* * *

By February a number of the passengers and crew were exhibiting symptoms of scurvy. They had the red patches of skin haemorrhaging, with a soreness of the tongue and a swelling of the gums which made eating uncomfortable. Others were further troubled by the swelling of their feet and legs.

Stocks of salt beef, oatmeal and dried peas had run out and very little salt pork remained. The passengers began sniffing the air as an aroma of grilled rat drifted from the seamen's quarters. Soon they, too, began trapping the large black rodents. The flavour reminded them of the hares they had eaten in the warmth of home parlours.

Margaret was almost four months pregnant. As her body grew thinner, the distension of her abdomen began to focus her mind upon the apparently insoluble problem. The marriage had still not been consummated.

Although it would take some time before her condition became apparent through the layers of her clothing, she could not imagine any way in which she could cope with the situation which would arise once it was made known. She knew the penalty for the sin of adultery, of which she must surely be accused, and that for the sin of fornication was hardly less. She could not bear to think upon the consequences once her shame was exposed for all to know. Susannah frequently mentioned the coming child which was due to be born a short time after her own. Margaret lived in constant fear that she would speak of it within the hearing of Deliverance Daniels.

Towards the end of February excitement began to mount. Eyes were turned towards the distant horizon with the hope of catching first sight of land. Attitudes changed. People who had bickered and quarrelled now approached the day when they would part company. The uneasy bond which had held them together was about to be broken.

For a week they had seen birds flying overhead. Now it seemed that they could sense the smell of approaching land, just as months ago they had caught the smell of the sea. Personal belongings were gathered together and packed ready for the moment of arrival.

It was the look-out, high up in the rigging, who first made out the hazy outline of land. Gradually they made their way

181

towards it, then down the coastline towards their destination. It was a cold, inhospitable landscape, frozen hard beneath a layer of snow and with trees bent away from the bitter north-easterly wind.

There was no sign of life in the icebound wilderness. Margaret's heart appeared both to lift and to drop at the same time. Yet, it was land; and the ice and snow were no worse than she had experienced in her own Cotswold hills. As they moved in close to shore, and her eyes adjusted to the landscape, she made out first a bird which she thought to be a pigeon, then several more, swooping their way from tree to tree.

At one point she thought she caught the movement of something larger in the trees — perhaps a man. 'Savages,' said someone close by, but the movement had gone almost before she had focused on it. She stood gazing in the hope that it would reappear but she could see nothing except the white, windswept landscape.

Then, almost taking her by surprise, they rounded a point and there was habitation — small houses tucked into areas of shelter, people waving their arms and shouting in excited greeting.

It seemed an age before they dropped anchor. They stood lining the deck, trying to make out the shouts and gesticulations of the people on shore. But, eventually, it was Margaret's turn to clamber over the side into the small boat to be rowed ashore. Her heart beat fast. As the shouts grew louder and clearer she caught the smell of woodsmoke from nearby chimneys.

Yet when her feet did at last touch upon solid land, it appeared to rise and fall beneath her feet with far greater motion than the sea. She tottered, blanching white, gulping at the unexpected sensation.

A woman reached out and took her arm. 'You're welcome, my dear. Welcome to this land and to the town of Boston.'

'Thank you,' she gasped, fearing that she would be sick. 'You've no idea how glad I am to be here at last.'

'Oh, yes, I have. I made the journey myself last year, though I came in summer, not in the teeth of winter.'

Margaret looked around her. Almost the entire population

of Boston had turned out to greet the new arrivals.

'It's always a great event when a ship arrives,' said the woman. 'We're hungry for the sight of new faces and it adds a little excitement to our lives.'

Margaret smiled. 'I wasn't sure what to expect. It's good to be greeted with such kindness.'

'This is God's land, my dear. We're seeding it with His Word and we endeavour to live according to our true consciences.'

'My husband's a minister of the church. He's come to serve the community of Ufferton.'

'Then you're indeed welcome. Come, we must find him and introduce him to my own. Then you must come eat with us. I guarantee you've not had a good meal since you left.'

The thought of food had an unpleasant effect upon Margaret's stomach. The woman took her arm and led her towards a group of people who were standing nearby. 'I'm Elizabeth,' she said, 'wife of Joshua Brown.'

'Margaret, and my husband is the Reverend Deliverance Daniels.'

She walked with a sense of unreality, still feeling the solid earth rising and falling beneath her feet. She hardly took in her surroundings or the people about her, greeting her with warmth. She was tired and cold. Above all, she was suddenly desperately homesick.

They were taken to a simple stone-built house beneath a roof of thatch where a young girl was preparing food. The aroma of it brought an added queasiness to Margaret's stomach. For weeks she had thought of good food: now she could not face the sight of it.

'You're very pale. You must rest with us for the night if you've no other plans.'

'We'll be making arrangements at first light,' said Deliverance Daniels. 'We must set out immediately for our destination. But we would accept the Lord's hand in guiding us to shelter for the night.'

'You'll not be setting out for Ufferton tomorrow,' commented Joshua. 'You've first to find a boat to take you up the coast, thence upriver to the settlement.'

'Who owns such a boat?'

'It'd be wise to wait until the weather breaks.'

'Then I'll go by land.' Deliverance Daniels did nothing to disguise his impatience. 'I'm within thirty miles of my destination.'

'Thirty miles you may be, but thirty miles of wilderness. It's no place to be in the depths of winter.'

'The Lord is with me.'

'I've no doubt. But you'll find no one here who'll agree to guide you in this weather.'

'But I've been months on this journey!'

'Then 'tis hardly wise to risk your life, and that of your wife, on the last thirty miles.' The settler sat and looked at him for a moment. 'This isn't England, Reverend Daniels. We've achieved much in the twenty-two years since our brothers first set foot on the shores at Plymouth, but there are thousands of miles of uncharted land out there. Take my word for it, it's best to be guided by those who'll take you at the right time – upriver.'

'You'll stay with us,' said Elizabeth. 'You're welcome to share whatever riches the Lord sees fit to bestow upon us.'

'I thank you,' said Deliverance Daniels testily. 'But I must be on my way at the very first opportunity.'

Next day they went to church. As she sat in the simple clapboard building, Margaret fingered her Bible and thought of her family in another church of Cotswold stone. Deliverance Daniels looked at her pointedly and she realized, in a confusion of shame and embarrassment, that she had been staring into space. She had hopelessly lost track of the sermon.

After the service they stood in groups outside the church, engaged in conversation.

'They've no need of another shoemaker in Boston,' said Thomas Norton. 'There'd not be enough work to keep my family fed. I've been thinking that we might make the journey to Ufferton and find out whether there's need for me there.'

Deliverance Daniels thought on it for a time. 'I see no reason why you shouldn't venture there. The community would doubtless welcome the presence of another God-fearing family.'

'Perhaps we could travel together?'

Margaret was delighted at the prospect of having Susannah's company.

'And I could be of help to Margaret,' said Susannah. 'When she gives birth to the child.'

Margaret felt a draining of blood from her head. For a moment she was certain that she would faint. She looked at Deliverance Daniels, cowering at the prospect of his reaction. But there was none.

'Your presence would be of the greatest value,' he said. Apart from the slightest initial hesitation, his face showed no emotion: his voice did not falter. 'I'd rést easy in the knowledge that she was in such capable hands.'

Margaret struggled to quell the whistling sound in her head; there was a sensation of pins and needles in her limbs.

'Are you unwell?' Susannah reached out and took her arm.

Her mouth had dropped open and she found herself staring at him. But he did not appear to notice. He had gone on to speak of something else.

'Are you feeling unwell?' asked Susannah again.

'What? Oh, no.'

'You're very pale.'

'No, I'm perfectly well.'

'I've got a good feeling about this land, haven't you? We're going to settle and make a decent life for our children.'

'Yes,' said Margaret, but she was still close to fainting.

She wondered what would happen when she was alone with him. She had seen her husband angry, but that anger had never as yet been turned upon her. She did not know what to expect.

This moment had been bound to arise, yet she had closed her mind to it, unable to cope. Now it was upon her and she must face whatever punishment lay in store. If only he had consummated the marriage! If only, just once, he had come to her. But her mother's plan had gone astray. And now her mother seemed so many miles away. Margaret was alone, in a foreign land.

She spent the next hours avoiding his eye yet at the same time staring at him, searching for some kind of reaction. There was none. As the time approached for them to be alone in their room, she could hardly disguise her fear. She walked up the stairs ahead of him, listening as he closed the latch upon them.

'You may say your prayers.'

'What?'

'Say your prayers and retire to your bed. You may dispense with your reading. I will find you an extra passage tomorrow.'

'Oh.' She had never been so frightened, nor so confused.

'There's something wrong?'

'What?'

'You're standing, staring into space as though you have suddenly become some sort of Bedlamite.'

'I'm sorry.'

'Then go to your bed. Or is there some urgent necessity which must occupy you in the middle of the night?'

'No, of course not.'

'Then go to your bed,' he said irritably. 'I'm quite worn out by the meeting of so many new people.'

'I'm sorry.'

'It would help if you were to stop saying you are sorry and commence to say your prayers, in order that I may have some peace in which to say my own.'

'I'm sorry,' she said again and went down on her knees.

For his part, Deliverance Daniels went and knelt in the corner. She would have been even more surprised had she been able to hear his supplication.

'Oh, Lord,' he begged silently, 'look down upon this, Thy servant. I, who am bowed down with the base impurity of an unclean heart, the loathsome sins of human flesh. Thou, who hast brought me to this land to do Thy Will, knowing that I am unworthy of the task.

'I am weak; filled with all that needs to be purified. Yet Thou bestowest upon me the bounteous gift of proclaiming Thy might to the far corners of this earth.

'In Thy goodness Thou hast led me across vast oceans, knowing that I am as an apple filled with vile crawling maggots which can lead to nought but stinking rottenness, save for the granting of Thy great mercy.'

He paused as Margaret moved behind him. The bed creaked and there was a small intake of breath as the sound

186

disclosed her movement. She crept, as quietly as she could, beneath the covers.

'Thou leadest me also to this woman,' he began again. 'Thou gavest her as helpmeet to walk beside me.

'Yet, by this very gift, Thou seekest to remind me daily of my wretchedness.'

The bed creaked again.

'Thou led me to her father's home. Thou gave her to me. And on that same day, as I stood upon the stairs, Thou made it known to me that Thou art, indeed, a vengeful God.

'But I will glory in Thy chastisement, Lord. I will carry this burden in punishment of my sins. For as long as Thou decrees it, I will bear Thy punishment of this bastard child.'

CHAPTER 9

In March, following the formation of the Western Association under Sir William Waller, Nehemiah was ordered to return to duty beside John Fletcher. He set out for Bristol and once again began the wearisome marching which would take him to Malmesbury, Gloucester, and on into Wales. But Waller chose to march at night. Partly to conceal his small force, and partly to use the element of surprise, he marched under cover of darkness. The tactic paid off. They took Malmesbury by storm and at Gloucester captured over sixteen hundred Royalist officers and men.

Nehemiah worked unstintingly, but his mind was constantly upon his family and upon his business back home in Dunscombe. With the departure of Margaret and the death of Samuel, the burden now fell heavily upon Tobias who was left with sole responsibility. A new apprentice had replaced Matthew Crawshaw, and a journeyman had been taken on immediately before Nehemiah's departure. But even with the promise of the additional help of one of Sir Henry's best men, Nehemiah knew it to be an untried team.

He worried about Anne, and thought constantly of Margaret. He wrestled with the dilemma of whether he should have confided in Sir Henry the true circumstances of Margaret's marriage and of Samuel's death; but by the time he had returned from Plymouth, Rupert had already sailed. There seemed little point after he had gone. Now, he was on his way to New England and Nehemiah could only hope that his presence would not endanger Margaret's relationship with her husband.

* * *

Margaret had been delighted with Ufferton from the moment she had first seen it. It had something to do with at last finding a place to settle after so many months of wandering; something to do with the tranquil beauty of the place. But most of all, it was the welcome she received.

A township of some twelve families, it swelled to fourteen with their arrival. Thomas Norton had been welcomed for his skills in leatherwork and very soon cottages had been built to accommodate them.

It was a good time to arrive. Harsh winter was giving way to spring, with its promise of new life and new beginnings. Winter had taken its toll, with two children dead and one man lost forever in the frozen wastes on the other side of the river, but now there was new leaf showing on the trees, a spirit of hope and vitality. The heads of marauding wolves still hung nailed to the door of the church but the people were re-emerging to face the challenge of this vast land which surrounded them.

There was something awe-inspiring in the knowledge that, while they had taken root in this one small area of the Americas, there were thousands of miles of empty, unknown territory stretching out beyond them.

Home for Margaret was a small cottage close to the church with an area of garden which she had begun tending with the devotion of one born to the soil. Already she had planted vegetables and herbs, and hens were scratching in the yard.

Beyond the garden, an area of woodland stretched down to the river then on again, a vast forest, as far as the eye could see. In the mists of early morning, deer cropped the grass in the meadow adjacent to the trees, squirrels were active after the long hibernation, and hares cavorted in the crazy ritual of spring courtship.

There were wild turkey eggs to be found in the scrub, ducks to be driven each morning down to the stream, and animals to tend. She knew that she could live here and be content.

At no time had Deliverance Daniels spoken to her on the subject of her pregnancy. Although her abdomen was now visibly distended, it was not mentioned. No reference was ever made to the coming child. Yet, to other people, she had more than once heard him speaking with apparent enthusiasm for approaching fatherhood.

To her he said nothing. He showed no emotion, no reaction, nothing which could indicate his feelings towards her or to the coming baby. It left her totally perplexed, yet at the same time grateful to have escaped so easily from what had seemed inevitable disgrace.

It caused her to fluctuate between moments of unease, when the uncertainty of it made her want to raise the subject herself and force it out into the open, and other moments when she closed her mind and refused to think about it.

There were still times when she looked at him, feeling her heart tremble at the sight of his features, the way he held his head. It was at those odd moments when he held his face at a certain angle, or when the betty lamp was casting a dim glow behind him − the movement of his body as he put on a shirt before the warmth of the fire.

She would smile at him shyly, half expecting some response. But she was always disappointed. He did not seem to notice her tentative approaches towards him. It seemed that the marriage would never be consummated.

Instead, the nun's habit was still produced from the saddlepack. She hated it. She dreaded the nights when he went to the corner and unlaced the bag, handing her the garment without comment, without raising his head to look her in the eye. He seemed both embarrassed and excited. She did not begin to understand the release which he obtained from it, but his need was evident.

Apart from her unease in this respect, life settled into a comfortable, predictable routine. Each morning began with prayer and an hour spent with her diary. It was an exercise imposed upon her by Deliverance Daniels during the journey down to Bristol and now she was well used to it.

For this hour she was required to search her mind, seeking out the smallest indiscretion, setting it down in ink upon the page for future contemplation. Only then could she turn to note down her uplifting thoughts: the overcoming of some minor temptation, a passage from the Bible which she had read with new understanding. It seemed that her failings far outweighed her spiritual growth. Set down here upon the page, she was constantly reminded of her human frailties.

Such a practised state of introspection was now quite easy to achieve before the hours of daylight. But, as dawn broke, Margaret could see the deer grazing the meadow. Time and again she was compelled to set down upon the page her loss of concentration. Deliverance Daniels moved her from her seat beside the window. She could no longer see the deer but he could not silence the dawn chorus of the birds.

It was but a few steps from the cottage to the church. A simple clapboard building beneath a roof of shingle and with shutters at the windows, it served both as church and meeting house. As Margaret sat, listening to the sounds of spring beyond the windows, she knew that yet again she must commit her lapse of concentration to the pages of her diary.

Dinner on Sundays was a pot of broth left simmering on the stove and afterwards, in the early afternoon, she joined the other women to discuss and analyse the sermon. Many times she was forced to blush and stammer, for how could she converse on minute interpretations of her husband's teaching when all the time her mind had been wandering amid the woodland?

There was provision after afternoon service for the hearing and judgement of offenders, though this was rarely used. The community experienced few problems with law and order.

There was, however, one such hearing on a Sunday afternoon in May. The thatcher, Nathaniel Smith, while drunk, had fallen from a roof. In doing so he had cracked three ribs which some said was sufficient punishment for the deed; but it was necessary for Nathaniel to stand shamefaced before the magistrates to explain his drunkenness.

'It's not the first time, Brother Nathaniel.'

There were three magistrates before whom he stood – Abel Finch, a farmer and long-established member of the community, William Green, wheelwright, and the Reverend Deliverance Daniels.

'No, Brother but 'twill be the last.'

'I remember hearing you say the same before us here on other occasions.'

'But this time it was different. I'll not do it again.'

'We're all aware of the occasion, Brother Nathaniel. We all rejoice in the birth of your son.'

'My wife has waited so long for the birth of a son, Brothers. I was so grateful to the Lord, I must have taken just a little drop too much.'

'The Lord,' said Deliverance Daniels, 'is not to be found in a cask of ale.'

'Oh, no, Brother, I didn't mean . . .'

'Then what did you mean? Did you not know, Brother Nathaniel, that the Lord has said, "Neither fornicators, nor idolaters, nor drunkards, nor revilers shall inherit the kingdom of God"?' Deliverance Daniels launched into a lengthy sermon upon the evils of excess, while Nathaniel Smith stood shamefaced, twisting his fingers within his leather jerkin.

When he had finished Abel Finch cleared his throat. 'I suggest, Brothers, the same punishment as before. Sister Helen shall stitch a large "D" to be worn upon his back for the next three months.'

Deliverance Daniels indicated disagreement. 'The law demands the whip,' he said.

Abel Finch looked slightly taken aback. 'It's permitted but it's not demanded.'

'Then I suggest this to be a fitting occasion on which to use it.'

Abel turned to William Green who looked uncomfortable but did not speak.

'It has always been found that the ridicule of one's brethren is punishment enough.'

'It hasn't stopped this man from repeating his sin.'

'In this instance there were special circumstances.'

'There are always special circumstances for every sin, Brother Abel. Are we all to claim such circumstances when we stand before the Lord on Judgement Day?'

Abel Finch said nothing for a moment, then decided to take a stand. 'I consider the whip to be excessive in this instance. I see no cause for its use.'

'Then we are divided.' Deliverance Daniels looked to William Green.

He deliberated in obvious discomfort. He shuffled his feet

beneath the table. 'If the Reverend Daniels believes it to be the Lord's requirement,' he said at last, 'then he has the greater understanding of such matters.'

Throughout it all Nathaniel Smith had looked from one to the other in a state of mounting alarm.

'A taste of the whip,' said Deliverance Daniels, 'will make certain that he curbs his weakness.'

'So be it,' said Abel Finch. 'But let it be known that I do not agree.'

The judgement was entered into the book, but there was a good deal of muttering and debate among the people assembled there.

Sentence was carried out on the green before the church. Margaret stood and watched along with others from the community. In England she had witnessed numerous men whipped for their crimes but, in this instance, it was not a sight which she found easy to accept. A short distance away stood Helen Smith, clutching her baby, in obvious distress. It seemed to Margaret that some lesser form of punishment would have been more appropriate; but she would not have voiced such thoughts against the opinion of her husband.

Deliverance Daniels stood beside her, watching intently. She did not look at him; yet, with each crack of the whip, it became increasingly obvious to her that some subtle tension was rising within him. When, surreptitiously, she did cast him a sidelong glance, she noted that his teeth were biting his lower lip.

Later, in the cottage parlour, she came across him handling his own whip, fingering it in a way which caused her to shudder. It was something about the way he touched it. He immediately put it down, but her feeling of unease increased.

That night when he reached for the saddlepack, the whip was lying on the chest beside the bed. In one moment of fear she thought that he was going to use it on her; but, instead, he knelt beside the bed. Their roles were reversed. She was standing, he kneeling, his back to her, his hands clasped in prayer.

She stood looking at him, uncertain of what was required of her.

'You'll use it.'

'What?'

He cast her a glance then flicked his eye towards the whip. 'Use it.'

She did not want to understand. He continued to pray, aloud but indistinctly.

She stood for some time until, eventually, he turned on her with taut impatience. 'USE it!'

It was said in a tone which made her reach out and pick up the whip.

'Oh, Lord, I am but a poor and sinful creature,' he muttered.

'How?'

He lifted the nightshirt from off his back.

'Oh.'

'Have mercy upon me and look down upon me in my wretched misery.'

She stood looking at him, letting the whip dangle loosely from her fingers.

'USE it!'

'No.'

'USE IT!'

She brought the whip down across his back.

'I am but vile soil upon which the base desires of weakened flesh seek root.' His voice rose.

She dropped the whip to the floor and held her hand clenched in a fist behind her back.

'Again.'

'No.'

'USE IT!'

She picked it up and hit him again.

'Teach me to love Thee and to glory in Thy chastisement . . . Again!'

A third time the whip came down.

'That I might be Thy chosen servant.' His voice had risen until he was crying out, arching his back and gasping with each crack of the whip. 'Again!'

She had had enough. She could not continue.

'Again!' he shouted.

She hit him once more.

'I am but wretched prey for Satan . . .' He let out an ascending gasp then shuddered with a convulsive movement which left him slumped sideways, groaning softly into the counterpane.

With trembling fingers she replaced the whip upon the bedside chest.

'The Lord is forgiving,' he said shakily, and rolled sideways so that he was sitting slumped on the floor.

He looked up at her, standing watching him, dressed in the nun's habit. His eyes filled with distaste. 'Take it off,' he ordered. 'At once.'

She hastened to remove the garment, quickly pulling it over her head. He always became angry if she did not remove it immediately. As usual she left it in a heap upon the floor for him to stuff back into the saddlepack.

'Go to bed,' he said shakily. 'I have things to do.'

She climbed into bed and covered herself with the counterpane.

He got up and went downstairs. He sat for a long time in the darkened parlour, until he kicked the ashes in the hearth and went back upstairs to bed.

Margaret heard every movement, though she pretended to be asleep.

She watched him next time she sat in church; watched him holding the rapt attention of the congregation with a sermon which had them sitting forward in their seats. She wondered what they would say if she were to reveal his sexual deviations.

Nearby, Luke Parker sat with Mary Finch, his finger just lightly touching the edge of her hand which she had placed on the seat beside her. They were betrothed. It was right and proper that they should look fondly upon one another, but as Margaret looked across at them she caught a glance of such gentle sweetness that it took her breath away.

It left her for some moments pondering the subject of love. It was not a subject upon which she normally spent much thought but there was something quite special about the love which Luke held for Mary.

She looked back towards Deliverance Daniels and pondered again, this time upon her feelings towards him. They were feelings born of duty — an unfaltering, unquestioning duty instilled since childhood in the knowledge that a woman must follow, no matter what, the man to whom she had made her vows. He was no less handsome than on the day when he first rode into Dunscombe. It all seemed such a long time ago.

This led her on to thoughts of her sisters and she tried not to dwell upon the thought that, had he not ridden into Dunscombe, they would not have succumbed to the fever. She thought of her wedding, of the reason for haste, and ended with Rupert and a flood of shame.

By comparison, any power she might hold over Deliverance Daniels paled into insignificance. She might be able to reveal his sexual propensities; but then, Deliverance Daniels knew that he was not the father of her coming child.

Less than twenty-four hours later Rupert walked into the settlement. He appeared at mid-day, walking down the street with the Native, Mawnauoi, who had brought him upriver by canoe.

The shock to Margaret was all the greater for it seemed that, by thinking of him, she had conjured him from her mind. She stood looking at him, her mouth agape in stupefaction.

'Rupert?'

He grabbed her about the waist and lifted her, swinging her round so that her feet left the ground. It was only when he kissed her that she overcame her shock sufficiently to push him away and to stand wiping her hand across her mouth.

'Why?'

Deliverance Daniels walked up behind them and stood looking Rupert over from head to foot. 'You're acquainted with this gentleman, my dear?'

'It's Rupert,' Margaret stammered. 'This is my cousin, Rupert Mainwaring. He's come from Dunscombe.'

'Then you're welcome, sir.' There was a distinct tone of rebuke in the statement which was directed towards them both. 'I suggest, my dear, that you go inside and make refreshment for our guest, rather than keep him standing in the street.'

'Yes, I'm sorry. It was such a shock.' She hurried inside

to stir the fire, still looking over her shoulder in total disbelief.

She busied herself with preparing food while her head buzzed with questions and with unease. She longed to have news of her family, yet she was fearful of Rupert's sudden appearance.

Her husband sat with him before the fire, posing his own questions concerning England and the course of the war. He did not invite her to join the conversation and, although Rupert repeatedly looked at her, imploring her to speak, she kept her eyes lowered and went on with her work.

Deliverance Daniels kept him in conversation all afternoon then ushered him away to the home of Abel Finch who, with the largest house in the settlement, would doubtless offer accommodation. Margaret had had no opportunity to speak alone with him.

It was not until early evening that Rupert had a chance to seek her out. Her shock was abating but she was no less disconcerted by his presence. 'How are my parents?' She kept her distance, avoiding his attempts to come close.

'They're well.'

'Thank God. And what of the others?'

'They're well. Tobias and Lucy are both recovered and Lucy's with child.'

'God be praised. And how's Samuel?'

He hesitated at her mention of her brother.

'What's wrong with him?' she asked immediately.

'He's . . .'

'What's wrong with Samuel?'

'Later,' he said gently. 'I'll tell you later about Samuel.'

'Tell me now.'

He looked at her and bit his lip.

'Now,' she demanded, in no doubt now that something was seriously amiss.

'There was . . . an accident.'

'What sort of accident?'

'A misunderstanding.'

'What sort of accident, Rupert? I want to know.'

'I don't know how to say this.'

'For pity's sake, just tell me.'

He shook his head. 'I didn't know about the pistol.'

'What pistol?'

'The one my comrade had behind his back.'

'You shot him!'

Rupert turned away from her and shook his head. 'An acquaintance of mine did. It was an accident; a terrible, terrible accident.'

'You shot my brother?' she repeated, unable to take in the facts he related, aware only that her brother was dead.

'I was trying to reason with him,' said Rupert. 'Just trying to reason. Then all of a sudden there was a shot and he fell down. He died a few minutes later.'

The sob rising in her throat almost choked her. 'Why?' she demanded.

'He had a sword. My comrade thought he was going to run me through.'

'What?' she demanded in disbelief. 'Samuel wouldn't have a sword.'

'He borrowed it from another man.'

'I don't believe you, Rupert. Samuel would never use a sword.'

'He was terribly angry.'

'Angry?'

'About you. About us.'

'Oh, God, no!' She held a hand to her face. 'Who told him about that?'

'I don't know.'

She felt sick. It was her fault that Samuel was dead. She began to cry, holding her head in her hands and sobbing bitterly. Rupert stepped forward to hold her.

'Go away.' She threw him off. 'Just leave me alone.'

'I'm so very, very sorry.'

'Sorry?' she shouted. 'Is that all you can say, that you're sorry? You've shot my brother.'

'I didn't shoot him,' he said dejectedly. 'I was trying to reason with him.'

'Why is it, Rupert, that everything you ever do seems to bring heartache upon us?'

He winced. 'I came to make amends somehow.'

'By coming here telling me that you've killed my brother?'

'By finding some way to set things straight.'

'Oh, go away, Rupert,' she said bitterly. 'Get out of my sight. Just go away and leave me alone.'

'Margaret . . .'

'Go away!' She turned and barged from the room, leaving him staring after her.

He called after her up the stairs but she had flung herself upon the bed and was sobbing bitterly into the counterpane.

He stood for a while, staring miserably about the empty room. It was a poor start. He wanted desperately to follow her but not only would it have been improper, it would have been useless. He turned slowly and made his way back to the home of Abel Finch.

For the remainder of the evening he sat before the farmhouse fire, endeavouring to make conversation; but his mind was upon Margaret. He wondered if she would agree to speak with him again.

In the chilly foreroom at the front of the house, Mary Finch and Luke Parker lay upon the floor. Between two blankets sewn at the sides and down the centre, they were free to talk of love.

'I can't wait for the day when we can be wed.' Luke tucked the blanket beneath her chin, wanting to keep her warm yet at the same time longing to slip his hand down inside its depths to touch her. 'I love you so.'

She smiled at him. 'I love you, too.'

A flickering betty lamp stood on the table beside them, casting shadows across her face.

He raised himself up on one elbow so that he was half-lying across her. He stroked her hair. 'Then we can . . .' He kissed her and, as he did so, moved his leg, wanting to lay it across her thigh. The division in the blanket prevented it.

She sensed his frustration and ran her fingers lightly across his face. 'Soon,' she whispered. 'Soon.'

It heightened his need and he pressed himself against her, seeking her body through the thick layer sewn between them. 'I don't think I can wait.'

'We must.'

'A whole month. And I'm going to die of love before then.'

She smiled. 'No, we shan't die. We've a whole lifetime to spend together.'

'It's just that I've never felt like this before. It's such an overpowering feeling.'

'I know.'

'And since we've been allowed to bundle like this . . .'

'I know,' she said again. 'My body aches for you.'

'Oh, Mary, how are we going to make a whole month go faster?'

She laughed at him gently. 'There's so much to do. A new dress to make; the cottage to be built.'

'I know I can't wait.'

'I'm going to wear flowers in my hair and have ribbons on my shoes.'

'Oh, Mary, I'm going to take such good care of you. And I'm going to bring you flowers every day of our lives until we're very, very old.'

She ran her finger across his lips and down the light stubble on his youthful chin. 'The greatest gift of all, my love, is that you love me.'

'Oh, I do, I do.' He grabbed her through the thick layer of blanket and kissed her again.

Next day Rupert sought Margaret out again. She was standing at the large table in her parlour, making pastry for a pie.

'Tell me of my family, Rupert.' She had her back to him and worked without looking up.

'It's as I told you yesterday — they're all well.'

'Those still living,' she said bitterly.

'Yes,' he said quietly, and wondered what he should say next.

'How's my father?'

'He was well, and at Dunscombe when I left.'

'But by now he'll have returned to the war.'

'Probably, but I can't be sure.'

'Oh, God, this hateful war,' she murmured to herself.

'He'll not be asked to wield a pike or fire a musket.'

'I notice you're not there,' she said in a voice which was full of meaning.

'No,' he said, then decided to grasp the nettle. 'Margaret, I've come to take you home.'

'What?' She turned round rapidly and looked at him for the first time.

'I've come to take you home.'

'Did my father send you?'

'No, but I've got a plan. I'm going to take you home to Oxford.'

'You said "home".'

'Home to England not to Dunscombe.'

'Why?'

'You're not happy here.'

'I'm . . .'

'I can see it. You're not happy with that man.'

She fought to control the reaction which she knew must have passed across her face.

'Please say you'll come.'

She used the opportunity to turn her back and return to making the pastry.

'I want to make amends. For what happened.'

She did not reply.

'I'll buy a house. For you, and for the child.'

She turned briefly and looked at him, floured hands raised above the table. 'You mean that you'll set me up as a whore?'

'No, of course not.'

'Then what?'

'I'll provide a home.'

'In sin and shame.'

'No, it wouldn't be like that. You'd have a home. You'd have care and comfort.'

'As a whore.'

'No,' he said again. 'You deliberately misunderstand me.'

'You have such a small opinion of me that you'd set me up in sin and shame?'

'No,' he said. 'No one need know . . .'

'No one need know?' she retorted. 'And how would you propose to keep it secret?'

'We'd say you were a widow.'

'Oh,' she said. 'And what of my husband? Have you thought of that?'

'I don't know yet. But somehow I'm going to get you away from here. He doesn't love you.'

She closed her eyes.

'Not like I do.'

'Oh, Rupert, everything you've ever done has caused me harm.'

'I'm sorry about the babe.'

She sucked in her breath. Under no circumstances must she admit to the true paternity of her child.

He nodded towards her abdomen. 'You're with child.'

'Yes.' There was no denying her state of pregnancy.

'And we both know it's mine.'

She must brazen it out.

'It was that night . . . in the stable.'

'How dare you? First you speak of me as a whore; now you say . . .'

'Aunt Anne told me. When I returned to Dunscombe.'

She was stopped short by that; then chose to gamble. Her mother would never have revealed the secret. 'She told you no such thing.'

'I've got to make amends.'

'What have I ever done to you Rupert? What have I ever done to make you follow me here and say these things?'

'I love you.'

'Love me!' She would have given anything to return to Dunscombe. But not to Oxford; and not with Rupert. 'Just go away.'

'Not unless I can take you with me.'

'You were as my brother, yet you violated and abused me. I gave you my friendship, yet you gave me nothing but heartache and pain.' She was kneading the dough, pummelling it with her knuckles, slapping it back and forth with much greater force than was required. 'And still you claim to love me.'

'I'd give you the whole world if you'd only allow me to.'

'Just go away.' She shook out a handful of flour, scattering it in all directions.

'Please, Margaret, I only want to love you and to look after you.'

'Oh, just go away! Get out of my life and leave me alone.'

'Will you think about it?'

She made no response but went on working, her back turned towards him. He left her undisturbed for some time, then said, 'I'll give you time. I realize it's a big step to think about. But it's the only way. He doesn't love you, Margaret, and you're not happy. I can see it. I'm going to take you back to England where I can look after you.'

The offer bit deep into her emotions. It was too close to her real desires.

'I'll come back tomorrow to see if you've had time to consider it.'

'Don't.' If she had turned round he would have seen her tears. She would never return to England. She had made her vows. 'And I'd advise you to leave before my husband sees you.'

Luke Parker stood waiting at the back of the church until Deliverance Daniels had finished at prayer. Then he approached him as he walked towards the door.

'You're not at your duties, Brother Luke.'

'I've been spared for an hour. There's a matter on which I badly need advice.'

'It must be pressing business to neglect your work.'

'I'm bowed down by conscience.'

'Oh?' Deliverance Daniels sent him a searching glance. 'And what ails your conscience?'

Luke flushed crimson. 'I can hardly say.'

'You come to speak of it and then you cannot say. How can you seek advice if you cannot say?'

'I've greatly sinned.'

'Oh?' Deliverance Daniels looked him over again. 'What kind of sin?'

'The worst.'

He swallowed audibly. 'They're all of mighty burden.'

'It was such a powerful feeling. It was as if the Devil Himself took hold of me. I couldn't control my need of her.'

Deliverance Daniels cast his eyes towards the heavens. 'Abomination of the flesh.'

Luke hung his head.

'He that committeth fornication sinneth against his own body and against the temple of the Lord. And he that sinneth against the Lord, shall be cast into eternal fire.'

Luke shuddered. 'I've brought shame on my family,' he said. 'And upon Mary.'

'He that lyeth with harlots shall be forever defiled.'

Luke jumped immediately to the defence of Mary. 'It wasn't with harlots: it was with my Mary.'

' "And I shall judge thee," saith the Lord; "Sodom and all her daughters." '

'Mary wasn't to blame. It was me. I couldn't stop myself.'

' "Vengeance is mine," saith the Lord. "I shall strip her and leave her naked and bare." '

'It's I who've sinned. Mary's as sweet and innocent as a newborn babe.'

'There's danger in the daughters of Eve,' said Deliverance Daniels. He was still staring into space but appeared now to be speaking more directly to Luke. 'They have the ability to draw us into sin. Beware of the innocence of woman. She'll drag you down into the depths of destruction.'

'Please tell me what I must do. I've got to make amends for what I've done against her.'

Deliverance Daniels folded his hands across his chest. 'Pray to the Lord. And stay away from the woman.'

The conversation had brought little relief to Luke. He returned to work feeling utterly wretched.

The following day a notice was posted upon the door of the church: Luke and Mary were to stand trial upon a charge of immorality.

The hearing took place the following Sunday. For days rumour and gossip surged around the community until, on Sunday, everyone sat, straining their ears to catch the soft, almost inaudible, responses of the two young people. Abel Finch was in acute discomfort. He refused to sit in judgement upon his own daughter; instead he was obliged to listen, torn between the embarrassment of the proceedings and his desire to protect her.

Mary and Luke were questioned and made to divulge their shame for all to hear. Their guilt was undenied: they had betrayed the trust of those who had allowed them to bundle. Their marriage date was set back by a further three months during which time they would wear the 'F' of the fornicator upon their backs. The punishment was not great but the effect upon their self-respect was long lasting and deeply felt.

As the weeks went by Margaret watched them many times

as they sat in church. The look of affection was still there but some inner light had been dimmed, clouded out by a permanent shadow of guilt and shame.

Rupert tried on numerous occasions to speak with Margaret but she steadfastly refused to discuss his plan. In fact she spoke very little, except to be polite in company. He began to waver in his interpretation of the situation, certain that she was unhappy, yet watching intently, seeking any sign of endearment which might pass between her and her husband, analysing every glance, every word they spoke. Worst of all was to watch as they walked together down the street and closed the door behind them. The time was rapidly approaching when he must make the journey down into Virginia. The prospect of leaving without her was unbearable.

He stood one morning in warm sunlight, leaning against the door of Thomas Norton's workshop. Thomas was making a shoe of goat leather while, nearby, a length of harness hung waiting to be repaired. Thomas chatted as he worked, looking up occasionally but concentrating upon stitching leather to leather.

'You're well settled here in Ufferton.'

'Yes, thank God. We took a great risk when we left England to start afresh.'

Rupert cast his eyes about the workshop. 'I think I'd soon die of boredom if I lived here long.'

'Why? It's a good place, full of God-fearing people.'

'I've been too long in Oxford. I'd miss the company of those who like to take some pleasure from living.'

'We take great pleasure in living.'

'I haven't played a single game of dice since I arrived.'

Thomas laughed. 'We don't spend much time in playing at the dice.'

'But I'm used to it. There's no harm in it.'

'I'm sure. But we take much simpler pleasures.'

'You've never seen such goings-on as there were in Oxford before I left. Since the King's been there the Court has gathered around him. You'd never believe the finery of those ladies − and the carriages! You'd think the whole of London had converged on Oxford.'

'I don't know much about London or about Oxford, but we did spend some time in Bristol before we sailed.'

'Bristol's a fine enough place but it's nothing compared to London, and now to Oxford.'

'It's not for me,' smiled Thomas. 'I'd rather be here, among people who've become good friends.'

'You haven't lived until you've spent the night roistering in grand company and slept at dawn with the music still ringing in your ears.'

'You're welcome to your music and your ladies in jewelled gowns.'

'And such a pain in your head the following day,' Rupert said, but then went quiet. 'But I don't drink much these days.'

In the meadow, beyond Rupert's shoulder, Thomas could see Susannah tethering the cow in its pasture. She was roundly pregnant. 'I'm more than content with the love of a good woman.' There was mud on her cheek. As he spoke, she lifted the back of her hand to brush it off.

'Yes,' said Rupert, still quiet. 'There's a lot to be said for the love of a good woman.'

'I thought long and hard about the wisdom of bringing Susannah and the children across the ocean, and in Boston I heard many accounts of men who'd brought their families here only to subject them to the most brutal hardships, then to lose them in death. I can well understand how it feels to bury a wife and bitterly regret having uprooted her from her own home village.'

'It must be even worse for the woman who buries her husband.'

'Yes,' said Thomas. He closed his eyes for a moment and shook his head. 'It doesn't do to think of a woman left unsupported to cope alone.'

'What do they do?'

'Some survive. Others choose to return to England.'

A spark ignited in the back of Rupert's mind.

'It depends on the circumstances,' went on Thomas. 'We try to help the widows but it's as much as most men can do to support their own families.'

Rupert did not reply. When he did eventually speak, it was more to himself than to Thomas. 'Without a doubt,' he said, 'a widow would be best served by going home.'

Thomas stopped work and glanced up at him. 'By the way, Susannah asked me to invite you to dinner.'

'What?'

'She's roasting a chicken.'

'Oh, thank you.'

'About eleven, then. We'll see you about eleven.'

'Yes,' said Rupert distractedly. 'That would be very pleasant.'

'We'll look forward to it.'

'Yes. But if you'll excuse me, there's something I must do first.'

'Of course.' Thomas watched as Rupert turned and walked away.

An hour before, Rupert had seen Deliverance Daniels ride out into the woodland. Now, before anything but the most vague of thoughts had formed in his mind, he rode out in the same direction.

He went down to the point where the river was fordable, then followed the clearly defined track up through the trees on the opposite bank. Here, on this side of the river, the woodland became dense forest but the path was clearly marked, laid down over the centuries by the feet of the native Indian population who regularly passed this way.

The path forged steeply upwards over rocky, uneven ground until it reached the top of a ravine which dropped away sharply to the right. Below was the river. Wide and languid upstream, it found itself here squeezed between sheer rock-face on either side, showing its anger by thundering over submerged boulders in a rage of white foam.

The horse picked its way warily, sensing the danger to its right, snorting with the effort of the climb. The thoughts in Rupert's mind were still unclear. He intended to catch up with the man ahead of him but he had no idea at this moment what he would actually do.

He came upon the Reverend Daniels sooner than expected and was surprised to see him a short distance ahead, dismounted from his horse and seated upon a high overhang of rock above the river.

Suddenly, it seemed so easy. Rupert knew that Daniels had not seen him, he was still within the cover of the trees while the minister was sitting, exposed, upon the outcrop of rock.

His heart began to thunder. He hated this man. He had not realized until this moment just how much he hated him. As Rupert watched him, he imagined Daniel's hands upon Margaret's body, his face buried in her neck.

He left his horse tethered and went on foot. One quick final dash out of the trees would be sufficient to catch his victim unawares. One determined push would send him hurtling one hundred feet into the river below.

He was panting before he was halfway there, partly from exertion, partly because he had been holding his breath. He paused, trying to compose himself by taking gasps of air through his mouth.

As he stood watching, Deliverance Daniels got up from his seat on the rock and walked back to his horse. A feeling of disappointment and anti-climax swept over Rupert so that he swore out loud. He continued to watch as Deliverance Daniels mounted the horse and rode away. The moment of opportunity had been lost.

Rupert was sweating profusely. He remained still for some time, feeling weak, reacting to the thoughts which had passed through his mind. He had actually intended to kill Deliverance Daniels.

Eventually he went back to his own horse and began to follow, still not knowing why but mesmerized by the other man and by the thoughts still running through his mind. He kept his distance under cover of the trees. The ground was level at this point, the path still keeping to the course of the river but a little further from the edge of the ravine. An area of tangled undergrowth separated him from the steep drop.

His mind was sufficiently composed by now to know that he might well have been seen to follow Deliverance Daniels from the settlement. It would have been of little use to free Margaret only to find himself charged with murder. The thought of the desperate course he was contemplating made the hair rise on the back of his neck.

The path began to descend, gradually in some places, more steeply in others, until the sound of water grew louder. He was back at river level.

A mile further, at a point where the river took a wide

sweeping loop, the path divided. Fresh horse droppings told him that Deliverance Daniels had kept to the river bank. The other path would cut across the bend.

A fresh thought hit Rupert. His heart began to hammer violently in his chest once more. An accident on the water would free Margaret for sure. He quickened his pace along the shorter route, knowing that he could get ahead.

His mind began to race. With the element of surprise, and with his superior strength, he stood a good chance. He would first need to drag the man from his horse, then roll with him down into the water. It called for a place where the bank was steep, but clear of undergrowth. It did not take Rupert long to find such a place.

He dismounted from his horse and left it concealed within the trees, then he crouched down and waited. He removed his boots and outer garments. He would be hindered by their weight, and it would not do to re-enter the settlement in sodden clothing.

A long time passed. His breath was painful in his chest and his temples pounded. There was no sign of Deliverance Daniels.

At last he got up from his hiding place and, still in his stockinged feet, began dodging from tree to tree, making his way upstream.

Deliverance Daniels had dismounted from his horse and was standing on a small beach of shingle where the steep bank had broken away to give access to the water. He was studying the flow of the river and it was obvious that he was thinking of making a crossing.

'Idiot!' Rupert exclaimed to himself. No one but a fool would attempt to cross the river at such a point. It was wide, fast flowing, and with swirling eddies of reeds where the current revolved upon itself.

The horse was nervous. Deliverance Daniels re-mounted and urged it out into the water, kicking hard as the animal stepped gingerly across the shingle. For the first third of the crossing it was submerged no deeper than its hocks but it pranced sideways, buffeted by the current.

Towards the centre of the river the bed dipped sharply. The horse stumbled; then, feeling the insecurity of its footing, it began first to flounder then to thrash wildly, sending silt and stones to cloud the frothing water.

Deliverance Daniels lost his grip. He slipped sideways, struggling to regain the saddle; but the horse was now swimming in deep water and a combination of panic and the swirling current caused him to lose hold completely.

He was swept at speed, the breath knocked from him, in water it was beyond his capacity to swim. Several times he went down, only to bob up again. Once he hit his back on a submerged boulder which halted his passage for a brief moment before the current gathered him up and swept him on.

Rupert watched in horror. It was one thing to plan a murder, another to stand and watch the man drown. Without any thought for himself, he stepped from the cover of the trees and stood on the bank, about to jump in and attempt a rescue. But Deliverance Daniels swept past at such speed that he knew he stood no chance. Rupert could do no more than stand helplessly and watch as the minister was swept away.

He should have been glad. Instead, he turned and vomited into the undergrowth. He went back to his horse, put on his boots and outer garments, and rode back to the settlement.

CHAPTER 10

Deliverance Daniels lay in a haze of pain and confusion. He was aware of being manhandled, but the pain in his back was excruciating. He had no idea where he was. He felt sick and bloated. Any attempt to open his eyes only brought a searing intensity of light and a pain to his head. He was rolled over on to his stomach. Immediately, a cascade of river water belched up from his insides, bringing little relief but leaving him choking and gasping for air.

He was dragged again, this time on to something which smelled of animal hide. It began to move, bumping across uneven ground. He heard the bark of a dog, somewhere near his head, and voices; but he could not make out what they were saying.

He was vaguely aware of arriving somewhere and of being carried, this time to an area which he realized to be under cover. The voices were muffled by whatever was above him but attempts to open his eyes gave no clue to his whereabouts. He was unable to focus before the pain caused him to close them again.

Something was pushed between his lips and he found himself swallowing on liquid poured into his mouth. Almost immediately he was sick, many times. Then, in weakness and exhaustion, he felt himself rolled over on to his stomach and allowed to sleep.

He did not know how long he slept. When he awoke he was vaguely aware of someone sitting nearby. It was not so much the sound of movement; more a sensing of another presence. He tried to open his eyes but the memory of the

213

pain restrained him. He lay for some time gradually focusing his mind upon his surroundings.

The smell was puzzling – not unfamiliar, but not consistent with his normal surroundings. It was the smell of woodsmoke but also of something like sawdust. There was an occasional voice but still he could not make out what was being said.

The pain had dulled to a sickening, deep-seated ache which seemed to come from his abdomen as much as his back. But his head was hurting less. He moved his fingers to touch the surface upon which he lay, and found that he was on a bed of horizontal poles covered with animal hide.

He risked opening his eyes but they revealed little at first. There was an absence of daylight; it was either early dawn or late dusk. From the feel of the atmosphere it was most likely dusk.

He thought again of the fact that he was inside an enclosed space and reached out to investigate the wall beside him. It was constructed of birchbark.

His movement had immediately brought the watcher to his side. In the same moment that he realized he was in a wigwam, he realized also that the woman beside him was a Pennacook squaw.

She kneeled down to touch him but he jerked back so sharply that it frightened her. In the dim light he could not see her properly but he sensed her fear. It only added to his own feelings of confusion and distaste. She hurriedly rose to her feet and left him.

He struggled to get up and found that he could not. The pain in his back prevented it and a feeling of weakness sent him gasping, back into a horizontal position.

The woman returned, stirring the fire outside the entrance to give more light. With her she had Mawnauoi.

Mawnauoi was the only Native whom Deliverance Daniels had previously met at close quarters. He did not like him. He had created a poor impression from the start when he had countered instruction to attend church with an amused disregard. Since then Mawnauoi had appeared in Ufferton on numerous occasions and Deliverance Daniels' first impression of him had not altered. There was a high-handed insolence about him which Daniels found both irritating and perplexing. He seemed totally incapable of taking orders or showing respect. Yet at the same time, he had a disturbing ability to place his interlocutor at a disadvantage which, to Deliverance Daniels, was utterly unacceptable.

Mawnauoi grinned. 'Drown. People empty.'

His mode of speech irritated Deliverance Daniels who did not reply.

'Much swallow. Now empty.'

He ignored the comment. He was not happy to be lying on his back with the other man at a higher level. He tried again to get up but found that he could not.

'Go to the settlement,' he ordered. 'Tell Abel Finch, or one of the other men, to bring transport to fetch me.'

'Much dark. Rest here till time of sun.'

'Didn't you hear me? This instant.' The thought of remaining in the wigwam all night brought a further feeling of discomfort.

'Not now. Take sun-up.'

Deliverance Daniels turned his head away. In the absence of knowing how to exert his authority, he chose to say nothing.

'Yinglees much trade for man's return.'

Deliverance Daniels turned and looked at him. He was appalled to think that the Pennacook might barter him. Yet, at the same time, he had an uncomfortable feeling that Mawnauoi was merely mocking him.

Mawnauoi settled down as if to chat. 'Mawnauoi speak good tongue. Learn much good.'

Deliverance Daniels sniffed, and said nothing.

'You got blankets?'

'No, I do not have blankets.'

'Trade much good for blankets.'

Deliverance Daniels sniffed again.

'Learn good. Yinglee man here; two, three summers ago. Teach good. Speak with gods. Make much magic.'

Deliverance Daniels had a disconcerting feeling that he was referring to his predecessor. He chose not to rise to the bait. 'English,' he corrected. 'We are not Yinglees.'

'Yinglee man teach good,' said Mawnauoi again.

His back was hurting. He was in no state to weather a confrontation. He closed his eyes and pretended to sleep.

He realized that the squaw had come to kneel beside him but did not open his eyes.

'Food,' said Mawnauoi. 'Much good food.'

It smelled appetizing. To his annoyance Deliverance Daniels realized that he was hungry. He propped himself painfully upon one elbow and took the bowl from between the woman's hands. It contained succotash made from fish, beans and corn. It offended his palate but the warm food inside his stomach brought an immediate feeling of comfort.

'Food good. Yinglee man's food . . .' Mawnauoi made a gesture of spitting on the floor. 'This food make plenty strong.'

Deliverance Daniels decided to try again. 'I really must insist that you go at once and fetch someone from Ufferton.'

'No fetch someone. Mawnauoi take. Mawnauoi take when sun . . .' He pointed with an arm to the required distance above the horizon.

'I've an injury to my back. I require someone to bring transport.'

'No injured. Man hit rock.' Mawnauoi laughed. 'Much colours soon.'

Deliverance Daniels realized that he was referring to bruising. He understood also, with some discomfort, that the Natives must have examined his body while he was unconscious. He put the bowl on the ground and lay down.

'Niccone see man in water. Fetch braves. We save.'

'I'm sure it's very good of you. But I need to go home.'

The consequence of having lifted himself in order to eat was to realize that he needed to urinate.

'You rest here. Much sleep. Grow strong.'

He resisted the urge for some time but it continued to grow. The pressure of a full bladder added to the pain in his bruised kidneys. Mawnauoi continued to sit and to give no indication of leaving. The woman had gone soon after he had finished eating but Mawnauoi sat on. Deliverance Daniels was disconcertingly suspicious that the Native was aware of his discomfort.

At last Mawnauoi said, 'Yinglee shoot water. Piss.'

Deliverance Daniels cringed with embarrassment and Mawnauoi laughed aloud.

'Piss much water. Swallow river.'

He went out chuckling to himself and was still grinning when he returned with a receptacle which he placed on the floor beside the bed.

Deliverance Daniels looked at him and waited. 'You may go outside.'

When the Native made no move to comply he repeated the instruction but he was rapidly beginning to realize that he could wait no longer. 'Well, at least turn your back.'

Mawnauoi continued to grin as though not understanding the instruction.

Deliverance Daniels fumbled in his clothing, sharply aware that never, in all his life, had he felt at such a disadvantage. When he had finished he turned his head towards the wall, ignoring Mawnauoi who continued to sit beside him. He was still chuckling.

'Why no speak? Yinglee man say Mawnauoi speak all times. Learn good.'

Deliverance Daniels had no intention of allowing Mawnauoi to practise upon him.

'You know man come last moon? Mawnauoi guide. Much travel. Across ocean.' He was referring to Rupert. 'Man talk plenty. Tell Mawnauoi many things.'

The reference to Rupert triggered a recent memory in Deliverance Daniels' mind. It was vague at first but the more he concentrated upon it the more certain he became. He had seen Rupert standing upon the riverbank. Perhaps it was he who had frightened the horse?

'Man have mighty fine brandy. Mawnauoi drunk; mighty fine drunk. You got brandy?'

'No, I have not.' He might have known that Rupert would be irresponsible enough to provide the Natives with strong drink. He was about to explain to Mawnauoi the evils of such indulgence when he was shocked from his intention by an eerie, wailing cry which sent a convulsion of fear coursing through his entire system. Surmounting the pain, he sat upright, looking about him.

'Shaman,' said Mawnauoi conversationally. 'Bring gods. Work much magic.'

The eerie wail rose and fell, accompanied by the shaking of a rattle and rhythmic drumbeats. It gained momentum then fell away, only to rise again.

It was to Deliverance Daniels as if the Devil Himself had revealed His presence but a stone's throw away. He raised his face to the heavens and pressed his hands together in an attitude of prayer.

' "And he cried out mightily with a strong voice saying, 'Babylon the Great is fallen and is become the habitation of devils and the hold of every foul spirit.' " '

Mawnauoi looked at him with amused perplexity.

' " 'Therefore shall her plagues come in one day, death and mourning, and famine; and she shall be utterly burned with fire; for strong is the Lord God who judgeth her.' " '

Mawnauoi, not understanding the sudden outburst, chose to ignore it. 'Shaman make medicine. Children sick. Many fever.'

' "And when the Lord saw it, he abhorred them. And He said, 'I will hide My face from them. For fire is kindled in Mine anger and shall burn unto the lowest hell. They shall be devoured with burning heat and with bitter destruction; the young man and the virgin, the suckling and the man with grey hairs. I will make Mine arrows drunk with blood and My sword shall devour flesh.' " '

Mawnauoi was growing bored. 'You wanna talk?' He prodded Deliverance Daniels to gain his attention but he continued to sit bolt upright, his eyes closed and his hands clasped in front of his chest. 'Or you no wanna talk?' Eventually he gave up and left him.

Deliverance Daniels continued to hold the position, oblivious to the pain in his back. 'O, Lord, have mercy on this Thy servant. Thou, who lifted me from the river and from the jaws of death, only to deliver me to this coven of witches at the very gates of Hell. How am I to do Thy Will? Thou, who sent me to this land of heathens, what must I do in this hive of demons and of sorcery? How am I to hone Thy sword of vengeance?'

He continued to pray for as long as the wailing continued. When at last it died away, he collapsed exhausted and lay with his eyes tight shut, his hands covering his ears, waiting for the morning.

Next morning Deliverance Daniels was escorted back to Ufferton. Lying on a travois, dragged along the ground by a dog, he found it yet another humiliating experience. He arrived at the settlement feeling thoroughly ill-tempered and when Mawnauoi offered to carry him into the cottage he curtly refused, walking stiffly and painfully up the path to the house.

By this time he had it firmly established in his mind that Rupert was in some way responsible for his near-drowning. The more he thought about it, the more convinced he became. He lost no time in making his accusation.

'In what way do you accuse him?' asked Abel Finch.

'He ran into my path, quite deliberately, with the intention of startling my horse.'

'Lies!' exclaimed Rupert. He was sitting astride a chair on the other side of the room. Margaret was stirring the cooking pot over the fire, listening intently.

'Then what have you to say about it?'

Rupert did not know what to say. He had done nothing, but the intention had been there.

'You were seen to enter the forest shortly after the Reverend Daniels.'

Rupert was still reeling from the realization that jealousy had almost driven him to kill.

'Caleb Clark saw you both ride by a short distance apart.'

It was unlikely that he would have carried it through, but he could not be sure.

'What have you to say?'

'There's nothing I can say. I don't deny I was in the forest.'

'But you did not frighten his horse?'

'Of course not.'

Margaret looked across at him with undisguised suspicion.

'I saw the man fall from his horse,' said Rupert. 'I was about to jump in and save him but it was no use. He was swept away before I could do anything.'

'The man lies. He deliberately stood and watched me swept away.'

'Well?' asked Abel Finch.

'I had no choice. He was taken too fast, swept with such speed that it was impossible to save him.'

'You did nothing?'

Rupert ran his tongue across his lip and swallowed. 'I thought for sure that the man had been drowned.'

'He deliberately set out to murder me.'

The word 'murder' again set the hair rising on the back of Rupert's neck.

'He did ride back into Ufferton to raise the alarm,' said Abel.

'When he thought it was too late. What better way to cover his tracks? I tell you, I saw him.'

'And you still claim he ran into your path with the intention of startling your horse?'

'He was in his undergarments, without doublet or breeches.'

Rupert seized upon the comment. 'And what would I be doing, on the banks of the river prancing about without doublet or breeches?'

'Waiting to startle my horse.'

'The man's mad! Destined for Bedlam.'

'There's no need for such comment,' said Abel. But he looked at Deliverance Daniels with some scepticism. 'Though it does seem unlikely.'

'The horse stumbled,' said Rupert. 'No one but a fool would cross the river at that point.'

'I saw him, I tell you. He ran out with the sole intention of startling my horse.'

Abel turned squarely to Rupert. 'Did you deliberately startle this man's horse?'

'No,' said Rupert thankfully. In this answer, at least, he could be truthful.

Margaret moved her position before the cooking pot. Rupert could sense her discomfiture from across the room.

'The man lies,' said Deliverance Daniels. 'May the Lord have mercy on his lying tongue.'

The three men looked at one another.

'I insist that he be charged with intent to murder. I shan't rest until I see him duly tried.'

'There's little evidence,' said Abel Finch, 'beyond your word.'

'You doubt my word?'

'No, but there's a possibility that in the shock of the mishap you may have been mistaken.'

'You're saying that I'm mad?'

Rupert grasped his own opportunity. 'And are you saying, sir, that my word is any less worthy than your own?'

'I am, indeed.'

'Then you question the word of a gentleman, sir.'

'You're no gentleman, sir.'

Abel Finch raised his hands. 'There's no need for this, Brothers. I suggest that we retire from the conversation for the moment and give the matter some further thought. We'll discuss it again when passions have cooled.'

He got up and drained the tankard which had rested upon his knee. 'I'm going home to my dinner. No doubt you'll be ready for your own.'

Rupert looked across at Margaret but her head was bent over the cooking pot. He gazed at her for a moment, willing her to look up, but she did not do so. At last he gave a sigh and turned to accompany Abel Finch back to his farm. She glanced at him as he passed. Her eyes were filled with suspicion and disbelief.

On the way back to the farm Abel coughed to clear his throat. 'You've almost completed your business in Ufferton.'

'I came to visit my cousin, and to sell my blankets in Boston.'

'Yes, but you've other business elsewhere.'

'I'm going on to Virginia to arrange a consignment of tobacco.'

'Then you'll soon want to be on your way.'

Rupert looked at him, beginning to realize what he was suggesting.

'This is a law-abiding community,' said Abel. 'It's rare that we need to sit in judgement upon our brethren; yet we've done so twice in the past few weeks.' The memory of Mary's face as she stood in the meeting house still burned in his mind. 'I've no stomach for yet another trial, especially one where the circumstances are in such doubt.'

Rupert lowered his eyes. 'You, too, question my word?'

'Let's just say it would be best if you were gone before next Sunday afternoon.'

'That's as good as saying that you doubt me.'

'I must doubt either you or the Reverend Daniels. In the

absence of further evidence it's a choice between the two of you. I wouldn't want to make an error of judgement.' Abel paused and looked at him. 'Particularly in view of the punishment which is bound to be demanded.'

Rupert gulped.

'There's no need to announce your departure. It would be sufficient to slip away before anyone has chance to delay you.'

'That would be as good as admitting the charge.'

Abel Finch looked at him. 'The choice is yours, my friend. Either you stay and chance your word against that of the Reverend Daniels; or you put some distance between him and yourself and so ensure that your neck remains whole and unblemished.'

'You call this justice?'

'You'll find Mawnauoi about three miles downriver. He'll guide you to wherever you want to go.'

'I should have the chance to prove my innocence!'

'You have; if you wish to chance your word against that of the Reverend Daniels. But there are those here who'd be reluctant to reject the word of a minister of God.'

Rupert spread his hands in a gesture of outraged injustice.

'The choice must be yours, my friend. I'm not able to help you any further.'

Later, after they had eaten their dinner, Rupert began collecting up his belongings. Abel made no comment except to wish him Godspeed.

He rode out, using the path which skirted the back of the settlement, thus avoiding the main street. He ached for opportunity to pass by Margaret's cottage, to see her one last time, to speak one last word. But he knew that she would disclose his departure to her husband. He kept close watch for her, hoping both that he might see her and that he might avoid her. But Margaret was busy inside her cottage.

When Deliverance Daniels learned that Rupert had left, he flew into a rage. He accused first Abel Finch, then Margaret, of complicity. He demanded that scouts should be sent out to bring him back. When no one seemed inclined to take such action, he sank into a long period of morose dissatisfaction with everyone.

Margaret had never seen him so angry. She went quietly

about her work, riding out his anger with passive submission, until eventually the debate concerning Rupert's guilt or innocence died down amongst the community.

Margaret's garden flourished. By mid-June it showed a growth of young lettuce, cucumber, radish and maize, while heartsease and mignonette grew amongst the thyme, rosemary, sage and lavender. She was eight months pregnant and the movement within her abdomen brought an ever-increasing awareness of the child growing within her.

Susannah, too, was near her time. On the last day of the month she gave birth to a son but three days later complained of feeling unwell, with a headache and feverishness. By the fourth day she was delirious.

'It's childbed fever,' said Esther Clark. She acted as midwife to the community and was well used to the symptoms of puerperal fever. She sent Caleb to catch two pigeons which she tied, live, to Susannah's feet but they did little to reduce the fever.

A rash broke out across her back, spreading to her neck and arms so that she could not bear the weight of her clothing upon her skin. She thrashed and called out in her delirium.

Margaret sat beside her day and night. She brought out her own book of remedies which had been given to her by her mother on the eve of her wedding. With Esther's help, she chose a cordial of rosewater with sage and nutmeg.

In her more lucid moments Susannah was well aware of her condition. 'Take care of my children,' she begged. 'I can't be taken and leave them motherless.'

'Hush,' said Margaret; but already in her mind she was adjusting to the prospect of having not one expected child, but four.

Thomas sat in his workroom stitching leather. He had not slept for days. A feeling of exhaustion and defeat hung over him. All the pleasure and self-fulfilment had ebbed away. All would be worthless without Susannah. He tried to pray but found that he was without sufficient faith: it left him feeling helpless and guilty.

But on the seventh day the fever began to subside and by the eighth Susannah lay in a quiet sleep.

'You'll grow strong again and rear your own children,' smiled Margaret.

'How's my baby?' She opened her eyes and smiled her thanks.

'He's been put to the breast of Martha Bracegirdle. He's in good hands.'

'And the children?'

'Safe at play. You've no need to fear.'

'May God be praised,' breathed Susannah and sank back into sleep.

In early July Nehemiah found himself in Bath. The two armies had been facing each other since June, first on a hill west of the city and now from the high ground of Lansdown. There was an air of nervous anticipation among the Parliamentarians who were heavily outnumbered.

'By how many?' Nehemiah and John Fletcher were preparing, as best they could, for the inevitable casualties.

'One thousand of our men to six thousand horse, foot and cannon.'

'And yet we're to attack?'

'Either we attack, or wait for them to do the same.'

'May God have mercy on us,' breathed Nehemiah, but he had long ago given up thoughts of one last battle.

The result was inevitable, but it was not without encountering fierce resistance that the Royalists succeeded in driving the Parliamentarians back to their second line of defence behind dry-stone walls.

John and Nehemiah stitched and staunched, leaving some of the wounded to the care of the women, others to drain their lifeforce into the soil. Nehemiah was drenched in blood and perspiration but he worked without thought for his own discomfort.

Eventually, in the middle of the night, Waller withdrew his force down into Bath.

'They're bound to follow us. We're at their mercy.'

'I doubt it,' said John Fletcher. 'Their leader has a mighty sore head.'

'How so?'

'Rumour has it that Sir Ralph Hopton was seated in a wagon with some of our men who had been taken prisoner.

One of them lit a pipe and in doing so dropped a spark into the gunpowder on which they were sitting.'

'Then they were blown to pieces.'

'Not all; Sir Ralph's alive, but it'll be some time before he feels fit to lead his men against us.'

The account proved to be true. The Royalist army marched away towards Devizes, leaving Waller and his men to catch their breath and to thank God for their deliverance.

Only a short time later Waller announced his intention of following. They marched the eighteen miles from Bath to Devizes and there encircled the Royalist army. They did not know that the King had dispatched a further three brigades of Horse.

There, on Roundway Down, Waller and his men were hopelessly defeated.

In the middle of the carnage Nehemiah stood up to stretch his back, briefly surveying the corpse of the man he had just failed to save. In the next moment he felt a blow upon his left arm. He looked down to see a bloody stump where once his hand had been. In the shock of it, he looked around for the hand and saw it lying, shattered, a few feet away. Then he fainted.

The next thing he knew John Fletcher was kneeling over him, inflicting pain such as he had never known. He wondered why, then remembered his hand lying beside the face of the dead musketeer. He fainted again.

'Rest easy, my friend.' Somehow he had been moved and was lying in a wagon. His arm was bound with cloth which was already steeped in blood. 'It's best that you sleep.'

'The injured men — I must go and attend to them.'

'You're in no state to attend to anyone but yourself. Get some rest and I'll call back later when I've more time.'

Nehemiah closed his eyes. 'What of the battle?'

'We've been cut to pieces. God only knows how we'll recoup from this one.'

'I wish to God,' said Nehemiah, 'that I could sometimes understand His purposes; but there are times when I fear I never shall.'

'Rest easy, my friend, and don't seek to question that which we can't change. Your task is to heal and regain your strength. In a few days' time I'll arrange for you to be transported home. Your time as my assistant has been ably spent.'

Nehemiah raised himself slightly. 'I can't leave you.'

'You'll be of little use without a hand. And it's time you went home to your family.' He walked away before Nehemiah had the chance to say more.

In the half-light of the wagon he lay listening to the activity outside – the sounds of retreat, the cries of the injured. He thought of Dunscombe and knew, with relief, that soon he would leave this hateful war behind. But he wondered what use he would be to his family with only one hand.

When he did return home he found that his presence, with or without his hand, was sorely needed. Tobias had met obstacles on every side. Not only was he working with a newly assembled workforce, he was also experiencing difficulty in distributing the finished cloth.

Every road leading towards Oxford or out of London was threatened by Royalist garrisons. Much of the cloth had previously been transported by Tom Cox but his pack-horse train was no longer able to travel safely along the roads. It was not so much the goods which were at risk as the horses themselves. Cavalry officers, with men and large quantities of baggage to move, chose to ignore the King's proclamation against pillage. They cast envious eyes upon strings of sturdy Galloways or Suffolk Punches. Tom Cox devised many ways of avoiding such attention but there were traffic spies in alehouses and along the road. It was inevitable that the extent of his usefulness was curtailed.

'I shall be mighty glad when this dreadful war's ended,' said Tobias with feeling.

'Amen to that.'

'But to what end now that Sir William's army has been cut to pieces?'

Nehemiah shrugged. 'It's up to My Lord Essex now to face the King. Though neither of them seems inclined to move from the comfort of London or of Oxford. I despair of My Lord Essex. I doubt he'll ever put his heart into this task which the Lord has set him. I don't know how he'll ever dare to stand before his Maker on Judgement Day.'

He spoke with a vehemence which Tobias had never seen

in him before. 'This war has had an ill effect upon us all, Father. We must try somehow to get on with our lives now that you're home again.'

'I still hold him responsible for not ending the whole affair at Edgehill. He could have seen an end to the war that day and men could have returned to their families instead of lying, rotting, in distant soil.'

'It must have been truly dreadful to have witnessed it.'

'Now he sits in London, and the King holds Court in Oxford. And neither of them does anything to bring about a final conclusion.'

'You've done your part, Father. You must leave it now to those in command.'

'I only wish to God that I could have faith in their desire to see it through.'

Tobias reached out and touched him on the shoulder. 'You're home now; home with Mother and with the rest of us. And Rupert will be back soon with news of Margaret.'

'Yes,' sighed Nehemiah. 'Rupert. I only hope to God that I haven't made an equal error of judgement.'

The wedding of Mary Finch to Luke Parker was intended to be a joyous occasion, but the spectre of guilt still hung over them.

Here in New England the wedding ceremony had been stripped of all pagan custom. This was a civil contract of inheritance and property though there was no less joy in the bringing together of a newly wedded pair. They stood in the parlour of the farmhouse, before Abel as magistrate, while each pledged themself to the other.

As Margaret watched she recalled again the circumstances of her own wedding, her mother and the now dead children. Tears sprang at the memory of the frail Bibby-Anne, and the pain of leaving her. She looked down at her finger and remembered how it had disturbed her mother that she did not wear a ring. Few wore wedding rings here in New England.

The baby kicked and reminded her how close she was to giving birth.

Deliverance Daniels used the occasion to get up and preach a sermon concerning the virtues of chastity and the

227

denouncement of sin. It was hot. Margaret was uncomfortable, squeezed into a corner with her belly distended. It was not long before her thoughts wandered again, back home to Dunscombe and to the sheep upon the hills.

When at last it was over she was glad to move and to go outside where she was free to breathe fresh air and to stretch her abdomen. A slight pain ran through her and she winced.

There was wedding cake to eat, a haunch of venison, numerous hams and tarts. Ducks and hens had been roasting all morning and there was fresh-baked bread and cheese. The men helped themselves to sackposset and rum, and exchanged views concerning the effect of the weather upon crops or the breeding of a good new foal from Abel's stallion.

In the middle of it all Mawnauoi came along, looking expectant.

Abel raised a tankard and held it towards him. 'Come, help yourself, my friend. There's plenty for all.'

Deliverance Daniels turned his back.

'Much laughter,' grinned Mawnauoi. 'Mawnauoi hear many paces. Come look, see.'

'You're more than welcome. And there's meat and cheese on the table.'

Deliverance Daniels waited until Mawnauoi had moved a short distance away then turned to confront Abel. 'Do you not know that the Lord has commanded us to remain separate from all that is unclean?'

'I see no harm in offering a little hospitality.'

'Witchcraft, man. The heathen practise witchcraft.'

Abel stifled a sigh. He had had this conversation many times.

'Haven't I told you a hundred times? I heard it with my own ears.'

'I agree that it's our duty to bring true worship to the Indians,' Abel said. 'But they're not easily convinced.'

'Then they must be shown.'

'You're not the first to try, Reverend Daniels. If you can find a way then I'll readily join you; but I'll have nothing to do with any action which causes disharmony between us and the Pennacook.'

'Brother, we have the might of God on our side.'

'That's as maybe. But I've no wish to endanger the friendship which has been built between us.'

Deliverance Daniels gave him a disdainful glance. 'You have much to learn, Brother, in the ways of the Lord.'

Abel made a slight movement of his head and looked at him sideways. 'That is why, Reverend Daniels, you have been sent here to teach us.'

Deliverance Daniels prickled visibly at the double-edged comment but chose to ignore it. 'I've wrestled long and hard with the nature of the task before me,' he said. 'The Lord has made clear his disapprobation of the vile practices which go on among these heathen. But it has yet to be revealed how I'm required to deal with them.'

'Whatever action you may decide to take,' Abel reiterated seriously, 'it's of paramount importance that we retain the friendship of these people. It was Gettonahenan, Mawnauoi's own father, who sold us this land. Our lives depend upon the continued goodwill and friendship between our peoples.'

'We must nurture the seeding of the true church.'

'True, but we must be grateful for the opportunity to live in peace and harmony.'

'We must also,' said Deliverance Daniels, 'be grateful for the opportunity to do God's Will.'

Margaret walked away from the main body of the assembled guests. She was not feeling well and wanted to be on her own. She walked past the animal pens and an area where young apple trees had been planted, and out towards a field of growing maize. In a quiet corner she squatted to relieve herself. There was an uncomfortable pressure on her bladder.

She was not used to seeing maize. Already it was shoulder high, showing bulges along its thick stems where cobs were forming, but she was yet to see the large golden heads of seed. The Pennacook had taught the settlers how to grow it, just as they had taught them how to grow pumpkins and squash, and how to bring seaweed from the coast as fertilizer. They had told them of the best areas in which to fish, and of new ways in which to hunt.

She liked the Pennacook. She had seen little of them, except from a distance, but she had watched their birchbark canoes upon the river manned by dark-skinned braves. They had no horses. She had watched the women passing by with papooses on their backs. She would have liked to have spoken with them but they could not understand her; and she knew that her husband was not in favour of associating with them.

On one occasion she had come upon their village set in a clearing near the river — a collection of dome-shaped wigwams made from overlapping strips of birchbark, standing amid fields of new-sown corn. People had been sitting eating near a fire. They had not seen her and she had not made herself known. She had stood for some time watching them.

Mawnauoi had come up behind her, quietly, and had startled her. He had laughed and invited her to join the women but she had refused and had hurried away. She had spoken to him on several occasions since. He was always smiling.

She found a tree stump and sat upon it. The pains in her abdomen were becoming more evident and she knew what it meant. She tried not to think of her mother and of the pains of childbirth, but she was afraid. She felt alone and wondered if she would die, as Susannah had almost done. She thought, at first, that it would not matter but her sense of survival was strong. She wondered if her mother was pregnant again, then remembered that her father had been away. She had never known a year in which her mother had not been pregnant. And what of Lucy?

There had been dancing at Lucy's wedding. There was no dancing here by the law of Massachusetts. But there was happiness of a different kind. There was the happiness of being among good friends who relied upon one another. And there was a freedom which she could not define. It was in the bearing of the women — a newly budded emancipation which she found intriguing and exciting. There were those women who stood beside their men in a way she had not known in England.

The pain came again, enough to make her fold her arms across her belly. She would be glad when it was over.

In the shadow of a large tree beside the house, Thomas Norton stood talking to Deliverance Daniels.

'God's blessing upon them,' said Thomas, nodding towards the newly wedded couple. 'It's good to see the seeding of a new family.'

'It's the Lord's command,' said Deliverance Daniels, 'to multiply and fill the earth.'

The whole world looked good to Thomas now that Susannah was alive and gaining strength. 'There's nothing on God's earth,' he said, 'like the love of a beautiful woman.'

'It's an onerous burden upon us all to keep them in the path of righteousness, Brother. Left to her own devices, she is easily lured.'

'Mary's a comely maid,' said Thomas. 'Young Luke's a lucky man.'

'You've a short memory, Brother. It's no time at all since she was leading him into abject sin.'

'It seemed a pity . . .' Thomas carefully measured his words. He had been among those who had disapproved of bringing charges against them. 'It seemed a pity to cause a cloud upon the marriage.'

'It wasn't we who caused the cloud, Brother, it was they.'

'But to wear the mark of fornication! It was very hard and shamed them deeply.'

'And what would you have had us do?'

'Abel would gladly have paid the usual ten pounds' fine.'

'And would that have been a punishment upon the pair?'

'The punishment was in public knowledge.'

'Would you have preferred to have them whipped?'

'No, of course not.'

'Then I would suggest, Brother, that you leave the matter of discipline to the magistrates who are required to deal with it. It wouldn't do for everyone to meddle in the affairs of justice.'

Thomas smiled inwardly at his ability to ruffle the other man. He did not like him but found him intriguing. He returned to the subject of women. 'I've always been most fortunate with the women in my life,' he said. 'Susannah, a host of sisters, sisters-in-law, and of course my dear mother. Mother was one of the most wonderful women I've ever known.'

There was something odd about the way in which Deliverance Daniels set his jaw.

231

'And what of you? Do you have sisters? A mother?'

The minister took time to reply, then said slowly: 'I knew little of her.'

'I'm sorry. A woman's love is worth more than pearls.'

'It's a culpable heart which is easily diverted to all that which is lewd and base.'

Thomas raised an eyebrow. 'I've not found it so.'

'I was well grounded in an understanding of such matters by my father. It's well that we remember always that they are the daughters of Eve.'

'Your father was not a lover of women.'

'My father was a lover of all mankind; but most of all he loved his God. My father was the greatest preacher I have ever known.' As he said it he held his palms pressed close together beneath his chin.

'Your father was a preacher.'

'And *what* a preacher! I've known crowds of two thousand gather just to hear him speak. There wasn't one verse in the Scriptures which he couldn't repeat from memory.'

'You, too, are well versed in the Scriptures.'

'He taught me well. And beat me when the Devil strove to steal away my concentration.'

'I don't care for beating.'

'It was done with kindness and a love of God. He taught me from an age when I was barely breeched to search my heart and seek out all that is vile and seeded from the Devil.'

'I don't care for beating,' said Thomas again.

'We must not flinch from what is required to cleanse our hearts.'

'I teach my own children with a gentler hand.'

'Then you'll be sorry, Brother, when you find that they fall prey to sloth and lack of zeal.'

'Maybe, but I'll keep my whip for use on horses.'

'The whip . . .' There was a strange look again on the face of Deliverance Daniels. 'The whip,' he said, 'can prove to be a most useful aid. It can be truly . . . beneficial.'

Margaret got up from her seat on the tree stump and went to find the midwife. 'Sister, I'm going home now. I'd be most grateful if you'd come by in an hour or so.'

'I'll come with you now.'

Esther Clark helped her home and put her to bed. The two women sat together for several hours. During the late evening, just after the betty lamp had been lit, Margaret gave birth to a healthy girl.

Deliverance Daniels did not look at the baby. From other people, Margaret heard accounts of his pride in 'his' new daughter. A special prayer of thanks was offered up in church on Sunday. To Margaret he said nothing.

It was not until a week later, when she was newly risen from her childbed, that he came into the room and said simply: 'The child will be called Jessica.'

She did not question it, nor did she invite him to look at the baby lying in her cradle.

She went to stir the fire beneath the cooking pot. On a table nearby was an open book and beside it, in his diary, he had been listing Greek and Hebrew names. She ran her eye down them until she came to one which had been underlined.

Jessica: 'Yah is Watching'.

CHAPTER 11
Spring 1648

Five years had passed, two of them in peace. Pitched battles, indecision, and turning tides had at last brought supremacy to the Parliamentarians – that final tide surging onwards following the formation of the New Model Army with its Lieutenant General of Horse, Oliver Cromwell.

But victory did not sit easily upon the victors. There was indecision in their midst. An army is reluctant to disband when there are arrears of pay, and Parliament soon found the New Model a formidable force.

And few knew what to do about the King. Their plans to set up a Commonwealth with him at its head did not succeed, not least because, though beaten, he was in no mood to co-operate.

Rupert rode into Dunscombe to speak with his father.

'We've need to raise funds and support.'

'Again? To what end?'

'To victory, of course. The King's far from defeated.'

Sir Henry heaved a tired sigh. 'Rupert, I can't understand your continued involvement in these matters. I had hoped . . .'

'These are trumped-up leaders sitting in Parliament. They're nothing but soldiers out for their own ends.'

'We all know that, Rupert, but it'll do no good to bring about a second civil war.'

'No one relishes war, Father . . .'

'I well remember,' said Sir Henry, 'how you once went to the Americas to get away from it.'

Rupert lowered his eyes.

'Yet when you returned, you re-entered the conflict with a fervour much greater than you'd ever shown before.'

'Yes, Father,' said Rupert quietly.

'Anyone would think you wanted to get yourself killed, the reckless way you plunged yourself back into the most foolhardy situations.'

'The Cause is just.'

'Why, Rupert? I could have arranged for you to be spared further fighting. I could have kept you usefully employed in the Americas.'

'Yes, Father.'

'I could have had your wife and child sent out to join you.'

Again Rupert lowered his eyes.

'But, no, you insisted on throwing yourself back into battle. It's a miracle you're still alive.'

'Yes,' he said, but it was almost with a hint of disappointment.

'And now, two years later, you come to me saying there's to be another civil war.'

'The King's not beaten, Father. There's still a chance of setting matters straight, if we can just raise sufficient men and funds.'

Sir Henry shook his head. 'Don't look to me. I'd rather use marl to fertilize my crops, not rotting corpses.'

'You speak like all the others. How's the King ever to regain his rightful authority if he doesn't have the support of his people?'

'He'll have little support for intrigue which will lead to a second civil war.'

'You're wrong there, Father. How many do you know who've had their lands and property sequestered? How are they ever to get them back unless we fight for what's right?'

'They were given opportunity to compound and have their lands returned.'

'Yes, but at enormous expense. They've got to pay vast fines — and all because they served a Cause which was just and right.'

'I pity those who lost their land, but I'm not about to join them by having my own sequestered.'

'You know we've no choice, Father. There'll be no justice until the King regains his rightful throne.'

Sir Henry heaved another sigh. 'Isn't it enough that your own uncle tends his business with the use of only one hand?'

'I'm sorry about Uncle Nehemiah. But that doesn't mean that we have to abandon our rights and kneel to the dogs who are seated in Parliament.'

'Then it must be done by compromise. This country has got to be brought back to true stability.'

'But Parliament's dominated by the army, Father. We can't have men like Cromwell, and Ireton, and Lilburne leading us. They're our enemies.'

'The war is over, Rupert.'

'No, it's not over. We're far from beaten. The King's only waiting for more men to join us before . . .'

'I'd have thought you had better things to do, now that you've affairs of your own to deal with.'

Rupert hesitated.

'You're a man of wealth now that Sir John is dead.'

'My own father-in-law slain by these people and you expect me to knuckle down and submit to them!'

'He died on the battlefield like hundreds of other good men. And there's no way that we're going to bring them back by shedding even more blood.' Sir Henry paused and looked at his son. 'Sir John left you onerous duties along with his fortune. It's up to you to see that his business interests are sustained.'

'They're well attended to. I've good men on my staff.'

'But you're not there. A business needs the master at the helm.'

'I'm well in touch with what's going on.'

Sir Henry sighed. 'And that fine house in Chiswick . . . you hardly venture near the place let alone your wife and children.'

'Isobel's well cared for and my affairs keep me on the move a great deal of the time.' It was Rupert's turn to sigh. 'But it grieves me that I see so little of my children.'

'Consumption's a dreadful torment,' commented Sir Henry. 'And it's worse still when children are afflicted.'

'Yes,' Rupert said with a sincere sense of sadness. 'Children born of a woman with consumption are often frail.'

'You must guard your son's health, Rupert.'

'He's a fine boy.' Rupert smiled at the thought of him. 'It saddens me greatly that he's ailing.'

'He's your heir. And, by that token, mine also.'

'And my little Lucinda. You know, last time I went to Chiswick she came toddling to me calling "Papa".'

' 'Tis a wonder she knows you at all,' said Sir Henry tartly. 'You see so little of her.'

The comment hurt Rupert. 'I've great love for my children,' he said. 'It saddens me that I so rarely see them.'

'If you were home more often, you'd have more by now.'

Rupert thought, as he often did, of another child in New England. He knew it to be a daughter; knew also that her name was Jessica. 'Life's a funny thing,' he said absently. 'We should be happy with our children.'

Sir Henry looked at him. 'You must guard your son's health. Consumption is a dreadful robber of human life.'

'I know.' The pain returned to Rupert's eyes. 'One feels so helpless in the face of sickness.'

His father placed a hand on his shoulder. 'I've lost too many of your own brothers and sisters.'

'I know, Father. It's an onerous duty being a parent.'

'You must attend to your business,' said Sir Henry. 'Make sure that you've something worthwhile to pass down to them.'

Rupert knew that he was a disappointment to his father. 'If we can just bring a rightful end to this conflict with Parliament, Father, I'll gladly spend more time in Chiswick and devote myself to the business.'

Sir Henry nodded.

'But in the meantime, I've more pressing matters than my own.'

'Oh?'

'I've fifty men camped in the wood.'

'You have what!'

'Fifty men camped in the wood.'

'You've so little thought for this house and for your family that you endanger your own mother by bringing men to camp in the wood? Don't you know there were soldiers passing through the village this very day?'

'Good God!'

'Have you gone mad?'

'I'm sorry, Father. I'd no idea. My intelligence was that they were miles away.'

'Then your intelligence was wrong.'

'I'm sorry, Father. I'll go at once. I'll have them away from here within the hour.'

'Why did you come?'

'To see you, Father. We're on our way to join up with the Scots. The King has struck a deal.'

'I see.'

'Each time I go off on matters such as these, I always wonder if I will ever . . . As I was passing so close, I came to see you.'

Sir Henry's face softened slightly. 'I wish to God that you'd distance yourself from this intrigue. I've no wish to lose another son.' He grasped Rupert by the shoulders and embraced him.

'I'm sorry, Father. When it's all over I'll endeavour to lead a more settled life.'

'Henry . . .?' Elizabeth appeared at the door. There was a tremor in her voice. 'There are soldiers at the gate.'

'What!'

Before there was time to react, she was brushed aside by a large man wearing a buff coat. He was accompanied by others. Rupert and Sir Henry exchanged anxious looks then stood and waited for the inevitable charge.

'Sir Henry Mainwaring, in the name of the army and of Parliament, you are charged with treason. You'll come with us now, and will accompany us back to London where you'll be duly tried.'

'Oh, God, Henry!' Elizabeth reached out for her husband but was restrained by the men who stood behind her.

'Rupert Mainwaring, you too are charged . . .'

She would remember always the sound of horses' hooves on the courtyard cobbles as they took away her husband and her only son.

That evening found them encamped at the roadside not far from Witney. Sir Henry sat hunched, in a daze, thinking inconsequentially of an unfinished business deal because he could not bring himself to think of his wife and family left abandoned, without support or protection.

'Father,' Rupert hissed at him twice before gaining his attention, 'don't do anything to draw attention but there are friends . . .'

'Where?'

'On the other side of those trees.' Rupert moved his eyes but not his head. 'Beyond the copse.'

'How do you know?'

'When you're trained in these things, there are ways of knowing.'

Sir Henry had seen no such indication.

'You see those horses, the two on the right?' Rupert again moved his eyes. 'Their ropes have been loosened.'

Sir Henry looked towards a row of horses tethered some thirty yards away.

'The ones on the far end.'

'Oh.'

'I'm going to make a run for it.'

Sir Henry looked around again. 'You can't,' he said. 'There are soldiers everywhere.'

'I've got to or I'm as good as dead. I haven't a hope if I'm brought to trial.'

Sir Henry nodded reluctantly. He knew it to be true.

'What of you, Father?'

'What about me?'

'You can either come with me, or you can stay.'

Sir Henry thought on it for only a moment. 'I've got to stay,' he said. 'I've done no wrong.'

'I agree. But I had to give you the choice.'

Sir Henry shrugged. 'I can't be found guilty of something I knew nothing about.'

'I'm sorry, Father.' Rupert put out a hand and clasped the other man's forearm. 'I'll never forgive myself for bringing this upon you.'

'You didn't know.'

'I truly didn't. I would never have come if I had.'

Rupert stared at the ground for a moment. 'I'll find some way, Father, of getting word in your defence. I'm not sure how, but I'll find some way of making it quite plain that you had no knowledge my troops were in the wood.'

Sir Henry sighed. 'I can only speak what's true, and trust

that someone has the decency to believe me. I've never taken part in intrigue.'

'I'll find some way of making the situation quite plain.'

'What of these friends?'

'They're over there.' He looked towards the copse. 'I'm waiting for the signal.'

'But you'll be killed.'

'I'll be killed if I stay. Or imprisoned, which is worse.'

'But you could . . .'

'I'm well known, Father. I don't stand a chance.'

Sir Henry nodded. Rupert's allegiance and intrigues were known to all. 'I don't know how you've managed to avoid having your own property sequestered.'

Rupert gave a wry smile. 'By playing all hands. It's not been easy.'

'You'll lose it now.'

'Yes,' he said quietly. 'I can only ask for your help in that.' He looked earnestly at his father. 'Father, take care of Isobel and the children.'

'I'll do my best.'

The two men clasped hands. 'I leave them in your care. They're bound to lose their home.'

'Take care, my son.'

At that moment confusion erupted around them. A large group of horsemen came thundering out of the copse, causing noise and distraction. Soldiers were running everywhere, dropping plates of food, reaching for their weapons.

Rupert began to run, legging it towards the row of horses. Sir Henry could only stand and watch.

Rupert had made it to the horse and was about to grab its mane and vault up on to its back when Sir Henry saw a soldier with his musket raised, about to fire.

'No!' He launched himself forward.

Another soldier, thinking that he, too, was about to escape, raised his own musket and aimed it at Sir Henry's back.

Sir Henry had taken only a few steps when he felt the impact, the thud of lead. It pushed him forward a further three paces before he stumbled to the ground, his face smashing into the hard uneven turf. There was blood coming up into his mouth. He could taste it.

He looked up long enough to see Rupert upon the horse racing for the trees. The shot had missed.

A few moments later, Sir Henry was dead.

Rupert was unaware of his father's fate. He galloped full pelt for the copse where he was given a fresh saddled horse on which he raced towards a safe haven in a nearby town. From there he set off again and spent the next eight weeks in running and hiding, until at last he made the shores of Holland.

Nehemiah was doing his best to be of assistance to Elizabeth but the activity all around them was distressing her greatly. Soldiers were looking into chests, turning their contents on to the floor. Others were tapping on the carved panelling of the walls, testing for hidden cavities.

'They're demanding the deeds of the house, Nehemiah. Is that what they're looking for?'

'I doubt it,' he said. 'They're probably busy on other matters.'

'I don't know where they are. I don't know anything about the affairs of the estate. How am I to know where the deeds are kept?'

'They'll come to light. I suspect they're searching for more than deeds.'

'But what? We can't have done anything to justify this sort of treatment. They're claiming that Henry was plotting treason. I just don't believe that he'd do such a thing.' She looked at Nehemiah, imploring him to make sense of the situation for her. She was eaten up with grief and confusion. 'Will you tell them, Nehemiah, please? Tell them that they've made some dreadful mistake. My husband would never be party to treason.'

Nehemiah could not divulge the thoughts which were passing through his head. He, too, doubted Sir Henry's part in the affair but he was more than willing to believe Rupert capable of anything.

'We must make some plans for your future,' he said gently.

'They can't take this house away from me, Nehemiah.

242

It's our home. It's always been our home. Even as children . . .'

'It's to be sequestered. We must make arrangements for you, and for the children.'

'I won't go. They can't make me.'

'They can,' he said.

Her defiance collapsed immediately. She had never been called upon to do anything which demanded initiative. Without Sir Henry's guidance, she was at a complete loss. 'Help me, Nehemiah, please.'

The door opened and a tall good-looking man came in. There was something vaguely familiar about him but Nehemiah gave it little thought. The man looked twice at Nehemiah, then back to Elizabeth.

'The deeds, Lady Mainwaring, I must have the deeds.' He said it firmly, but not unkindly.

'She doesn't know where they are,' said Nehemiah.

'Then who would?'

'I don't know,' she said, becoming distressed. 'I don't know anything about my husband's affairs. How am I to know about my husband's affairs?'

'I'm sorry, Lady Mainwaring. I know what this must mean to you. It's as distressing for me as it is for you, but I've got my duty to perform.'

'Duty!' She turned away from him. 'What duty is it that leaves my husband lying yonder?' She nodded forlornly towards the room where her husband's body lay waiting to be buried. 'What duty is it that kills an honourable man like my husband?'

'It wouldn't serve any purpose to set out the reasons,' he said. 'But it would have been better had he not attempted to escape. He would have been fairly tried in London and released if he were innocent.'

Elizabeth still did not look at him.

'And there were fifty men camped on the estate all ready to admit their part in the plot.'.

'Perhaps he didn't know,' put in Nehemiah.

The man looked at him closely, then studied him again. 'That would seem hard to believe. And Rupert Mainwaring's well known for his part in the King's intrigues.'

There seemed little that Nehemiah could say in the

circumstances. The man continued to look at him, scrutinizing him until Nehemiah became uncomfortable.

'Hawkins,' he exclaimed at last. 'I've got it now.'

'Sir?'

'Edgehill, man, or have you saved so many that you've forgotten?'

It was Nehemiah's turn to study him. There was definitely something familiar about him and the reminder of Edgehill brought it back. 'Captain Mosely, sir, it's good to see you again.'

'I wish it were in other circumstances, but I've never forgotten.'

'You're fully recovered, sir.' He recalled now the slight limp as the man had entered the room.

'I owe you my life, Hawkins. I'd have been dead for sure if you hadn't rescued me when I was trapped beneath that horse.'

'I only did my duty, sir.'

'Maybe, but you saved my life.'

Elizabeth had been looking from one to the other, feeling abandoned.

Nehemiah put out a hand and touched her lightly on the arm. 'Lady Mainwaring is the sister of my wife, sir. She speaks true when she says that Sir Henry was an honourable man. I don't believe him to be guilty of treason.'

'It's a pity, then, that he'll have no chance to prove it. I, too, spoke the truth when I said he would have been given a fair trial.'

'It's too late for everything,' said Elizabeth, beginning to weep. She could see no point in discussion of trials, fair or not. 'There was no need to take my husband. He'd done nothing wrong.'

Captain Mosely did not attempt to pursue the comment. 'If you'd care to go to your room,' he said, 'we'll get one of your women to assist you.'

'I don't want to go anywhere,' she said bitterly. 'Soon enough there'll be nowhere for me to go.'

Captain Mosely spoke even more gently. 'You realize, Lady Mainwaring, that Parliament doesn't hold a widow responsible for her husband's wrong-doing. You're entitled to one-fifth of the value of your husband's estate, but you'd need to go and plead your case to the County Committee.'

'How could I plead my case? I'm just a woman. I don't know how to plead my case.'

'I'm sure that Hawkins, here, would assist you.'

'You know full well that I'd never be capable of doing such things.'

Captain Mosely let the subject rest and turned instead to Nehemiah. 'Hawkins, I told you once that I'd repay your deed. I've long wrestled with my conscience because I wasn't able to keep that promise. Is there anything that I can do for you now?'

Nehemiah hesitated, knowing that he could not ask the impossible. 'If only, sir, it were possible to spare this lady. I'd do anything to plead the well-being of Sir Henry's household.'

'I've already said that she's entitled to a portion of the estate. She'll not be troubled more than I'm obliged to do.'

'But she's to lose her home, sir. It's been the family home for generations. If only there were some way, sir, to spare the house.'

'That's impossible, Hawkins. You know that I'm under orders, the same as any.'

'I know, sir, which is why I knew I couldn't ask.'

Captain Mosely stood and looked at him for a long time. There was a serious, troubled expression upon his face. Then he went over to the window where he turned and stared for a further time into the distance. Behind him Elizabeth and Nehemiah stood glancing at one another, not knowing what to do.

At last he turned. 'This is a mighty difficult task you set before me, Hawkins. But I gave my word, and I can't break it.'

'Sir . . .'

'I pledged my word to God, Hawkins, as well as to you. I pledged that I'd do whatever was asked of me. There's no way that I can leave the house in the keeping of Sir Henry's household . . .'

'No, sir, I know you can't.'

'But there may be some other way.'

'Sir?'

'You're a worthy Parliamentarian, Hawkins.'

'No more than any other, sir.'

'You fought well for the Cause.'

'I did very little, sir.' Nehemiah was torn between a natural playing down of his role and the need to capitalize upon it. 'But I did try to do what was required of me.'

'And I see you gave your hand.' Captain Mosely nodded towards the stump in Nehemiah's sleeve.

'At Roundway Down, sir, in 'forty-three.'

'Perhaps you should be rewarded for your bravery.'

'Rewarded, sir? I'm only asking for the one favour you offered me. I'm only asking for this lady to be allowed to live in peace.'

'I've already explained that I can't do that. But I'll try to have the estate passed over to you.'

'*Me*, sir?' Nehemiah could not believe his ears.

'I don't know yet how I'm going to achieve it.' Captain Mosely was looking seriously troubled. 'But somehow I've got to convince my superiors that it's the rightful action.'

Nehemiah was standing with his mouth open, unable to speak. 'I didn't mean . . .'

'I pledged to God that I'd repay the gift of my life with whatever favour you might ask. I'd have done anything which was within my power but this is stretching that power to its very limits.'

'I'm sorry, sir.'

Elizabeth was clutching hold of Nehemiah's arm, digging her fingernails into the cloth of his sleeve.

'I didn't mean to cause you anguish, sir.'

'It's not you, Hawkins. The Almighty has a way of exacting the full price. And I suppose it's little enough payment for the gift of my life.' He turned and walked towards the door. 'Leave it with me, and don't say a word to anyone. I'll see what I can do.'

He strode out of the room, leaving Nehemiah still gaping in astonishment.

Nehemiah never learned how Captain Mosely succeeded in carrying through the pledge. There were many in power who would have been glad to acquire the estate. Indeed, a large acreage of the land was quickly absorbed into that of adjoining landowners: but, in due course, the deeds of the house, and a few surrounding acres, were transferred into the name of Hawkins.

Elizabeth was grateful beyond words, knowing that she and her children had been rescued from certain disaster: but Nehemiah was left with a problem. He was left not only astonished but with a feeling of total inadequacy. He had no idea how to run the property. On the spur of the moment when he had requested that the house be saved, he had given no thought to its future management. Now, he found himself responsible for it and totally out of his depth.

'You must farm the land, Father,' said Tobias. 'And produce wool.' They were standing just inside the heavy carved door of Oakbourne House, the staircase behind them, the garden and farmland stretching out before them. 'You know how many times you've complained of the price of wool. You can produce your own.'

Nehemiah looked out towards the acres which were now his. 'I don't know anything about farming,' he said. 'Or about sheep.'

'You've got men to help you. Good men. Sir Henry's workers were the very best. They'll be grateful beyond words that you've saved Oakbourne from the hands of a less worthy master. They'll be only too glad to instruct you.'

The thought of the estate workers laid an even greater burden of responsibility upon Nehemiah. 'All those families dependent on me. How on earth do I support us and the households of these men?'

'You'll have to learn the skills, Father, and quickly. Most of them have gone with the adjoining land but there are a few good ones left.'

'I don't think I can.'

'Of course you can, Father. I know you can.'

'Could I?' It was the first time Nehemiah had realized the need for support and guidance from his son. Tobias had matured into an upright, capable man. Nehemiah was newly aware of the person he had become. 'I'm a master weaver; there's no way I can run the business and take care of this place at the same time.'

'I'll run the business,' said Tobias.

'You?'

247

'I ran it while you were away. There's no difference now, when you're close by.'

'Yes, but . . .' It was one thing to leave Tobias temporarily in charge, another to hand over completely. 'You'd never manage alone.'

'I wouldn't be alone. I'd have you to come to whenever I needed advice. I managed before, when things were at their lowest ebb. Surely I can manage now, when you're here and we've got a good team.'

Nehemiah realized that his dilemma was within himself. He clapped Tobias on the shoulder. 'You're a worthy son. I don't doubt your ability, merely my own.'

'It would work, Father. I know it would.'

Nehemiah looked about him, at the large hall with doors leading off into spacious rooms. His own house had become cramped now that Tobias had a family. Lucy had given birth to a son in the autumn of '44 and, despite two further miscarriages, they now had two boys and a daughter. Anne, too, despite her fears that her childbearing days had ended, had given birth to another son. William was three years old.

'I'd be more at home at the loom than aping the work of a gentleman.'

'You've got no choice, Father. This place has been thrust upon you. Somehow you've got to manage it. You can leave the business with me and concentrate on learning the skills of running the estate.'

'I don't know where to start.'

'I've told you, the men will help you.'

Nehemiah was still looking about him, bemused.

'And don't tell me you wouldn't like to live here in this house. Mother would love it.'

'Yes,' said Nehemiah, 'she's always missed it. Since the day I took her away.'

'Then bring her back. She'll help and support you. And Aunt Elizabeth needs you. She'll never manage alone.'

'Yes, I suppose you're right. And you could do with the space.'

'I didn't mean . . .'

'I know,' said Nehemiah. 'You weren't intending to throw me out of my own home. But there's no doubt that you could use the space.'

248

Tobias was deeply embarrassed.

'Next year there'll be another child, and doubtless more to come.'

'We'd been thinking about finding a cottage of our own.'

'You won't need to now. You can have the house.'

Tobias had turned scarlet. He stumbled on his words. 'I'd take good care of it for you, Father. I'd work well.'

'I know you would, my son. And with God's help you'll succeed.'

In an atmosphere of closeness and enhanced mutual affection, Nehemiah put an arm about his son's shoulders and, for a few moments, they embraced.

'I must get back to work,' said Tobias at last. 'There's cloth to be finished ready for tomorrow.'

Nehemiah came out of his own thoughts and prepared to go with him.

'You stay here, Father, I can manage alone. I'll leave you to get used to the place.' Tobias cast a glance up the wide oak staircase which stood behind them. 'You'll cut a fine figure at the head of those stairs.'

Nehemiah grinned back uncertainly.

He waited until Tobias had left then walked round the house, opening doors to rooms he had never before entered, touching objects with a combined sense of reverence and awe.

Elizabeth came out of her bedroom and held out a hand to him. 'I'm grateful to you, Nehemiah.'

'If Sir Henry . . .'

'Nothing will bring my husband back,' she said sadly. 'But at least you've saved Oakbourne.'

'I only hope that I can hold it together.'

'You'll succeed,' she said. 'The men are behind you. They'll work hard to your bidding.'

'I hope you don't mind,' he said, 'but I've made plans. I'm . . . I'm intending to move in.'

'Of course. You're master now.'

'But if you think . . .'

'You're the master,' she said. 'It's God's Will that you should run the estate.'

'I'll do my best.'

She turned away from him and hesitated. 'Do you wish me to go?'

'Go?'

'Do you want me to leave?' She was looking frightened but endeavouring to cover it up.'

'No, of course not.'

'But if you wish . . .'

'This is your home,' he said. 'It will always be your home.'

She was immensely relieved. 'I thank you, Nehemiah. I don't know where I would have gone.'

'It's your home,' he said. 'For as long as you wish to remain here.'

'I thank you, and I am most grateful to you.'

'Anne will be glad to return,' he said, trying to lighten the conversation.

'Yes,' said Elizabeth. 'She has always loved this house.'

He stood for a moment, not sure what to say next.

'Of course,' she said, 'when Rupert returns . . .'

Nehemiah felt acutely uncomfortable. 'You realize the situation concerning Rupert?'

'Yes.'

'That he's fleeing for his life? That he'll be forced into exile?'

'Yes,' she said. 'They've got a lot to answer for.'

Nehemiah was uncertain how to respond.

'But when he comes home . . .' she said.

'It may be a long time.'

'Oh, I'm sure it won't. They'll find out they're wrong. Then he can come home.'

Nehemiah lowered his eyes and looked away. He would face the situation of Rupert's return when the time came. At this moment he had no wish to over-emphasize to Elizabeth that the deeds of Oakbourne House had been transferred into the name of Hawkins.

Jessica was almost five years old. She was a robust child, with the golden skin and dark chestnut hair of her mother, and with grey eyes which could have been traced to Rupert. But she was also a secretive child. When she smiled, the large grey eyes did not reveal that part of her which had to be concealed. She was a very young child to hold such secrets.

For the past four years the women of the community had commiserated with Margaret for her apparent inability to conceive again. 'You must drink mares' milk each morning.' Or 'Raise the foot of your bed a little higher than the head.' Margaret smiled and said nothing. The marriage had never been consummated.

Each morning Margaret sat with her daughter and taught her to read. Each evening Deliverance Daniels sat with her and taught her to search her mind.

'What thoughts have passed through your head this day?'

She was well used to the question. 'I've been good, Papa.'

'But what of your bad thoughts? You must tell me now in order that you may repent to God.'

'I pinched the puppy-dog when it stole my oatcake.'

'And why did you have oatcake?'

'Because I was hungry, Papa.'

'But it wasn't dinner time.'

'No, Papa, but I was hungry . . .'

'We must guard at all times, Jessica, against the sin of gluttony. The Lord gives us food with which to serve Him. We eat it three times a day to give us strength; but we do not fall prey to gluttony.'

He picked up a pen and wrote on the open page before her: 'I must guard always against the sin of gluttony.'

'Soon you'll be old enough to write the words yourself,' he said, and placed the pen in her hand so that she could make a mark upon the page.

He had never found the need to beat her. She was totally compliant and did not resist his ministrations. He had thought about it on occasions and had wondered if he were failing in his duty, but when she turned her large grey eyes on him he found that they had an effect upon him which he had not expected. He put off thoughts of physical chastisement and resorted instead to quoting from the Scriptures.

'Go, fetch me the bag lying in the corner.' He had brought her a gift: a newly cured rabbit skin given to him by Ezra Bracegirdle. He would have Thomas Norton make it into a pair of slippers.

She went to the corner. There were two bags lying there. She chose the wrong one. She was just about to withdraw

251

the long black nun's habit when he realized what had happened and stopped her.

'No,' he said sharply. 'Not that one.' He began stuffing the habit back into the bag.

He was deeply embarrassed. Jessica stood looking at him, sensing, but not understanding, his confusion.

'The other one,' he said, swallowing hard. 'I intended you to bring the other one.'

Deliverance Daniels rarely touched the habit, except at moments when there was an aching urgency in his loins. Even then, he viewed it in different ways at different stages. When it came out of the bag, it heightened the urgency to an intensity which demanded to be satisfied, with the aid of the whip. When it went back into the bag, he was beset with a sense of deep self-loathing and disgust.

He never viewed it for what it was – the garment which had been worn by his mother.

When she had left the home of his father so many years ago she had returned to the religion of her upbringing and had worn the habit behind high stone walls where she was forever unreachable. Had he tried, he could have remembered the day on which she had walked away. He had been in an adjoining room, watching, listening, cowering beneath the angry accusations which his father had been hurling upon her.

But he had chosen not to remember. He had clung, instead, to a blank cold emptiness which was almost memory, but not quite.

When Margaret wore the garment, it was different again. She was not Margaret. She had no part in this base confusion of his carnal drive. It was the garment which was significant – and the whip: fused and confusing, combining a father whose love was real, urging him onwards towards salvation, and a woman with tender kisses who had fed him sweetmeats.

But he did not remember the woman.

'I meant the other one,' he said again, stuffing the last of the black fabric into the bag.

It had been just before he set out on the journey to New England that he had received the bundle of assorted items. Someone had sent them to him – the remains of his mother.

He had thrown most of them away but had kept the habit, he did not know why. Its effect upon him had been as immediate as it had been alarming. Now he threw the bag with undue force into the corner of the room.

Jessica hung back. She was used to sidestepping his outbursts of anger but this time she knew that he was not angry with her. She had initiated it by selecting the wrong bag, but he was not angry with her. She kept quiet and waited.

He took several deep breaths through his nose, with his eyes tight closed; then he walked out of the room. She had not been given the gift which he had brought for her. She knew better than to ask for it, or even to wonder what it was.

She was used to being confused by him. There was a bond which held the two of them together: it could not be severed, could not be shared with anyone − not even her mother. They had a secret which was known to no one, except to God: she was something called a 'bastard'.

Four new families had joined the community. Their numbers counterbalanced the children who had been taken in an epidemic of scarlet fever, and two women who had died in childbirth. Another two had been widowed. Within days of arriving, John Smith had lost both legs in an accident whilst felling a tree.

In April, Richard Fullwood rode in. A quiet-spoken young man, he had come to farm.

He took over a sizeable strip of land further upriver and immediately set about the process of building a house and clearing the vegetation from areas which were to become his fields. The craftsmen of the community each played their part but it was Richard who rolled up his sleeves each morning at daybreak and prepared to hack his way through dense scrub and knee-high vegetation.

Margaret saw him at work on a number of occasions when she went upriver. It was an area rich in wild fruits and herbs, and she was used to walking there with Jessica. She became accustomed to stopping and passing the time of day with him, admiring the hard work and effort he was putting into the venture. Several times he stopped, glad of the chance to lean on his mattock, sweating from the effort of grubbing out the stubborn roots of a tree or hacking at knee-high thistles or dock.

As time went by, their neighbourly pleasantries turned into more lengthy conversation. Some chance comment would arouse interest, lead to questions, give rise to others, until soon they found themselves in animated discussion.

The friendship developed in such a relaxed, unselfconscious manner that neither gave any thought to the impropriety of the situation. They were rarely seen by others and, when in company, instinctively withdrew, retaining a polite distance, observing without question the restrictions of the society which bound them. Yet, alone, they increasingly dropped the barriers and discovered a growing number of reasons to find themselves in the same place at the same time.

He explained to her the problems and the pleasures of farming, told her of the crops he would grow, the animals he intended to breed. She spoke to him of weaving, of the Cotswold hills, of home; asked questions concerning the flatter land of his native Suffolk.

She liked the way in which he listened to her when she spoke, prepared to accept the opinions of a woman and to stimulate her curiosity. There was a quiet easy informality about their relationship for which she knew of no other words but 'family feeling'. And they laughed. It was good to laugh.

She listened to him, too, when he spoke in the Meeting House. It was not that he spoke often, or forcibly, but when he did offer an opinion, it was always expressed with tolerance and with a gentle strength. He reminded her of Tobias or Samuel but, even more, of her father.

Once he had touched her, quite accidentally, a mere brush of hands. She was surprised at the warmth of his skin.

Jessica was always with them. At any time she could have reported the meetings to Deliverance Daniels. But Jessica knew instinctively which subjects would arouse his disapproval, and she did not mention it.

They were walking one day along the edge of a newly ploughed field, a small oasis amid the rank vegetation.

'Why did you come to Ufferton?' Margaret was searching for barberry root to dye some cloth, while he had a bag of seed slung over his shoulder, broadcasting it across the soil as they worked parallel to one another.

'To farm, of course.'

'But you could have farmed in Suffolk.'

'There were older brothers to inherit my father's land. And I'd got no wish to become a physician or a lawyer.'

'But you do have some knowledge of doctoring?'

'A little, but my heart wasn't in it. It's here, in the land.' He made an expansive gesture with his hands. 'Just look at this place. And I wanted the adventure of New England. A man can carve out his own destiny here. No barriers; no waiting for something he knows he can never acquire. If he puts in enough toil, there's no end to what he can achieve. It's just one vast expanse of untilled soil.'

'I'm still not convinced we should take it from the Indians.'

He looked at her. 'We haven't taken it. We've bought it.'

'But they don't seem to understand. They don't realize that land goes hand in hand with wealth and status.'

'They don't have the same values. They see things differently.'

'Just because they're different, it doesn't mean they're any less worthy.'

'I didn't say it did.'

She looked up at him and posed the question again. 'Is it right to take their land?'

'We've only bought that which they've willingly sold. And we've brought them trade.'

'I still say they're unaware of its value.'

'Their values are different,' he repeated. 'But I do accept that we mustn't take unfair advantage of those differences.'

They were nearing the corner of the field. 'Your house is almost ready,' she said, looking up. 'Brother Nathaniel's almost finished the roof.'

'Next week, perhaps I may move in. I've been camping out like a vagabond.'

'You should find yourself a good woman to look after you.'

He smiled at that. 'I shall manage quite well with the help of Sister Ruth. She's glad of the opportunity since Edward died.'

'There are fathers in the community with other ideas.'

'There are always fathers with other ideas.'

She had found some barberry root and began scrabbling in the soil. 'But you've never chosen to marry?'

He laughed. 'So far I've managed to avoid it.'

He stood and waited for her while she gathered the root and put it into a bag.

'It must be difficult for a man to make a choice,' she said. 'Especially when there are a number of daughters available.'

'It must be worse for a maid. She's got no choice at all.'

She shrugged. 'Oh, I don't know. It's just the way of things.'

'Perhaps if I'd been offered someone like you . . .'

It was the first time he had ever made her feel uncomfortable. She blushed, then regretted it. She covered her embarrassment by retracing her steps to retrieve Jessica who had stopped to crouch at the side of the field, sifting through a pile of loose stones which had been cleared from the soil. Margaret lifted her to her feet and brushed the dirt from her hands.

When she returned to Richard, he changed the subject. 'It'll take me years to get this farm the way I want it,' he said. 'I've got these two fields planted and another ready for the plough, but it'll take me a lifetime to get it right.'

'What do you intend to do next?'

He nodded to an area of woodland a short distance away. 'Next year I'll clear the trees over there, but those roots go deep. And I've got an idea how we could dam the stream. I must discuss it with the Brothers.'

She laughed at him as he became carried away by enthusiasm.

'You can laugh,' he said, 'but some day you'll be standing here on the finest farm in the whole of New England.'

'Don't you ever miss home?'

'Sometimes. How about you?'

'Yes,' she said. 'I miss it a lot.'

He smiled at her then stretched his arm towards the horizon. 'But just look at this place,' he said. 'Such scope, so much reward, so much freedom.'

She nodded. 'I must be getting back to the cottage. It must be almost eleven.' She glanced up at the sun which was approaching its highest point. 'My husband will be home soon for his dinner.'

'He's divided the community.'

'What?' She looked at him sharply in response to such outspoken comment.

'There are many here who don't share his views.'

'He's a godly man,' she said. 'He understands the Scriptures.'

'But not the Pennacook.'

She was not sure how to respond. 'He's concerned about their witchcraft,' she said. 'The Scriptures say that it's abhorrent to the Lord.'

'And what do you think?'

'It's not for me to think. My husband knows better than I do what's abhorrent to the Lord.'

He smiled. 'You're concerned about their welfare, yet you've no views of your own?'

He had embarrassed her again.

'You've such strong opinions, then you've none.'

She tried to analyse her thoughts in order to form some kind of reply. He was aware of her dilemma and took steps to release her. 'You're a strange mixture,' he said. 'You must forgive me: I'm not used to speaking with women such as you.'

She was still trying to come to grips with her own response to his comment, but he said, 'Shall I see you again tomorrow?'

'I don't know. My husband may have need of me.'

'Yes, of course.' He let it ride a moment then said, 'I saw some good turkey eggs over in the scrub this morning.'

'Oh,' she replied. 'Well, perhaps then. If I can get away.'

He smiled and raised his hand in a gesture of farewell as she turned and began to walk back to the cottage. 'I'll keep watch for you, just in case. I'll be working over there.'

'Yes,' she called back. 'I'll look out for you.'

She took Jessica's hand and together they ran back along the course of the river. The sun was glinting on the water and there was a feeling of warmth and well-being about her. She had been happier, more contented, in these past few weeks than at any time since she had left Dunscombe.

* * *

Deliverance Daniels was far from content. He was deeply troubled by his inability to make any impression upon the idolatrous behaviour of the Natives, and less than satisfied with the attitude of the settlers towards his efforts.

The Pennacook were not interested in his expositions on Biblical condemnation of their ways. Those who could hold quite adequate conversations with the settlers quite suddenly developed an irritating inability to understand the language whenever he appeared. It infuriated him when they smiled good-naturedly at all he said, then showed more interest in the binding and the decoration upon his Bible than in the authority of its content.

He had counted upon the support and co-operation of the settlers but had soon learned that, while they talked of a need to bring the Church to the heathen, they showed far more concern for the need to conserve peace and friendship at all costs.

He had never forgotten the fear of demonism which had rooted him to his bed on the night of his near-drowning. He had preached sermon after sermon on the subject, which had served only to split the community into factions. Some had called for firm action, praying daily for guidance from the Lord. Others had called for tolerance. Most had referred to the vulnerability of the settlers. They were out-numbered, and none relished the possibility of angering the surrounding tribe.

The Pennacook had grown aware of the divided feeling towards them, becoming suspicious and mistrustful.

Argument had raged but nothing had been decided. Action had been demanded but nothing had been done. Now, five years later, Deliverance Daniels continued to campaign for righteous vengeance. Some ignored him; others did nothing. Most chose to close their minds, only to experience guilt because of their lack of courage in supporting him.

Deliverance Daniels scoured his own conscience, searching inwardly for the sin which denied him God's guidance. It was yet another example of his own base unworthiness which caused the Lord to chastise him by withholding the means of serving Him.

He made one more effort when he met Mawnauoi on his way home for dinner.

'Mawnauoi, I must speak with you concerning the Lord.'

'You want fish?' Mawnauoi held out a large salmon which he had caught that morning.

'It's of the utmost importance that you tell your people.'

'Mighty big fish. Give much fight.'

'He's a most merciful God,' persisted the minister. 'But we are beholden to serve Him.'

Mawnauoi swung the salmon back and forth on a short loop of sinew threaded through its gill. 'How much you trade?'

Deliverance Daniels had met this type of resistance many times before. 'I've no wish to trade. I've need to speak with you, and you're well aware of the fact.'

'What you want speak? Mawnauoi speak plenty. Learn much good. You wanna speak hunting? You come, Mawnauoi show place for big fish.' He spread his arms shoulder width. 'Plenty big fish.'

He waited for Deliverance Daniels' response. When there was none, he said, 'You wanna trade hat?' He pointed to the high copotain hat. 'Mawnauoi like plenty hat. Mawnauoi trade big fish. You trade Yinglee hat. Give fish.'

'English,' snapped Deliverance Daniels. 'Not Yinglee.'

Mawnauoi reached out to touch the hat.

Deliverance Daniels drew back. 'I have no wish to trade and you are not so dull-witted that you don't know that perfectly well.'

Mawnauoi's face clouded.

'Now be quiet and listen to me. The Lord has need to teach your people of truth and righteousness.'

'Who you call stupid?'

'He has sent me to this land and it's my duty to preach His Word.'

'Who you call stupid?' the Native asked again.

'Oh, for goodness' sake, man! Will you just be quiet and listen?'

'No be quiet. Mawnauoi not stupid. Yinglee man stupid. Mawnauoi catch big fish. You catch big fish? Tch!' He spat derisively and held his hands to measure a distance of some six inches. 'Yinglee man, little fish. Mawnauoi make long journey; know many places. You know many places? Tch!

Yinglee lost over little hill. Need Mawnauoi guide. Yinglee know nothing without Mawnauoi.'

'We are not Yinglee. We are English.'

'Yinglee man know nothing without Mawnauoi.'

Deliverance Daniels felt compelled to raise his voice. 'The Lord God has made it clear: "I will make My Holy name known in the midst of the people; and the heathen shall know that I am the Lord, the Holy One of Israel." '

'You want fish or not?'

'No! I do not want fish.'

Mawnauoi shrugged. 'Mawnauoi go now.' He swung the huge salmon in an arc before him, bringing it to rest across his left shoulder. In doing so, it hit Deliverance Daniels a sickening blow in his solar plexus, making him gasp.

It appeared to have been an accident and yet, there was a look on Mawnauoi's face which infuriated Deliverance Daniels. He stood gasping, holding his hands across his stomach.

'Mighty big fish,' apologized Mawnauoi. 'Need much room.'

'Mawnauoi . . .'

But already the Native was walking away, the large salmon swinging across his shoulder.

Deliverance Daniels went home feeling angry and frustrated. As soon as he reached the cottage he took some water and washed himself thoroughly. It was not just the smell of the fish; it was something he always did when he had been in contact with the Natives.

The next day was hot. Margaret scratched in the dry soil beneath the bushes until she unearthed some more barberry root, then searched for turkey eggs. But it was too hot to work. Jessica had found an area of shade in a secluded hollow and was already seated there, her bare toes trailing in the water of a stream. Margaret went and sat beside her.

Almost immediately they were joined by Richard who had seen her stop work. 'May I sit down?'

She indicated a patch of turf beside her and he sat down, arching his back to relieve the strain of guiding the plough.

Neither of them spoke. Both rested, glad of the cool shade, gazing at the water. A little later Margaret looked across at Jessica who had fallen asleep, her plump little body slumped sideways against a tussock of grass, her forearm across her eyes to protect them from the sun.

They exchanged smiles at the endearing sight of her, and Margaret lay back, feeling the cool grasses upon her neck. There was a hum of insects and the sound of water but, beyond that, there was silence, save for the intermittent calls of birds from the woodland. She closed her eyes and drifted in contentment.

Richard reached out a finger and touched the back of her hand. It was a pleasant sensation. She did not move. He ran it back and forth, gradually lengthening the motion until he was stroking her arm; then he rolled over so that he was looking down at her. She opened her eyes and smiled, knowing that he was about to kiss her, yet giving no thought to resistance.

It was the sweetest, most tender emotion she had ever experienced. She opened her lips for more, slowly turning her face to invite the soft light kisses across her cheekbone and down the side of her jaw. She arched her neck, baring her throat to receive the caress of his lips above the line of her collar.

His hand was upon her waist, gently squeezing through the layers of cloth. She sighed with the pleasure of it and reached out her own hand, cupping it round the back of his neck with her fingers in his hair — such soft hair, with loose waves and curls. She found herself entwining it within her fingers, taking handfuls and massaging his scalp.

Her body was moving rhythmically of its own volition, without instruction from her — a pleasant, flowing sensation which brought soft unbidden sounds to her lips, bitten off between her teeth. She reached out to kiss his face as he brought it close — kissing, caressing, her whole being caught up in one overwhelming feeling of pleasure and anticipation.

When he reached his hand beneath the layers of her clothing she cried out aloud so that Jessica stirred in her sleep, turning over and gently murmuring as she settled back into slumber.

He kissed her again. She moved to accommodate him, co-operating with his movements, eager yet tender, urgent and yet with all the time in the world to bask in the pleasure

261

of this new sensation which felt as though she had been familiar with it always.

When the moment of climax came he called out her name, softly and with a tenderness which brought the surging intensity of her own response to fill her with the quivering, gasping pleasure of fulfilment.

She lay happy and speechless, not wanting to move, contented in a way she had never dreamed possible. She lay and thought of that look between Luke and Mary, of the unspoken bond between her mother and father. She knew now what it had meant.

'I shouldn't have done that.'

She turned to him and smiled.

'Can you ever forgive me?'

'Forgive?' For a moment the question seemed incongruous.

'It was wrong of me,' he said. 'I got carried away.'

'It seemed so right.'

'Yes, I know. But I shouldn't have done it.'

'I think I love you,' she said, and brought his face down to kiss him again.

'And I love you,' he breathed. 'But I had no right.'

She knew it to be true. They had just committed one of the gravest sins it was possible to commit. Yet, for the life of her, she could not feel remorse. 'It was as if it was always meant to be.'

'Yes,' he breathed. 'Oh, yes.' He buried his face deep within the crook of her neck and kissed her. 'May God forgive me, my dearest girl, but I love you.'

CHAPTER 12

Margaret was happy. She met with Richard and they made love at every possible opportunity. She had never been so happy. Her whole existence had taken on new meaning. Each morning she awoke with an invigorating feeling of new purpose.

They took risks — hasty, impetuous risks — and got away with them. More than once she slipped away in the evening while her husband was at prayer, meeting Richard in the cool darkness of the woodland beyond the garden, then slipped back, just as quietly, to be sitting demurely, if a little pink-cheeked, at her needlework when her husband returned to the parlour.

The moments together were snatched and savoured, relived during the times when they were apart. They did not speak of the future, of tomorrow, only of the present delirious moments when they were happy and together.

Within weeks she knew that she was pregnant. She knew that soon enough it must come to light. Some day she would be forced to face reality. But not yet.

There could be no future. From the inevitable moment when their love became known they would be condemned and punished by the entire community. There would be no one who would condone the relationship. Long after the marks of the whip had faded from their flesh, the lash of public awareness would inflict far deeper scars upon them.

Summer ripened into harvest time and still their secret remained undiscovered. Richard had harvested three fields of corn, there was hay in a newly erected barn. In October the community celebrated Harvest Home.

After church on Sunday a table was laid on which were served a goose and two turkeys, fattened on the stubble fields where they had competed with the gleaners. Housewives had baked pies. There were venison and fresh cranberries gathered from the damp bogland at the bend of the river.

Richard walked up casually beside Margaret and entwined his fingers within her own under cover of the tablecloth. 'I'll go for a stroll down to the large oak in a moment or two. I'll wait there in case you can get away.'

She looked about her. Jessica was playing happily with Susannah's children; her husband was engaged in conversation outside the church door. 'I've got duties here beside the table for a while but I'll come as soon as I can.'

He gave her fingers a squeeze, helped himself to a piece of apple tart, and moved away as casually as he had arrived.

It was half an hour before she could join him. He was sitting waiting in a quiet glade where they had met many times before.

She kissed the top of his head as she sat down beside him. Immediately he enfolded her in his arms, kissing her hairline, her eyes, and finally her lips. 'I thought you weren't going to make it.'

'I got away as soon as I could.'

'I know, and you'll soon be missed.'

She touched his eyelids with the tip of her nose. 'I've got a few minutes.' Then she gave out a little moan, burying her face in his neck as he caressed her hair and ran his hand down the length of her spine.

He continued to move his hand round to her stomach and back up towards her breasts. He stopped at waist level and returned to her abdomen, running it back and forth across the area which was becoming slightly distended.

'You're with child?'

She nodded.

He said nothing for a while; then, quietly, almost as if to himself, 'And it could so easily be mine.'

'It is yours.' A feeling of quiet gentle warmth seeped through her. She had never spoken to him of her relationship with her husband. It would not have been right. She did not tell him now but took his face and held it before her. 'I know it's yours.'

His eyes held such an intensity of love that it brought a taut sensation to her loins but, as she held his face, she watched the expression change – a succession of emotions mirrored in rapid succession across his eyes, until eventually he tore himself away from her and stood up.

'What's the matter?'

He went and stood facing a tree, his forehead pressed against the bark. She did not understand the sudden change and went to stand beside him.

'Richard?'

She placed a hand on his back but he did not respond.

'What's the matter?' she asked again.

'Don't you see?'

'What have I done?'

'Oh, not you, my love. It's me.' He turned back to her. 'Don't you see? It's what I've done to you.'

'You've done nothing but love me.'

He shook his head. 'I've been utterly, completely, selfish.'

'No.'

'In the name of love I've thought only of myself.'

'You've given me everything.'

'I've given you nothing.' He beat his fist against the tree. 'God, how could I have been so selfish!'

'You're the most unselfish person I've ever met.'

'If I were unselfish,' he said, 'I wouldn't have loved you. I wouldn't have touched you.' There were tears in his eyes which she wiped away with the tip of a finger. 'I would never have let you know how I felt about you.'

'But I loved you too.'

'I would never have placed you in such danger.'

'I'll take more care. We'll only meet when we can be certain that we'll not be seen.'

'There's always danger. You know as well as I do that it's only a matter of time before we're seen or someone realizes how we feel about one another.'

'I'll only come in the night, when my husband's asleep.'

'No, that's not enough.'

'Then what?'

'We shall have to stop meeting.'

She let out a small cry.

'And I shall have to watch you, knowing that I can't have you. Every day, knowing that I can't hold you; knowing that I can't touch you; knowing that I'll never be able to hold you, ever again.'

'No,' she cried. 'I can't bear it.'

'But we must.'

She was sobbing. 'Don't talk like that. I'd die if you stopped loving me.'

'God, how am I ever going to find the strength to keep us apart.'

'No,' she cried. 'No, I won't let you.'

'We must,' he said. He took hold of her and held her by the shoulders. 'Before it's too late. Before we're seen and the wrath of the whole community is brought down on our heads.'

'I can't do it, Richard. Please don't make me.'

He dropped his arms against his sides and went again to beat his fist against the tree. 'Oh, Margaret, it's so unfair. I've watched that man. I've watched him with you. He's never so much as touched your arm. He could never love you the way I do.'

'He's . . .'

'Though, God, if he did . . .' He smashed his fist hard against the tree. 'I swear I'd near die of jealousy.'

'He's a good husband,' she said. 'He's provided for my needs.'

'What needs? He couldn't possibly know what makes you happy and alive. Not like I do.'

'Nobody's ever treated me the way you do.'

'He could never love you. Not really love you.'

'It's a different kind of love.'

'That's not love.'

'Richard?'

'I can't bear to think of it,' he said. 'Not you, with him.'

'You know I'd rather be with you.'

'But you're not. And never will be. And I shall have to watch you with him, knowing that the child you're carrying could so easily be mine.'

'It is yours. I know it's yours.'

He bit his lip.

'Take my word for it, the child is yours.'

He stared at her intently for a while, then walked off a distance and stood in thought. 'Look,' he said, as he came back, 'I'm going to take you away.'

'What?'

'I'm going to take you away.'

'I can't. My husband—'

'To hell with your husband.'

'Richard!' She was shocked.

'Far away, where no one will know.'

'It's not possible,' she said. 'I've taken my vows. I can't break them.'

He looked at her. 'You've broken them already. With me.'

Guilt rose in her throat. 'It doesn't seem like that to me.'

'I know, but in the eyes of the rest of the community we've committed the gravest sin. We've no choice but to go away.'

'Where could we go?'

'To Plymouth or one of the other townships.'

'And within months someone from Ufferton will go there to trade. We'll be seen and our shame will be magnified.'

'Then far away. Virginia. Somewhere where no one will be able to find us.'

'And how would we find our way? We could never make such a journey alone.'

'Mawnauoi will guide us. We could even take ship over to Barbados.'

'And my husband would force him to disclose our whereabouts. He'd have us brought back and we'd be punished.'

Richard stopped at the thought of punishment. 'Yes,' he said. 'He'd demand the maximum penalty.'

She nodded. 'He's often spoken of adultery as a capital crime.'

'He'd demand our lives.'

'Yes,' she said softly. 'And he'd see that sentence was carried through.'

Richard drew breath sharply, his shoulders drooping. He turned again and walked away from her.

She followed and tried to hold him, trying to turn him back towards her, but he refused.

'I've got no choice,' he said at last, his back still towards her. 'I must be the one to go.'

'Dearheart . . .'

'If it were just me,' he said quietly, 'I'd take the chance. But it's not. We'd both suffer. I can't take that risk. If I take you with me, he'll seek us out. And I can't stay here, knowing that one false move, one unguarded word or action will bring down condemnation upon your head. I'd never forgive myself for bringing destruction on you.'

'No.'

'I must go away.'

'No, Richard.' She clawed at his back. 'We'll both stay here. We'll be careful. We won't even look at one another when there are people around.'

'I'll have to make arrangements,' he went on. 'I'll sell the farm.'

'Not the farm!'

'To hell with it.'

'But it means so much to you.'

'It means nothing, if I can't have you.'

She was crying. He turned to face her, holding her at arm's length. Tears were streaming down his cheeks. 'Go back to the celebration,' he said, 'before you're missed. Tomorrow, I'll start making arrangements to leave.'

'Don't, please.'

'And you must take care not to let your feelings show. Try not to be sad when I'm gone.'

'How could I help it?'

'Then try not to show it. Your safety depends on hiding it from everyone.'

'I can't do it. I know I can't.'

'You must.' He turned her and gave her a gentle push. 'Go now,' he said. 'Before someone realizes you're missing and comes looking for you.'

'I can't do it, Richard. Please don't make me.'

'Now. And don't come looking for me again. I'll try not to let our paths cross while I'm making arrangements to leave.' He gave her a more forcible thrust away from him.

'Richard . . .'

'And, please,' he said, causing her to stop, 'don't look at me when I eventually ride away. If I saw you looking at me . . . if you looked at me . . . I don't think I could go through with it.'

She gulped, unable to speak; but he had turned away from her again and was standing staring at the tree.

She stumbled back towards the sound of raised voices and of laughter. Discretion made her pause and compose herself before she faced them, but she was deathly pale and trembling.

Later that night her husband went to the corner of their room for the bag and the whip. Without comment she put on the habit and, as he knelt beside the bed, cracked the whip across his back.

He looked up in astonishment. She had never hit him so hard. He gave her a searching stare but she seemed lost in a world of her own. She brought the whip down again.

He took several more blows until, eventually, he was forced to cringe before the onslaught and crawl on hands and knees across the floor to remove the whip from her hand. He was angry and also perplexed. Her fingers were clenched white about the handle of the whip and she was crying.

'You may go to bed now,' he said unsteadily. 'And remove that . . . thing.'

She said nothing but took off the habit and stood clad in her undergarments. The light was behind her. She realized that he was looking at her, his eyes fixed upon her abdomen, and a feeling of stone-cold defiance rose within her. She turned slightly and stood deliberately silhouetted against the lamp.

'You . . .!' Colour was staining his cheeks.

She said nothing but continued to stand, defiantly staring back at him.

'Jezebel! Mother of all harlots!' The sinews of his neck were taut. 'May the dogs eat the flesh from your bones. May you be as dung upon the face of the field.'

There was no feeling in her — only stone-cold numbness. 'Who is this man?'

She flinched, believing he was about to hit her, but the abuse was verbal.

'I'll have you brought to your knees before the Lord.'

Still she said nothing.

'Who is this man?'

'I'll not tell you.'

'Then I shall have every man in this community questioned until the truth is revealed. And you shall be made to pay for your defiance.'

Slowly, she lifted her head and swallowed. She ran the tip of her tongue nervously across her upper lip. 'If you take any action at all, I shall tell the whole community why the child can't be yours.'

She waited, expecting an even greater onslaught of anger: but it did not come. Instead he sank to his knees as though all the lifeforce had been drained from him. He collapsed on the floor, slumped with his head in his hands.

'Husband?' A strange ambivalence drove her to reach out a hand.

He ignored her.

'Are you ill?'

He continued to ignore her but raised his face to the ceiling and, with tears trickling down his cheeks, began: 'Oh Lord, what must I do?' His voice was filled with pathetic pleading. 'Why dost Thou withhold Thy love from me? Why must Thou heap Thy vengeance upon me?'

'Husband?'

She stood for a long time waiting for him to turn on her with the anger which she felt certain must come. Yet he appeared totally to have dismissed her: it was as though she did not exist. He was completely submerged within his own misery.

At last she drew backwards, one step at a time, no longer daring to draw attention to herself. She kept her eyes fixed upon him and, step by step, made her way out of the room and down the stairs.

Once there, the full impact of her action began to hit her. She knelt before the fire trying to absorb some of its warmth but could not control the shivering which had taken hold of her. She piled on more fuel and crouched with her arms clasped around her knees, her head slumped forward upon her chest. She waited for him to come down and to confront her, but he did not do so.

She remained there all night, waking with a start in the

early hours of the morning to find that the fire had burned low. She added a few small pieces of wood, raking the ashes quietly, fearing that he would hear her.

She did not know what to do. There was nowhere for her to go. It was dark outside. No one in the community would take her in — no one but Richard; and even he might be angry for her foolhardiness. She could not go upstairs where her husband lay. There was nothing for her to do but to remain crouched before the fire, dreading the coming of morning.

That same night, Deliverance Daniels had a vision. He saw first the full ferocity of the destruction of Sodom and Gomorrah — fire and brimstone and the mighty vengeance of the Lord. He felt the heat of burning, smelled the scorching of flesh; closed his ears to the screams of the people, for there was nowhere for them to hide. The mountains broke open with His fury and the rivers spewed forth fire.

Then, suddenly, all was calm. The scene had changed to one of green fields. He was David, the young shepherd boy, with a sling in his hand. The air was very calm and still. He could hear the song of birds. Then a voice rang out across the heavens saying: 'Go, slay Mine enemies with thy sling; for thou art chosen, and by thy hand shall this land be brought to destruction, that the people may know that I am God.'

Then it was gone and he awoke. He looked around the darkened room, taking time to reorientate himself to the dim shapes and smells of the New England cottage. He knew now what he must do. He understood the purpose of the deprivations which God had imposed upon him. He had been tested — just as Job had been tested by the withdrawal of His presence — and he had won through: he had been chosen.

He fell to his knees and thanked the Lord for His bounteous kindness.

Margaret watched the coming of dawn and waited for her husband's tread upon the stairs. But he did not come down. Instead, he remained upon his knees, oblivious to the growing pain in his joints or the need to eat.

Jessica stumbled to the parlour, still sleep-filled,

demanding her breakfast. Margaret fed her, insisting with unusual severity that she eat quietly then play outside.

At dinnertime she prepared food but left it in the cooking pot when her husband did not appear. By mid-afternoon she could bear it no longer. She took Jessica by the hand and went to Richard, not bothering to conceal her destination from the people whom she passed. She found him in the barn.

He listened as she told him what had happened, holding her in an attempt to stop her trembling.

'I can't leave now,' he said when she had completed her account. 'It's too late to protect you by leaving.'

It was in one way an enormous relief. She closed her eyes and pressed herself against him. 'I just couldn't bear to think of you leaving.'

'I'll need to be there to stand by you when the accusations are made.'

Jessica gazed at them both. She was puzzled and disturbed by her mother's distress, anxious and yet not understanding. It was obvious that some calamity was about to descend upon them all. She wondered if, in some mysterious way, she had been the cause of it.

She had never seen them openly embrace. She had seen them often enough when they had thought themselves unobserved, but never like this. They took no notice of her now, ignoring her as she stood, her head buzzing with unasked questions, needing comfort yet wary of approaching them.

She tugged at her mother's skirt but Margaret did not look down. She tried several times but Margaret was caught up in her own emotions, ignoring the appeal. In the end she turned and walked away, crouching in a corner of the barn amongst the hens, watching every movement which her mother made.

'We must be brave,' Richard said. 'One of the first things he'll do is to post the notice of our trial.'

She clung to him. 'Our friends will shun us.'

'They'll more than shun us. We'll be lower than the filth on the ground.'

'It doesn't seem fair. It doesn't seem to me, in my deepest heart, that I've done anything wrong.'

'I know, my sweet; that's because we love. But in the eyes of the others it's a dreadful sin.'

She looked up at him. 'I don't regret it,' she said. 'Not one moment of it.'

He smiled at her. 'Nor I. But I shall never forgive myself for what I've brought upon you.'

In the corner of the barn Jessica continued to sit. She did not take her eyes from her mother's face.

'Why did you tell him?'

'I don't know. I couldn't stand it,' she said. 'I just had to tell him.'

'But I was about to protect you by leaving.'

'I would still have been with child.'

'He wouldn't have known. He'd have accepted it as his own.'

'He'd have known,' she said. 'You can take my word for it.'

Richard's mind raced again through the five years of Margaret's childlessness. He wondered if Deliverance Daniels were impotent. Margaret's loyalty would not allow her to tell him and he knew it.

'You're quite sure it's mine?'

'I know it is.'

He wanted desperately to ask but knew that she would not tell him.

Jessica shifted her position but kept her eyes upon her mother.

'I must go to him,' said Richard. 'I shall have to confront him.'

'No. He doesn't know it's you.'

'Then I must tell him.'

'No, please don't. It'll be soon enough when I'm brought to trial.'

'I can't do that. And by that time every man in Ufferton will be under suspicion. It'll cause disharmony throughout the entire community.'

'Then not until tomorrow. Not until after the notice is posted. Leave it a few more hours before we both have to face his wrath.'

'I can't possibly leave you to face it alone.'

'Please,' she begged. 'Just until tomorrow.'

He was reluctant.

'Please,' she said. 'Do this one thing for me.'

'Well, only until tomorrow. But the moment that the notice is posted on the church door, I must make myself known.'

She kissed him softly on the cheek. 'Thank you,' she said. 'Now I must be getting back. He'll be looking for me.'

He held on to her, fearing to let her go.

'Please,' she said. 'It'll be worse if I'm not there.'

'Then let me come with you.'

'No. I'll call you if I'm in trouble.'

'Take care, and come running if you need me.'

She nodded and kissed him again, gently pulling away from his hold. 'I love you,' she whispered. 'Nothing can change that.'

'I love you too. But take care, my love.'

Margaret looked around for the first time for Jessica. 'Oh, there you are.' She picked her up and gave her a hug. But the child held herself stiffly and did not respond.

Deliverance Daniels had not been aware of their absence. He was still on his knees. As Margaret let herself into the cottage she stopped and listened but all was silent. She crept halfway up the stairs where she could see him through the partly open doorway. She re-heated the cooking pot in case he should ask for food, but still he did not come down.

As dusk fell, she curled up with Jessica before the parlour fire and prepared to spend a second night upon the floor.

Just before midnight Deliverance Daniels walked through the parlour and out of the door. Margaret heard him and, while remaining perfectly still, opened her eyes. In the light from the fire she could see him quite clearly. In particular, she noticed his eyes: there was a blank, fixed expression in them as though he was in some kind of trance.

Over the past five years Deliverance Daniels had ridden past the Pennacook village on many occasions. This time he went on foot. In other circumstances he would have had difficulty finding his way through the forest at night but, in his present state of heightened consciousness, it seemed that he remembered every blade of grass, every twist and turn of the path, every boulder over which he must pick up his feet.

A strong wind buffeted him in areas of exposed ground, tugging at the cloak slung carelessly across his shoulders. A pale moon glided in and out of the clouds, causing shadows.

There were few Natives in the village that night: most were away on a hunting trip. Only the old and the children remained along with three women who were menstruating and thus confined to a wigwam on the edge of the clearing. There was no sound or movement except for that caused by the wind. The embers of a small cooking fire glowed intermittently a short distance from the women's wigwam.

Deliverance Daniels strode into the clearing. He had been gathering dry brush as he went, holding it as a bundle in his hands. When he saw the cooking fire he realized that he need not even pause to create a spark. He plunged the dry brush into the embers, waiting only until the fire took hold before hurling it against the side of the women's wigwam.

The rapid ferocity of the ensuing blaze took him by surprise. The dry overlapping strips of birchbark went up like a torch. The strong wind sent sparks and flames whipping and whirling into the dark night sky. The shock of it sent him several paces backwards.

A woman emerged, screaming and ablaze. He retreated further, back into the cover of the trees. He had fired only one wigwam: his mission had been to raze them all. He had failed.

Old men ran from their beds. Under cover of the trees, he stood watching as though he had no part in it. They rolled the woman in the dust, beating the flames with their hands. The remaining two women were dragged from the fast-collapsing structure, but they were already dead.

The screams were hideous. When those of the woman died away, they were taken up by the old men who sent a wailing into the night sky which caused Deliverance Daniels' blood to run cold.

He should have marched out among them and fired the remainder of the village, but he did not. The momentum had gone from him: the screams had been too real. He slunk back into deeper cover, fearful that the wailing men would sense his presence and turn their anguish upon him.

The fear was sufficient to keep him silent until he had put a good distance between himself and the village. Then he stumbled and finally ran, falling and picking himself up, falling again and tearing his way through the undergrowth as he made his way back towards Ufferton.

At the cottage he flung himself inside the door, leaving it wide ajar, stumbling to the corner of the parlour where he curled himself into a foetal ball upon the floor.

The noise awoke Margaret with a start. She watched as he stumbled across the floor; continued to watch as he lay in the corner. She dared not move. Jessica stirred. Her mother pressed a hand upon her back, urging her back into sleep.

She lay still for a long time, afraid to draw attention to herself, but at last she rose silently and crept in a wide arc around him. In the half-light of approaching dawn he lay tight-curled, whimpering like some hunted animal.

She put out a hand, cautiously, then withdrew it, afraid that he might turn on her. She went back to the fire, closing the door as she passed, and crouched down, keeping silent but not taking her eyes from the dark shivering shape in the corner.

Deliverance Daniels lay in a wretched world of his own. To only part succeed was to fail again. There was to be no reward − only the anguish of the chosen: the anguish of David who had slain ten thousand; of Moses chosen to slaughter the entire nation of the Midianites; the suffering of Abraham called upon to sacrifice his son.

When it came time for people to be up and about, Margaret went to summon help. Inclination urged her towards Richard, discretion directed her towards Abel Finch. Abel accompanied her back to the cottage and stood for some time looking down at Deliverance Daniels huddled in the corner. He was a steadfast, practical man but did not understand madness and feared it more.

'Reverend Daniels,' he said at last, 'what ails you?'

Deliverance Daniels stopped snivelling, responding to his name.

'Speak to me, man. What ails you?'

He looked up, staring through barely focused eyes.

'Are you taken sick? Or are you injured in some way?'

He continued to stare.

'You're soaking wet, man. Where have you been in the dead of night?'

Deliverance Daniels put a hand to his clothing, patting it as though surprised to find himself wet.

'Where have you been?'

'On the work of the Lord.' He responded like a questioned child.

'In the dead of night?'

'It was as I was told to do.'

'By whom? Is someone sick? I didn't know of it.'

Deliverance Daniels looked up towards the heavens. 'And by thy hand shall this land be brought to destruction.'

Abel Finch was becoming increasingly alarmed.

'And thou shall declare His glory among the heathen.'

'Heathen?'

'And His marvellous works . . .'

'What heathen?'

'That they shall know that I am God.'

'What heathen?' Abel went down on one knee, grabbing a handful of clothing. 'Listen to me, man.' He half-lifted Deliverance Daniels from the floor. 'Where have you been?'

'It's as I told you.'

'You've told me nothing. Where have you been?' Abel was shaking him now.

'Why are you angry with me, when I've done nothing but serve the Lord?'

'Where have you been?'

'And they shall be brought to destruction with fire and brimstone.'

'May the Lord have mercy upon us.' Abel let go of the clothing, allowing the minister to fall back upon the floor. He got up off his knee.

Margaret had been standing behind him, confused and frightened.

'I must go at once and see if I can undo the damage which has been done.'

'I don't understand,' she said. 'I don't understand what my husband has done.'

'Nor do I, but I've got the gravest suspicions.' He made

for the door. 'Help me summon the Brothers. Tell them to bring their weapons. We must prepare for attack.'

Margaret, confused, went with him into the street. Soon people were running everywhere, summoning neighbours from cottages and from their fields.

'Get everyone inside the church,' Abel instructed. 'Prepare to defend yourselves.'

'What's happened?'

'I don't know, but I'm going to the Pennacook village to see if I can speak with the Natives.'

'That would be madness.'

'Maybe, but someone must tell those people that we had no part in whatever happened last night.' He climbed up on to his horse and rode out before anyone could think clearly enough to stop him.

Abel knew he was riding into probable danger but the lives of everyone in the community depended upon him. Over the years he had had a good deal of contact with the Pennacook, aiming to forge a friendship and an understanding which would enable the two cultures to co-exist. He had sat many hours discussing their mutual welfare and had traded with them over beaver skins which were used, in turn, to trade with the ships which made port at Boston.

He had learned from the *sachem* and from the old men of the tribe who had shared the wisdom and knowledge passed down over generations. It was true that his conscience pricked concerning the matter of their idolatry, but it was counterbalanced by his gratitude to a people who had allowed the white man into their territory and allowed him to live in peace and harmony.

He reached the vicinity of the village unchallenged. He had seen no one. There were moments when his skin had tightened, sensing that he was being watched, but it was his imagination. The Natives had not yet returned from their hunting trip. Only the old and the children were there.

He rode into the clearing, highly aware of his vulnerability, but again unchallenged. He saw at once the evidence of the fire. The centre of the conflagration was now a heap of ashes but a large area of surrounding grass had been burned and several bushes and trees had been scorched.

Sasketupe was sitting beside his wigwam. An old man

278

now, Abel had known him since he first came to New England.

'Hail, friend.' He waited for some kind of adverse response but there was none. Sasketupe looked old and sad. By a gesture, Abel asked permission and, when given it, lowered himself down beside him.

'There's sorrow in your village.'

'Fire. Three squaws.' He looked up at Abel with sad eyes. 'Niccone, daughter of Sasketupe.'

'Oh, Sasketupe, I'm so sorry.'

'With squaw of Ketottug; and Seaseap, sister of Pausochu and squaw of Bequoquowes.'

In a closely related community Abel knew that many would be mourning the loss. 'I'm so sorry,' he said again.

'Gods protect. Only women. Chiefs and braves not danger. Men go hunting.'

Abel looked around him, saying nothing for a while. Then, striving to keep his voice level, he asked: 'What caused it? The fire, what was the cause of it?'

'Cooking fire,' said Sasketupe. 'Spark. Big wind.' He made an explosion with his hands. 'Pow!'

'Oh.' It was a feeling of anticlimax. Abel felt clammy and cold. He offered up a silent prayer to his own God, not knowing whether it was in thanks for being spared, or whether for forgiveness for having wrongly accused a Brother.

'There's some way in which our community can be of help to you?'

'No, not for white man: this for our people.' Sasketupe turned and looked at him. 'Friend go now. Sasketupe old man.'

'Yes.' Abel rose from his seat beside him. He had never seen Sasketupe look so old. He knew Niccone to have been a favourite daughter.

The two men touched one another and made a gesture of peace; then Sasketupe returned to staring at the ground beside his feet.

Abel re-mounted his horse and rode away. Once out of the clearing, the full shock of the encounter hit him. The relief was enormous but the confusion even greater. He was angry, yet uncertain. The Pennacook believed the incident to have been caused by a spark from the cooking fire, yet he knew he was right. Deliverance Daniels had placed the entire community in jeopardy.

When he reached the settlement he paused only long enough to cancel the alert before making straight for the cottage.

Deliverance Daniels was sitting dejectedly before the parlour fire. Margaret had not been able to get him to the church but had sent Jessica there with Susannah. She had persuaded him to cross the room and sit in front of the fire. She had heated some broth but he had refused to eat it.

Abel Finch burst into the room without waiting for an invitation. He strode across the floor. Others had followed him from the church and a crowd gathered at the door, straining to hear some word of explanation.

'The fire,' demanded Abel. 'Did you cause that fire?'

Deliverance Daniels looked up at him. 'The Lord commanded it.'

'Blasphemy!' retorted Abel. 'The Lord does not command murder.'

'I'm but a weak man. The Lord commanded and I did not succeed.'

'What made you do it?'

'It was all that I could manage.'

'You stinking Bedlamite! Don't you realize you risked the lives of every man, woman and child in this community?'

'It was the Will of the Lord.'

'Will of the Lord,' said Abel derisively. 'More like the Will of the Devil.'

There was an intake of breath from those standing at the door.

'I tell you this,' said Abel, announcing himself to Deliverance Daniels and to the people, 'within the hour there'll be a hearing before the magistrates. You'll be judged and tried before your Brethren for what you've done this day.' He turned on his heel and strode out of the door.

The crowd parted to let him through. Several craned their necks, staring at the Reverend Daniels seated before the fire, then a hubbub broke out. Everyone started to talk at once.

Margaret watched them disperse. 'What fire?' she asked herself, but dared not ask her husband.

Richard was among the last to go. She saw him on the edge of the crowd and made towards him but he made a small quick gesture with his hand which held her back. There was a need for discretion.

Within the hour Margaret found herself seated in the church beside Susannah. In front of her, before three magistrates, her husband stood where she and Richard had been expecting to stand. Susannah reached out and squeezed her hand but Margaret was in a daze. Far away on the opposite side of the church she could see Richard, his head turned away from her: he seemed remote. On their way into church she had tried to catch his eye but he had looked away and she had felt hurt. In some strange way she felt abandoned.

'What have you to say for your conduct?' Abel Finch was seated between William Green and Caleb Clark.

'Only that I have failed.' Deliverance Daniels stood with slumped shoulders, his voice a passive monotone.

'In what manner?'

' "By thy hand shall this land be brought to destruction that the people may know that I am God." '

There was an intake of breath among those listening — some awed, most dismayed.

'Are you seriously saying that the Lord commanded you to destroy the Pennacook village?'

The people were uneasy, finding themselves on uncomfortable ground.

'I tell you only what you ask. The Lord commanded: and I have failed.'

'The man's crazed in the brain,' whispered Caleb Clark; but William Green looked decidedly uneasy.

'May we venture to ask,' said Abel Finch, 'if you will try again?'

'I'm but a poor servant and despised of the Lord.'

'Will you try again?' persisted Abel.

'I'll pray for courage; and for strength.'

A murmur went round.

Abel conferred with the two men beside him. 'The man's a positive danger,' he said. 'We've a situation which calls for firm action to safeguard the community.'

'But if the Reverend Daniels is chosen,' said William Green, 'then we must listen.'

'The man's not chosen: he's suffering madness.'

'How can we know? The Lord works in mysterious ways. Who are we to question His servant?'

'We question a man,' said Caleb, 'who has misused his authority as minister of this church to threaten the safety of the entire community.'

'I agree,' said Abel. 'It's a matter of time before he brings about a bloody conflict.'

'But if he's chosen . . .'

'We can't place our women and children at risk,' said Caleb. 'If the Pennacook got wind of his intention we'd never sleep safe in our beds. And I'd rather be tending my fields than manning a cannon.'

'May God have mercy,' said Abel. 'Our lives would be shattered.'

'May God have mercy if we condemn His chosen servant. The Reverend Daniels has been warning us for five years about the sorcery of the heathen.'

' 'Tis an abomination on the face of the earth,' began Deliverance Daniels, who had overheard the comment. 'The Lord will cleanse the filth and stench from this place so that all shall know that He is God.'

Abel Finch turned to the people. 'Is there anyone here who wishes to speak on behalf of the accused?'

'He's a man of God,' said Ezra Bracegirdle, rising and speaking quietly. 'And I don't want to be associated with condemning a man of God.'

'This is the man,' shouted Nathaniel Smith, rising from his seat on the opposite side of the church, 'who had me whipped for celebrating the birth of my son.'

'Aye, and rightly so. Drunkenness is abhorrent to the Lord. The Reverend Daniels has stood steadfast in his condemnation of sin.'

'And he's taught us many things of His bounteous goodness,' said someone else.

'How about condemnation of his own sin?' called someone from the back.

There was some laughter which was rapidly quelled.

'He came here to teach us concerning the laws of God.'

'Aye, and he's taught us to argue amongst ourselves. And now to fear for our lives.'

'Perhaps we should pray,' suggested another voice. 'The Lord will guide us.'

'And who will lead us?' asked someone else. 'We were a year without a preacher before the Reverend Daniels arrived.'

A young girl had been whispering to her mother near the back of the church. The woman, pale and shaken, turned and whispered to her husband. He, in his turn, got up and walked to the front where he spoke quietly into the ear of Abel Finch.

All comment stopped: it was obvious that something new and of import had been introduced. Abel raised his hand, though it was unnecessary: there was complete silence. Everyone waited while he conferred with the other two.

At last he turned to Deliverance Daniels. 'It would seem that you are further accused of an act of depravity.'

A loud gasp resounded round the church. Then there was a moment of total silence, followed by babble. Abel Finch held up his hand.

Deliverance Daniels looked as though he might be sick.

'What say you to this charge? You are accused of placing your hands upon a young maiden of this community in a manner which is lewd and depraved.'

The girl was hurriedly removed from the building by her mother. The babble had not died down. Abel raised his hand again but to no avail. For a full two minutes he allowed the hearing to lapse while the people talked amongst themselves.

Deliverance Daniels was seen to be praying. He was in tears.

'What say you to this charge?' asked Abel Finch again.

In the meantime two other women had whispered to their husbands, unburdening themselves of incidents which they had kept hidden. The men went forward to confer with the magistrates.

There was a further recess before Abel Finch announced, 'We have three such charges that you used your position as minister of this church to gain the confidence of these women, then did act in a manner both lewd and depraved. Are there any more gathered here who wish to speak?'

Everyone looked at everyone else.

'I meant them no harm,' said Deliverance Daniels brokenly. 'It was each on only one occasion; and I did nothing but touch them lightly upon their person.'

The babble broke out again. Abel Finch had difficulty in keeping order.

'You admit the charge?'

'I meant them no harm.' He was weeping so that it was difficult to hear him. 'The Devil is a formidable adversary. And I'm but a weak and wretched creature.'

Margaret half rose. She felt that she should go to him. Susannah held her back, placing her arms about her in a gesture of comfort and compassion. Margaret turned towards Richard but he was not looking at her. He showed no emotion, except that he had grown pale.

'This is a serious matter,' said Abel Finch. 'It calls for the most serious deliberation.'

They were all required to sit for a further time while the magistrates conferred. It was obvious that they were divided two-to-one. The women continued to look at one another, wondering if any more held secrets they were not prepared to divulge. Others looked towards Margaret — some with pity, others with curiosity.

Jessica sat wide-eyed, not understanding. Her sympathy lay with the man who was crying.

The magistrates got up and removed themselves from the congregation. The were seen to kneel and pray.

At last they returned. 'The sentence,' said Abel, 'has not been reached without a great deal of heart-searching and prayer.' He turned to Deliverance Daniels. 'Reverend Daniels, you are a disgrace and an insult to this church. Your behaviour is a profanity in the name of God, and you are a danger, not only to this community, but to the entire land. You are banished from this settlement. Our doors are closed against you.'

He waited for the reaction from the people, then went on: 'Not only this, but we shall make it our duty to notify all other townships of your actions. I've no doubt that they'll be as unwelcoming of your presence as we are here in Ufferton. Thus you will be banished into the wilderness where you can do least harm.'

He looked towards the congregation and went on by way of explanation: 'This land is vast, and by God's good grace we've been allowed to live in peace and prosperity. We owe it to our Brothers in other parts to live in equal peace. For each is affected by the fortunes of the other. You've all heard of the slaughter which can arise from conflict with the Indians; and conflict in Plymouth or Providence will soon mean conflict in Boston or Salem. We've a duty to our Brothers, and to ourselves, to protect them from this man.'

'Amen.'

Ezra Bracegirdle stood up. 'Brothers, this is our minister – a man of God.'

'You've heard the evidence.'

'It's our duty to follow him and listen to his guidance, even though the way may be difficult to understand.'

'Brother Ezra,' said Abel gravely, 'you're at liberty to follow your conscience. But, if you do, you must follow him into the wilderness.'

'Then I and my family will go with him.'

There was an audible gasp of dismay from Martha Bracegirdle. Everyone turned to look at her.

'Do you know what you're saying?'

'I only know that I must trust in God, and in His servant.'

Another babble had broken out.

'So be it,' said Abel. 'We shan't stand in your way.'

Martha Bracegirdle was in obvious distress. Several women of the congregation went to assist her.

Abel Finch turned to Margaret. 'Sister Margaret,' he said, 'you're a respected member of this community. I personally wish it to be known that, if you decide to remain here amongst us, we shall offer succour and support to yourself and your child.'

'I must go with my husband.'

Susannah grabbed hold of her. 'No. You've been given the opportunity to stay.'

Margaret smiled thinly and gently pulled herself free. 'I've no choice,' she said. 'It's my duty.'

Abel Finch waited for the hubbub to die down again then said, 'Is there anyone else who chooses to follow the Reverend Daniels into the wilderness?'

Susannah was whispering urgently into Margaret's ear;

285

but Margaret ignored her. She was in state of shock but she was bound by her vows to follow her husband.

There was a long pause while everyone looked at everyone else. William Green was seen to have his eyes closed, his face turned towards the floor. He was in obvious discomfort.

'I go,' said Richard. He stood up as all eyes turned towards him. Another gasp went round the church.

Abel Finch did not disguise his surprise. 'You've never before shown any great respect for the views of the Reverend Daniels.'

Margaret wanted to cry out; but Richard did not so much as glance in her direction.

'It's a matter between myself and my conscience,' he said. 'I don't agree with all the views of the Reverend Daniels but he is our minister. Brother Ezra's right when he says that it's our duty to give him our strength and support.'

Abel Finch looked at him for some time as though about to challenge his motives. Then he said, 'I'll not deny that I'm surprised. I wouldn't have expected it.'

'Our Brothers gained foothold in this land in order to establish freedom of conscience,' said Richard. 'That's why many of you are seated here today.'

'Aye,' said Abel. 'I'll grant it's not for me to question your conscience.'

Someone else spoke up. 'We came here to follow the true religion not a madman who preys on women.'

It brought other comments in its wake.

'He should be hanged before he does more harm.'

'It amounts to the same thing once he's banished into the wilderness.'

'But what if he kills more Indians? It's we who'll suffer. It's this settlement they'll come to when they seek vengeance.'

'The Pennacook will be told,' said Abel Finch, 'that he has no part in this community. They in turn will be asked to inform the Wampanoag, the Massachuseuk and the Nipmuck. For the sake of those accompanying him we shan't mention the cause of the fire, but we'll tell them that he's been punished for breaking our laws. They'll understand that.'

'For the love of God, let's hang him before he does more harm.'

'If he harms the Indians,' said Abel, 'then he must face their wrath. We shall make it clear to them that he's been banished from our midst. He has no part in our society and is as dead to our eyes.'

He stopped and looked first at Deliverance Daniels, then at Richard and Ezra Bracegirdle. 'Brothers, I can only beg of you for your own sake, and for the sake of the women, keep close watch on him at all times. The lives of each one of you will depend upon it.'

CHAPTER 13

That evening Margaret sat with Richard in the cottage, awaiting the arrival of Ezra and Martha Bracegirdle. Deliverance Daniels was upstairs upon his knees. He took no part in their discussions of that evening, nor on any subsequent occasion: he appeared to be trapped in some dimension of his own.

'We've two choices,' said Richard. They sat on stools before the fire, their hands touching. 'We can strike inland, or we can work our way round to the coast and find passage on a ship.'

The thought of Dunscombe was suddenly overwhelming. 'I want to go home,' said Margaret.

'Of course, my love. But if you go home, you realize that I can't go with you.'

'Why not?'

'The reason's obvious. Your family couldn't accept our love, any more than the people of Ufferton.'

It was true. However they might disguise the reason for Richard's presence, it would take no time for her father to see through to the true relationship.

She felt him squeeze her hand and returned the pressure. 'I'll go with you,' she said. 'Wherever you choose.'

He leaned over and kissed her on the cheek.

'At least we shall be free to love,' she said.

'Not free,' he replied quietly. 'Ezra and Sister Martha won't accept it either. Whatever we decide to do this evening, one thing's for sure: we're going to need complete unity. Our lives will depend on it. If we do anything which causes disharmony, it will bring about the downfall of us all. It's going to be difficult enough to survive as it is.'

Distress registered upon her face.

'Have patience, my love. Give it time. Eventually we'll find the place and the opportunity. Until then we must be discreet.' He glanced up at the ceiling. 'At least your husband allows us freedom to sit here like this. I haven't heard a sound from him since I arrived.'

'He frightens me, he's behaving so strangely. He doesn't seem to understand what's going on or to care. He just stays on his knees, and stares.'

'We must watch him constantly once we're in unknown territory. Never let him out of our sight.'

They heard Ezra and Martha outside the door. 'Come in,' Margaret called. As she said it, Richard moved so that he was standing on the far side of the hearth. Margaret remained seated but took her needlework in her hand.

'Is the Reverend Daniels joining us?' asked Ezra.

'He's upstairs at prayer.'

'Then how are we going to decide what we must do?'

'I think, Brother,' said Richard, 'we must make decisions for ourselves at this stage. The Reverend Daniels doesn't seem able to take part.'

'I suppose you're right,' said Ezra dubiously. 'If the Lord has need to guide us, the Reverend Daniels will make it known.'

He took the pot of ale which Margaret handed him and sat on a stool beside the fire. Martha perched on the edge of her seat, declining Margaret's invitation to draw a little closer. She seemed confused and distracted.

'We've a unique opportunity,' began Richard, 'to strike out and set up a new community of our own.'

They all nodded but no one was convinced.

'It will take courage, but if we stand together we can succeed.'

'Where do we go?'

'We could return to England,' said Richard. 'But I, for one, choose to remain here.'

'And where does the Reverend Daniels choose to go?'

'He hasn't said.'

'Then perhaps we should ask.' He glanced at the stairs,

then at Richard and at Margaret. Margaret did not know what to say but Richard shrugged in a gesture of useless invitation. Ezra got up and went upstairs.

He was gone for some time. When he returned he said, 'He doesn't seem inclined to discuss the matter.'

Richard gave another gesture. 'Then the choice must be ours.'

Ezra bit his lip and sighed. He would have given a great deal for Divine guidance. Instead, he paced the floor. 'I suppose . . .' he said at last, 'the Lord sent the Reverend Daniels to this country. I suppose we must assume that he's meant to stay.'

'I agree,' said Richard. 'We must find somewhere to settle and build up a life of our own.'

'But where?'

'Far enough away for us to be unknown. We'll be made unwelcome anywhere that our story has been told. I suggest we continue inland until such time as we find some suitable place.'

'Towards unknown territory?'

'If we try to settle anywhere along the seaboard we'll be hounded.'

'But we can't just set up a new settlement,' put in Margaret. 'It calls for patents, permission from the King.'

'We'll first find the place,' said Richard kindly, 'and think about obtaining permission later.' He took a mouthful of ale and placed the mug on the mantel. 'We can follow the river at first but it will turn north and keep us too close to the area we need to leave. At that point we shall have to strike out west.'

'We'd be lost without the river.'

'Some sixty miles or so due west we should meet the Connecticut.'

'We'd be mad striking out across country,' said Ezra. 'We'd be lost before we'd made half that journey.'

'It's only about sixty miles, then we can follow the Connecticut.'

'Sixty miles of wilderness. We'll go round in circles.'

'Not if we watch the sun.'

'We're not travellers, any of us. We've none of us got experience in finding our way sixty miles across dense forest.

We'd do best to go round the coastline and find the Connecticut that way.'

'We'd be unwelcome anywhere along the coast,' repeated Richard. 'Our story will spread before us. There's no point in remaining in populated areas. We shall be constantly chased away.'

'Then what do we do?'

'Strike out west,' said Richard. 'And trust in God.'

Ezra went quiet and thought for a while. 'I suppose you're right,' he said at last. 'If it's God's Will that we go, He'll see to it that we survive.'

'Good man,' said Richard, though he was far from certain. Survival depended upon a great deal more than finding their way sixty miles to the next river. He decided to change the subject. 'We must get moving quickly,' he said. 'Not only must we find somewhere, we must have time to set up shelter and prepare for the winter.'

'It's already October,' said Margaret. 'We don't have much time.'

Richard smiled. He wanted to touch her, to comfort her, but instead he remained standing where he was on the opposite side of the hearth. 'If we can just get through that first winter,' he said, 'we can make canoes. I can go downriver for supplies and seek out a place where we can settle permanently. But first we must reach that river, or some other suitable place, and dig in for the winter.'

'I'm afraid,' said Martha. It was the first time she had spoken.

'So am I,' said Margaret. She reached out a hand and touched her. 'But the men will look after us.'

'And I'm with child.'

'So am I,' she said, and glanced over to catch a look from Richard. It was only fleeting. Almost immediately he turned away.

'We've a week,' he said. 'The Brothers have given us longer but the later we leave, the less time we shall have to find shelter.'

'What shall we take?'

'As many provisions as we can carry. Flour, salt, spices for pickling. We can hunt game but there'll not be much else.'

'At least there'll be fruit,' said Margaret. 'The bushes are laden with it.'

'Then we'll forage as we go,' said Richard. 'Save as many of our provisions as we can for winter.'

'We'll need pack animals,' said Ezra. 'I've one good beast.'

'And I've another two. I'll do a deal with Brother Caleb tomorrow; he's got one to spare.'

'And goats.'

'One male, two female. We shall need to breed.'

'I've got my good oak chest,' put in Martha.

'Forget the chest,' snorted Ezra with impatience. 'We've no room for chests.'

'But how am I to set up home without a chest?'

Ezra's impatience turned to exasperation, but Richard said kindly, 'It's going to be a very frugal home at first, I'm afraid, Sister. We have first to think of survival. We'll think of furnishings later.'

Martha began to weep. 'But I've never been without my chest.' She was deeply distressed. She was more concerned about leaving it than with leaving her home.

Margaret knew how she felt. The prospect was awesome. It was not possible to visualize the enormity of walking out into the unknown — only the sadness of losing a beloved chest. She touched Martha's arm again. 'We'll manage,' she said. 'Trust me.'

Martha smiled thinly but was not consoled.

'Guns,' said Richard. 'Is your musket in good order?'

'Of course,' said Ezra.

'And I've two. I bought a second from William this afternoon in exchange for my cow.'

He turned to Margaret. 'Can you fire a musket?'

'I don't know but I can learn.'

'And the Reverend Daniels,' said Ezra. 'He's got a musket.'

'I think, Brother,' said Richard, 'that we'd best carry the musket for the Reverend Daniels.'

Ezra conceded the point. 'I suppose you're right. It will be up to all of us to protect him with our lives.'

On the morning of departure the whole of Ufferton turned

out to watch them go. Many were visibly distressed.

Susannah wept. She begged Margaret again to stay. 'You've been given opportunity to remain,' she said. 'Stay here with us. We'll take care of you and Jessica.'

Margaret returned the hug, holding on to her and kissing her cheek. 'I must go with my husband,' she said gently.

The four pack animals were heavily laden with provisions, tools, ammunition, warm clothing for the winter. Jessica and Joel Bracegirdle were of roughly the same age. They were able to walk beside their parents; but Isaac Bracegirdle was an infant of eighteen months and would need to be carried. Martha was six months pregnant.

Margaret was fit and strong, well used to handling pack animals. She was in her fourth month of pregnancy and quite capable of helping with the goats and the children as well as with the many other tasks which she would be called upon to do.

They stood around for the goodbyes, feeling awkward. People did not know what to say. Many still feared the decision which had been made. They attempted to speak with Deliverance Daniels but he seemed incapable of conversation. It seemed heartless to expel others who had been their friends. Many would have begged a reversal of the decision had they not feared the Reverend Daniels more.

Margaret said yet another farewell to Susannah and Thomas Norton and their children. They now had six: Margaret had been present at the birth of each of the younger four. She kissed them all, clinging to them at the last.

'Goodbye, Aunt Margaret,' said the children, but they did not fully understand.

Martha stood, a hand on each of her children, looking lost.

At last Richard gave the signal to be off and there was no more to be said. The pack ponies tossed their heads and set forth, adjusting to their loads. Children ran with them, taken up with the spirit of adventure, until all but the most daring turned back to their parents. Jed Taylor was the last to go. Jessica watched him as he tailed off and was left behind. She did not like him. More than once he had pinched her while she sat in church.

Now all was quiet — just the creaking of leather, the sound of feet and hooves on the grassy path. Little was spoken. Each was lost in their own thoughts.

They walked upriver, past Richard's farm with its three fields neatly harvested. He looked at it as he passed, revealing nothing of the thoughts which were in his mind.

The pack ponies were strung together in line, the goats tied at their side. One person could lead them. The others made their way as the terrain dictated — sometimes as a group, sometimes in single file where the path was narrow. At this stage they were following a well-worn Native track.

Deliverance Daniels walked alone, a short distance from the others, mumbling distractedly to himself. He did not appear to be fully aware of their circumstances.

The children were used to walking long distances but, after several hours, Joel Bracegirdle began to complain. He began to dawdle, then sat down and refused to move.

'My legs are hurting. And I'm thirsty.'

Richard scooped water from the river into his hands. When the child had drunk from it he swept him up to sit upon his shoulders. 'Here,' he said, 'you're the lookout. Watch out for bears.'

The goats were perverse. They got themselves beneath the hooves of the ponies and endeavoured to forage. Their ropes became entangled in the thorny undergrowth beside the path, so that they hindered the plodding progress of the pack.

Margaret poked at them with a stick, keeping them moving and in line. She took her turn in carrying the infant, Isaac, who was sleeping, a dead-weight upon her chest. As she walked she gathered handfuls of nuts, throwing them into a bag slung across her shoulder. She and Martha were training their eyes to seek out every edible root and berry, slipping them into the bags as they passed.

At mid-day Ezra caught a turkey. It lifted their spirits. They began to talk of the sight, the taste, the smell of it as it would roast on the spit at the end of the day.

Jessica kept walking, refusing to acknowledge that she was tired. A short distance away Deliverance Daniels still mumbled to himself. She wondered why he no longer spoke to her or appeared to notice her. It was ten days since he had sat with her before the open book. She wondered which of her sins had caused him to withdraw from her.

His last words to her, as always, had been, 'Beware the sin of lust for you are more vulnerable even than all the other daughters of Eve. A cat will after its kind, and after all you are a . . .?' He had held the final inflection of his voice by way of the usual question.

'A bastard, Papa.'

'A bastard. And let us never forget it. It's our secret. Remember always in our prayers to seek the bounteous kindness of the Lord who knows all things and is forgiving.'

Towards evening they collapsed exhausted beside the river bank, too tired any longer to think of food.

'We must eat,' said Richard. 'And build shelters.'

'It's not cold,' said Ezra. 'We can lay where we are in the open.'

'You'll be sorry, come morning. It'll be cold in the early hours. And we must get used to building. By the time winter arrives we've got to be skilled in providing protection.'

They made their first attempt at erecting a Native wigwam. While the turkey roasted, they cut saplings, staking them in a circle and bending them inwards at the top to form a dome. The Natives would have laid on layers of birch or elm bark. They chose, instead, a covering of fresh-cut branches.

'We must learn the art of stripping bark,' said Richard. 'But, for today, this should provide sufficient shelter.'

The finished structure bore little resemblance to the wigwams they had seen in the Pennacook village but they were pleased with their efforts. They allocated it to Ezra and Martha then set about building another two, placing them in a triangle with the animals at the centre.

'We must keep the provisions beside us as we sleep or lose them to wild beasts.'

It was dark by the time they had finished. They ate the turkey and fell into their beds.

Margaret lay in the darkness listening to the sounds of the wilderness. An animal came near — possibly a wolf — causing the pack ponies to become restless; but the fire was still burning and it came no closer. On one side of her Jessica slept, curled on her side, breathing rhythmically. On the other side Deliverance Daniels snored through an open mouth. It was cold and she was glad that Richard had made them build shelters.

She thought of him lying a few yards away and wondered if he were sleeping or awake. Her body ached from the strain of the day and she longed for the caress of his hands upon the small of her back. She was sorely tempted to get up and go to him, but, as she moved, Jessica complained at the sudden loss of her mother's warmth: Deliverance Daniels rolled over on to his side, mumbling in his sleep. She settled back upon the hard soil and tried to get some rest.

They were up again at dawn, subdued at the prospect of setting out again through the seemingly endless forest. It was frightening to think of it stretching out in all directions around them, knowing that Ufferton lay behind them and that they had nowhere to go. They walked in silence, broken only now and then by the grizzling of the infant, Isaac, and the complaints of Joel.

Martha Bracegirdle walked in a daze, as though she had given up wondering why she had been called upon to leave her home, expecting that at any moment she would wake from some unpleasant dream.

But it was on the third day when the real exhaustion set in. Leg muscles cramped and a feeling of utter despondency settled upon them all. The trees closed in around them and they had the desperate feeling of being lost, even though they were still following the river.

Joel Bracegirdle sat down and cried, asking repeatedly to be taken home. He refused to be carried, or to ride on the pack ponies. He demanded only to return home to the pet dog he had left behind.

Jessica kept walking. Her small feet were blistered but she refused to allow the pain to show upon her face. Several times she sidled up to Deliverance Daniels, wanting to take hold of his hand, but he appeared not to notice her. Richard picked her up and carried her but she held herself stiffly and was glad when he set her down. She did not like him.

Towards mid-afternoon they came to the turn in the river. They stopped to rest, spending far too long, but fearful of leaving its security to set out across featureless forest. Richard checked the sun. He knew which direction was west but had started to doubt his own abilities. He re-checked repeatedly and measured with his eye a distant landmark, though it was difficult to gain any perspective of distance when hemmed in by trees.

'Just a few more hours,' he said, 'then we can eat. Tomorrow's the Sabbath; we can take the day to rest.'

It was a strange Sunday. Deliverance Daniels stirred himself to lead them in worship, performing as if by rote and barely acknowledging the presence of those about him. Several times he trailed off into passages of self-condemnatory abuse which were as embarrassing as they were confusing. He took an hour and a half over the preaching of his sermon: its theme bore no relevance to their present circumstances.

Inactivity only served to heighten their awareness of the total isolation in which they found themselves. In all directions there was nothing but forest, no sound but for the call of birds and the occasional scurrying of an animal. The trees were a spectacular array of red and gold but already the leaves were falling, fluttering with a soft rustling *plop* to form a growing carpet upon the forest floor. It augured coming hardship.

They were almost glad to set off again, making sure that the sun was at their backs, heading once more into the seemingly impenetrable forest. The undergrowth tore at their clothing and the canopy of trees obscured their vision. It had the effect of mesmerizing them into believing that they were walking in circles. Richard kept his eye continually on the sun, watching its passage across the sky, experiencing panic when it went behind cloud.

In a small clearing they came upon an old Native village but it was long abandoned. They spent time contemplating the possibility of using it for their own winter stopover but they were fearful that the Natives might return.

'And we're still too close to Ufferton,' said Richard. 'Let's keep going, at least until we get to the Connecticut.'

'But there's water here. It's as good a place as any.'

'Not if the Indians return.'

'I'm tired,' said Martha plaintively. 'And the children have walked as far as they can go.' She was carrying Isaac, resting him upon her distended belly. Wisps of hair had escaped her cap, falling across her tired face. She brushed them back with the heel of a grubby hand.

Richard felt sorry for her. He took Isaac from her, relieving her of the burden. 'I'm sorry, Sister. I know you're tired but we must keep moving.'

'Surely we could stay for just a little while?'

'The longer we remain, the less time we shall have to prepare for winter. We've homes to build, or we shall freeze.'

Martha shook her head forlornly. She still did not understand why Ezra had made them leave their cottage.

'I know you're tired,' said Richard again, 'but we must keep walking. It would be worse still to settle here, then find that we have to move again when the frost is in the ground.'

They walked for a further week and came one morning to a point where the ground fell away before them to the valley floor. Below was a ribbon of water. It was the Connecticut.

'We made it,' said Richard but it was with a feeling of anticlimax. They had arrived but they had nowhere to go. The walk had ended: but the task of survival had only just begun.

Margaret found herself weeping, whether from relief or from apprehension she did not know. She dashed away the tears with the back of her hand, knowing that this was neither the time nor the place to exhibit signs of weakness and exhaustion. Isaac had been sick for two days, feverish and fretful, with a cough which kept them all awake at night. She saw, growing in a patch of sunlight, a herb for which she had been searching. She gathered it up into her bag along with the nuts and berries. She would pound it into a potion.

She increased her stride and, taking Jessica by the hand, they ran the last few yards, laughing as they tried to keep their foothold.

The next day was spent searching for the spot on which to build their homes.

'It must be on level ground,' said Richard, 'sheltered from the winds and high enough above the river in case it floods. This area will serve for the winter. Come spring we'll search for somewhere more permanent.'

They cut down trees, shaping the timbers and laying them

horizontally within a framework of upright posts. The heavy work fell upon Ezra and Richard. Deliverance Daniels did nothing to assist. He spent his time upon his knees or staring at the water. Margaret and Martha trimmed the branches, heaving and straining upon the heavy loads, while the children cleared the twigs. Martha was now almost seven months pregnant, Margaret nearly five.

They worked for several days but at the end of it they were not pleased with the result. The walls were unstable and, although they attempted to caulk the gaps with mud and turf, the house was far from watertight.

'This won't do,' said Richard at last. He threw down his axe and looked about him. 'The snow and winds will freeze us in our beds.'

'It's the best we can do.'

'Then we shall die.'

'My husband's a tanner,' complained Martha. 'He's never been called upon to build a house.'

'And I'm a farmer,' said Richard. 'But still we'll die.' He stopped and smiled at her by way of apology. 'I'm sorry,' he said, 'we're none of us used to this. But we've got to protect ourselves from the ice and winds.'

He walked off on his own for a while and when he returned he said: 'We start again.'

There was a unanimous groan.

'Again,' he repeated, and pointed to a south-facing slope a short distance away. 'If we can't build, then we must dig. We'll construct our homes so that the winds will blow over us.'

They dug out a small section, some three feet deep, to form a terrace on the side of the hill. Then, placing two uprights and a horizontal timber towards the front of it, they proceeded to lay on a sloping roof, taking it down to meet the slope of the hill at the back and on both sides. It was like a man-made cave. They used first a layer of small birch trunks, then a covering of branches and reeds, and finally a close layer of turf, tightly filling the gaps to make it waterproof.

'Now we've only got the front to worry about, and that's facing south.'

It was dark inside with no windows and only a narrow

doorway covered by a blanket. They would cook outside but, come winter, there would be only a small outlet for the smoke.

It was November. It had taken them the best part of a week to build this one shelter, in addition to the time they had wasted on the house. The weather was growing noticeably colder and the daylight hours short. At night they huddled inside the temporary wigwams, fretting about their lack of progress. It would be necessary to build another two shelters, along with one for the animals.

There was no time for the men to hunt. Margaret and Martha searched for food, boiling up pots of broth, making the most of any small mammal they managed to trap. While it boiled, they fetched and carried, heaving upon the lengths of timber, trimming the branches from newly felled trees. The children worked beside them, gathering branches and bundles of reeds, laying them in piles beside the framework of the roof.

Baby Isaac continued to cough. Margaret searched for herbs, but found nothing to ease it.

It rained while they were building the final shelter, making it difficult to dig into the hillside, slipping and sliding in the mud. Tempers were frayed and Richard found himself quarrelling with Ezra and speaking sharply to Martha, who was eventually allowed to take shelter with the children away from the downpour. Clothing was saturated and filthy. They had nowhere to dry it, except in the already constructed shelters, where it steamed, adding to the already unpleasant smoke-filled atmosphere.

But, on the day of completion, the sun shone. The men went out to hunt and came back with a deer which they roasted, rewarding themselves with a few of the provisions they had been so carefully saving. It was a feast.

Deliverance Daniels kept his distance, chewing mechanically upon the food which Margaret placed before him. He rarely spoke, except for the constant mumbling. Jessica went and sat beside him. When no one was looking, she gave him the tastiest morsels from her bowl.

During the weeks since they left Ufferton there had been little opportunity for Margaret and Richard to be alone. Living in such close proximity, they were always observed.

Little had passed between them beyond the occasional loving glance, a whispered comment, a brief touch of hands.

Later on that night, she took the risk of slipping away from her husband's shelter. She crouched over the snoring figure, satisfied that he was deeply asleep then, tucking a blanket more closely around the sleeping Jessica, she quietly left.

Jessica stirred, thinking that her mother was going to relieve herself. When she did not return, the child went to search for her. Outside Richard Fullwood's shelter she heard muffled whispers. When she peeped inside they were there together. She dropped the blanket door as silently as it had been lifted and went back to Deliverance Daniels. In the cold lonely stillness of the night she took her bedding and snuggled down against his stiff unresponsive body.

Beneath a blanket of their own, Margaret and Richard made love, seeking assurance, giving comfort and relief to tired bodies.

'It's been so long.'

'I know, but we must take care. We can only survive if we avoid friction amongst ourselves. Ezra and Sister Martha would never accept our love.'

'But it's such a waste. We could be happy and together.'

He kissed her lightly on the brow. 'Have patience, my love. Somehow I shall find a way.'

It rained again while she was there, pattering against the turf of the roof, but beneath their blanket they were snug and warm. The wind blew over the top of the shelter, deflected by the hill and by the slope of the roof.

She waited until there was a lull in the storm then scuttled back to her own shelter, dodging the raindrops plopping from bare branches, taking special care as she skirted round the shelter of Martha and Ezra Bracegirdle. When she got back to her own shelter she groped about in the darkness, wondering why Jessica had moved her bedding. She found her pressed close against the side of Deliverance Daniels. She did not see that Jessica was awake — and watching.

Shortly before Christmas the snow came — a thick blanket of white silence.

It had become increasingly difficult to forage for food

and they had begun, reluctantly, to use their stock of provisions. One sack of flour had been spoiled – placed beneath a fault in the structure of the roof. Unnoticed, the damp had seeped through until, one morning, they found the flour congealed. Others had been nibbled by small rodents which found their way in through cracks in the walls and by the open door. They began devising means of trapping them and preventing access.

Isaac continued to cough. He had lost weight and had become shrivelled and blue. Margaret and Martha had more time now. They took turns to sit with him, laying him across their lap, massaging his back as he fought to catch his breath.

The men set traps and hunted but the deep covering of snow made the going difficult. There was constant danger of losing their way in the uniform whiteness.

The pack ponies were no longer able to graze. As weeks passed, their ribs began to show.

'It would be foolish to slaughter them,' said Richard. 'In spring we'll need them to move on and re-settle.'

It was not a wise decision. By the time two died, there was little flesh left on their bones to replenish the stewpot.

The goats were less fussy in their foraging. Each morning the children led them out to feed upon the seemingly inedible scrub. Jessica's shoes had worn thin and she plodded through snow with her feet bound in the skins of squirrels.

In January Isaac died. It had been inevitable but no one had spoken of it. They carried him out on to the hillside and laid him to rest in a spot where the first rays of spring sunshine would warm the soil.

Martha stood and wept. She was eight and a half months pregnant and asked herself repeatedly why God required her to be standing here. She had followed in obedience when Ezra had chosen to leave England. She had set up home for him in New England, far removed from the large bustling family she had left behind in Salisbury. She had followed again when he left Ufferton. Now she stood beside the grave of her child, fearing for another which she carried in her womb.

Margaret led her back down the hillside, knowing there were no words to comfort her, offering instead a bowl of broth to warm the chill from her bones. They were all suffering with coughs. As they sat, silent and grieving, the intermittent wheezing only served to remind them all of the child they had lost. And it was cold — so very cold.

Less than a week later Ezra went out to track a deer. A thick layer of fresh snow had fallen overnight and by mid-morning it was snowing again. A strong wind was causing it to drift.

The going was too difficult. He gave up and turned for home, struggling thigh-deep in places. Large flakes stung his eyes, making it difficult to see. He kept calm, beating down flutters of panic as the swirling snow obscured his vision. He was within half a mile of home but nothing was familiar.

He came to a tree and felt sure that he had passed it only minutes before. Panic welled again. He was walking in circles. He looked around for landmarks but there were none. He was hemmed in, isolated by a blanket of white where nothing was recognizable. In that moment he knew the true meaning of wilderness.

It was sufficient to cause him to lose control. He began to run, stumbling mindlessly from tree to tree, looking for something, anything, which was familiar. He was on the side of a steep bluff and, in his panic, placed his foot upon snow which gave way beneath his weight. He slipped and fell. At first he thought that he would slide only a short distance but he gained momentum, hurtling headlong past rocks and trees until he landed with a heavy thud in a drift. He struck the back of his neck and lost consciousness.

When he came round it took some time to recall what had happened. He lay bemused, his body temperature already beginning to fall dramatically. By the time he began to dig himself out of the drift it had fallen even lower. He wondered why he could not think clearly, and why he was devoid of all sense of urgency and of direction. In his stupor he did not realize that he was cold but continued to flounder about, stumbling from tree to tree with very little purpose.

Richard grew anxious, sure that Ezra would have taken shelter from the blizzard, but by late afternoon when it had eased he went out to look for him. Darkness was approaching and there was danger that they could both become lost. He found him lying in a heap of snow, making no attempt to find his way, thinking only to sleep. He was but a few hundred yards from home.

Richard hauled him to his feet. 'Come on, Ezra, you've got to walk.'

But Ezra barely recognized his name. He was a small man, smaller than Richard, but it was with great difficulty that Richard succeeded in dragging him back to the warmth of the fire. He was suffering from concussion and from the effects of the cold: there was evidence of frostbite to his nose and fingers.

Martha nursed her husband. When the pains of labour began, she lay down beside him. In the early hours of the morning she gave birth to a blue-tinged, undersized boy.

'What will you call him?' Margaret asked.

'Ezra. It had best be Ezra.'

The unmistakable meaning brought tears to Margaret's eyes. She doubted that the baby would survive to perpetuate the name.

Later, when Martha was sleeping, she went in search of Richard. There was no longer any need to guard her actions. With her husband oblivious to all that went on around him, there was no one left to see. But she had underestimated the children. Jessica missed nothing.

She found him chopping wood. 'You look tired, my love.'

He took her in his arms. 'And you. You've been up all night.' Her hands and fingers were cold. He took them to his lips and kissed them.

She stroked his face. 'I sometimes wish we could just go home.'

There was nothing he could do but draw her to him, holding her and giving comfort by his touch.

'I'm so afraid for Ezra. His fingers are black.'

'I know,' he said. 'I'm going to need your help.'

She knew what he meant. 'Oh, God.' She stood looking at him, biting her lower lip. 'What will you use?'

'The axe,' he said. 'I'll see that it's sharp.'

She nodded and closed her eyes. 'We'll move him first. It wouldn't do for Martha to see.'

Ezra did not recover from the trauma of losing his hands. He remained unconscious for three days. On the fourth he

305

slipped quietly into death. The baby survived him by less than twelve hours.

The ground was frozen hard but they dug a grave as best they could and laid the baby beside him. They covered it with boulders to protect them from the wolves.

Deliverance Daniels was called upon to conduct the funeral service. He made no mention of the fact that it was for his sake that Ezra had followed; that it was for his sake that Martha now stood on a windswept hillside beside another grave. She looked at him, dazed and perplexed. It was not for her to question a man of God.

The weather closed in around them. A bitter north wind swept down the valley, whining through the trees. Days slowed, dragging in tune with their own despondency. Martha functioned as one who had given up hope. She looked lost and confused with no inclination remaining to question that which could not be answered.

Richard now hunted alone for game to feed four adults and two children. He felled trees for firewood, leaving the women to chop them into manageable pieces. Margaret was in her eighth month of pregnancy and her belly got in the way. She was tired and her back ached after hours of hard toil but she did not complain. She was only too well aware of the weight of responsibility which rested upon Richard.

They were at their lowest ebb; but, with the coming of March, evenings lengthened. There were signs of spring. They began to speak, hesitantly, of plans — of building a canoe, and of going downstream to reconnoitre the surrounding area for a spot where they could permanently settle.

'There are settlements on the Connecticut,' said Richard. 'I'll get supplies.'

They were freer now to be together. In deference to Martha's feelings they did not exhibit the true nature of their relationship but they were more relaxed in their behaviour. On this occasion all three sat together in Martha's shelter.

'I'll take care of things,' said Margaret. 'While you're away.'

She had voiced his own unease. He was not happy at the thought of leaving the women unprotected.

'I'll sound out the nearest settlement,' he said. 'See if we can join them.'

'I'd like that,' said Martha. It was the first time she had shown any enthusiasm. 'It would be so good to live in a cottage again, and to sit in a parlour.'

'But would we be welcome?'

'I don't know. I doubt that our story will have travelled as far as the Connecticut settlements, but one can never tell. There are many who trade round the coast and up this river.'

It reminded Margaret that, with the coming of spring, other inhabitants could pass this way. The realization brought mixed feelings. It was a long time since they had seen anyone.

'And what if we *are* known?'

'Then I'll buy seed, and we must set out again. Far enough to find a place of our own, somewhere we can plant our crops and make a life for ourselves away from interference.'

Martha gave a stifled sigh and closed her eyes.

'There's no reason, Sister, why you wouldn't be made welcome nearby. It's not you they would fear — only the Reverend Daniels. If you wished to stay, I could arrange to leave you in their safe keeping.'

Martha shook her head, afraid to move on yet afraid to be left in the care of strangers.

'Let's hope,' said Margaret, 'that we can all settle.' She beat down the rising hope that she and Richard might at last be alone. Her husband no longer noticed anything which passed between them. But the thought of abandoning Martha left her feeling guilty and disloyal.

'We must keep watch for the Indians,' said Richard. 'The Pocomtuc are known to inhabit these parts.'

'We've seen no one since we left Ufferton.'

'Not in winter, maybe, but they can't be far away.'

Margaret bit her lip. They had become complacent concerning the threat which Deliverance Daniels posed to them all. He was harmless enough in the prison of his own self-condemnatory torment. Placed in proximity to the Natives, it could well be a different matter. She offered up a small inward prayer that the Pocomtuc would not make their presence known until after Richard's return.

He looked at her, knowing the thoughts which were

passing through her mind — the same thoughts which were passing through his own. He wondered again if he should take the party with him downriver and not leave them alone. But he decided against it. His best course was to paddle the canoe and to sound out the inhabitants of the nearest settlement, then to return with all speed. He could do no more than offer up his own prayer that the Pocomtuc were in some other part of the territory.

'In a few weeks' time,' he said, 'when the floodmelt has lowered, I'll be ready to go downriver and check things out. We can't tell what's best for us until I've sounded out the settlements in these parts.'

A few days later Margaret gave birth to a baby girl. Small but sturdy, she showed no ill effects from the hardships and deprivations of the previous months.

'She's beautiful,' breathed Richard. He stood beside her, gazing down at the tiny wrinkled face which nuzzled Margaret's breast. He reached out to touch a tiny hand which flexed and curled around his finger.

Margaret smiled. 'She has your hair.'

'Margaret . . .?'

He was tempted again to seek reassurance but she answered him with a single glance.

'But not my nose,' he smiled. 'She's been spared my nose.'

She laughed and drew her arm closer round the baby to protect her from the draught. 'What shall we name her?'

'I don't know. Oh, Margaret, it's such a responsibility! We've got to find a good place to settle; build ourselves a proper home.'

She smiled at him. 'It means a lot to you to have a child?'

'I hadn't realized. But now I see her . . .' He stroked his finger across her face. 'I want what's best for her — and for you, my love. I want to build a proper home for her to grow up in. I want to . . . Oh, God, we could do so much if only . . .'

'We'll find a way,' she said tenderly. 'Somehow we'll work it out.' He took them both in his arms, clasping them tight. 'I'm so glad you're both mine.'

'Shall we name her Abigail?' she asked softly.

'Abigail? Why Abigail?'

'Because,' she smiled, 'it means "Her father rejoiceth".'

Mawnauoi awoke with a start, feeling the sharp prick of straw on the back of his neck. It was morning but he did not remember how he had spent the previous night. He had come into Ufferton to trade skins and had accepted, in part, a bottle of brandy which he had drunk before the moon had risen to its full height. His head hurt and it took him some time to work out where he was. He was in Caleb's barn.

His mouth was dry and he spat out flakes of corn husk as he rolled over and attempted to stand. His head throbbed and he swayed on hands and knees, asking himself why an experience, so good the previous night, always left him feeling so bad the following day. He gave up the attempt to stand, promising himself a further hour before he forced himself upon his feet.

From the other side of the wooden slats he could hear voices.

'I've slaughtered three cows but the hides'll be wasted. There's not a decent tanner for miles around now that Brother Ezra's gone.'

'He was a fool. Waste of a good tanner.'

'You can't argue with a man who follows his conscience.'

'Conscience.' Caleb spat at the thought of it. 'What conscience follows a defiler of women?'

'Same as Richard Fullwood. Though I'll never know why he chose to go.'

There was a moment of quiet before Caleb said, 'I still feel badly sometimes about the way we all gained from their going.'

'Fair and square. We paid fair and square. And did deals for anything they could carry.'

'They'd little time to haggle over the price of their land.'

'We paid them fair. There's not a man here who made profit at their expense.'

'It depends how you assess it,' said Caleb. 'Richard Fullwood broke his back to prepare those fields.'

'And then went willingly to abandon them. They couldn't have been so dear to him that he'd go off and leave them.'

'I'll never understand. And with a madman.'

'Some still say he was a man of God.'

'Man of God?' said Caleb derisively. 'More like the Devil.'

'Have caution, Brother, we still don't know it wasn't truly a vision.'

'Vision! We'd have known about visions if the Pennacook had come to hear of it.'

Mawnauoi had been paying scant attention. He caught the last comment and lifted himself painfully up on one elbow.

'Amen to that.'

'We'd not be standing here discussing the distribution of land if they'd wreaked their vengeance upon us.'

Vengeance for what?

'Thank the Lord it was only squaws. If it had been braves they might have enquired further.'

Mawnauoi staggered to his feet. He forgot the pain in his head.

'To set out purposely to burn the village — the man had to be mad.'

Mawnauoi did not stay to hear more. He shook the last of the drunken stupor from his head and went to find his father, the *sachem*.

Gettonahenan listened to all that Mawnauoi said. 'This is a bad thing which you tell me, my son.' He stood, sad-faced, taking in the news.

'The Yinglees make a mockery of our people.'

'It's a sad heart which hears these things.'

'I'll summon the braves. We make ready.'

But Gettonahenan raised his hand. 'And then the white man will come with their guns.'

'We have men brave as the bear, fast as the deer.'

'We stand no chance against the white men's guns.'

'Our braves will fight the white men's guns.'

'And we shall die.'

'Then we die with honour.'

'And our village will be wiped out. The white men will move on and kill our brothers. Soon all our villages will be wiped out.'

'But we can't live with dishonour. We can't allow the Yinglees to do this to our people.'

'We have lived in peace with the white men. They have been our friends.'

'They're friends no more.'

'They have punished this man, and have sent him out where he must surely die.'

'They have brought dishonour upon our people.'

'We shan't forget what you have learned this day, but we'll not go out and risk the white men's guns.'

'I can't believe you say these things.'

'Take heed, my son, of one who is older and wiser. We shall not forget but we will not make war.'

Mawnauoi made to speak again but his father raised his hand. 'I, Gettonahenan, *sachem* of this tribe, have spoken. I will not risk my people to the white men's guns.'

Mawnauoi went into the forest and cried out his anguish to the sky. He remained there for three days refusing to eat. Instead, he worked himself into a state of frenzy, determined that he alone would avenge the deaths of his people.

Richard had succeeded in constructing a birchbark canoe which was reasonably watertight.

'I'll be gone a week,' he said. 'If I find no settlement in that time, I'll return.'

'I fear for you, my love. What if an accident should befall you?'

'I'll not take chances, and I can swim. If I meet rapids, then I'll pick up the canoe and carry it. I've watched the Pennacook do it many times.'

'But the river's flowing high and fast following the thaw, and there's no knowing what dangers may lie along it.'

'I'll not take chances,' he said again. 'I'll be back with you soon.'

Margaret was not consoled. 'I couldn't bear it if you were harmed.'

He took her in his arms and kissed her. 'I'll be back before you know it, with news of the settlements and whether we'll be welcomed.'

She nodded, fighting back the tears. 'When will you leave?'

'Tomorrow. I want you to be brave and to look after Martha and the children.'

Mawnauoi made his way with speed across the forest. He

was sure-footed and swift as the mountain lion. He knew how to live off the forest and where to find water. He reached the Connecticut and began to reconnoitre upriver and down, searching for signs of habitation.

At nightfall Margaret slipped away from her husband's shelter and went for the last time to Richard's bed. All were sleeping. Jessica was nestled in the corner of Martha's shelter where she had fallen into slumber while playing. They had covered her with a blanket and left her peacefully where she lay.

'Is the Reverend Daniels asleep?'

She nodded. 'And I checked on the children before I came. Jessica's with Martha for the night.'

He lifted the blankets and furs to let her nestle next to the warmth of his body, positioning himself to accept her cold feet against the backs of his knees. She shivered, pressing herself close and laying her head in the curve of his shoulder.

'I love you, my sweet.' He took her cold hands, placing them against his stomach.

'What would I do if you didn't come back?'

'Hush,' he said. 'Of course I'll come back. I'll be back to take care of you and of the children. We've a baby daughter now to take care of together.'

She nodded and for a while they said nothing. Then he reached out for his skinning knife which lay nearby. He handed it to her. 'I want you to take this.'

'But why? You need it more than I.'

'There are wild beasts about, and who knows what might be moving now that the thaw has come?'

'I've got the musket. You need the knife much more than I do.'

'I'd be happier if you took it, just in case.' He held her close. 'Keep watch at all times. I'm concerned about leaving you alone.'

'We've seen no one.'

'And if the Pocomtuc pass by, keep the Reverend Daniels inside his shelter. Use the musket to keep him there if needs be.'

'I can't hold my own husband at the point of a musket.'

312

'Keep him inside and don't let him emerge till I get back. On no account must we let him have access to the Indians.'

Margaret shook her head. She did not like the idea.

'They'll only be passing but it's important that he has no contact with them, or opportunity to follow. It'd be best that he didn't know they were here at all but that might not be possible.'

She was filled with unease.

'They'll probably go round you. But who knows? We haven't asked permission to be here.'

'How could we?'

'I know, but it could be that we're on some area they'd object to our inhabiting.'

She looked at him.

'I'm sorry, my love. I wish to God that I didn't have to leave you. But the best I can do is to get back as fast as I can. One of us has to go.'

'I'll be all right,' she said shakily.

'Of course you will.' He bit back on his own unease. 'I've such great faith in you. And I place you in God's good keeping.'

She kissed him and laid her head again into the curve of his shoulder. 'I shall miss you so.'

'And I. But wherever I may be you'll always be there too. There's a corner of me forever filled by you. You live there.'

'Oh, I love you, sweet. I couldn't bear it if you didn't come back to me.'

'I shall come back.' He rolled over, facing her and taking her more closely into his arms. He felt himself rising, thrusting into her, seeking expression, seeking to console. They made love, reaching heights which left them breathless and gasping, until at last they collapsed quivering and panting, entwined one within the other.

'I love you,' he whispered. 'You're my life, my whole existence.'

She should have got up and returned to her own shelter but instead they fell asleep still entwined one within the other.

A few hours earlier Mawnauoi had found the first signs of

313

habitation — a few footprints, twigs snapped and ripped from low-growing branches. He could even tell the height of the man who had passed that way. He came upon a patch of undergrowth flattened by a hunter laying in wait, then, a little further, an area where trees had been felled. He knew that he had arrived.

In the first glimmer of daylight, just at the moment of dawn, Margaret lay dreaming. She was floating on water — a strange merger of the Connecticut and that gentle fast-flowing river which passed through Dunscombe. She recognized landmarks as she bobbed by, reaching out to grasp at objects which dissolved and slipped away, no longer recognizable. It was time to be waking but both she and Richard remained deeply asleep. She was swept on, lazy and languid.

Suddenly a convulsive movement. She was submerged. A rush of water, drenching her, leaving her gasping. In that same moment she was awake. The water was warm. She knew that it was blood.

Someone was standing over her, a vague shape against the dim light of the open door. In that same moment at which he moved towards her, she reached for the skinning knife which lay beside the bed. It was by luck that her hand fell immediately upon it; by luck again that she aimed it accurately. It was not done with any conscious precision but as she lunged upwards she felt the blade enter, sliding in beneath the ribcage.

There was the sound of an inward gasp and a moment later Mawnauoi fell upon her, the full weight of his body across her face.

She struggled for air, spitting and choking, throwing him off with a force she had not known she possessed.

Shock had her in its grip, but she looked down at Richard who lay beside her. His throat had been cut.

The other man's body lay across them both, his blood oozing to combine with Richard's.

Margaret screamed — a strange piercing sound which penetrated the early morning, echoing out across the hillside, reverberating from tree to tree, sending birds soaring in alarm, on and on until the sound of it became apparent to her own ears and she wondered from whence it came. She made a conscious effort to stop the spasms which were paining her throat but still the noise emerged, gradually lessening in intensity until it was a gasping whimper.

Jessica came to investigate – cautiously, drawn by the sound of her mother's distress but fearful of the terror in the scream. She stood in the doorway looking at the scene before her, her eyes gradually adjusting to the dim interior of the windowless shelter.

Her presence was sufficient to bring Margaret partially to her senses. She got up from the floor, turning Jessica by the shoulders and pushing her away, doing it more by instinct than by conscious effort.

They were joined by Martha, drawn also by the scream. She gazed at them both, her face turned grey-white, and her mouth dropping open.

She was looking at the blood. Margaret glanced down and became aware again of her condition – drenched, and with her hair and clothing thick with red.

Her head swam; then, in her frenzy to rid herself of her clothing, she tore at it, clawing with fingers at fastenings which would not open, tugging and pulling, writhing to free herself until she stood naked, her hands, her face, her head still caked with blood.

Martha appeared to gain some animation and grasped her arm, dragging her to the river. There they dunked her head, turning the colour of the flowing river, scrubbing until she was clean. It was ice-cold in this early morning but both were oblivious to the chill, thinking only to scrub and to be free of red.

Jessica stood on, watching but taking no part, wondering but asking no questions, knowing but denying conscious thought. She turned and walked over to the shelter where she believed Deliverance Daniels to be sleeping.

She saw him immediately upon entering. He was kneeling in an attitude of prayer, propped against a half-empty flour sack, his head turned to one side. He had been scalped.

'Papa?' There was a mixture of pity and bereavement, an instant sense of loss. She tugged at his sleeve but she knew that he was dead.

Margaret came in behind her, a blanket slung round her,

held tight to cover her nakedness. Her hair still dripped with water from the river. She saw Deliverance Daniels kneeling beside the sack but went immediately to the corner where, under a thick covering of blankets and furs, unnoticed and unharmed, the baby Abigail lay sleeping.

She gathered her up into her arms, letting go the tears which coursed down her face in uncontrolled emotion — crying, crying, as though she would never stop.

Jessica stood and watched, needing comfort but afraid to approach, feeling the first seeds of jealousy take root as she looked at the baby cradled in her mother's arms.

'Mama.' She tugged at the blanket until, eventually, Margaret looked down. 'Papa's hurt, Mama.'

'I know,' said Margaret tightly. She took a single deep inward breath as though trying to compose herself. Then, placing a hand on Jessica's head, she said: 'Come with Mama. I'll get you something warm to drink.'

For three days they did nothing about the bodies lying unburied in the shelters. Margaret could not bear to go and look at Richard, but neither could she bear to lose him. Eventually she accepted the inevitable and went with Martha to the spot where Ezra and the baby lay. They dug a hole large enough for two and dragged into it the bodies of Richard and Deliverance Daniels. Her lover and her husband lay side by side. It seemed somehow right that they should be together.

There was no ceremony, no prayer. Jessica waited until the women had left, then laid one single early flower upon the grave, taking great care that it was placed to the side under which Deliverance Daniels lay.

They rolled Mawnauoi into the river, dragging him to the bank then toppling him off, watching him float face-down like a large log to be carried by the current, slowly at first then gathered up by faster water in midstream to be swept away. Margaret was past feeling. An ice-cold barrier had descended, defending her from pain.

For a further week they went through the motions of numbed normality — two women alone with their children, going through the rituals of daily routine.

At last Martha voiced her fear. 'What shall we do?'

'Return to Ufferton.'

'But how?'

Margaret sighed and looked up towards the sky. 'We walk towards the point of the rising sun.'

'We shall never find our way.'

Margaret knew even better than Martha that it had been far easier to find a river crossing north—south across their path than it would be to find a small settlement placed like a dot beyond ninety miles of forest. 'We walk to the east,' she said. 'Sooner or later we must hit the coast. There'll be someone there who'll guide us back to Ufferton.'

Martha was filled with dread. 'We'll not survive.'

'We'll not survive if we remain here. We've got no choice.'

'It makes no difference,' said Martha plaintively. 'We'll all be dead.'

'For the sake of the children we've got to try. There's no way we can remain here alone. We must take the children and go home.'

Martha heartened slightly at the thought of home. The following morning they loaded up the remaining pack pony and set out, heading into the forest, back in the direction from whence they came.

It was a strange feeling as they left the clearing, abandoning the shelters which had housed them. Margaret looked at the shelter where she had lain with Richard. She remembered again the night of love, the face dead beside her on the pillow with no opportunity to say goodbye. She went back and set fire to the shelter. She could not bear to leave his blood spilled upon the ground.

They walked day after day, week after week. Shock still held Margaret in numbed distraction, the memory of Richard's death too painful to accept yet with her at every waking hour. At times she turned, expecting to see him there, expecting comfort, only to experience yet again the knowledge that he was gone, never to return. Over and over she repeated his words: 'Wherever I may be, you will be there too.' But he was nowhere − in a hole in the ground in a place she had left behind. He had not kept his promise. She had been deserted. She could not believe in heaven and felt no guilt in her inability to do so. God had been wrong to take him and she could not forgive.

But then she would look at Abigail and know that he had

317

not gone. Already Abigail bore his features. She was flesh of his flesh, born of his love. So long as she cherished this baby, Richard would not die. He would live on. Every time she looked at his child he would be there.

Jessica walked alone. She did not ask for comfort. She did not ask Margaret why she had been sleeping in Richard Fullwood's bed. Martha, too, did not comment. She did not want to know.

They did not know how long they walked. Again and again they stopped, too tired and dispirited to carry on, until necessity forced them to continue, walking always towards the rising sun. Eventually, one day, they came upon a township and were taken in, fed and comforted, until they were fit and strong enough to be escorted back to Ufferton.

They came to it at last, one gentle sun-warmed day in mid-summer. The first person they saw was Susannah Norton.

CHAPTER 14

It had taken a year for the New Model Army to put down the Royalists and the Scots to bring an end to the Second Civil War. There were still those in Parliament who saw the possibility of restoring a chastened King. Others, including Cromwell, had had enough. On 30 January 1649 Charles Stuart strode through Whitehall Palace and out on to the scaffold where he was to place his head upon the block.

He went with a courage and dignity which stayed long in the memories of those who watched. When the content of his final speech was written up into pamphlet form and widely distributed, it was this which remained in the minds of the people while memories of tyranny rapidly receded.

For Nehemiah it had been a year of transition. Largely freed from his responsibilities as master weaver, he had put his mind to Oakbourne House. Sheep grazed the hills and he had learned quickly from a loyal staff. But he had learned equally quickly that without the sequestered land of the estate and the resources of Sir Henry's fortune, he could be no more than an inadequate caretaker. With hard work he could maintain some kind of equilibrium but it would not be possible to undertake any major repair. He could foresee that any setback by way of disease or bad harvest could bring disaster.

News had come of the death of Isobel. She had gone to live with her mother following the sequestration of her home but, despite care, her health had declined. And now the tuberculosis which had killed her was remorselessly sapping the strength of her two children. The girl would survive her by less than a year and the boy, a puny, ashen-skinned child, was already coughing up blood along with the yellow sputum.

Elizabeth grieved for her grandchildren whom she had never seen. She grieved for her dead husband, and for her absent son still exiled in Holland. She never fully came to terms with the reasons for their loss. She endeavoured to assist in the running of Oakbourne House but the spirit had gone from her: she was as an old woman.

The burden of domestic duties fell upon Anne, who was forty-four and again pregnant. A young girl worked with her as servant, another as dairymaid. Sarah and Rachael were of an age to assist with the work and with the care of their four-year-old brother, William. But Anne was tired: this time when she lay down upon her childbed, she did not get up.

Nehemiah stood in the hall of the house which had suddenly grown cold, echoing and unwelcoming. He wondered upon the purpose of it all. It had taken four months for news to reach him that Margaret had been widowed. He went now to find pen and parchment. It took another three months to reach New England but the message was clear – 'Come home, my daughter.'

In the early summer of 1650 Margaret stepped with her two children on to the quayside at Bristol. She was met by Tom Cox with his string of Galloways and it seemed in that moment of warm greeting that she had been gone for seven months rather than seven years. As she rode with him out of Bristol, up through Wiltshire towards her beloved Cotswold hills, she found herself taking in great gulping breaths of air as though trying to draw back into herself the very essence of her approaching home.

The hedgerows were alive with foxglove, scabious, the yellow heads of dandelion and coltsfoot.

Her father had grown older – grey-haired and with blackened teeth. He kept the stump of his hand hidden within his sleeve. But he took her in his arms and she knew again the old familiar warmth of his love.

'I was sorry to hear of your husband's death.'

She nodded and cried into his shoulder, thinking again of Richard. It was always there – that aching, unspoken void – and yet she had never once been able to speak of his love.

In New England she had been called upon to give account of the way in which he had died, repeating it again and again for those with need to hear but never once mentioning the love they had shared. Martha had not referred to it and no one had suspected the true nature of their relationship. It had been a strange, disconcerting condition – the widow of one man, grieving for another.

She went with Nehemiah across the hills to the churchyard where they stood together beside the graves of her mother, laid to rest with the baby in her arms, of Samuel and of the three children.

'What use am I to be standing here?' asked Nehemiah. 'What use am I, with so many gone?'

'I'm here, Father, and I need your strength.'

He took her hand and led her back to Dunscombe.

For nine years they lived, and worked, and cared for one another. They worked hard but Nehemiah was now in his mid-sixties and increasingly the burden fell upon Margaret. At thirty-five she was fitter than most women of her age – not least because she had been saved the rigours of repeated pregnancies – but the hours of work were long. She could see a deterioration in the house and it grieved her that they had insufficient income with which to maintain it. Tobias helped where he could but the weaving business, though stable, was sufficient only for the upkeep of his own growing family.

The memory of Richard remained with her as a festering open wound, too painful to touch, refusing to heal.

Her daughters were growing fast and her brother William, born to Anne in '45, was a lad of fourteen. A strong, willing boy, he took pleasure in working beside the men. He could remember little of Anne and looked upon Margaret as a mother. Her sisters, Rachael and Sarah, both now married, had children of their own.

Each Sunday throughout the years Nehemiah had walked the four miles across the hills to place a single flower upon Anne's grave.

Jessica was no longer a child. A ripe-breasted fifteen year

old, she harboured some hidden smouldering flame which Margaret feared and could not understand. She could not reach her, could not make contact. She realized now, with a growing awareness, that she had never really known her daughter. There had always been that stiffness which had not responded to hugs.

She found herself comparing the two girls — Abigail, so much like Richard that it brought a pain to her throat, and Jessica, who held herself apart and would be like no one. The one placid and willing, the other fiery and stubbornly defiant. Abigail, still only ten, worked twice as hard as her sister.

Jessica, for her part, did not care. She did not want to be reached — and certainly not by her mother. She ignored her sister, admitting neither to hatred nor to jealousy of her. She got on well with William, for they were of much the same age, but even he did not understand her. She harboured a feeling, deep within her. Some day, somehow, she would stand up above all others and tell the world that she was there.

It had started with the secret. Memories had dimmed, but she could still recall the evenings on which she had sat with Deliverance Daniels before the open book. When she had eventually learned the meaning of 'bastard', it was not he whom she had come to hate — it was her mother. She had caused the stigma and robbed Jessica of respectability. It seemed more just to blame her mother rather than the man who had merely told her of her plight.

For years she had waited for the secret to be divulged; waited to be exposed. Yet it was never mentioned. At times she had openly challenged her mother, wordlessly confronting her with open stare, but Margaret had not responded: she had merely seemed confused.

The sense of waiting had not diminished with the passage of time — that deep inner humiliation, the constant fear of exposure. But, little by little, it had been joined by another emotion — that of defiance. Instead of waiting, she would stand up and tell the world, 'I'm here'.

Her mother did not begin to know what went on inside her. Jessica held her in contempt; the same contempt with which she recalled the man whose name also was never mentioned — Richard Fullwood.

She sat now and thought of him on this day in early autumn. It was warm and she had been sent into the orchard to gather apples. But the basket was only half filled and she chose instead to sit on the grass with the sun-warmed tree at her back. She knew that she would be chastised, that Abigail would have spent the entire afternoon making cheeses or stirring great boiling pans of conserve. It was always the same at this time of year with her mother fraught and short-tempered, declaring that she would never get sufficient meat preserved, or vegetables pickled, before the onset of winter.

She sat now and thought of the times when she had watched her mother with Richard Fullwood, thinking themselves to be unobserved. She had watched them panting and gasping, her mother crying out in some kind of pleasurable agony. And she had been disgusted. She had watched Deliverance Daniels, cut off and alone. She had understood what it meant to be lonely.

This was the same woman who now sat in church, her hands folded in her lap; the same woman who chastised Jessica when she found it impossible to concentrate upon the sermon. No one suspected that she had writhed upon the bare soil while Deliverance Daniels had read his Bible.

Jessica had difficulty in recalling the faces of those who had passed. Her memories were fragments, made up and embellished into a whole which had become hazy and distorted with the years. She wondered if Richard Fullwood were her father. She could not remember how long he had been on the edge of their lives. It was confusing and painful.

She hated men, yet she found them attractive. It was a paradox with which she had not yet begun to come to terms. She found herself watching them, fascinated by the opposite poles of her emotions. And she was constantly chastised when discovered to be doing so. She felt herself oppressed, unwilling to take on the role of subservience which was expected of her. What was more, she knew that this very reluctance made her attractive to the men she watched. She knew that, when she was not looking at them, they were looking at her.

She heard movement behind her and got up reluctantly, expecting it to be some member of the family come to harry her into action: it was not. Someone was stealing apples. It was not that Jessica cared about the apples, but she resented the theft. She shouted.

The man turned but made no attempt to cover his actions. He stood looking at her, taking a bite from the apple which he held in his hand.

'I can pay.'

'That's not the point. You didn't ask.'

'Sure, you've more than enough. You'll be having plenty here to share with others.'

'You didn't ask,' she said again.

'I'll be asking now. Can I be having some apples to go with the duck which is roasting on me fire?'

'No doubt also taken from our pond.'

He grinned and she knew that she was right. 'I can pay. If you'll just be coming back with me to my wagon, I'll pay in kind.'

'What form of kind?'

'If you'll just be coming back with me, you can have your choice.'

'I've no intention of accompanying you anywhere.'

'Then you'll never be knowing what I've got to offer.'

It was an obvious ploy. She knew that she should not be holding this conversation, but there was something roguishly likeable about him.

'You're a stranger in these parts.'

'Just passing through.'

'On route to where?'

'To London, unless the fancy takes me somewhere else.'

'It's a wonder you're not locked up,' she said, sizing him up to be a vagrant.

'Sure and I am, quite often. During the year of the major generals in forty-five, I was after spending more time locked up than on the road.' He grinned. 'I'll be trusting your father isn't the magistrate?'

She laughed and shook her head. 'But I do know who is.'

'Then I must be after paying you. I really do have some things in my wagon.'

'What sort of things?'

'Some pieces of silk, some oils as sweet as the sunrise. I took them from a sailor who couldn't hold his drink.'

'You stole them, too.'

'I did not. I won them fair in a game of dice.'

'From a sailor foxed with drink.'

He laughed. 'Sure, it wasn't my fault he couldn't hold it. Though I did buy the ale.'

'I don't want your things,' she said. 'But you're welcome to the apples.'

'You can still be coming and looking at them, if you'll be wanting to.'

'No, my mother wouldn't like it.'

He smiled. 'No, we mustn't be after having such well-bred young ladies talking to the likes of Joseph.'

She returned the smile and picked up the basket. She could not stay there and pick apples while he remained yet she knew that she would be chastised for the half-empty basket. She began to walk towards the house.

'I'll still be here tomorrow, if you change your mind. I'm camped in the wood.'

She smiled again but did not look round. She waited in the small yard behind the pig pens where she could stand and watch him unobserved from behind the wall. When he had gone she returned to fill the basket.

Next day, when she was sent into the village, she was half relieved, half disappointed, to find that he had gone. The evidence of his camp fire remained but he had moved on.

She thought of him over the next few days. His aura of freedom contrasted sharply with her own sense of oppression. So it was with a feeling of surprise that she saw him the following week, camped in the spot where he had said he would be.

'I thought you had gone.'

'Business to be doing, but now I'm back.'

'Oh.'

'I'll be off again when I've had a bite to eat.' He indicated another roasting duck which she knew would have been stolen from her grandfather's pond. 'I'll be off to the Michaelmas Fair at Stow.'

'Then you'll see my Uncle Tobias. He'll be there with his cloth.'

'Or maybe Burford,' he put in hurriedly. 'Would you be after wanting to come?'

She shook her head and laughed at such an unthinkable invitation.

'Sure, there's lots of things you'd like to see.'

'I know. I've been to Stow.'

'But not to Burford.'

'I expect the fair at Burford's much the same as the one at Stow.'

'Ah, now that's where you're wrong. The next town's always better than the one before it. 'Tis why I keep moving.'

'Much more likely to evade the magistrates.'

He grinned. 'There's always that other side of the hill, another ford to cross. Sure, I bet you've never been more than an old man's spit away from this very place.'

'I came from New England when I was small.'

He looked at her as though she were returning a tall story. 'And have you ever been to Burford?'

'No.'

'Well there you are. I'll be having you back within the week.'

'That's quite ridiculous and you know it.'

'Ah,' he said, 'but 'twould be fun.' There was a glint in his eye which made her smile.

'Fun, maybe, but quite unthinkable.'

She had stood too long talking to him. She smiled her farewell and started to walk on.

'What would they be after doing to you?' he called after her. 'Whip you? Lock you up and beat you?'

'No, of course not.'

'Then what? You'll be wanting to come, I can tell.'

'I must be going,' she said. 'My mother needs me.'

'What would they do?' he asked again.

'I don't know, but my mother would be angry beyond words.'

'Pity. You'd have been liking Burford.' He went back to his fire as if dismissing her. She felt rejected.

She began to think about her mother's anger. Such an escapade would make her so angry, so distressed, that Jessica could hardly picture the scene. There was a certain fascination in thinking of her mother so distressed — about her. It might even be worth the consequences, just to find out how much she cared.

She was dawdling down the track, totally lost in thought. Joseph crouched over his fire, watching her from beneath his eyebrows.

She could perhaps go for just a few hours. It would be sufficient to give her mother a fright. She could tell him that she would go to Burford, then she would change her mind and insist that he bring her back. She could claim on her return that he had forced her against her will. They would believe her word against his. That way she would get the man into trouble, too. There was a certain sense of power in that. And, after all, he was used to trouble: he wouldn't hold it against her. She bit her lower lip between her teeth and felt her pulse rate quicken.

As she turned back towards him, Joseph removed the duck from the spit and dowsed the fire. Wordlessly, he threw the few surrounding items into the wagon and made room for her. She climbed in and crouched down out of sight. The wagon moved off out of the village. No one took much notice, no one saw her go. Not a word had been spoken.

The wagon was fusty, crammed with items which she could half see in the dim light — old books and jars, a chart showing signs of the zodiac: he obviously practised as quack doctor when the opportunity arose. There were a couple of barrels containing liquid which she could hear sloshing, a coil of rope against which she rested her head. In a corner was a pile of clothing and a grubby blanket spiked with straw. On top of it were thrown a basket of apples and yet another duck, ready for plucking.

It made her think of the bird which he had removed from his spit and of the fact that she had been returning home to the family dinner. They would be missing her by now. Her mother would be angry — too early yet to be worried. She searched around for the bird and found it in a corner near her feet. It was grubby, with grit and fluff sticking to the greasy skin. She brushed it off and began picking at it with her fingers.

It was half-eaten by the time he stopped, a good distance from the village.

'You can be coming out now. There's not a soul about and we can be having a bite of dinner.' He looked at the half-eaten duck and raised an eyebrow. 'And 'tis a good thing your mother will be having one less cheese on her dairy shelf.' He reached into the wagon for a large cheese.

'You steal everything,' she said. 'That's my mother's cheese.'

' 'Tis just as well, seeing as you stole my dinner.'

He gave her a piece of the cheese with some bread and threw her an apple.

'How long have you been travelling?'

'Sure 'tis many a day — since I were but a baby in me Daddy's arms.' He began to tell her tales, far-fetched but none the less enjoyable. He was a born storyteller.

'I don't believe you've done half those things.'

'Well, who'll be knowing? And if I've done the other half, then I'll have been doing a devil of a lot more than you, in your cosy little sheltered life.'

'I've been to New England.'

Again he looked at her as though not believing. ' 'Tis time to be on our way afore we're seen,' was all he said.

By early evening she decided that enough time had elapsed for her to return home. She had worked out in detail the story she would tell.

'I want to go back now,' she said. 'I've changed my mind.'

He looked at her with an amused lift of the eyebrows. 'We've only just set out.'

'I know, but I've changed my mind.'

'Tomorrow, maybe, you'll not be wanting to go tonight.'

'Now,' she said. 'I want to go home.'

He placed his hands on his hips and looked at her. 'You'll be free to go but 'tis dark it'll be soon and I'm doubting that you know the way.'

It was true. She had not taken note of the route: she had been hiding in the wagon. 'Will you take me, now, please?'

He seemed amused by the request. 'Sure, I'm going to Burford then on to London.'

'You could take me home first.'

'And lose a day? I'd be late for the fair.'

'I'd pay. My grandfather would give you money.'

He laughed. ' 'Tis more likely he'd lay a stick about me ears. I may be a traveller, but 'tis not stupid I am.'

'Please,' she said. 'My mother will be so angry.'

'You were knowing that afore you started out.'

'I know but it seems different now.'

He smiled as though relenting. 'Tomorrow,' he said. 'I'll be taking you home tomorrow. Sure, it'd be after getting dark afore we were halfway there.'

She was tempted to throw a tantrum, but sensed that it would not bring the required result. She sat and sulked. The thought of spending the night in the open did not appeal to her.

The family would be searching for her by now. By morning they would be beside themselves with worry. She thought of her mother. It would give her a terrible fright. There was nothing she could do. She decided to settle down and make the most of it. She would go home at first light.

After supper he came and lay down beside her. It frightened her. She got up and moved away.

'You'll be wanting to come back by the fire,' he said. 'You'll be getting cold over there.'

'I'd rather stay here.'

He laughed and came over to lie with her again.

'Stop it,' she said, becoming increasingly alarmed.

She tried to get up again but he caught her by the ankle, tripping her so that she fell, grazing her hands on the uneven ground. She was angry, and fear was turning her throat dry. He merely held on to her ankle, making it impossible for her to get up, leaving her feeling humiliated and defenceless.

'Now don't be telling me that you're going to be behaving like the young well-brought-up lady you are.'

'If you don't leave me alone . . .' she threatened.

'And what will you be after doing?'

'I'll scream.'

He laughed at that. 'If it'll be after making you feel any better.'

'I *will* scream.'

'Go ahead.'

She felt vulnerable and ridiculous. A scream which is not instant and spontaneous is difficult to achieve. She prepared her dry throat.

'There's no one as'll be hearing you,' he said. He was finding it amusing, teasing her with her own vulnerability.

She did scream — not loud, a forced shout which achieved

329

nothing but to send a barn owl clattering out of a nearby tree.

'There. Now will you just be coming here so we can be getting on with what you came to do.'

'What do you mean?' The knowledge that no one would hear was frightening. No matter how loud she screamed, she knew that no one would come to her aid. 'What do you mean — what I came to do?'

'Sure 'tis what all young ladies will be after doing, if they're given half a chance.'

She decided to try reasoning with him. 'Look,' she said, 'I think there's been a misunderstanding. I didn't really mean to come.'

Teasing was turning to irritation. 'You'll not be telling me that you didn't know exactly what you were intending to do when you got in the wagon?'

'I wanted to frighten my mother. I . . .'

'You were wanting to know how it would feel to lie with Joseph. And now that you're after getting the chance, you'll be going all coy on me.'

'No, I didn't.'

'If you'll just be coming here like a good girl, I'll be after giving you the treat of a lifetime.'

'Leave me alone!' she shouted. 'I want to go home.'

'You'll be coming here.'

'No.'

He was still holding her ankle. He pulled on it, attempting to drag her towards him, but she resisted, clutching out at the grass and nearby plants in an effort to use them as an anchor. They proved to be stinging nettles and she gave out a yelp of pain. At the same time he changed position, throwing himself across her, catching her face and kissing her.

Her hand was stinging and painful but she had no intention of giving up her resistance. She used it to hit him.

He hit her in return — a hard stunning blow with the flat of his hand which sent her reeling, banging the back of her head against the hard soil.

She was stunned. No one had ever hit her before. She lay speechless, more from the fact that he had hit her than from the pain.

'Now,' he said, more gently, 'will you just be coming here, like the good girl you are?'

'Please,' she said. 'You don't understand. I . . .'

'Come and give Joseph a nice big kiss.'

'Won't.' She slapped him hard across the face.

He hit her again. ''Tis enough I'll be after having,' he said. 'Sure if there's one thing I can't abide, 'tis a woman who says as she will, then says as she won't.'

'I never . . .'

He put his knee in her stomach while he removed his belt.

'If you'll not be doing it the easy way, then we'll be after doing it the other.' He wrapped the belt around his hand and she was in no doubt that he would use it.

Without his belt, it was easy for him to divest himself of his breeches.

She squirmed on the ground, trying to inch away from him, but she was in great fear that he would do her serious harm. He was a small man but strong and she could feel the sexual tension in the pressure of his body. She looked again at the belt wound round his hand and knew that she would be foolish to resist.

He took her without consideration, it seemed almost without pleasure, merely using her then rolling off when he was through. She thought of her mother with Richard Fullwood and wondered what it was all about.

She lay there feeling dirty and ashamed. The stars came out and she lay watching them against the dark night sky, knowing that those same stars shone above Dunscombe, making home seem both haven and very far away.

Another thought was forming in her mind. She could not go home. One part of her told her that she had done no more than she had seen her mother do. But her mother was no longer the same woman who had rolled upon the soil. She would not understand. And what of her grandfather, the gentle, kind Nehemiah, who loved his God and would not tolerate sin? He would be sickened by the very thought of her. She knew without doubt that she could not go home.

Next morning when Joseph awoke he made no mention of the previous night. They ate breakfast and prepared to move off as though it were the expected thing to do. No mention was made of returning to Dunscombe.

A mist lay across the hills, shredding with the coming of day to reveal the warm clear autumnal sunshine.

''Tis a fine day,' he said. 'Sure, 'tis glad I am to be alive on such a day.'

She did not reply and he did not appear to notice.

She hardly spoke as they stowed away the last of the items into the wagon and began to walk, heading off away from Dunscombe towards the distant horizon.

Margaret had not slept all night. They had started searching during the early evening, growing ever more concerned as dusk fell, casting shadows which deceived the eye. During the afternoon she had been cross and anxious, wondering what had happened to prevent Jessica returning home for her dinner, imagining her idling away her time somewhere and avoiding her chores. But everyone, always, came home for dinner. Even Jessica would not miss coming home for hers.

By evening she was distraught, sending family and servants in all directions, making enquiries, becoming ever more worried as those enquiries came to nought. Several people had seen her in the village, some in the wood. After that nothing. Where could she be? Someone had mentioned the tinker in the wood. But he had been seen leaving Dunscombe: he had been alone.

They searched the wood and found his campfire, beat down the surrounding undergrowth, half fearing what they might find. There had been nothing.

Someone else had mentioned another traveller passing through. Tobias had set out to follow, only to return alone. William was gone a longer time. He took a horse and went to find the tinker but there were many tracks he could have taken − and Joseph had taken care to keep well away from habitation. William searched in vain, passing within a short distance of Joseph's camp, only to miss it and return home despondent.

In darkness they had used lanthorns and flares, joined now by others from the village who turned out in numbers, organizing themselves into search parties. But still nothing was found.

Just before midnight they called off the search. It was useless searching in darkness. For the past three hours they had known they stood no chance in darkness but no one had wanted to be the first to call it off. Eventually they admitted defeat and went home to their beds.

The family stayed awake, sitting with candles at the windows as if hoping that the light would somehow draw her like a moth to its flame. Margaret prowled the rooms, going repeatedly into the garden, calling, calling until her voice was hoarse, stumbling through the undergrowth which surrounded the orchard, beating with a stick in the darkness.

'Come inside, Mama.' Abigail took hold of her hand.

'What are you doing here, child?'

'I came to find you, Mama.'

'It's very late. You should be in bed.'

'You're cold, Mama. Your hands are cold.'

Margaret took control of herself and smiled. 'I'm perfectly all right, my love, but you shouldn't be out here alone in the darkness.'

'I came to bring you home, Mama. I was worried about you.'

'Thank you, child.' Margaret took her and wrapped her in her arms.'

'Mama?'

'Yes, child?'

'What do you think has happened to Jessica?'

'I don't know, I only wish to God I did.'

'Will she come home?'

'Of course she'll come home.'

'But why . . .?'

'I don't know, child. Stop asking me questions. Of course she'll come home. And when she does . . .' Her voice rose tightly towards a hint of hysteria. 'And when she does, I swear I'll give her the beating of her life.'

At Burford the hiring fair was in full swing, the wide main street crammed with sheep, and with people. Men and women stood in lines, each with a symbol of their trade — the shepherd with a tuft of wool, the dairymaid with her pail, the housemaid with her mop — come to gain employment for the coming year.

Carts were set out, heaped with produce. A man with a bear danced on a street corner.

Housewives walked along lines of girls until they found the maid of their choice then sealed the deal with a hiring penny which the girl took to be spent on ribbons or trinkets from a pedlar's tray.

A puppet theatre entertained the crowd; on another corner a one-legged man juggled with sticks.

Joseph dispensed pills and potions from the back of the wagon, selling powdered unicorn horn which Jessica knew to be ground-down grit collected that morning from beneath a dry-stone wall. He also sold the pieces of silk and the aromatic oil taken from the sailor. He was doing good trade.

By suppertime the proceeds were gone, spent in the alehouse. He returned to the wagon, drunk and quarrelsome, together with another man, each with an arm supporting the other. She kept out of their way as they continued to drink, bickering as they shared a jug of ale.

They were too drunk to pay her much heed but, next morning, Joseph called her over.

She was afraid of his mood, afraid to disobey. She was afraid of being abandoned, of being left alone. But, most of all, she was afraid to go home.

The other man looked her over with an unpleasant glint in his eye. 'All that remains in me pockets for an hour in the wagon, Joseph, my friend.'

Jessica had no difficulty in understanding the object of his offer.

'I doubt you'll be after having anything there but fluff.'

'And the shilling lifted from the fine gentleman who was sitting behind us in the alehouse last night.'

''Tis an old rogue you are. I didn't see.'

'Nor did the gentleman, or we wouldn't be sitting here this morning.'

Joseph laughed and examined the silver coin, turning it between his fingers. He beckoned to Jessica who remained standing, feeling sick.

''Tis pleasure our companion's about to give you.'

She shook her head.

'And a gift if you please him.'

'She'll please me all right, but you've got the shilling.'

Joseph beckoned again. Jessica backed off, biting her lip between her teeth.

'I'd rather not.'

The man laughed and took a step towards her. 'Come here, my pretty.'

'No.' She shook her head.

He laughed again. 'She's got spirit. I like a bit of spirit.'

Jessica stood mesmerized then managed to turn and began to run.

He moved with remarkable speed and agility — caught her, swung her round and ran his hand across her breast.

'Don't.' She flinched, feeling her whole body repulsed by his touch. 'I can't. I don't want to.'

'For sure you do.'

He touched her again, but this time she knocked away his hand, reaching out at the same time to claw his face with her finger nails.

It only served to spur him on. 'Will you put up a fight?' He sprang into the stance of a wrestler, laughing and pretending to defend himself. 'I like a bit of a tumble.'

He jabbed at her, feigning a fight, but each time touching her in ever more intimate parts of her body.

She gathered a large globule of saliva into her mouth and spat, accurately, into his face. It took him by surprise, then he roared with laughter, shaking his head and jabbing at her again.

'For sure, Joseph, 'tis a right little vixen you have here.'

There seemed nothing she could do to repel him. She tried kicking out at him but he was an accomplished wrestler, well used to quick moves. He merely sidestepped her flailing hands and feet. Joseph stood on the sidelines, urging him on.

He continued to jab at her, having his way no matter how she tried to deter him. At last she gave way to the sheer hopelessness of the situation and stood looking at him as a rabbit watches a snake.

Immediately, he came to her, grabbed her about the waist and lifted her bodily into the wagon. She continued to kick and to struggle, hating Joseph, hating the man. But in the end he had his way.

That night Joseph brought another man to her. When she refused, he hit her again. He took the money which the man handed to him and went to the alehouse.

Jessica lay in the darkness, sickened by the smell of sweat

and sex, sickened most of all by herself. She thought again of the housewives hiring their servants but they had all gone home, the sheep had been sold. The streets were deserted except for the few remaining revellers who were spending their gain. She knew now, beyond a shadow of a doubt, that she could never go home.

Next morning when Joseph packed up his possessions and prepared to move off, she went with him, making towards London without comment or protest.

Back at Dunscombe, the entire village continued to search for her, scouring riverbank and woodland, thinking first to find a sick or injured girl, later a body. There was no sign of her.

William and Tobias again set out in search of the tinker but it seemed that he had disappeared without trace. At one hamlet someone thought they had seen him, but they could not be sure, and there had been no evidence of a girl. In fact, they were searching in the wrong direction for Joseph had deliberately set out to the north and had then doubled back in a wide arc to escape detection. In open countryside it was quite possible to keep to tracks where he was unlikely to be seen.

Margaret refused to sleep, sitting at night with a candle beside the window, and during the day going out to beat down the bracken, peering into the backs of barns, into cavities formed by rocks or tree stumps. She thought of all the words left unspoken, the reassurances of love, the fact that her last words to Jessica had been of chastisement not affection. She could not cry, yet her lungs ached from the need to give vent to her grief. If only Richard were here, he would know what to do. Her mind screamed out in need of him.

She searched tirelessly. Even after the villagers had abandoned hope, she did not give up. She kept her eyes alert, raking the countryside for some sign, some clue which would give her hope, or some depression in the undergrowth which could lead her to what she feared most.

In the meantime, Jessica was moving ever farther away from home.

CHAPTER 15

Jessica arrived in London at a time of turmoil for the city. Cromwell's death the previous year had led to a power struggle which was gaining momentum. In the latest move, the army had taken over the government, dismissing the Rump Parliament. Richard Cromwell had succeeded his father for only a matter of months before he was pushed aside. Since then, there had been Royalist uprisings, Parliamentary intrigue and counter-intrigue. It had caused moderate men to turn their thoughts to a return to a more stable monarchy.

The army was no longer the same cohesive revolutionary force of its former days. Deserters roamed the streets, without purpose or means of support, seeking to survive by guile and open lawlessness. They added to the hundreds of beggars and thieves already snatching a subsistence living in squalid back alleys.

What was more, General Monck was known to oppose the recent move of his fellow officers. He commanded the most powerful section of the army and, although at present in Scotland, it seemed likely that he would march south to restore the Rump.

Intrigue and uncertainty hung in the air but Jessica was aware only of noise and of people. She retained some faint childhood memory of passing through Bristol but had never seen so large a city. Three square miles, housing some two hundred and fifty thousand people, it was a hive of activity, wealth and squalor.

Wealth was abundant in the clothes of fine gentlemen, in the large houses, each with its own gardens and orchards,

337

in the carriages and coaches which forced their way through crowded streets. Squalor was everywhere, from the dunghills and open drains, to the ragged bundles of orphaned infants who held out limp hands to passers-by.

Workshops lined narrow streets, each with open door through which the noise and smells of ironworker or baker pervaded the air. Apprentice boys ran errands, dodging between the feet of housewives and of street vendors selling trays of hot pies, fruit and oysters.

The wagon rattled slowly through Holborn, across the Fleet Ditch to St Sepulchre's church and the conduit which gathered water from surrounding springs; on through the crowds of Newgate Market, into Cheapside, where they turned off down Old Jewry and Coleman Street; out through the turreted Moorgate in the London Wall, to the green of Moorfields.

They set up camp in a small area of scrub — keeping well away from the walls of Bedlam which stood on the north-east corner — and lit a fire. Joseph had taken to sleeping at the end of each day's trek, leaving Jessica to prepare a meal. She did so without comment. He was pleasant and easy-going when she did as he required, but she had learned to avoid his hasty temper.

Next day he went off into the city to seek out old cronies. He took her with him, fearing that she would run away if he left her unguarded.

'Just leave me here,' she said. 'I wouldn't even know where to run.'

But he took her with him. 'You'll be staying close by,' he said. 'You'll be after earning Joseph a few dinners afore I let you go.'

Laundrymaids had come to lay out sodden linen to dry upon the grass of Moorfields, families to walk in the autumnal sunshine. They passed through Finsburyfields and Spitalfields where fine ladies rode in carriages and gentlemen were at sport with bow and arrow, on down Bishopsgate Street to Shoreditch, down Petticoat Lane to Whitechapel. Here and there Joseph stopped to talk but he had not found the friends he sought.

At last, back within the walls of the city, he found a group of men in a squalid tavern.

'You'll be after sitting there upon that stool.'

He pushed her into a corner where he could keep an eye on her then went off to drink with his friends. The men leered at her from across the room and she could tell that they were discussing her.

Eventually Joseph came back to join her, bringing with him an eel pie and a pot of ale. He pushed the pie towards her and she ate ravenously. She had not eaten all day.

'Sure and we'll be after having it all worked out,' he said. 'Tomorrow, I'll be after taking you down to Goldsmiths' Hall. We'll be having a little job for you to do.'

'What sort of job?'

''Tis one as will suit a fine lady like yourself who turns her nose at the giving of favours.'

She looked at him sideways.

'You'll be after being our kinchin. That way 'tis all promise and none of the giving.'

'Your what?'

He looked at her and sighed. 'Sure you'll not be knowing anything at all.'

'What's a kinchin?'

'You fine ladies! You'll not be knowing the half of it. A kinchin stands and looks inviting.'

'You mean, be a loose woman?' She felt sick. Her life was to become one of prostitution.

'I mean, after getting your catch, you'll be after bringing him down the alley. You'll be after leaving the rest to us.'

'I couldn't do that.'

'And why not?'

'It wouldn't be right.'

'Sure, 'tis honest coney-catching. And how else is a man to make a living in this god-damned city?'

'You'd hurt him.'

'We'd do no such thing: not if he's behaving himself. We'll be after asking no more than his purse; and maybe his clothes, if they're worth taking.'

'You'd take a man's clothes!'

'And why not? He'll be having plenty more at home to keep him from the cold.'

'But it wouldn't be right.'

'Wouldn't be right,' he mocked. 'And would it be right

339

for those fine gentlemen to swagger around in their clothes and jewels when the likes of Joseph has not a coat to put on his back?' He swaggered up and down, mimicking the gentlemen he intended to rob. 'Sure, in the name of justice, they should be after thanking us for setting the balance straight.'

She shook her head.

'Besides,' he said, 'it makes more sense to take the purse: 'tis better than to take a single coin in return for favours.'

She sighed and turned away. 'It's wrong,' she said. 'It's terribly wrong.'

'Sure, you're too well brought up,' he scoffed. 'There's a devil of a lot you've still to learn.'

Next day he took her to the entrance of Goldsmiths' Hall in Foster Lane.

''Tis here you'll be working,' he said.

She looked at the fine gentlemen milling about, horrified at the prospect of what she was required to do. 'I can't do it,' she insisted. 'Why can't you find something else for me to do?'

''Tis like I've been telling you — 'tis easy as falling off a greasy pole.'

He walked her up and down the lane, into Paternoster Row and Cheapside, until she was familiar with her surroundings.

'You'll be after picking them up here,' he said. 'There's plenty to be choosing from.'

'I don't know which ones . . .'

'And I wouldn't be after upsetting my friends, if I were you. You wouldn't be liking them when they're angry.'

He took her back to an alley at the junction of Foster Lane and Cheapside. 'When you've found your man,' he said, 'you'll be after bringing him for a little walk down here. We'll be waiting to give him the time o' day.'

'I can't do it,' she said. 'I really can't.'

'You'll have met my friends,' he said, pointing in the direction of the men sitting, drinking, in a nearby alehouse. 'I'll be after letting them have a little word with you, if you like.'

'No.'

'Then I suggest you'll be after getting back to the Hall, afore they're after getting impatient.'

She returned to Goldsmiths' Hall and sauntered up and down the lane, gazing into shops and doorways. She did not know how to approach the gentlemen and she had even less inclination to try.

After a time Joseph came and tapped her on the shoulder. It made her jump. ''Tis taking you a terrible long time.'

'I don't know how.'

He heaved a sigh. 'Just be getting on with it. My friends are tired of waiting.'

There was a smell of drink on him and he rolled slightly as he walked away. She wondered about the state of his cronies.

'And don't be after thinking of slipping off, 'cause I've a pair of eyes what's after watching you.'

She looked around, wondering who it could be, but there were a number of rough men and urchin children standing about. Any one of them could have been watching her.

'Half an hour,' he said. 'Then we'll be after losing patience.'

She summoned all her courage and approached a man in a blue waistcoat and white linen shirt. 'Excuse me, sir.'

'Madam.' He made a leg. 'I may be of service?'

'You'd like to take a walk?'

She saw the look of repugnance in his eyes, felt ashamed and immediately wanted to stammer out some kind of apology; but he pushed her to one side with an utterance of contempt.

She felt dirty and filled with self-disgust, fearing that all about had witnessed the incident; but no one appeared to be concerned by it.

'Madam.' A voice by her side made her jump. 'I should be most honoured to walk with you.'

'Oh.' She swung round, breaking into a sweat.

A man stood beside her, large, middle-aged, wearing a doublet of scarlet damascene beneath a cloak lined in a deeper shade of red.

'Oh,' she said again. Now that she had achieved her aim she felt incapable of seeing it through. She made a conscious effort to compose herself.

341

He stood for a few moments, waiting for her to speak, then took the initiative. 'Perhaps,' he said, 'I may suggest we go this way towards a little place I know?'

'No,' she said hastily, 'I would prefer to go down here.'

'By all means.' He took her hand, placing it upon his forearm, and she led him away from Goldsmiths' Hall, down Foster Lane towards the alley.

'Must we go far?'

'No, sir, it's just a little step down here.' She was aware of the tremor in her voice.

She looked about for Joseph, wondering where he would be. There was no sign of him. They had turned into the alley and had taken more than a dozen paces but nothing happened. The knowledge that they were about to be confronted only added to her tension. Her nerves were stretched taut.

Suddenly, a man stepped from a doorway, then Joseph, then another and another. Four men surrounded them.

'Move!' Joseph was speaking to her. 'St Paul's Churchyard — wait for us there. And don't be going back near Goldsmiths' in case he's after coming looking for you.'

Her mind had been diverted from the gentleman who had been torn from her arm and bundled into a nearby doorway.

'Don't hurt him . . .'

'Move!' ordered Joseph, and she went.

'Bitch!' she heard the man shouting after her. 'Mother of all dogs!' But then the cry became muffled. She covered her ears and ran, hurtling out of the alley.

She knew the way to St Paul's Churchyard. Joseph had taken her there earlier in the day before going to Goldsmiths' Hall. As she made her way towards it she thought seriously of running away. Joseph and his cronies were well occupied and would not see her go. But the thought frightened her further with a feeling of utter loneliness and isolation. She knew no one in this great city and she had nowhere to go. She looked around at the people in the streets, imagining that she recognized faces as the same ones watching her outside Goldsmiths' Hall. She was doubtless being followed to prevent her escape. She cringed at the thought of what would happen to her if she ran and was brought back to Joseph and his cronies.

She thought of the gentleman who had been bundled into the doorway and feared that he would be brutally treated.

For an incongruous moment she saw vividly before her the face of her grandfather – the gentle, kind Nehemiah – and was overwhelmed by the desire to go home. But she could not. She was dirty and unchaste.

After half an hour Joseph appeared. 'As fine a set of clothes as I'll be after seeing in many a day,' he said. 'And a big fat purse into the bargain. You'll be after choosing well at your first attempt.'

'What have you done to him?'

He laughed. 'Sure and 'tis nothing we've done but tickle the fine gentleman a little until he was seeing fit to be handing over all his gold.'

'Did you hurt him?'

'I dare say he'll be after having a slight pain in the head for a day or two.' He laughed again. 'But 'tis nothing that'll not be set right. The poor wee man did get his head in the way of me fist.'

She closed her eyes. 'Can we go now?'

'Go?' said Joseph. 'And where would you be after going?'

'Back . . . away . . .' She wanted to be anywhere but here. St Paul's Churchyard was the centre of the book trade and all around her gentlemen were browsing at bookstalls or exchanging pleasantries. She had no doubt that she had been sent here for a purpose.

'And why would we be going anywhere, when there's fine gentlemen to be had for the taking?'

'But you've got the purse. I brought the man to you.'

'And now you'll be bringing us another,' he said. 'And if you'll be after being a very good girl, I'll be giving you a groat.'

'Please, couldn't we just go?'

'No,' he said brutishly. 'You'll be after doing as you're told.'

She flinched, drawing backwards.

'That one over there,' he said. 'He'll be having the look of riches about him.'

'I couldn't,' she said. 'I couldn't possibly approach a gentleman such as that.'

'You're a lady,' he said. 'Sure, and what's the point of

us having a lady if you can't be after talking to fine gentlemen?'

She sighed. 'I'm not a lady. I'm really very ordinary.'

'You'll be after being a stinking mess at the bottom of the Fleet Ditch if you'll not be after doing as you're told!' he threw at her.

'And you'll be having a hemp halter round your neck,' she threw back.

It was a foolhardy act of defiance. He brought the side of his hand in a stinging blow across her face.

'You'll just be getting on with it,' he said. 'I'll not be after spending all day in standing here talking about it.'

She put a hand to her cheek, cradling the tingling flesh.

'And when you've got your gentleman, you'll be after bringing him to Joseph in the alley over there.' He indicated a narrow alley a short distance away.

After he had gone she looked around for the extravagantly dressed gentleman to whom Joseph had referred. He had moved away and was in conversation with others. She was relieved and looked for someone else.

In all she found four men for Joseph and his cronies that day. They were well pleased and drank away a good portion of their gains in The Bear at the foot of London Bridge. They sat her in a corner of the room where they could keep her in sight and later they all used her in a squalid drunken orgy beneath the wagon. She wondered if she might kill herself.

In the course of the next month she found many more victims, moving each time from pitch to pitch in order to avoid being recognized by the men who had previously been robbed. She was degraded and demoralized to a point where she almost thought she did not care. She had given up all ideas of running away. She had been provided with ample evidence that she was watched by a succession of wretched men and waifs only too eager to earn a coin by reporting her whereabouts. She was a good source of income to Joseph and his cronies who had no intention of letting her go.

One cold, damp, mizzling afternoon she stood outside the Cockpit Playhouse a short distance from Whitehall Palace. The play was about to start and people were arriving – on foot, in carriages and in chairs. Ladies in elegant clothes contrasted with her own stained and crumpled dress. She had been wearing it since she had left home and it had become increasingly ragged. The effect had been that over the course of time she had been less able to pick up elegant gentlemen and the content of their purses had diminished in proportion. It had angered Joseph who, more than once, had cuffed her about the ear for her inability to keep up the flow of income.

She had begun to protest that he should buy her a new dress from his takings but then she had held back, believing that he might lose interest in holding her if her usefulness had ended.

She was tired, the lethargy of hopelessness sucking her down. She felt soiled in body and in mind as well as in her dress.

A man came up and said, 'How much?' She looked like a prostitute now.

She named a low price and led him towards the alley where Joseph and his cronies were waiting. She no longer gave much thought to the ritual. Her own self-preservation was at stake and she had given up concerning herself with the welfare of the victims. She no longer asked what had happened to them. She did not want to know.

Whitehall was a maze of squalid back alleys, courtyards, stables, chapels, orchards, royal presence chambers, and stinking hovels. There was no shortage of dark places in which Joseph could hide.

She led the man towards King Street, passing between the back of a royal storehouse and a row of crumbling cottages, knowing this to be the place where Joseph and his cronies lay in wait.

They stepped out as Jessica turned the corner, intending to grasp the man and to drag him into a nearby doorway. But he was prepared. He drew a sword, taking all of them by surprise, not least Jessica who jumped back and squealed.

At the same moment a number of his friends ran down the alley behind them, all brandishing swords or pistols. She recognized one as a gentleman whom she had lured into another alley some two or three weeks before.

'It's a set-up!' Joseph drew a knife but at the same time

345

prepared to run. Their assailants were laying about the robbers in the confines of the alleyway.

One of Joseph's cronies was shot in the leg and hobbled away howling in agony, his breeches stained red. Another spurted blood from a deep gash across his face. Joseph fell to the ground, his arm lying awkwardly outstretched, his sleeve slashed open showing exposed raw flesh. The artery had been severed. She watched mesmerized as blood pumped into the filth and debris amid which he was sprawled.

'Begone, wench,' she was roughly pushed to one side, 'before I lay about you like the scum you frequent with.' It was the man whom she had recognized. 'And be thankful that I'm a gentleman.'

She was still mesmerized by the sight of Joseph sprawled before her, pumping blood.

'And spare your pity for that son of Belial lying yonder. He'll be dead before you've time to shed a tear.'

She turned and ran, trembling and faint, hardly able to control her feet as she stumbled away from the alley.

'Search the wretch,' she heard the man say to another crouching over Joseph. 'If I can't have back the purse he stole from me, I'll have another which he took from some other poor fool.'

She found a dark corner into which to crawl and lay there for hours, trembling uncontrollably, feeling sick. The savage sight had dredged up long-buried childhood memories of her mother drenched in Richard Fullwood's blood. She was utterly alone.

As time went by she began to think about her plight. She had nowhere to go. She considered returning to Joseph's wagon but remembered also the one man who had made his escape. He would doubtless have the same idea and she had no wish to meet up with him there.

The thought of food made her feel even more sick but self-preservation told her that soon enough she would need to eat. She had no way of acquiring it.

After two days of aimless wandering she did what she knew she had to do. She accepted the offer made by a man and went with him to a pile of filthy straw in a stableyard. It bought her a hot eel pie and a piece of bread.

The man paid her and was pleased. It seemed almost

respectable and most certainly preferable to seeing him robbed.

After that she made use of her body just enough to enable her to eat. And, at night, she found somewhere to crawl away from the cold damp city air. The nights were growing colder. She did not know how she would survive the winter. She wanted to pray but could not bring herself to do so.

Margaret closed the diary in which she still wrote each morning and evening. She was tired and arched her back to relieve the strain of the day. Nehemiah was far from well. He was eaten up with rheumatism and recently had begun to complain of pain in his lower abdomen. He spent a long time trying to pass water and each time he returned from his efforts his face was grey and drawn.

She got down on her knees beside the bed. 'Oh, Lord, preserve my father in his aging days. He has been a good man and has served Thee well these many years.'

She wondered if she should get up and go to him, to see if he had settled for the night: yet she had checked on him only an hour before. She was putting off the prayer which she made each evening and from which she drew no comfort.

'Lord, preserve my daughter in her every need. She has been gone from us these many weeks. In Thy mercy, watch over her and keep her safe. Oh, Lord, let her be alive and not lying undiscovered, rotting in some lonely place.'

She began to weep. 'Lord, Thou who knows all things, who decrees that the sins of the fathers shall be visited even unto the third and fourth generation. Lord have mercy upon the child of this sinful woman. I can't bear to think that she must suffer for my deeds. I know she's headstrong and lacking in humility, but she's deserving of Thy charity. Oh, Lord, she's a worthy child and I've not loved her enough.'

She stopped and laid her head upon the counterpane. 'Bring back my child, I beg Thee, Lord. Bring her back, and lay some other kind of punishment upon my head.'

One late afternoon of a dank November day, Jessica sought shelter in the Royal Exchange between Cornhill and Threadneedle Street. She was not looking for men. She had eaten that day and, in any case, the gentlemen here were too grand to look at her in her dishevelled clothing.

The Exchange had a central paved quadrangle around which a covered walkway gave access to shops and warehouses. She sauntered within its shelter, escaping from the chill of the heavy mist-filled air. Dusk was falling and, with it, a thick soot-laden fog. Upstairs were more shops, even more opulent than those on the ground floor, and looking down on her from niches built into the walls, were life-size statues. All around, knots of extravagantly dressed merchants discussed business while ladies shopped and beggars like herself sought shelter from the cold.

''Ere what's your game?'

'I beg your pardon?' She was confronted by a young girl of about her own age, pregnant, wearing a good dress of lilac taffeta.

'What you doin' on me pitch?'

'Sorry, nothing. I'm really not doing anything.'

'What you doin' round 'ere, anyway?' the girl said, but this time with a different tone. 'You ain't no usual kind o' doxy.'

Jessica did not know what to say.

'You don't talk like no doxy.'

'I'm sorry. I really didn't mean you any harm.'

The girl looked her over from head to foot. 'What's a lady like you doin' 'ere dressed like that?'

'I'm no lady.'

'Well, you ain't yer usual sort o' doxy and that's for sure.'

There was a simple rough-hewn kindness about the girl which touched Jessica. It was a long time since anyone had addressed her kindly.

'What you doin' 'ere?'

'Wishing I was somewhere else.'

'Ah.' The girl looked at her knowingly. 'Come up with the carrier, did yer?'

'No, with the tinker, actually.' Jessica found herself briefly outlining the circumstances of her journey to London.

'You stupid pisspot! What you go and leave a good 'ouse and family for to come up 'ere and do this?'

'It does seem rather foolish now.'

'Foolish? You oughta be locked away.' The girl continued to look her over for a while. 'What was it like, this 'ouse?'

'Just a house.'

'Big?'

'Quite big, I suppose.'

''Ow many rooms?'

'I don't know. I never counted.'

'You must be mad! No one leaves an 'ouse like that and comes and stands 'ere.'

'I did, and I wish I hadn't now.'

'You'd best go 'ome.'

'I can't. Not after what I've done.'

'You ain't done nothin' yet. Only what you was made to do.'

'I don't think they'd see it like that. I can't go home.'

The girl looked at her again and smiled. 'You got anywhere t' sleep tonight?'

'No. I haven't had anywhere for days.'

'Pretty murky night,' said the girl, glancing up at the encroaching fog. 'What's yer name?'

'Jessica.'

'I'm Bridget. Want t' come 'ome with me f' the night?'

Jessica wondered if it were a trick but the girl seemed genuine and it did not sound like an improper suggestion. In any case, she felt she had very little left to lose. 'That's incredibly kind.'

Bridget shrugged. 'It ain't much but it's out o' the weather.'

'What reason could you possibly have to be so kind?'

'Don't know, luv,' the girl joked. 'Let's just say I got an 'eart o' gold.'

'You certainly have,' Jessica said gratefully.

Bridget glanced about her. 'Might as well be gettin' orf,' she said. 'These geezers'll all be goin' 'ome soon and I could do with gettin' out o' this weather.'

'Where do you live?' asked Jessica.

'Southwark. T'other side o' bridge.'

'It's very kind,' she said again. 'I don't know why you should.'

'Nor do I,' laughed Bridget. 'But I ain't never taken no lady 'ome.'

As they set out the darkening sky pressed down the fog more thickly about them, made worse by the emissions from the premises of soap boilers, dyers, tanners and ironworkers. The smoke from coal fires was quite unlike the woodsmoke of Dunscombe. Flecks of black soot irritated their eyes and made them cough.

Apprentice boys were putting up the shutters on the shops and people, heads down against the fog, were hurrying home to their supper. Schoolchildren were returning from their lessons, barging through the crowds, and empty produce carts trundled, avoiding horsemen and coaches, while dairymaids herded home the cows from their pasture.

They walked down Gracechurch Street and Fish Street to the foot of London Bridge, where foul-mouthed fishwives, relieved of their heavy trays, were spending their takings in the alehouses. Mudcaked beggars scavenged the river banks for some means of surviving the following day.

They crossed the bridge, narrow and congested with people and vehicles, hemmed in on both sides by the houses and shops built along its length. With their heads down low, they did not look up at the shrivelled heads which hung from poles above the tower guarding the drawbridge. The river was wide and the bridge, some twenty arches, was the widest Jessica had ever seen. She had crossed it on a number of occasions in the past weeks and never failed to compare it with the pack-horse bridge above the river at Dunscombe.

On the far side they passed The Bear at the Bridge Foot in which Joseph and his cronies had frequently spent their time, then went on into streets which became progressively more seedy. Here were the bear garden, the cockpits, the homes of the poor. The streets were a warren of foul-smelling alleys which wound their way between overcrowded tenements. Once large old houses, these had long ago been abandoned by the wealthy and now housed whole families crowded into single rooms, filling the air with the stench of overcrowding and poverty.

Home for Bridget was a room on the second floor of one such house. They made their way up the rotting staircase, glad to be out of the fog and the increasing darkness. Even inside the room it was damp and cold but there was a feeling of protection and safety within its walls.

''Ere, set yer arse down on that stool.' Bridget lit a tallow candle. 'I'll just nip out and buy us an 'ot mutton pie.'

Jessica realized that she was hungry. She held her hands above the few pieces of coal which Bridget had set smoking in the grate, and looked about her, thinking of Dunscombe and of roaring log fires. A rat came out and scuttled about the floor but, finding no food, it went back beneath the floorboards to search elsewhere.

The family would be at their supper now. Afterwards, in the warmth of the firelight, her grandfather would instruct that the book should be taken down and read. She had never cared much for the times spent with the family; she had never felt a part of it; but at this moment she thought of the reading.

''Ere you are, then. Get this inside yer. You'll feel better after a bit o' grub.' Bridget reappeared and handed her a pie.

'Thanks.'

They sat facing one another, nibbling the hot pastry between their fingers.

'We'd best be gettin' yer another dress.'

'What?' It was something so far outside the scope of Jessica's present boundaries that she stammered upon the very idea of it. 'What for? I can't.'

'Well you can't be workin' in a dress like that. You look like one o' them sluts what's from them whore 'ouses down Bride Lane and Cheapside.'

Jessica was still struggling with the very suggestion of obtaining a new dress. 'What sort of work?'

'Don't you want t' work alongside me?'

'Well, yes, of course. What sort of work? I hadn't thought . . .'

'You'd do well down the Exchange. I can just see them geezers take t' you.'

'But why?' asked Jessica. 'It's your pitch.'

Bridget shrugged. 'Gets lonely sometimes. Could do with a friend.'

Jessica smiled at her in pure appreciation. 'Thank you,' she said. 'You're enormously kind.'

'Not bad yerself.' Bridget grinned. 'I'm quite took with you. I gets a bit fed up with all them other doxies what's round 'ere. Ain't got no class. Not like you. I can just see them geezers down the Exchange takin' t' you.'

'But it's your pitch. I couldn't knuckle in on it.'

'Plenty for both,' said Bridget. 'And we'll see them other doxies orf together.'

'About the dress . . .?' began Jessica.

'Well it just so 'appens . . .' said Bridget, getting up and going to a simple wooden chest. 'It just so 'appens as me dear old pa did give me one only t'other week. That means I got two.'

'But I couldn't . . .'

'I can't wear two,' she said. 'Not at the same time. And you can pay me back one o' these days.' She laughed and dug Jessica in the ribs. 'When you've got yerself set up with one o' them fine gen'lemen.'

'I can't take your dress,' insisted Jessica, but Bridget held it out before her. It was of red silk with velvet trimmings, one of the prettiest dresses Jessica had ever seen.

''E come by it by way o' 'is business,' said Bridget darkly.

'Oh?'

She did not elucidate.

'But I can't possibly take it. It's much too good.'

'Just call it a loan,' said Bridget. 'Can't 'ave you workin' 'longside me lookin' like that.'

Jessica looked down at her clothes. 'I do look a bit of a mess.'

'D'you want a wash?'

'Yes, please.'

'There's a drop o' water over there. Bought it from the carrier this mornin'.'

'Thanks.'

Jessica washed herself and put on the dress. She felt much better to be fed and warm and clothed in a decent dress again.

'You look a treat in that dress,' Bridget said. 'Me old pa d be proud o' you.'

'Where does he live?'

'Over at Wappin'.'

She did not go on and Jessica did not like to ask. 'I'll pay you back,' she said. 'You can be sure of it.'

Bridget made a gesture with her hands. 'Who cares, luv?

It'll be good t' 'ave a bit o' company round the place.'

'About the work,' said Jessica, 'what do you want me to do?'

'Just pick up yer gen'lemen and take 'em round to the apothecary's shop. I got an arrangement. Second door at the top o' the stairs. But you gotta pay 'im.'

'Oh.'

''Alf yer takin's at the end o' the day. In return for a potion.'

'What's the potion for?'

Bridget laughed. 'T' stop you gettin' like this,' she said, and pointed to her own distended belly.

Jessica closed her eyes and swallowed. She did not want to be confronted with what she knew to be inevitable.

'What's the matter? You gone already?'

'I'm not sure, but I think I must be.'

Bridget laughed again. 'Well, there's one thing about bein' big-bellied,' she said, 'it stops you 'avin' t' worry about gettin' that way again f' the next nine months.'

'Doesn't it bother you?'

'There ain't much point in worryin' about it, luv. And them potions don't work 'alf the time, anyway.'

'About the gentlemen . . .'

'Just stick t' the better toffs, luv. Don't 'ave no truck with none o' them others. And don't get taken in by none o' them soldiers. Tell you all sorts o' tales, they will, but the army ain't been paid for months.'

'Yes,' said Jessica. 'What about pay?'

'Shillin' a bout. There's some as'll give more, but don't take no less.'

It seemed a lot. 'I'll pay you back.'

Bridget pointed to the half-eaten pie which Jessica had left near the fire to keep warm when she had gone to wash. 'Eat up, luv, else it'll get cold. And I've got us a drop o' gin f' afterwards.'

'You're very kind,' said Jessica for the umpteenth time.

'Will you stop yer goin' on about it, and just eat up yer pie?'

Later, beneath the luxury of a blanket, Jessica lay in the darkness, listening to sounds beyond the window. She felt secure for the first time in many weeks. The fog, thickened by the smoke from thousands of coal fires, had the effect of heightening the silence, echoing anything which broke it – the bark of a dog, the sudden piercing cry of a baby in a room at the top of the stairs, lone footsteps in the street below. There were few about after ten o'clock except those who chose the cover of darkness.

She lay and thought of Dunscombe. She thought of Margaret and found her mind wandering yet again over those old well-worn paths of confused memories – Deliverance Daniels reading his Bible in the candlelight, her mother lying gasping and sighing in the arms of Richard Fullwood. Here, in her new-found security, she remembered again that she did not like her mother.

For her part, Margaret lay in her own bed thinking of Jessica. It was foggy in Dunscombe too, but a different kind of fog – a thick grey mizzle; it brought the same heightened silence but was pierced by different sounds.

She lay and thought of Jessica lying somewhere, exposed and unprotected, ill and uncared for. But maybe she was dead. Perhaps it would be better if she were. It was the not knowing which was so excruciatingly painful. She went again over all the things left unsaid, gestures never made. She should have given her more time, more opportunity for conversation. But Jessica had not wanted conversation and there had been so little time, so much to do.

There were so many jobs waiting to be done tomorrow. The men had been killing pigs and cows ready for winter. There were carcasses to be dressed, hams to prepare for smoking. She had not made sufficient conserves, and apples were still lying rotting in the orchard.

There was sickness among the sheep. Only this morning the shepherd, Goodman, had reported a dozen deaths. She knew only too well that widespread disease in the flock could bring the estate to economic disaster. And there were so many families dependent upon it.

She was tired – too tired to sleep. She spent even more time these days helping Nehemiah. Each day she found herself giving one more hour, taking over one more duty.

Had Jessica fallen somewhere, become trapped, perished undiscovered?

Or had she been taken by force? The thought of abduction was almost too much for her to bear — pictures of cruelty and degradation, misery beyond imagination.

'Dear God, watch over my daughter. Or take her soul into Thy keeping.'

The cry of an owl cut distantly through the fog-laden air. It was so damp out there. Jessica would be drenched. Her body would be lying sodden, decomposing, denied a decent burial. But perhaps she was huddled in a barn somewhere, in a doorway on some squalid street, unable to find protection from the all-pervading dampness, wracked with coughing, covered in sores.

'Richard,' she screamed silently, 'Richard — why aren't you here?'

The girls had a good day. They giggled a lot. It had seemed to Jessica that she would never laugh again but now a new world of optimism had opened up for her. She was immensely grateful.

That evening they sat before their small coal fire, sipping gin.

''Ere, 'ow much d'you make?'

'Six shillings but the apothecary took four. I've still got two.'

'Not bad f' a start. We'll soon 'ave you eatin' cake.'

'I only need enough to pay you back.'

'You look t' me as if yer used t' eatin' cake.'

Jessica laughed. 'I really wasn't wealthy, you know. My grandfather has a dreadful struggle.'

'Don't know about that, luv, but I never did know anyone as lived in an 'ouse like that afore.'

Jessica smiled. 'He spends half his time worrying as to how he can afford to keep it going.'

'Did you get yer potion?'

'Yes,' said Jessica. And, with that, all the newfound optimism receded. 'For what it's worth.' She put a hand to her face.

'You sure yer gone?'

'Pretty certain. I've got to be.'

'Never mind, luv.' Bridget reached out and touched her on the arm. 'Best take it, anyway, just t' be on the safe side.'

'What is it?'

'Dunno.' She shrugged. 'Some sort o' mixture what 'e makes up. Probably thyme and lavender, I reckon, with a bit o' bracken. Or maybe it's 'oneysuckle or rue. You 'eats it up and swallows it down quick.'

'There doesn't seem much point.'

'Best do it anyway, and we'll get 'im t' make you up some cover shame. That might do the trick.'

'Did you try some?'

'Yeah,' she laughed. 'Didn't work f' me.'

'Then there doesn't seem much point,' she said again.

'Come on, luv. It ain't that bad,' said Bridget. 'We could do with a couple o' little nippers about the place.'

'How far gone are you?'

'Seven months.' She pointed to her abdomen. 'Just look at this bump.'

'I don't know, Bridget.' Jessica sighed and shook her head. 'This isn't such a good idea — the gentlemen, I mean. There must be other ways of making money.'

Bridget sat back and allowed her to continue.

'I mean . . .' Jessica hesitated then put in hurriedly: 'Of course I'll do it till I've paid you back.'

Bridget shrugged. 'Then what?'

'Oh I don't know. But there must be other things I could do.'

''Ow much d'you say you made today?'

'Two shillings. Why?'

'And 'ow much d'you reckon you'd get if you were some nice respectable laundrymaid or somethin'?'

'I don't know. I'm not sure how much my mother paid.'

'Lucky if you got 'alf that much in an 'ole week.'

'I'd get my food and a bed.'

Bridget spread her hands to indicate the room in which they were sitting. 'You got food and a bed 'ere.'

'I know, but . . .'

'And this way there's always the chance you'll get set up by some toff as fancies you. A lady like you'd stand a good chance o' gettin' set up by some toff.'

'I don't know . . .'

'I'll come and visit you,' grinned Bridget, 'when you gets set up.'

Jessica was not convinced. 'I still say I'd prefer something a little more respectable.'

'You could always go 'ome.'

'Oh, no,' she said quickly. 'I couldn't do that.'

'Look, luv.' Bridget lowered her voice and came to kneel on the floor before her. 'If you went 'ome and explained, they'd understand.'

'You don't know my mother.'

'But if she loves you . . .'

'I'm not sure she does.'

'Course she loves you! She's a lady.'

Jessica laughed bitterly. 'What difference does it make – being a lady?'

'But she's yer ma.'

'Ah, yes but who's my pa?'

Bridget let a few moments elapse. 'What's she like, yer ma?'

'Oh, I don't know . . . just a person. Very respectable. Or so you'd think.'

'You ain't never said nothin' about yer pa.'

Jessica heaved a great sigh. 'And thereby hangs a tale.' She recounted what little she could remember, confused and altered with the passage of time. 'I think it could have been that man Fullwood but I'm not sure.'

'And the man you called yer pa . . .?'

'He was a good man. She treated him shamefully.'

Bridget thought on it for a while. 'Don't make no difference, do it, whether they're toffs or ordinary folk? They're all the same.'

Jessica was deep in her own thoughts. 'I was always so ashamed.'

'What of?'

'Of being a . . . a bastard.'

Bridget laughed at that. 'Cor blimey, luv, you ain't the first what's been a bastard.'

'I know, but . . . it's different here, in London. In Dunscombe, well – oh, Bridget, I waited for years to be found out. I felt so different, so ashamed.'

''Tweren't your fault. 'Tweren't nothin' t' do with you 'ow you was born.'

'No one else seems to think of it like that.'

Bridget pondered for a while. 'Did anyone ever say anythin'?'

'No. No one ever said a word.'

'Then 'ow can you be sure?'

'Oh, I know. Papa told me quite definitely. I remember it well. He said, "You are a bastard".'

'Well, never mind, luv. Yer grown up now and no one's found out. It ain't as if it's common knowledge.'

'It matters to me,' said Jessica firmly. 'I'll never forgive her.'

Bridget looked at her seriously. 'That's a big thing to say – that you'll never forgive yer own ma.'

'I know, Bridget, but it's true. I'll never forget the way she deceived him. She thought I didn't know about it, but I watched them. I remember.'

She began to cry. Bridget took both her hands.

'And you should see her now. So pious! So respectable! Butter wouldn't melt in her mouth.'

'Don't cry, luv.'

'I hate her, Bridget, I really hate her.'

'You don't 'ate 'er, luv.'

'And I'll tell you something else,' sobbed Jessica, 'I'm glad I ran away. I'm never ever going back.'

'Come on, drink up yer gin.' Bridget got up and poured them each another good measure from a clay jug. 'Then I've got a clyster you oughta use,' she said as she handed it to her. 'Rue and castor oil and camphor. You washes yerself out with it.'

'Thank you, Bridget. You're very good to me.'

Later, as they lay in the darkness, Bridget called across: 'I'm glad you come, Jess. Things was gettin' a bit lonely round 'ere all by meself.'

'You saved me from the most dreadful state.'

'You'd 'ave got yerself out of it, one way or t'other.'

'I'm not sure. I think I might have gone under.'

Bridget rolled over and made herself comfortable. 'Never mind, luv, yer 'ere now.'

'Yes,' said Jessica. 'But Bridget . . .'

'Yeah?'

'When I've paid you back, I think I'll find some other kind of work.'

CHAPTER 16

December was bitterly cold. Although the girls tried to keep the small fire burning at night, several times they awoke to find that their dresses, damp when removed the previous evening, had frozen. They sought whatever shelter they could find in the quadrangle of the Exchange but eventually they abandoned their pitch in favour of the coffee houses which abounded in the area. Here it was warm and, in exchange for a further share of their takings, they were allowed to sit unobtrusively in a corner to catch the eye of potential clients.

By this time Jessica knew for sure that she was pregnant. She had tried a number of potions from the apothecary but, when these had all proved unsuccessful, she had reluctantly taken Bridget's example and tried to accept her condition philosophically.

Talk in the coffee houses was of increasing civil unrest. On 5 December the apprentice boys had openly mobbed the soldiers whose numbers were deserting in force. General Monck had still not appeared on the scene, but had moved his troops down to the Scottish border where they were poised to march south.

Change was in the air; the atmosphere was charged with rumour and speculation. On 19 December, the Commander-in-Chief of the army capitulated to the demands of the Common Council of the City of London and promised a free parliament. It was the only way he could ensure that his men would be paid.

It was on this day that Bridget flopped down upon a stool

and announced: 'I'm fed up with this lark. Me belly's too big.' She was eight months pregnant and the effort of climbing the stairs at the end of each day was exhausting her. 'Blessed if I ain't orf 'ome.'

'Home?'

'To Wappin'. I'll get shot o' this belly in a week or two.' She looked across at Jessica. 'You wanna come?'

'I don't know.'

'I was gonna take you there anyway, for Christmas.'

Jessica thought of her own home. Throughout all the years of the Commonwealth religious festivals had been abolished, but old customs die hard. Behind closed doors most families cooked a goose and ate mince pies and plum broth.

'We always 'ave a right old knees up at Christmas,' said Bridget.

'It's against the law.'

'Well, we all know that don't we, luv? We all know some soldier's likely to come bargin' in and take the food what's on yer table — but it ain't nothin' but show. Nobody's bothered really and there ain't much as they can do about it, anyhow.' She grinned. 'Even the toffs get caught every now and then and they gets fined for goin' to the play 'ouses. So it's not just us what's at it.'

Jessica nodded. 'Even my grandfather likes to celebrate Christmas and he's very godly.'

'Well, there you are, then. And, any'ow, there ain't no one gonna bother us this year. The army don't know whether it's on its arse or its elbow.'

Jessica had been stirring the fire. She brought a mug of warmed ale which she placed between Bridget's cold hands. 'Here, drink this. It'll warm you.'

'Thanks, luv. You comin' then?'

'Would your family mind?'

She laughed. 'There's that many of 'em, they'd 'ardly notice.'

'Well if you're really sure . . . it would be nice.'

'That's settled then. We'll go t'morrer.'

Next morning they hired a wherry from just below the bridge and were rowed downstream towards Wapping.

The river was as much a hive of activity as were the streets.

With only one bridge, there was a constant crossing and re-crossing of wherries taking people from one bank to the other.

'They say as there's near on two thousand wherries round these parts,' commented Bridget.

'It looks as though they're all round here.'

They passed beneath the vast stone walls of the Tower, oars rhythmically cutting the water, avoiding other craft which ferried cross-stream and passing beneath the large ocean-going vessels which moved more slowly to their mooring places.

Squalid shanty settlements lined the banks, the homes of seamen and dockworkers, built around a maze of wharfs and piers. Narrow, foul-smelling creeks spilled forth filth and garbage into the main flow. There were children in the mud of low tide, begging with black-caked hands from the seamen of newly berthed ships or grubbing for small items of cargo dropped in the passage from ship to wharf. Everywhere was noise and activity: anchorsmiths, chandlers, ropemakers, sailmakers, carpenters, shipwrights.

'What work does your father do?'

'Bit o' this, a bit o' t'other. Mostly on the account.'

'What?'

'On the account.'

'Your father's a pirate?' Jessica was shocked.

Bridget was slightly put out by her response. 'It's only takin' a bit of what some toff don't need.'

'You mean he goes out and steals from ships?'

'What's wrong with that? It's what everybody does round 'ere.'

'Everyone?'

'Well, not everybody. Just most of us.'

'I hadn't realized.'

'Me pa, me brothers, most of me uncles — nearly all the blokes what's round our way.'

'Oh I see.'

Bridget gave her a reassuring nudge. 'You don't ask no questions,' she said kindly, 'And you don't get told no lies.'

'Oh,' said Jessica again.

'Well, what d'you expect? All them ships coming up 'ere loaded down with all sorts o' stuff. They ain't gonna miss a few, are they? Any'ow, them rich geezers up in them ware'ouses . . . it's what they expect. They've got enough. And there's people like us, what's got mouths t' feed and nothin' t' put in 'em. What d'you expect?'

There was a certain logic to it. Jessica sat and pondered for a while on the morality she had come to accept since she came to London. 'But what if they get caught?'

'They don't.'

'What, never?'

Bridget shrugged. 'Well, who's t' catch 'em? Navy's only got one ketch 'tween 'ere and Gravesend. Can't be everywhere, can they? When they're patrollin' down the bottom end, what's to stop us up 'ere? An' if someone spies 'em up round these parts, you can always go down to Tilbury.'

'I suppose.'

'They ain't really bothered, any'ow. Sometimes they rounds up a few. Do it 'cause they thinks as what it scares the pants orf us. Makes a real show of it, they do. Comes and 'angs 'em over there.' They were approaching Wapping and she pointed to the gallows just coming into view on the docks.

Jessica shuddered.

'They gets about four or five of 'em and bungs 'em in the Marshalsea. Then they puts word round as what there's goin' to be an 'anging. You should see the crowds what gets down 'ere then. Climbs up on the roof tops, on the ships, sits up in the riggin' — anywhere so's they can get a good eyeful. Then this geezer with a silver oar leads the procession, over the bridge, all the way down 'ere. Then they 'angs 'em.'

'Oh.'

'Over there. Do it at low water and leaves 'em there till the tide's flowed over 'em three times afore they cuts 'em down.'

Jessica was almost glad that they had reached the steps and had other matters to occupy them. They paid the wherryman and began to walk through the narrow alleyways between the buildings.

'Did you know,' Bridget was enjoying her role as guide, 'they say as what there's thirty-seven ale'ouses 'ere in Wappin'?'

'I can believe it.'

It seemed that there was one on every corner. The streets were filthy and there was an overpowering stench of excreta. They wound through a maze of alleys until Jessica was lost.

''Ere we are.' They were in front of a house, similar to all the others, squeezed between yet another alehouse and a ropemaker's workshop.

It was filled with people. Although Bridget ran to each, calling them by name, Jessica was never to learn the relationship between them all. It was a miscellany of extended family — aunts, uncles, in-laws, children — all intermixed and intermarried in a manner which seemed totally incomprehensible to her. People came and went at all hours of the day and night; a pot of boiling stew was kept permanently over the fire from which everyone helped themselves at will.

When it came time to sleep, the girls cleared themselves a space upon the floor. No one appeared to resent the further overcrowding.

There was a feeling of warmth and fraternal acceptance which absorbed Jessica into its midst. Almost at once she overcame her initial disconcertedness at their occupation. For the first time she experienced the pleasure of being part of a family.

Two days before Christmas, they all went out as a crowd to gather boughs of bay and holly, screaming encouragement to the two boys who climbed the tallest tree for mistletoe. Geese and turkeys appeared as if from nowhere. The women fell over one another baking pies and tarts. It seemed a disorganized tangle of hands, laughter and children underfoot, but in spite of everything, a growing pile of food was stacked ready for Christmas.

In the middle of it all Bridget gave birth to a boy who was unceremoniously absorbed into the whole, wet-nursed by any woman with a breast to spare, crooned over by so many that it was soon difficult to tell to whom he belonged. She named him Ben.

The men got drunk — riotously, morbidly, aggressively drunk — telling tall stories and reminiscing, fighting and being pummelled into submission by stronger or more sober kin. One man sat and cried for the wife he had lost.

They banked up the fire, roasted chestnuts and told tales of ghosts and fairies; then they cleared everyone back against the walls to play ' The Dun is in the Mire'. It caused a near riot. They lifted the heavy log of wood, attempting to drop it upon one another's toes. It began with laughter and ended with bloody noses.

It took two days to consume the quantities of food and strong drink, another to nurse sick heads. On the fourth, the atmosphere changed. There was an air of subdued tension and excitement in the air. Jessica sensed it but Bridget only said: 'Don't ask no questions. Remember what I told you, and you won't get told no lies.'

Late that night, when the girls were supposed to be asleep, the men smeared their faces with blackened ashes from the hearth and went out.

The following morning there was horseplay and elation. A quantity of bales was stacked about the room and there was a strong heady aroma of spices.

'They'll be wantin' us to go orf up Smithfield t'morrer,' said Bridget.

'What for?'

'T' get rid o' the stuff.'

Jessica was shocked. 'Why us?'

''Cause it's our job, silly. It's always the women what sells the stuff.'

'Oh.' Jessica thought for a while, then ventured: 'Supposing we get caught?'

'We won't.'

'But they'll ask questions. What do we say?'

'They won't,' her friend said again. 'People won't wanna know, just s' long as they're gettin' a bargain.'

Jessica was far from happy. She wanted to ask if anyone had been harmed in the course of the raid; but, as she looked around at the laughing men, they did not seem capable of deliberate brutality. It was another question best left unasked.

'We'll take a bit at a time,' said Bridget. 'We spreads ourselves out a bit: that way, we'll 'ave it all got rid of in no time at all.'

The two girls went together to Smithfield, trundling a cart through crowded streets. There was a quantity of sugar, some tobacco, spices, a couple of casks of wine, some ivory.

Wealthy and poor came to buy or to haggle. No one questioned the origin of the goods. A quantity of opium was bought in its entirety by a gentleman dressed in expensive green brocade with a cloak of velvet.

'Told you it'd be easy.'

But Jessica found herself continually looking over her shoulder.

At Oakbourne, Christmas had been a more subdued occasion than at Wapping. Margaret carried out her duties in providing food and extra comfort for the household but her heart was not in it. She was concerned about Nehemiah and her mind roamed endlessly over her fears for Jessica.

She watched the weather, at one moment picturing a dishevelled creature shivering on some distant doorstep or in the back of a barn, next moment the decomposition of an undiscovered body, sodden and ugly, torn at by foxes.

And, all the time, she held in her mind that one thought: that it might not have happened had she loved her daughter more.

Abigail came to her mother and entwined her fingers within her work-calloused hand. 'You're cold, Mama. Shall I fetch you a warmer cloak?'

Margaret looked down at her and smiled. She had been standing gazing out across the hills. She did not know how long she had been there but Abigail was right: she was very cold.

'I'll come in now,' she said. 'There are pies to bake and I haven't attended to the men in the barn.'

'I'll help you, Mama.'

'Thank you, child.' She was so like Richard that it made Margaret's heart ache just to look at her. It was in her face, her voice, the way she held her head. She wanted to call out his name but no one here at Dunscombe had ever known of him.

Jessica had had Rupert's eyes. But, there again, no one but Nehemiah knew of Jessica's parentage. And Nehemiah had never mentioned it, not even to Margaret. She herself had almost wiped it from her thoughts — except when she had looked at Jessica's eyes.

'Come with me, Mama. I'll get you something warm to drink.' Abigail was not yet eleven but already she was so hardworking, so thoughtful.

Margaret had spoken recently with Tom Cox who had said there was talk in London of restoring a monarch. The Commonwealth had not proved popular and the army was disintegrating with no one strong enough to lead it since Cromwell had died. It occurred to her that, with the return of a king, Rupert would be free to return from exile.

He had written letters to his mother during her lifetime, telling her of his wanderings around Europe, on the fringes of royalty as a follower of the Prince of Wales. But now Elizabeth was dead — passed on peacefully in her sleep some three years ago at the age of fifty-four.

In the early days Nehemiah had worried about Rupert's return and about his reaction to the fact that Oakbourne had passed out of his hands. But Rupert's letters had shown no animosity. Now, twelve years later, Nehemiah was well-established in the community as master of Oakbourne.

Rupert's house in Chiswick had also been sequestered. Margaret wondered where he would choose to live if he returned to England. The thought brought back the feelings of unease which the years had masked. She assumed that it would be in London on the fringe of the Court in company with his returning friends. He seemed a remote figure after so many years of absence. He must undoubtedly have changed after the years of wandering. But of one thing she was certain: her ill-feeling towards him had not diminished in the slightest degree.

The days following Christmas passed into their second week and still Bridget showed not the slightest inclination to return to the room in Southwark. 'It's warm 'ere,' she said. 'We've got us a good fire.'

The men went out on another raid. This time Jessica did not question her part in disposing of the loot. It seemed an appropriate way of repaying hospitality.

Everywhere in the city, talk continued to be centred upon political change. General Monck had arrived in London and was leading a new government. There was talk of elections.

It was widely predicted that the Prince of Wales would be invited to ascend the throne as Charles the Second.

The girls had time on their hands. They wandered about the city taking in the sights. Outside the Tower they watched visitors from other lands who spoke in strange foreign tongues.

'They comes from all over t' look at London,' said Bridget. 'There's all sorts o' things what you can see in there.'

'What kind of things?'

'Fierce wild beasts like what you've never seen afore.'

Jessica looked at her, disbelieving.

'Strike me if I tells a lie. There's lions and all sorts o' wild beasts. You can go in and look at 'em, if you like.'

'I don't think I'd want to.'

'Got 'em walled up so's they can't get at you, but you can see 'em if you pays. We'll go in one day, when we've got us some money.'

'Does it cost a lot?'

'Dunno, but they says as there's plenty o' geezers in there what's 'oldin' out their 'ands.'

They wandered around St Paul's Churchyard where the booksellers gathered.

'Can we get out of here?' said Jessica. 'It brings back bad memories.'

'Why?'

'I remember standing here with Joseph.' She looked around uncomfortably. 'And I 'm always afraid someone's going to recognize me.'

'Come on then.'

They passed a bookstall. 'Can you read?'

'Yes,' said Jessica, 'My mother taught me.'

'Cor! I forgets sometimes w'at a lady you are.'

'I've told you,' said Jessica quietly, 'I'm no lady.'

At Smithfield they sat and watched the bawds waiting to procure young girls who had come up from the country with the carriers.

'Stupid little pisspots! Oughta 'ave stayed where they come from.'

Jessica turned to her and smiled. 'Don't go back to the Exchange, Bridget.'

'Why not?'

'Stay with your family. You're happy there.'

'What about you?'

'It's time for me to move on.'

Bridget's face clouded. 'There's no need, luv. Yer welcome t' stay.'

'I'm eating their food and I've still got to pay you back.'

Bridget shrugged. 'You does yer bit up 'ere at the Market. It pays for yer grub.'

'But I've got to pay you for the dress.'

'Sod the dress. And nobody's bothered if you wants t' stay.'

'Thanks,' smiled Jessica. 'But I've got to move on.'

'We'll go t'morrer.'

'No,' said Jessica. 'I want you to stay.'

'I ain't lettin' you go orf alone.'

'Why on earth did you do it, Bridget?'

'Do what?'

'Go up to the Exchange. You were all right in Wapping with your family. Why did you go to work at the Exchange?'

'Dunno, luv,' she shrugged. 'Wasn't much t' do round Wappin'. Seemed as good a place t' be as any.'

'That's no reason. There was no need to go and sell yourself.'

Bridget just laughed and poked her in the ribs. 'It's like a lot o' other things, luv; seemed like a good idea at the time.'

It was no explanation but Jessica knew it was all she was going to get. 'Don't go back, please.'

Bridget smiled and looked at her steadily for some time. 'Yer a good mate,' she said. 'I'm glad you come back with me that night.'

'I'll go back to Southwark,' said Jessica. 'Just until I've paid you back.'

'Sod the bleedin' dress,' repeated Bridget.

'No, I've got to pay you back. I'll go and live in our place in Southwark. But I want you to stay at Wapping.'

'Yer a cussed little bleeder. If it weren't f' little Ben . . .'

'Stay with him, Bridget. He's better off in Wapping.'

Jessica returned to the room in Southwark but it was lonely on her own. There was no more of the fun and companionship, only the degradation of the gentlemen and the room above the apothecary's shop.

It was very cold. Bridget had insisted upon giving her a warm cloak but it only added to her sense of indebtedness. Each evening when she climbed the stairs her feet and fingers were numb and she would sit for a long time over the little coal fire, waiting for it to throw out some heat.

On one particularly bitter day, she sat in a coffee house warming herself and looking for potential clients. Outside, the air was filled with white flakes which settled and turned colour in the open sewers and beneath the wheels of passing carts and carriages. People walked with their heads held low against the biting wind.

Jessica felt unwell, sick of her way of life and of being alone. She thought perhaps she would cultivate the interest of some gentleman in the hope that he would set her up in some form of greater comfort; but the thought sickened her more than the role she already played.

Her stomach ached. It had been troubling her all day in a vague sort of way. She thought it was the chill in the air. But, as she sat in the coffee house, the ache became a more definite pain, growing until it caused her to suck in her breath and hold her stomach in her hands.

A gentleman approached. 'I'm sorry, sir,' she said, 'but I must just sit here a while and take a rest.'

The pain did not ease: in fact it grew worse, lessening at times but then intensifying to a greater degree. At last she abandoned her seat in the coffee house and walked home, dragging her feet through the thickening snow. It seemed a very long way.

At last, in the room at Southwark, she threw herself down on the truckle bed without bothering to light the fire; then regretted it. She was extremely cold. She knew she must take off her dress. Above all else, she must not spoil her only dress. But she was so cold.

The pain was intensifying. She rolled off the bed and crawled on her knees to the fire, lit it and lay before it waiting for the warmth. After half an hour she forced herself to remove the dress and to lie tightly rolled in the blanket.

She must have slept for, when she opened her eyes, it was dark outside the window. She was thirsty but could not summon the energy to crawl across the cold room to get herself something to drink.

She realized that she was bleeding. A feeling of warm stickiness alerted her to it and investigation proved that she was bleeding heavily. Her reaction was one of relief. She knew that she was aborting the baby.

But relief was soon crowded out by a sense of pain. It washed over her in waves, causing her to feel sick and to sweat despite the cold.

'Just hang on,' she told herself. 'It'll be worth it when it's ended.'

But it did not end. The pains went on all night and the blanket was saturated. She tried to crawl about in an effort to find something to absorb the flow but there was little in the room apart from the bare essentials. She could not use the dress.

She felt faint. In the early hours of the morning she began to realize that she was in real danger. She needed help.

She called but no one came. If anyone heard, they did not respond. She went on calling but the strength of her voice diminished to a whimper.

'Oh, God, please send someone to help me.'

She thought of her mother. She would have known what to do. But her mother would have been appalled to learn of the pregnancy. And, in any case, she hated her mother. She did not want her mother here. But just the same . . .

She slept again, drifting off into a strange kind of half-sleep which brought little relief but confused her as to time. She thought it was still the early hours of the morning when there was a sound at the door.

'Cor blimey, luv, what on earth you doin' there?' Bridget came in and threw herself down on her knees beside her.

'Oh, Bridget, thank God you're here!'

'What's goin' on? 'Ere, shift over so's I can make you a bit more comfy.' Bridget lifted Jessica's head and put something beneath it, then covered her with her own cloak.

She re-lit the fire which had gone out and warmed some ale.

''Ang on,' she said, 'I'll soon be back.'

She went out of the room, leaving Jessica alone. After

a time she became panic-stricken, fearing that she had been abandoned, but at last Bridget returned with an elderly man.

''Ere, I found this geezer with a cart. 'E'll get us back t' Wappin'.'

Jessica felt herself hauled down the stairs and laid amongst the produce in the cart. It began to move, rattling and thumping through crowded snow-lined streets. Buildings looked strange from this prostrate angle, their jutting upper stories appearing to close in above her head. The jolting of the cart rolled her from side to side, thumping her head against a woven basket.

''Ang on, luv, just 'ang on. We'll soon 'ave you back at Wappin'.'

By the time they arrived, Jessica knew little of it. She felt too ill to care.

''Ere, come on out you lot,' Bridget shouted. 'Our Jess is in trouble.'

Strong willing hands lifted her from the cart and carried her into the warmth of the house. Women closed in on all sides, ministering to her. She gave herself up to them with an intense feeling of relief and gratitude.

Next day Bridget sat beside her bed. 'You feelin' better, luv?'

Jessica nodded. 'I think I'd have died if you hadn't come.'

'Good job I turned up then.'

Jessica looked at her. 'What would I do without you, Bridget?'

'Dunno, luv. But it just goes t' prove you ain't no good up there all on yer own.'

They both laughed.

'You lost the little nipper.'

'Thank God for that.'

Bridget inclined her head. 'They ain't so bad. Just look at me little Ben.'

'Oh, Bridget, little Ben is beautiful. I didn't mean . . .'

'I know, luv, yer better orf without it.'

Jessica nodded. 'It feels like a fresh beginning.'

'You'd best not go back. T' the gen'lemen, I mean.'

'No. I must never go back.'

Bridget smiled with satisfaction. 'Then you'd best stay 'ere.'

But Jessica shook her head. 'As soon as I'm well I must get up and look for something else.'

'You'll stay where you are,' said a woman nearby. 'We've not saved you from yer Maker so's you can go running orf again.'

'Sorry,' said Jessica.

'Give it a couple o' weeks or so,' the woman smiled. 'You'll soon be 'ale 'n' 'earty.'

It was proving to be a hard winter for Margaret. Nehemiah refused to acknowledge the seriousness of his illness but the pain in his abdomen was gradually incapacitating him.

The weather was unremitting, with cold snow-laden winds which piled drifts against walls and hedges, bearing down trees beneath its weight so that their branches swayed sullenly in downturned grace.

The sheep had been herded to the lower slopes but, even here, were overcome by drifts. Nehemiah spent one bitterly cold night with his men digging them out, only to lose a good number later for want of fodder.

The chill exacerbated his pain and he limped home hardly able to stand. Margaret put him to bed and tried to warm him but the icy chill would not release its hold. For three days she replaced warming pans as they cooled and fed him with warm broth until at last the yellow-grey pallor of his skin gave way to a more healthy colour.

'You must stay in bed,' she insisted. 'Until you're quite well.'

He chafed to be free to resume his duties. 'There's work to be done. And it's still snowing outside.'

'I know, Father, but you're not fit to be out in it.'

'I must. Who else will do it if I'm not there?'

'I will.' She forced down the knowledge that soon enough he would not be there at all.

That night the wind howled around the house, rising until it reached storm force, rattling windows and sending unsecured objects thudding and skidding with muted crashes into thick snow.

Margaret lay in her bed listening to the creaking of the heavy-laden elm tree which stood beside the house. If only Richard were here! The unremitting need for him gnawed at her in the white-filled darkness of reflected snow. Richard would have warmed her bed, he would have calmed her fears.

She began to drift in near-sleep through the forest and fields of New England, remembering the touch of his hand upon her back, the upturn of his mouth in laughter. She remembered the way he would cup her face within his fingers when he kissed her.

She thought of Jessica – of a Jessica alive and destitute, exposed to this bitter wind.

Suddenly a crash, much louder than all the others, and the sound of splintering wood. It seemed as if the whole roof were caving in around her.

She shot from the bed and ran to the window from where it was quite clear that the tree had split, sending one huge bough crashing against the house.

By the time she had dressed and run downstairs there were other members of the household gathered. They were standing huddled together gazing up towards the roof.

''Tis difficult t' see, Missus. 'Tis difficult to know how much damage be caused.'

Margaret put a hand to her brow and peered upwards, swaying on her feet as she was buffeted by the strong wind.

'There's a sizeable hole.' In the light of pre-dawn and reflected snow she could just see a gaping void with a large splintered branch protruding from it. 'But we won't know the full extent till morning.' She turned to see Nehemiah hobbling to join her, a cloak pulled tight around him, clutched to his abdomen.

'Father, what are you doing here?'

'What's happened?'

'The tree's come down – or part of it. You must go back to bed.' The wind snatched at her words, taking her breath.

'I can't. I must attend to what's got to be done.'

'There's little that can be done until daylight,' she said. 'We can't see clearly and it's too dangerous in this storm.'

Nehemiah took a few more steps but was in obvious distress.

'Go back to bed, Father. You'll take chill again in this biting wind. It'll do you no good to be standing here.'

She called to a servant. 'Take the Master back to bed, Aggie, and get him a warming pan.'

'What's to be done, Missus?' A man came running up beside her, stumbling through the snow.

'Persuade the Master he must go back to his bed, William,' she said. 'Then go and check on the rest of the men. Is your cottage all right?'

'We're all right, Missus, though we've lost some thatch.'

She spent the next hour trudging through snow, ensuring the well-being of the families on the estate. There was nothing, at this stage, which could be done about the roof. She helped soothe frightened children, gave instructions for the start of repairs, and herded together a gaggle of straying geese.

At the coming of daylight she stood eating bread and cheese before the kitchen fire, flexing fingers which tingled as they thawed. The servants began to gather about her in ones and twos, stamping the snow from their boots and blowing on their hands. Margaret gave them all food and warm ale.

'Wind's slackening, Missus. I'll get out ladder and go check on the roof.'

'No, Albert, it's too dangerous. I'll not risk your safety. We'll clear the boughs which have fallen to the ground. It will give us an area in which to work better. By the time we've done that, the wind may have eased. Those with damage to their own cottages may go home and attend to it.'

'I'll tend the flock,' said Goodman. He pulled his sheepskin jerkin tight about him and made to launch out into the snow.

'I'd rather you stayed,' said Margaret. 'I've need of you here.'

He looked uncomfortable. 'Master 'd want me to tend flock.'

'You've a boy quite capable of watching the sheep,' she said. 'And we've already checked that they're together and secure.'

'What do Master say?'

'I've no idea what he says,' she said firmly. 'I'm telling you that I need you here.'

'I think you'd best go ask Master.'

Margaret straightened her shoulders. 'The Master is ill in his bed and I have no intention of disturbing him.'

'Then I'll just go tend sheep.'

'You will stay here,' she commanded. She surprised herself by the authority in her voice. He looked taken aback; several people standing about shuffled their feet.

Goodman took one pace backwards but kept his face set in an expression of stolid defiance. 'I'll not be takin' orders from no woman, Missus.'

Margaret set her own jaw though her heart was hammering. All eyes were upon her. 'You will do as you are told, Goodman. When the Master is up and well you may refer to him.'

'This bain't be no matter of the kitchen, Missus. This be man's work.'

'Yes,' she retorted, 'this is a matter of great concern to the estate and thus to us all. And if you wish to remain here and keep your job, I suggest that you go this instant and arm yourself with an axe in order that you may start to clear the tree which has fallen against this house.' It was bluff. Under no circumstances would she have evicted Goodman's wife and children.

'We'll see what Master do 'ave to say,' he said sullenly.

'You do that. But in the meantime, I suggest you go and fetch an axe.'

He went out mumbling to himself. ''Tweren't seen the like o' this in Sir Henry's day.'

'My father's Master now,' she threw after him. 'And has been these past twelve years.'

The other men standing nearby lowered their eyes, pretending they had not witnessed the exchange of words. 'We'll just be getting on, Missus, now 'tis getting daylight. 'Twill take us best part o' morning to clear that tree.'

Fourteen-year-old William came and stood at her side. 'Shall I speak to the men for you, Margaret?'

She declined with a smile of appreciation. 'I need you to support me, William,' she said. 'You're my man-brother now.'

They worked all day, the young and able women working with the men while the others kept supplied a constant source of warmth and nourishment. By late afternoon, as an early

375

winter dusk descended, Margaret was able to report their progress to her father.

Nehemiah sat in his bed, a shawl about his shoulders, fretting that he could not get up.

'The tree's been cleared,' she said, 'and we've pulled down another bough which was threatening to fall.'

'What of the roof?'

She sighed. 'There's extensive damage,' she said. 'There's a great gaping hole and the main timbers are splintered.'

He was seriously concerned. 'Is it in danger of collapse?'

'Not now. It's shored for the present and the hole's been covered against further falls of snow.'

'It's bad news,' he said. 'I don't know what we can do.'

'I'll get the men to do the best they can tomorrow. But I'm afraid they can only patch it.'

He nodded. 'It's work for skilled craftsmen, not the men of the estate.'

'It'll cost money.'

'More than we have.'

'I know,' she said, and they both fell silent. 'And there's damage to the barn,' she said after a while. 'The stable's collapsed and a number of windows are broken.'

'It's bad news,' he said. 'Very bad news.'

She sat looking at him, her hands resting in her lap. 'How much?' she asked after a while. 'How much do we have?'

'Not enough,' he said.

'But how much?'

'Margaret,' he said, 'we're doing very little more than living from hand to mouth. Our expenses have been greater than the money earned and now that we've lost so many sheep . . .'

'I know, Father,' she said, only too aware of the answer to her own question. 'What can we do?'

'I don't know, child. I really don't know.'

'Perhaps Tobias . . .'

'No,' he said. 'Tobias has little enough to support his own family.'

She heaved a sigh. 'I shouldn't worry you, Father, with these matters.'

'Who else should bear the load?'

'But when you're ill . . .'

'I must get up.' He began to fidget with the bed coverings. 'It's too much to expect you to carry such burdens for me.'

'Stay where you are,' she said. 'There's nothing anyone can do till morning.'

She piled a few more logs upon his fire before going downstairs to carry out the many chores which had been left undone. 'Try to get some rest, Father,' she said. 'I'll come back later. We'll talk about it then.'

Late at night she made her own way to bed and knelt for a long time in prayer. Then she went to a small chest in the corner of the room. It was filled with mementos of her life, small items brought back with her from New England, a book which had belonged to Richard. She took it to her breast and breathed his name.

At the bottom, wrapped in a piece of cloth, were several pieces of her mother's jewellery, given to Margaret by Nehemiah shortly after her arrival home. It was all that remained of Anne's early womanhood, daughter of a good family here at Oakbourne. Margaret wondered again what was the story behind her marriage to a young journeyman weaver, but she understood much more clearly now the meaning of love. She took out the jewellery, piece by piece, and fingered it. It seemed a fitting purpose that she had in mind.

A week later she set out, riding a horse which plodded hock-deep through the snow, towards the nearest sizeable town.

Nehemiah had wept when she had told him of her intention. He had taken the jewellery and had slept with it beneath his pillow, returning it to her only that morning as she was about to set out.

'I'll get a good price for it,' she said.

'Yes,' he nodded. 'Make sure you're not cheated.'

Although the snow was deep, a blue sky had replaced the leaden grey and the wind had dropped to a light breeze. The snow was thawing slightly, causing white accumulations to slide with a soft *plop* from the branches of trees. Snow crystals caught the light, sparking colour.

The road was well known to her but she took great care for it was impossible to see what lay beneath the deep white blanket and landmarks had all taken on new character.

Mid-morning, she stopped at a village inn, hoping both to warm herself and to rest her horse. The innkeeper's wife brought her mulled ale and cleared a space for her beside the fire.

'You travelling alone, my dear?'

'Yes,' she smiled. 'I'm well used to it.'

'It's not wise for a woman to travel alone.'

For a brief moment Margaret wondered if she should have brought William but he had been needed at Oakbourne. 'I'm well used to it,' she said again. 'And I know the way.'

'There's a stranger about,' said the woman darkly. 'Been seen over yonder.'

'What sort of stranger?'

The woman made a speculative gesture with her mouth. 'Could be up to no good.'

'Really?' Margaret felt a slight chill of alarm. 'But surely there's been no rogues on this road for years. Not since they hanged Jake Habgood.'

'And good riddance.' The woman crossed herself. 'Terrorized these parts no end.'

'Then who do you think this new one might be?'

'No idea, my dear. I only knows as that my husband saw him yesterday, acting very strange.'

'Really?'

'Yes, my dear, didn't like the look of him at all.'

'Oh dear.' Margaret looked around at the people listening to the conversation. 'Well I'm not carrying anything of value.' One never knew who might be listening.

'That's just as well, my dear. But 'twouldn't be nice to get stopped when you're on your own.'

'No,' she agreed. 'Let's hope he chooses to be in some other part this morning.'

When she set out again she went with added caution, checking for fresh prints of hooves or feet, taking particular care at crossroads and at areas providing cover close to the road. She was only too aware that in deep snow she was unable to urge her horse into any kind of hurried escape.

An hour later she had almost reached her destination. She must pass through one small area of woodland, then open countryside in which she would be able to see a good distance in all directions.

She was nervous in the woodland. It was little more than a copse but the trees were thick, made thicker still at the perimeter by drifted snow. She put her hand on the saddlepack and plodded on, looking always to right and left. There was no sign of foot or hoof prints apart from those of travellers along the road. Anyone lying in wait would have been bound to leave some kind of telltale track off the main thoroughfare.

The attack when it came was so sudden that it made her gasp. Suddenly there was a sound behind her, feet slipping and slithering through the deep banked snow. However he had got there, he had achieved it without leaving prints. He grabbed her from behind, pulling her backwards and sideways from the horse so that she lost balance and fell sprawling into the wet snow.

It was the indignity as well as the shock which left her gasping. Her first instinct was to scramble to her feet, re-arranging her clothing. The man had already righted himself and had grabbed the bridle of her horse.

'How dare you!'

He was a filthy, dishevelled creature, with dirt-caked skin and matted hair. When he opened his mouth he showed blackened teeth worn down to stumps. He took no notice of her protest and gave his attention to steadying the horse which had taken fright.

'You leave it alone.' It was an inane thing to say but the first to enter her mind. She was at a great disadvantage stumbling about in the deep mass of wet snow; and she kept her eyes upon the heavy piece of wood which he held in his hand like a club.

He had the horse under control and began removing the saddlepack. She launched herself at his back and began clawing and tearing, but he whirled round and with his arm sent her flying, floundering backwards through the snow so that once again she found herself lying helpless, looking up at him.

For a brief moment he stood over her, threatening her with the club, but then turned away and began rifling through the saddlepack. Some items he discarded to the ground, others were stuffed into his clothing.

When he came to the jewellery stowed at the bottom of

379

the bag he let out a loud guttural sound of discovery. He had not spoken: the sound made her wonder if he were dumb.

He worked quickly, giving her no time for thought. Even had she been able to do so, she would have been hard pressed to form any kind of retaliatory plan. He was clearly a footpad of the very worst kind who would not have hesitated to use the club upon her.

Almost before she knew it he had turned away and was forging a path back into cover of the trees. She watched him go, anger, fear, shock and helplessness warring in the invective which she hurled after him. Almost immediately she realized the sinfulness of the words she had used and was left with a sense of guilt to add to her distress.

There was no point in continuing the journey. She turned the horse and, still trembling, started back towards Dunscombe.

By the time she arrived she had rehearsed a number of ways in which she could break the news to her father. In the event, Nehemiah thought first of her own welfare.

'He hurt you, child?'

'No, Father. But he would have done if I'd put up any kind of resistance.'

'You poor child.' He took her in his arms and comforted her like an infant. 'I should never have let you go.'

'How many times have I made that journey alone?' she protested. 'And never come to harm.'

'I should have asked Tobias.'

She looked at him. 'Then we would have had to share with him the knowledge . . .'

'Yes,' he said. 'It would not have done to distress him by knowing of our troubles.'

'He'll know soon enough,' she said wearily. 'We've no money now to mend the roof.'

'No,' he said, and took her back into his arms.

'What are we going to do, Father?'

'I don't know, child, I just don't know.' He rocked her back and forth.

'I've failed you, Father.'

'Child.' He held her away from him and looked into her face. 'How can you say such a thing? You have been the best daughter that any man could ever have. And since your mother . . .'

'I've lost her jewellery, Father. It's even worse than selling it.'

'Don't talk like that, child. She would have been the last to condemn you.'

She put her head back to his shoulder. 'Do you ever wish, Father, that we were back at the old house and just working at the loom?'

'Yes,' he said quietly. 'I'm just a simple master weaver.'

She looked up at him and smiled. 'We'll think differently tomorrow when we've come up with something. Or in the spring when the lambs are gambolling and the orchard is full of blossom.'

'Yes,' he said, but without conviction.

His despair spurred into life her own survival instincts. 'We'll think of something, Father.'

'I don't know what.'

'We'll find some way, just wait and see.'

'If only,' he sighed, 'if only I weren't so tired.'

She looked at him and bit her lip. 'Leave it to me, Father. There's no need for you to worry yourself about it.'

'I can't leave you to carry my burdens.'

'May God help me,' she said, 'I'll find some way to mend that roof.'

He smiled at her sadly and stroked her hair. 'You always were a fighter, child.'

'You taught me how, Father.' But she was deeply distressed by the death of his own fighting spirit.

Next day she gave instructions for further reinforcement of the roof repair but knew that it would not be adequate for any length of time. Although the hole was covered, there was a strong likelihood that the damp would seep through, causing further damage to the already deteriorating structure. There was extensive damage to the timbers and the men had discovered additional damage caused by rot when they had gone into the roof to examine them. It would require skilled craftsmanship to replace both the timbers and a large section of the stone tiles.

She could only pray that somehow they would find the money to pay for it; but she had no idea where to turn.

CHAPTER 17

Jessica's health improved. Three weeks after her miscarriage the girls were able to venture out again, first to nearby places, later into the city. They made their first visit to the theatre. At the Salisbury Court, just off Fleet Street, Jessica walked into an experience which held her enthralled.

The play was *The Rump*. There was little doubt to the politically aware that the characters Bertlam and Woodfleet were caricatures of the army generals Lambert and Fleetwood, but this fact passed over her head. While the audience rocked with laughter, Jessica's thoughts were only of the atmosphere and of the people upon the stage.

'You like it 'ere,' commented Bridget.

'Yes,' she said. 'There's something about it.' She did not yet recognize it but her visit had evoked that old yearning to stand up above the crowd and to be noticed.

'We'll come again.'

'No,' said Jessica. 'I've got an idea.' She pointed to the orange-sellers with their trays. 'I think I've discovered what I'll do.'

Bridget was shocked. 'Don't talk daft. That's worse'n with the gen'lemen.'

'It's only selling oranges.'

'You must be jokin', luv. They does more'n sell oranges.'

'But I needn't. I'd simply refuse.'

'You must be jokin',' said her friend. 'Them's a load o' doxies.'

'You wait and see. And it's a way of getting into the theatre.'

'You'd never get away with it.'

'Yes, I will, you wait and see.'

Bridget was still looking uncertain. 'Well, I s'pose we could give it a try . . .'

'Not we: *I'll* give it a try.'

'Look, luv,' Bridget turned and said determinedly, 'if you thinks as how I'm gonna let you do that on yer own, then yer a bigger pisspot than I thought.'

'But what about little Ben?'

'We'll bring 'im with us.'

'We couldn't.'

'Why not? Cor blimey, we ain't the first t' bring a little nipper with us.'

'No,' said Jessica. 'You look after little Ben. I'll sell the oranges.'

'Yer not doin' it on yer own,' Bridget said again.

Jessica looked uncertain. 'Would he be all right?'

'Course 'e would. We could take turns t' carry 'im.'

Jessica was still far from certain. 'Well, all right,' she said reluctantly. 'We'll give it a try.'

The arrangement worked well. The girls carried their tray of oranges around the theatres — not only to the Salisbury, but to the Cockpit and the Red Bull Playhouse in Clerkenwell. Ben went with them: while one carried the tray, the other carried him.

Over the years of the Commonwealth playgoing had been illegal, yet several theatres had succeeded in remaining open. Now that the old order was crumbling there was no one to care. The theatres were packed.

''Ere!' Bridget got breathless rushing from one to the other. 'Why can't we just stay put in one of 'em?'

'Sorry.' Jessica lifted Ben from her and took her turn in carrying him. 'I want to watch all the plays.'

'You ain't supposed t' see 'em all in a day. But yer always was a rum'n,' commented Bridget.

'Sorry,' said Jessica again. 'I'll take the tray. You go and put your feet up in the alehouse.'

'You must be jokin'. Takes two of us t' see orf them geezers.'

'We've done all right so far. They've got the message.'

'Yeah,' grinned Bridget. 'And got us a right rum

384

reputation – a couple o' doxies what don't give.'

'We're not doxies,' said Jessica with feeling. 'I shall never ever again be a whore.'

'Maybe,' said Bridget. 'But I'm still not lettin' you go in there alone.'

They bought themselves an eel pie then set out again for the Cockpit where they stood at the back watching the play.

'If there was a woman on the stage . . .'

'Don't talk daft! There ain't never been a woman on the stage. Well, I did see one once but she were one o' them foreigners.'

'But don't you see?' Jessica indicated the balding, middle-aged actor who was playing the part of a young girl. 'If there was a real young maid up there, it would be so much better.'

Bridget giggled. ''Adn't thought of it afore. S'pose it is a bit daft. Better get some of these 'ere doxies up there on the stage.' There were more than half a dozen prostitutes in the theatre looking for clients. 'They could parade theirselves up there f' all t' see.'

'No, a real maid: one who would do it properly.'

'You must be daft. There ain't never been a woman up there. Wouldn't be allowed.'

'You'll see. One of these days . . .' Jessica thought on it for a while. 'And you know what?'

'What?'

'I'm going to be there when it does.'

Bridget looked at her.

'I'm going to be an actoress.'

'You're addled in the brain.'

'No, I'm not. I'm going to be a woman player on the stage.'

Bridget shook her head and gave up. 'Come on,' she said. 'Me feet's killin' me standin' 'ere and we ain't sold 'ardly any oranges. You've 'ad a few rum ideas in yer time, but that one near on beats the lot.' She adjusted the weight of the tray and made to move off.

'Bridget?'

'What?'

'Are you really tired of spending time in the theatres?'

Bridget stopped, turned round and grinned. 'Cor blimey, luv, you don't 'alf take things t' 'eart. We might as well

385

be 'ere as anywhere else. But we gotta sell these 'ere oranges.'

'But you're not as keen on it as I am.'

'No one's s' keen on it as what you are.'

'And another thing . . .'

'What?'

'We're not earning much. And I haven't paid you for the dress.'

'Cor blimey.' Bridget rolled up her eyes in exasperation. ' 'Ow many times d'you 'ave t' be told? Sod the bleedin' dress.'

'I'll pay you sometime. You know I will.'

'The only way as you'll ever get rich is if you goes 'ome.'

'No,' she said sharply.

'Or if yer takes up with one o' them geezers sittin' over there.'

'Never.'

'Well, you wouldn't make much bein' an actoress, and that's f' sure.'

'No, I suppose I wouldn't.'

Bridget stopped and looked at her for a moment, then said kindly: 'Is that what you really wants? T' be a player?'

'Yes,' she said, 'I really do.'

'Then I s'pose that's what you'll 'ave t' be.'

Jessica's confidence was beginning to wane. 'Perhaps I am mad after all?'

'If that's what you want, we'll 'ave you up on that stage afore you know it.'

'I'm a woman.'

'Well,' grinned Bridget, 'we'll just 'ave t' make 'em see different.'

'You are good to me, Bridget.'

''Ere cop 'old o' this tray,' she said. 'An' see if you can sell some o' these 'ere oranges. Yer better lookin' than what I am.'

Next day they kept their eyes open until they saw the manager of a troupe of actors whom they had seen many times sitting in a coffee house near the Salisbury Court. They went in and sat for a long time staring at him from across the room.

''Ere are you goin' t' go over there and speak t' 'im?' asked Bridget at last. 'Or am I?'

'I'll go.' Jessica took a deep breath and launched herself across the room.

The man looked up as she approached.

'Sir, may I speak?'

He indicated with his hand that she should sit opposite him.

Bridget hoisted Ben up on her shoulder and moved across the room so that she was seated on a bench nearby.

'I have this notion,' began Jessica hesitantly, 'that it would add to the enjoyment of the play if a woman were to take part.'

The man lifted an eyebrow.

She went on to explain her views upon the subject, then concluded: 'And I should very much like to be an actoress, sir.'

'A most interesting suggestion,' he said; but the lecherous glint in his eye had not escaped her notice. 'If you'll just accompany me back to my lodgings, we'll discuss it further.'

'Could we not discuss it here?'

'We'll be much more comfortable at my lodgings, my dear.' He rose and offered her his arm.

''Ere, I'm famished.' Bridget got up and nudged her. 'This is my friend . . .'

'Let's get out o' 'ere and get summat t' eat.'

Jessica half apologized for Bridget's rudeness but had recognized as easily as her friend that the man had thoughts other than of acting on his mind. 'If you'll excuse me, sir, I must be leaving with my friend. Perhaps we could discuss it some other time?'

'Lot o' bleedin' good, 'e was,' commented Bridget as they walked away.

Jessica was despondent. 'He didn't take me seriously.'

'They ain't none of 'em goin' t' take you seriously. There's only one thing on them geezers' minds and it sure as 'ell ain't acting.'

'Someone's got to take me seriously.'

'Dunno who. But we ain't done yet, luv. We'll try the lot of 'em until we finds someone as does.'

Jessica nodded. 'We mustn't be put off at the first attempt. We'll keep going until we find someone who's prepared to listen.'

Over the following weeks and months they tried many times to speak with both managers and others associated with the theatre but no one was prepared to accept Jessica as a member of their company. She became increasingly despondent but at no time did she consider abandoning her dream. She was determined that one day, somehow, she would stand upon the stage.

On 1 May, Parliament voted for the restoration of the monarchy. The Fleet was despatched to bring home the new King from Holland.

On 29 May the girls made certain that they were up early. By dawn they were out in the streets of the city, hoping to reserve themselves a good vantage point; but others had been there all night. It was almost impossible to squeeze their way through the crowds, let alone to find a position from which to see. Twenty thousand people lined the streets. Cut-purses were everywhere, blind beggars and children crushed beneath trampling feet.

Everywhere was a feeling of abandonment, as though the populace was trying to throw off, overnight, the strictures of the past fifteen years. Many were drunk. Prostitutes were doing good trade. From windows hung brightly coloured tapestries and the conduits had been decked with flowers and with greenery. From church steeples bells were ringing.

They pushed their way through the crowds, holding Ben between them to protect him from the jostling throng. At the Strand, with its great houses belonging to the wealthy, they manoeuvred themselves into a position from which they could climb up on to a cart. It was still not possible to see clearly but at least they were a little higher than the heads of those in front of them. Behind them, young men and boys had clambered into the gardens of the houses and climbed the trees.

They stood for hours, taking it in turns to shoulder Ben's weight. The cart swayed as people pushed and jostled, threatening to collapse as more and more climbed up on it.

At last the procession came – colour and noise. They caught only the briefest glimpse of the King. The crowd surged forward as he approached, further obscuring their view. A slim, swarthy man – today his thirtieth birthday

– he looked strained from the journey, as though he would be glad to reach Whitehall Palace, now but a short distance ahead.

Behind came the gentlemen with their ladies on fine horses decorated with plumes, the Lord Mayor and aldermen in robes of scarlet lined with fur, sheriffs with gold chains about their necks, Livery Companies with their banners, each with a pageant on a stage carried by relays of men depicting their respective trades – the Mercers, the Grocers, the Clothworkers, the Merchant Taylors, the Goldsmiths, the Fishmongers – twenty-four in all. There were squadrons of horse and foot, trumpeters in black velvet with cloth of gold, jugglers and morris dancers, musicians and acrobats.

It took seven hours for the procession to pass. Along the road to London the crowds had fallen in behind, adding to the numbers who paraded through the narrow city streets, growing all the time as more and more lengthened its tail. Old and young, walking with dignity or the worse for drink, scholars and milkmaids. In the middle of it all, a group of apprentice boys were trying to kick a football.

It went on all day and when the girls went next day to visit Bridget's family in Wapping they learned that the men had taken advantage of the occasion to make another raid. This time one of their number had not returned. All were quiet and subdued, giving comfort to one another and to the widow. No one mentioned the two seamen who had also lost their lives.

Bridget shed a tear for a favourite uncle, cuddling Ben and crying into his hair. 'We'll go up t'morrer while the crowds is still about,' she said. 'It'll be easy t' get shot o' the stuff.'

It was. Within an hour the cart was empty. And afterwards, they went again to the theatre.

Margaret used the back of her hand to brush the hair from her face. She was in the fields, supervising the haymaking. It was hot. Nearby, Nehemiah sat in the shade of a tree, pale and drawn. He still put up a pretence of taking charge but over the months he had done less and less. After an hour or two she asked one of the men to escort him home.

'I can manage, Father, and you're tired by the heat.'

He was reluctant to leave but she persuaded him to go. 'You can come back later when you've had a rest.'

They were all there — every member of the household who could be spared from their duties, every member of the family. There had been a period of rain and it was imperative to use this present warm spell in which to gather in the hay. Sarah and Rachael had taken time from their own home chores and had brought their children — the older ones to assist, the younger to play or to sleep in the shade. Abigail wielded the long wooden rake alongside her aunts, stopping every now and then to brush the hair from her eyes. William worked beside the men.

As Margaret looked about her she was painfully aware of the awesome responsibility which fell upon her. Nehemiah was aging daily and the pains were growing worse. She was surrounded by people who looked to her for guidance and for employment. The roof of the house was leaking badly. It had been patched and re-patched but nothing had been done by way of major repair. In addition to the sheep taken by disease, they had lost many lambs in the winter snow.

She sighed and went back to her work. Richard would have known what to do.

A horseman came out of the wood and rode across the fields towards them. The sun was in Margaret's eyes and she took little notice of him until the man beside her said: 'Well, to the mercy of God — 'tis Master's son.'

'Master?'

She looked again, shielding her eyes from the glare of the sun. It was Rupert.

He was older — seventeen years older than when she had seen him last — but there was no mistaking the way he sat his horse.

He called out and waved. 'Hello, everybody, I'm back. I'm back!'

He had put on weight — an unhealthy flabbiness — and looked tired from the journey. Through Margaret's mind raced a thousand thoughts.

'Margaret, it's so good to see you.' He made straight for her on dismounting from his horse.

'Good-day, Rupert.' She fought to control the tremor in her voice. 'I'm glad to see you safe and well.'

'Oh, it's so good to be home.'

She wasn't sure she liked the sound of that 'home'.

'You've no idea how long I've waited for this day.'

'You're welcome,' she said tightly.

'You are in health?'

'I am, and trust you are, too.'

'I'm very well.' He reached out in an attempt to take hold of her hand but she moved.

'You've been gone a long time.'

'I have indeed. ' He stood and looked at her. 'And you haven't aged a day.'

She made a dismissive gesture and tucked her work-calloused hands inside her apron.

'Not since the day I last saw you.'

'The day you last saw me,' she said in a low voice, 'I seem to remember that you were accused of the attempted murder of my husband.'

'Oh!' He flinched as though she had slapped him. 'I didn't actually harm him, you know,' he said eventually.

'Actually?'

'I would have saved him, had he not been swept away so fast.' Nevertheless, he looked uncomfortable.

'Actually?' she repeated.

'I'll not deny it was in my mind.'

She exhaled slowly.

'But I would never have been able to see it through.'

People were looking askance at them. They became aware of it.

Margaret coughed. She realized she was being less than courteous to a visitor, particularly one who had previously been heir to Oakbourne. She made a conscious effort to change the subject. 'You've had a long journey,' she said. 'I'll get someone to prepare you some food.'

'Thank you.'

He looked around at the people standing about them. Some did not know him. Others remembered him too well. They blamed him for the death of Sir Henry, while Sarah and Rachael still retained painful memories of their brother Samuel.

'It's good to be home.'

Each nodded recognition and extended a greeting — some

genuinely warm, others accompanied by some murmured aside.

'I've been gone too long.'

Again the servants made polite responses then went back to their work, leaving Margaret alone with him.

'I'm sorry, Margaret.'

'Sorry?'

'But I was so terribly jealous.'

She looked at him.

'Of your husband. And I could see . . .'

She continued to look at him, offering no assistance as he struggled for words.

'I could see . . . Margaret, he didn't love you.'

She closed her eyes.

'Not like I . . .'

'I don't want to hear it, Rupert. I'd rather you didn't continue.'

'No, of course not,' he said quietly. 'We'll talk about it some other time.'

They stood looking at one another uncomfortably, neither knowing what to say.

'It was such a long time to be away.' He shook his head sadly. 'And I missed you so.'

'Aunt Elizabeth read me your letters,' she put in hurriedly.

'Yes.' He seemed to shake himself. 'She kept me informed.'

'She was always very pleased to receive them.'

'I'm extremely grateful to you,' he said. 'And to Uncle Nehemiah. He cared for her well.'

'We did our best.'

'After my father . . . Well, she could so easily have lost her home.'

'Indeed,' said Margaret coldly. 'It would have been as well if you'd thought of that at the time.'

He was deeply hurt. 'They claim he tried to run.'

'So I believe.'

'He didn't, you know. He was going to stand trial.'

'I've no idea of the truth, Rupert, but it's much too late now.'

'Yes,' he agreed. 'Much too late.'

He let some time elapse before he spoke again. 'I did send word, you know, to clear his name.'

'So I hear.'

'But it was too late.'

'Much too late.'

'Yes,' he said, and went quiet again.

'You blame me, Margaret,' he said after a while.

'What else am I expected to do?'

'I didn't mean to involve him. Not for a moment.'

'Rupert,' she said, 'if you hadn't taken men on to Sir Henry's estate he wouldn't have been arrested.'

'No.'

'And if he hadn't been in that camp on the road to Witney, he wouldn't have been shot.'

'Agreed,' he sighed.

'Then what am I supposed to say? That I don't hold you responsible? That you're in no way to blame for your own father's death?'

'I know,' he sighed. 'I do understand how you feel.'

'Your mother would have been pleased to see you,' she said a little more kindly. 'She went painlessly, and at peace.'

'But before I was able to return.'

'Unfortunately, yes.'

'Yet another thing for which I hate those damned Parliamentarians.'

'Yes,' she said quietly. 'She never did come to terms with your exile.'

He stood deep in his own thoughts, looking about him. 'I would have given anything to come back just once, to see her.'

'And Isobel and the children?'

'Yes,' he said sadly. 'I never saw the children again.'

She wanted to ask him his intentions but did not know how.

He continued to stand, looking about him. 'Which one is ours?'

'What?'

'Jessica.' He indicated the women working in the field. 'Which one is she?'

Pain closed up Margaret's throat. She could rarely bring

herself to speak of Jessica by name and certainly not to Rupert.

'That one,' he said. 'I'll wager it's that one.'

She swallowed and attempted to control her voice. 'My daughter has . . .' she began. 'My daughter has . . . gone away.'

'Away?'

Tears were smarting in her eyes. She did not want him to see.

'Where?'

'She's . . .'

Goodman came up and saved her from immediate distress. 'Master, they say as old King's son is coming back.'

Margaret prickled at the term 'Master': it was the shepherd who had used it when Rupert had first arrived.

'Here already, Goodman, and seated in Whitehall.' Rupert slapped him on the shoulder. 'All's well with England. Those damned Parliamentarians have had their day.'

''Tis been a long time, sir.'

'It has indeed, Goodman, but the years of insanity are at an end.'

'Good to have you home, sir.' Goodman touched his forelock and returned to his work.

Home. Again Margaret wanted to ask Rupert his intentions. She turned over in her mind ways of approaching the subject.

'Father isn't here,' she said. 'He's taken to his bed.'

'How is he? I must go at once and greet him.'

'He'll not want to see you,' she said. 'He's not well.'

'Of course he'll want to see me,' he said, but his expression was pained.

'I don't see why.'

'I only want to greet him. I've been gone a long time.'

'And it seems you've forgotten a lot of things while you've been away. Father still remembers the manner of Samuel's death.'

He closed his eyes and sighed. 'So long ago,' he said, 'and yet memories never fade.'

'He was my brother.'

'And my cousin.'

She gave him a sideways glance of contempt.

'And Uncle Nehemiah still holds it against me?'

'Why shouldn't he?'

'Because,' he said, 'it was an accident.' He gave a gesture of hopeless resignation. 'I've explained so many times — it was an accident.'

'So you said at the time.'

'And can say no more. It was as much a tragedy to me as to anyone else. I loved Samuel.'

'We all loved him,' she said, 'but it was you who shot him.'

'I didn't shoot him . . .'

'It doesn't matter any more just how he died,' Margaret cut him short, 'it only matters that he's dead.'

He sighed. 'And Uncle Nehemiah still refuses to speak to me because of it?'

'Doubtless he'll speak to you, seeing that you're here in his home. But Father's a sick man: I don't want him upset by recalling things which are best forgotten.'

'It's not I who am recalling them,' he said. 'In the few minutes I've been standing here, you've raised half the misfortunes which have ever befallen this family!'

'Yes,' she retorted, 'and you've had part in most of them.'

He stepped back and stood looking at her for a long time. Then his face softened. 'Oh, Margaret, enough of this.' He reached out in an effort to touch her. 'Is this any way for us to meet after I've spent the last twelve years wandering like a vagabond in foreign lands, unable to return home? Take my hand and let's be friends.'

She pulled back, refusing to let him touch her. 'I'll get someone to prepare refreshment,' she said. 'You can rest before you're on your way.'

He stood for a moment as though about to make some new attempt to take hold of her. 'I'll go up to the house,' he sighed at last, 'and wash some of the grime from my face. I've been eating dust these past miles.'

'Jane?' Margaret called to a young girl, issuing instructions for the preparation of food and ale.

'My father's resting,' she said as Rupert turned to go. 'I don't want him disturbed.'

'I'll not disturb him.' He climbed up on to his horse. 'And

I'll come back shortly to give you a hand. It'll be good to be haymaking again, after all these years.'

She watched him go, her stomach churning.

Later that evening she sat with him in the long oak-panelled room overlooking the garden. The heat had not gone from the day and Margaret sat beside the open window, trying to catch the breeze. Outside, the sun was setting in a blaze of orange light.

'A glass of sack before you're on your way?'

Convention had dictated she should invite him to share the family meal, but it was still not clear where he intended to spend the night.

He nodded. 'I'll be glad of my bed. It's been a long and tiring day.'

It had been a sombre meal – polite stilted conversation had been made over an underlying feeling of unease. Nehemiah had eaten in his room, persuaded by Margaret to stay there and rest. Abigail and William did not know this stranger – but they had heard of him. Eventually, after the reading, everyone had excused themselves to their beds, leaving Margaret and Rupert alone.

'You've a room at the alehouse?'

He smiled at her. 'May I not stay here?'

She tensed. 'I thought . . .'

'My old room's free. I checked with a servant. It would be so good to sleep in my old bed again.'

'You had no right . . .'

'I'm sorry,' he said. 'I meant no discourtesy.'

She looked at him for a moment. 'You do realize, Rupert, that Oakbourne belongs to my father.'

'Of course. How could I not know?'

'Just so long as we have things straight.'

He smiled at her. 'It was a clever move on his part to keep it in the family.'

She was not sure what to say.

'He's made a good job of looking after it.'

'He's worked hard,' she said. 'It hasn't been easy for him.'

'I'm sure. And now that he's ill, he'll be glad to be relieved of the responsibility.'

'What do you mean?'

'He'll be glad I'm back.'

Margaret coughed out a small bitter laugh. 'Rupert, whatever he feels, I can assure you he'll not be glad to have you back.'

He sat and looked at his hands.

'You've caused nothing but trouble in this family, yet you think that you can just walk back in as though nothing has happened! As though all those years, all those events, can just be wiped away.'

'What have I done?' he asked simply. 'Tell me, what have I ever done but love you?'

'How about Samuel?' she retorted. 'And my husband? Even your own father!' She had left out herself.

'There's an explanation for every one of them,' he said quietly. 'But no one chooses to listen.'

'The list is too long,' she said. 'It denies you any credibility.'

He was still sitting staring at his hands. 'After all these years, I had hoped that you'd look a little more kindly upon me. It's what kept me going, all that time. Through all that damnable boredom and misery wandering about in foreign parts. I had hoped that memories would have eased and that you'd welcome me back just a little more kindly.'

'You ask too much,' she said. 'Too much has happened.'

'Is it too much to believe that I may have changed?'

She raised a sceptical eyebrow.

'I've done a great many foolish things in my time; I'm not proud of any of them. But I have had time to think. There's not much else to do when you're kicking your heels far from home.'

He looked at her hoping for some kind of encouragement but she gave him none.

'I was young. In twelve years I've had time to think. There are many things I wish I had done differently.'

She was determined not to be moved by the obvious sincerity of his words.

'Only one thing hasn't changed,' he said, 'my love for you. I've loved you steadfastly since you were in your cradle, and it grows with the years.'

Thoughts of Richard rose like a huge painful lump in her throat and she fought to swallow it down.

'What did you mean, Rupert — he'll be glad to be relieved of the responsibility?'

'Now I'm back, he'll be glad of my help.'

'Really?'

'I'll be only too pleased to help him in any way I can.' He stopped and measured his words carefully. 'You do realize,' he said, 'now that the King has returned, it's only a matter of time before he orders the return of all sequestered land to its rightful owners.'

'What?'

'It's only fair. Sequestration was totally unjust.'

The statement left her floundering.

'It's as well for us that Oakbourne was retained within the family.'

'What?'

'It'll cause much fewer problems when it comes to sorting matters out.'

'I don't believe you, Rupert. Oakbourne belongs to my father.'

'Of course it does. But very shortly it will be returned to me.'

'No,' she said. 'That can't be right.'

'I can assure you it's the King's intent.'

She set her jaw and stared out of the window in brooding silence. The setting sun was casting dark rivers of shadow beneath the trees.

He came and knelt before her, trying to take her hands in his own, but she drew them back into her lap. 'Come, my love,' he said. 'Let's not quarrel. I've no intention of taking my land forcibly from Uncle Nehemiah.'

'Then he won't give it.'

'I only want to be of help to him — and to you. You've worked too hard. It's time you took a rest.' He looked at her and smiled. 'I can take the burden from your shoulders now I'm home.'

'You're not home, Rupert. Oakbourne belongs to my father.'

'He's worked long and hard but it's time to bring the estate back to the condition in which my father left it.'

She smarted at the reference to the deterioration of the estate.

'I've noticed that the roof . . .'

'Yes,' she said curtly.

'And there are various other major calls for repair.'

'Father did his best. He was always short of . . .'

'Money,' he finished for her gently. 'It's as well that I set aside a good portion of my own before Cromwell's robbers could get their hands on it.'

'You still have Sir John's?'

'Not all of it. Just a good portion which I happened to put by in a safe place.'

'The house in Chiswick,' she said suddenly, seizing upon the thought as it entered her head. 'It will be returned to you when the land is handed back.'

'I doubt it,' he said. 'The new owner has been astute enough to swap sides. It's quite amazing how a staunch Parliamentarian can suddenly become an ardent supporter of the King.'

'But that can't be right. If one property must be returned, then . . .'

'The King needs all the supporters he can get,' he said. 'He's not going to anger his new friends.'

She heaved a sigh, totally unable to come to terms with the politics of today.

'And, in any case, I'd be of little help to you in Chiswick. I'm much more use to you at home.'

'You're not home.'

'I never did like the house at Chiswick,' he continued. 'This is my home.'

'Poor Isobel. You were cruel to that poor woman.'

'I hope not,' he said. 'I gave her every care and comfort.'

'But not yourself.'

'You know why.'

'And your children,' she put in. 'Those poor children.'

'I loved my children,' he said with feeling. 'It breaks my heart to have lost them.'

He ran one finger across his eye and she realized that, in this instance at least, she could share his grief.

'Isobel . . .' she began.

'You know why I couldn't love Isobel. I did try, truly I did, after you were gone. But it was no use. I could never love anyone but you.'

She lowered her eyes. 'You must have hurt that woman, Rupert.'

'I know, but I loved you so.'

'You know nothing of love,' she said quietly.

He smiled. 'But you must admit that I do know about steadfastness? Despite all your rebuffs, I still come back, still loving you more than ever before.'

'I don't know why,' she retorted. 'I've never given you a moment's encouragement.'

'Nor do I. It'd be a lot easier not to bother.' He smiled again. 'But somehow I've got no choice.'

She got up. 'You must excuse me, Rupert. It's getting late and there are matters which must be attended to before I can rest. I must be up early in the morning to gather the hay.'

'Marry me, Margaret.'

She stopped for an instant, then continued as though she had not heard. 'You're welcome to stay the night. I'll get Jane to prepare a room.'

'Marry me and everything will be all right.'

She stopped again and said evenly, 'I can't marry you, Rupert. You know I'll never marry you.'

'Don't say "never". Just think about it for a while. You'll see it's for the best.'

'For whom, Rupert?'

'For everyone. For you, for me, Uncle Nehemiah, the family, the household — and not least for Oakbourne.'

'The family, and Oakbourne, are quite suited as they are.'

'Are they?'

She looked away.

'I could make quite certain that everyone's livelihood is secured.'

'Your own sisters may well have been glad to receive you,' she said, 'but they're all married and settled. As for my family, I can assure you . . .'

'I'd give you every care and comfort that it's in my power to provide. I'd spend the rest of my life in the sole pursuit of making you happy and content.'

'Rupert,' she said sharply, 'this is a pretty poor attempt at regaining Oakbourne. Tobias is my father's heir.'

'That's unkind,' he said. 'And totally unfair. I ask you for your own sake not for Oakbourne.'

'You seem pretty intent on regaining it.'

'I shall regain it soon, in any case,' he said. 'My wish to marry you has nothing to do with Oakbourne.'

'I suppose that then you'll throw us out.'

He smiled at her gently and extended his hand. 'You know very well that I would never throw you out.'

'Then what?'

'You'd be welcome here. But it would be a lot better if we were one family.'

'We were one family,' she said. 'Once. Before you spoiled everything.'

'Ah, yes,' he said. 'When I was as your brother.'

She smarted but said nothing.

'If only you had come with me that night before my betrothal. You were just a girl. If only we had run away, everything would have been different then.'

'It's no less foolish now than it was at the time,' she retorted.

'You wouldn't have gone to New England; I wouldn't have married Isobel.'

'And you wouldn't have had her fortune,' she put in sarcastically.

He shrugged. 'We'd still have had Oakbourne.'

'Perhaps, also,' she said equally sarcastically, 'Sir Henry might still be alive.'

'Yes,' he said quietly. 'He might.'

She got up again and made to leave the room. She wanted to end the conversation.

'And I could search for Jessica.'

'What?' She had been obliged to speak of Jessica's disappearance at the supper table.

'There may be some place you haven't looked; some stone left unturned.'

He was speaking figuratively but Margaret felt that she had personally turned every rock, every boulder within a wide radius of Dunscombe. She fought back the tears, unable to speak.

'I'll search,' he said. 'Somehow, somewhere, there must be someone who knows what happened to her. I'll search until I find her and I'll bring her back.'

He was stirring up the underlying pain, resurrecting hopes

which were best forgotten. 'Please,' she begged. 'My daughter is dead.'

'I won't believe that until I've proved it for myself.'

'Please, Rupert.' She put a hand to her face and walked towards the door. 'Go away and leave me to my pain.'

'I'm sorry, Margaret, but I'm determined to find her.'

'My daughter is dead.'

'She's my daughter, too.'

She stopped and bit her lip. 'Oh, just go away, Rupert. Leave me alone.'

She went into the garden and wept harsh dry tears in the fast-gathering dusk. Memories of Jessica, like ghosts, flitted among the darkening trees, tormenting her with her own guilt and pain.

At last, when the final candle had been extinguished in the house, she went inside to check on her father. He was not asleep.

'What did Rupert have to say?'

'You should be asleep, Father.'

'What did he say?'

'He's still the same old Rupert.'

'He wants Oakbourne back?'

'Yes, Father, he wants it back.'

'I knew he would.'

She smoothed his pillows and straightened the sheet.

'I always knew some day he'd ask for it back.'

She wavered between her need to talk with her father and the wisdom of urging him back to sleep. She plumped for conversation and sat down on the bed beside him. 'He says that the new King will order the return of land to its original owners.'

'I've no doubt he will.'

'But he can't, Father. It belongs to us.'

'A king can do anything he wishes, Margaret; once he's in power and it suits his purposes.'

'But Parliament . . .'

'The men of Parliament will be only too eager to keep on the right side of him. I can imagine them all scurrying to swap their places.'

'Then we'll wait until the order's made. We'll not give in until we must.'

Nehemiah looked at her with tired eyes. 'What's the point?' he said. 'Oakbourne belongs to Rupert. I always knew he'd take it back.'

'We'll fight.'

He shook his head. 'Rupert's the rightful heir to Oakbourne. It's been passed down for generations.'

'He lost that right.'

'No,' he said. 'That right of succession outweighs all others.'

'But that can't be. You've worked so hard.'

He put out a hand. 'I was a caretaker, child, just a caretaker.'

'I still say we should fight.'

'I've no wish to. And even if we did . . .' He spread his hand. 'What hope do we have of winning?'

'But . . .'

He stopped her before she could continue. 'Do we have lawyers? Do we have money to pay for them?'

'No,' she admitted. 'And Rupert has retained his fortune.'

'I thought he might have. He'd have made that safe long before he was sent into exile.'

'It doesn't seem fair.'

'But now we shall be without a home,' he said.

'He says we could stay.' She looked at him. 'But that's out of the question.'

He looked relieved. 'That's good,' he said. 'I can't imagine what we'd have done . . .'

'We can't, Father. We couldn't possibly live with Rupert.'

'Why not?'

'Father, have you forgotten?'

'No, child, I've not forgotten.' He took her hand. 'But your welfare and the welfare of this family are of far greater importance than any memories we may hold.'

'I can't believe it, Father.'

'Margaret.' He lifted her hand and held it to his lips. 'I shall be leaving soon.'

'Don't, Father.'

'I'm about to sup with my Maker. And I must think of you.'

She fought the desire to cry. 'Tobias . . .'

'Tobias has a family of his own.'

'He's heir to Oakbourne.'

'Rupert is heir to Oakbourne. Always has been. Tobias is happy at the loom. He's never nursed any great desire to be Master of Oakbourne.'

'But we can't just . . .'

'Yes we can. It's a way of securing your future.'

They sat and looked at one another for a long time.

'Margaret, in time he'll ask you to be his wife.'

'He already has.'

'Good. Then I can die in peace.'

'Father!'

'You're in need of the support and patronage of a husband.'

'I'll find work. I'll find some way . . .'

'No,' he said. 'It would not please me.'

She sat and thought for a while. 'Very well,' she said. 'I'll accept Rupert's offer of a home — if I must. But I see no reason to be his wife.'

'And what if he then marries someone else? What if he grows tired of waiting and marries another? Will she tolerate your presence here? No, child, you'd soon find yourself and your loved ones standing naked in the street.'

She heaved a sigh. 'What are you saying, Father?'

'I am asking that you marry Rupert.'

'I didn't think I would ever hear you say such a thing.'

'Nor I. But your need for care and support outweighs the bitterness we hold. He'll keep you fed and clothed and housed; in fact, I've no doubt he'll lavish all manner of luxuries upon you.'

'I don't care for luxuries.'

'I know that, child, but you need the care.'

'I still say that I could find some other way.'

'And what of Abigail? Has she ever known any home but this?'

'No.'

'Are you going to take her from the comfort of this house and put her in some hovel?'

Dear, sweet Abigail. 'No,' said Margaret. 'I couldn't do that.'

'Then you'd best secure her future along with your own. Make certain that this remains her home and that, in time, she's in a position to make a good marriage of her own. You'll not want to see her end as some drudge in poverty.'

'No,' she said, her mind already made up.

'It's not the first time,' he said gently, 'that you've made sacrifice for the good of your family.'

She lowered her eyes.

'I must ask you one more time in order that I may die in peace.'

She gripped his hand. 'You're not going yet.'

'A few more months, maybe. But we both know it won't be long.'

She brought her head down to rest upon his chest and he folded his arms about her.

'I love you, child. I'm sorry I couldn't have cared for you better.'

She began to cry. 'You've been the most wonderful father anyone could ever have.'

'But to leave you like this.'

'You're not going yet,' she began again.

'I wish that just once in your life you could have known of that pure true kind of love, the kind your mother and I had.'

'Yes, Father.'

She wept, her tears spilling on to the fabric of his nightshirt. She was crying for Richard.

CHAPTER 18

With the return of a monarch, there were many men who had formerly wielded power who now feared for their lives. Some made hasty plans to leave the country, but of those who stayed only ten went to their deaths. On 10 October the Regicides were brought to trial at the Sessions House before the Lord Mayor, General Monck, and a distinguished Bench of noblemen. The verdict was a foregone conclusion. During the course of the next week, the ten went, a few at a time, to the executioner.

On Saturday Bridget and Jessica were at Charing Cross, jostling for a place to watch the hanging of Major General Harrison. He was drawn through jeering crowds tied to a hurdle, then strung up and hanged. They stood and waited until he was cut down and disembowelled but could see little of it through the heads of the crowd. The corpse was quartered, the head and heart held aloft.

They cheered along with all the others in the crowd, little understanding, nor caring, the politics of the matter, merely caught up in the sense of occasion, the feeling of freedom which had abounded since the return of the King.

The quartered portions were taken, along with those of the other traitors, to hang from the gates of the city. They were a spectacle for a time but soon people took little notice as they shrivelled and decomposed to an ignominious end.

A few weeks later, to Jessica's amazement, her prediction came true. A woman stood on stage to play the part of Desdemona in *The Moor of Venice*. It had happened much sooner than she could have expected but it was in good measure due to the fact that the King had become a frequent visitor to the theatre. He had an eye for an attractive woman and much preferred to see one upon the stage, rather than to watch a man masquerading as a girl.

From that day, Bridget and Jessica stepped up their approaches to the managers of the theatre companies. But London had many gentlewomen left without dowry who had been trained to music and dancing. Competition was stiff.

The theatres, which had always been crowded, now became meeting places for those who wished to be seen in the vicinity of the King. When he was in attendance it was often impossible to find space inside. But the two girls knew each theatre well. They jostled with their tray until they found some suitable vantage point from which Jessica could see the stage. While she cradled Ben, Bridget would pass among the audience selling oranges.

Another Christmas came and passed, and several more river raids took place. Ben was a year old, so much a part of their life that he seemed to belong to them both. Jessica had stopped thinking of Dunscombe. She was content.

On 20 January she and Bridget were walking along Wych Street. It was Sunday and people were strolling home from church at St Clement Dane's. A feeling of relief was in the air that people were once more free to leave their homes.

For several days the Fifth Monarchy Men had rampaged through the streets, and the City Trained Bands had been out in force trying to catch them. An extreme religious sect, they expected the Second Coming of Christ and, when prayer failed, had chosen more violent means to usher in a millennium of rule by the saints under Jesus Christ. Twenty people had been killed and shop doors had been closed and barred; people had carried swords and pistols as protection.

It was the second uprising of these Monarchy Men. This time a number of them were captured, but not before they had caused chaos and had had the King's Lifeguard on the run. On 21 January they were due to be hanged.

And these were not the only notable hangings due to take place. Nine days later, on the twelfth anniversary of the execution of the former King, the bodies of Cromwell, his son-in-law Ireton, and John Bradshaw were due to be exhumed from their graves beneath Westminster Abbey. They were to be taken to Tyburn where they would be publicly hanged and their heads displayed in Westminster Hall.

It was a decision of Parliament which had brought mixed reactions from the people.

As the girls entered Drury Lane they saw a man turn off down a passageway to the left between the buildings.

''Ere,' said Bridget, 'that's old Killigrew.'

They recognized him well as the manager of the King's Theatre Company. Jessica's heart began to pound.

'I wonder what he's doing here?'

'Come on, afore we lose 'im. You can nab 'im again.'

They followed him down the passageway into a riding yard surrounded by buildings. They were between Drury Lane and Brydges Street. Thomas Killigrew was standing at the centre of the yard, hand on hip, looking about him.

'Forgive me, sir, if I approach you.'

He turned. 'How like you my new theatre?'

The girls looked about the empty yard hemmed in by buildings. Bridget twitched her nose in a gesture which conveyed 'addled in the brain'.

'I've this day leased this grand site from the Earl of Bedford. For the sum, I might add, of fifty pounds a year.'

They were suitably impressed.

'To erect a new playhouse.'

Jessica's eyes lit up.

'At an expected cost to myself of some one thousand five hundred pounds.'

They were even more impressed.

'What think you of it?'

'Magnificent,' said Jessica.

'Can you see it now?' He swept his arm in a grand gesture. 'You are standing, my dear ladies, upon the stage of the new Theatre Royal.'

Jessica's heart skipped a beat.

''Ere.' Bridget nudged her. 'Do yer stuff.'

'What? Oh, yes.' Jessica cleared her throat and swallowed. There were several roles which she knew by heart but she chose that of Desdemona. She cleared her throat again and launched into the part, holding herself with the stiff dignity which she knew to be correct, left hand pressed to her heart, the right flowing with elaborate eloquence.

When she had finished he applauded her with a tapping of his finger tips, lace cuffs rippling at his wrists. 'Splendid, my dear lady, that was positively splendid.'

She curtsied and blushed.

'I would have you for my company,' he said grandly.

She opened her mouth.

'Why have I not found your like before?'

She did not dare to tell him that she had approached him on a number of previous occasions and had been turned away.

'You have pleasing features.'

She blushed again.

'Do you know the play *The Silent Woman*?'

'Yes, sir. I saw it performed by your own company some three weeks ago on Twelfth Night.'

'Tell me of it.'

'Well, sir, Mr Kynaston played three parts. It was most impressive to see his performance as the gallant and as the other gentleman; but I feel, sir, that the part of the poor woman would have been best played by a woman actor.'

He threw back his head and laughed. 'I shall tell Kynaston of your view this very day. And next time you shall have the part. Can you play for me this poor woman?'

She took up her stance but he stopped her before she could begin to perform. 'But I see you best in some other, more dramatic, role. It's the dark hair, you know.'

He reached out and touched it with his fingers. 'Very pleasing.'

'Thank you, sir, I'm most honoured.'

He turned to walk away. 'Call on me tomorrow at an hour before noon. We shall discuss it then.'

As she watched him go she could hardly contain herself.

'You made it! You made it!' Bridget grabbed her and together the two girls danced a jig about the yard, whirling Ben between them, chuckling as his feet left the ground. 'I knew you would. Yer gonna be the grandest player in the 'ole of London.'

'And we,' said Jessica, 'are dancing in the Theatre Royal.'

'Oh, Lor', Ben. I do believe we just fell down the pit.'

Next day they went at the appointed time to a converted tennis court in Vere Street, presently being used by the King's Company as a theatre. Rehearsals were breaking up. It was obvious that Killigrew had forgotten the appointment.

'My dear ladies, I was about to withdraw to the ordinary to take my dinner.'

Jessica was bitterly disappointed.

'But you may come and watch me dine.' He issued the invitation as though it were a great honour.

He swept out followed by a number of the company. They went to an ordinary – a tavern – frequented by poets, authors and actors, where the girls watched Killigrew eat his way through a dish of oysters, a lamprey pie and a brace of woodcock, washed down with a quantity of malmsey and Nantz brandy. He had long been known as a jester and sharp wit favoured by the Court: people hung on his words.

After he had ordered syllabub and a dish of macaroons he appeared to remember that Jessica was there. He called her to him.

With the effect of the drink upon him, she did not like the look in his eye. She went to sit beside him. She knew of his reputation and by skilful movement managed to avoid his hand upon her knee, while at the same time smiling sweetly to defray offence.

'You'll join me in a little syllabub?'

'I'd be honoured, sir.'

He attempted to feed her from the dish but she picked up a spoon and made it obvious that she preferred to feed herself.

'You said, sir, that you'd have me in your company.' She thought that if she were not bold enough to raise the subject herself, his thoughts would be centred upon other matters.

'I did indeed.'

'And you'd tell me, sir, what is expected of me and what are my duties.'

He looked at her with a mixture of lechery and something which she feared might be boredom.

'You may report to the theatre tomorrow forenoon. You'll be required to assist and to learn. There's an apprenticeship of three months, after which you'll receive the sum of ten shillings a week.'

411

Jessica nodded approval.

'Out of it, you'll be required to supply your own petticoats, shoes, stockings, gloves and scarves.'

She nodded again.

'You'll report early to the theatre and you'll watch both rehearsals and plays. You'll learn the parts which are required of you. Do you dance?'

'Yes.' She half-lied. She had watched often enough, but she had no experience of performing.

'Then you shall dance for me tomorrow.'

She determined to practise all night.

Killigrew returned to his meal and appeared again to have dismissed her.

The two girls sat and watched until he had finished. Then, in the afternoon, they went back to the theatre to watch the play.

On the way home to Southwark Jessica was caught in a mixture of elation and apprehension.

'Ol' Killigrew and 'alf the company'll 'ave you in their beds afore the week's out,' predicted Bridget.

Jessica shook her head. She was deeply serious. 'I'm an actoress. I've told you before there's no way that I'll ever be a whore again.'

'You'll never make it, you know. If you don't do as they wants, they'll chuck you out.'

'I shall impress them so greatly with my acting that I'll turn their minds to other things.'

'You must be addled. Sellin' oranges is one thing — them actors is somethin' else. I give you a week afore yer lyin' on yer back.'

'I'm an actoress,' she said again. As she said it she flung wide her arms, causing passers-by to turn and stare.

Over the next months she worked as she had never worked before. Each play ran for only two or three days: there was constant learning and re-learning, and new tasks to perform. During these first three months of her apprenticeship she received no pay: it was Bridget who supported her and kept her going financially. While Ben toddled beside her, she sold oranges and took the proceeds home to Jessica.

Jessica maintained her determination to avoid the sexual advances of the men around her. It was not easy but, in time, they gave up. There were always plenty of prostitutes who were more than available. They began to accept her for the apprentice actress that she was — just so long as she knew her place and held her tongue.

There was constant rivalry between their King's Company and the Duke's. The Duke's Company had put on their first performance on 29 January and they, too, were building a new theatre. Theirs was to be at Lisles Tennis Court, Lincoln's Inn Fields, and it was due to open long before the Theatre Royal. On the other hand, Killigrew had secured the monopoly on the cream of the plays: Sir William D'Avenant was having to rehearse the Duke's in a whole new repertoire.

The King attended performances by both companies and each jostled for invitations to give private performances at the Cockpit Theatre in Whitehall Palace. It was important for prestige, and also for finance. The King paid ten pounds a play at the theatre, twenty pounds at Court.

Jessica enjoyed the excitement of visits to Whitehall, of being on the perimeter of Court extravagance, watching from the sidelines a kind of life of which she had not dreamed previously. But she was at her happiest when she was on stage, simply performing to the very best of her ability, standing up before an audience and declaring to the world: 'This is me, Jessica Daniels. Take me for what I am.'

Coronation Day was 23 April, St George's Day. On the previous day, a Monday, the two girls stood with Ben upon their shoulders, watching the procession which passed through the streets on its way to the Tower. The King was to be presented with the keys of the city. If the streets had been thronged on the day of his return from Holland, on this day they were even more so. The girls were jammed tight against the wall of a house and stood on tip-toe, peering past the heads of the crowd.

Richly embroidered horsecloths were outdone by the richness of the riders' clothes and companies of soldiers smartly dressed in white doublets — such a display of gold, silver and jewels as they had never seen. The King, accompanied by his brother the Duke of York, acknowledged the cheers of the crowd.

'Why aren't there any ladies in the procession?'

''E ain't got no Queen,' Bridget said knowledgeably. 'There ain't no women when there ain't a Queen.'

They stayed out all night, squeezing a place for themselves among the crowds who waited near Westminster Abbey. Ben slept with his head slumped sideways on Bridget's shoulder. Their legs were numb, their feet trampled upon, but they stood their ground, withstanding the pushing and jostling as more and more people joined the crowd with the coming of morning.

The ceremony was to be at eleven o'clock. They stood waiting, listening to the banter and good humour of the crowd, the occasional fight which broke out or a scuffle when some cut-purse was caught going about his business, until at last they witnessed a sight which Jessica was to remember for the rest of her days.

The procession came two abreast, walking along a length of blue cloth laid upon the ground, lined on either side by soldiers of horse and foot. First came the Aldermen, the Chaplains, the Gentlemen of the Privy Chamber, Judges, the choir of Westminster, Baronesses in crimson velvet lined with ermine and with long white dresses studded with diamonds, Viscountesses, Duchesses, their hair dressed with jewels and with their coronets carried in their hands, Dukes, Earls, Viscounts, Barons, wearing ermine capes, Knights of the Garter with gold chains, a star at their breast and a diamond garter at the knee, Bishops in black with flat four-cornered caps.

Next came those carrying the orb, the sceptre and the Crown, sparkling reds, blues and greens as April sunlight caught the precious stones, a Bishop with the Bible, others with the paten and the chalice.

The King was carried by eight Barons of the Cinque Ports under a canopy of cloth of gold, his train borne by the Master of the Robes and four young men who walked behind.

The girls were caught between the desire to gasp, holding their breath at the sheer grandeur of the occasion, and the desire to cheer and shout along with all the others in the crowd.

When the procession had passed they remained standing, listening to the singing, the shouting, the music which emanated from the Abbey.

The procession returned, in the same order as before but this time with their coronets upon their heads, the King wearing his crown and with the sceptre in his hand, back to Westminster Hall and to the banquet.

'I bet they've got more than mutton and turnip pie,' commented a spectator who had just bought one from a street vendor.

'Aye,' commented someone nearby. 'Old Cromwell's head 'll be looking down from its spike in there. I bet he'd have a thing or two to say if only his jaws could open.'

That evening there were bonfires in many parts of the city. People danced and drank until they were incapable of standing upon their feet. The weather, which had remained fine for the two days of the ceremonies, broke with a storm which brought thunder, lightning and torrential rain, putting paid to the firework displays which had been planned. Drunkards lay spewing where they fell, sprawled on dungheaps, oblivious to the rain which poured down upon them.

The girls went back to their room. They put Ben to bed then sat before the fire, hanging their heads to dry their hair in the warmth of the flames. They laughed and giggled as they recounted the excitement of all that they had seen. They had not slept for two days. They finally huddled together exhausted beneath a blanket, until dawn. Jessica had need to rise early next morning. She must return to work.

Some weeks later she sat preparing to go on stage. It was early afternoon and the theatre was already crowded, waiting for the play to commence at three-thirty. The King was due to attend, together with the Duke and Duchess of York and the King's mistress, Barbara Palmer. It was a liaison thought by some to be indelicate. He was newly betrothed to the Infanta Catherine of Braganza and waiting for her to be brought to England.

Jessica had been given a small part and, although she knew that the crowds were there more to be seen in the presence of the King than to watch the play, she did not care.

She was squeezed into a corner, endeavouring to prepare and to compose herself. It irritated her that the back-stage area was always so crowded. Extravagantly dressed men lounged about the walls, eyeing the actresses in their shifts, leaping forward to assist in the lacing of a bodice or the arranging of petticoats.

She brusquely refused the help of one man who stepped forward as she put the finishing touches to her hair. As she looked into the mirror she became aware of another — middle-aged and slightly overweight, with deep-set grey eyes in a sallow complexion. He was watching her intently from the other side of the room.

He stepped forward when he saw her look at him.

'You're Jessica Daniels?'

'I am.'

'I'm recently come from Dunscombe.'

He had dropped the name deliberately, watching for her reaction. She started and dropped her comb.

'Then it *is* you.'

'Sir?'

'*My* Jessica. It was the name. As soon as I heard it, I felt it was too much of a coincidence not to be true. I knew it must be you.' He was reaching out for her, trying to take hold of her, trying to draw her to him.

She resisted, shocked and not understanding, refusing to be touched by this stranger.

'I'm your father.'

'Father?' Her mind catapulted from Richard Fullwood to Deliverance Daniels, then back to the man in front of her. She shook her head. 'I don't know you, sir.'

'So like your mother. And the eyes . . . I do believe you take them from me.'

She was deeply embarrassed. 'I'm afraid you're mistaken, sir. I've never met you.'

'Indeed, you haven't. But I'm your father, just the same.'

She felt trapped here in the corner, unable to back away from him.

'Tell me you're from Dunscombe.'

She chose to lie. 'I know of no Dunscombe, sir.'

He appeared to ignore that. 'And that you disappeared beyond sight, some year and a half ago.'

'I know of no Dunscombe sir,' she repeated.

'Your mother has searched for you. She thinks you dead.'

The mention of her mother brought fresh tumult.

'She's never ceased to grieve since the day you left.'

'I'm sorry, sir, you're mistaken.' She was shocked and confused, could think of nothing but backing away from this stranger who insisted upon trying to take hold of her, and who knew far more of her than she found acceptable. 'I know of no Dunscombe and I must prepare for the play.'

'An actoress,' he said. 'You must tell me what happened and how you come to be upon the stage.'

She ignored the request and turned back to the mirror, attempting to attend to her make-up with shaking hands. 'If you'll excuse me, sir, I must have time to prepare.'

'You will have heard of me, Rupert Mainwaring, cousin of your mother.'

Jessica remembered hearing the name. She also remembered hearing veiled accounts of the reason for his exile.

'You'll be so pleased to know that Margaret is my wife.'

'Wife?'

'At long last. After so many years. My own dear, sweet Margaret is truly mine.'

'Your wife?'

'We were sweethearts as children, you know.'

'What?'

'Since she was a babe in the cradle I loved her so much, held her in my dreams. We were meant for one another yet it took all these years.'

Jessica was feeling sick. That same mother who had rolled in the grass, who had gasped and panted, deceived her husband as he sat reading his Bible. And all the time she had loved another — this man who stood before her now, pale-skinned and flabby from unhealthy living; this man who claimed to be her father.

'I must take you home to your family.'

'I have no home, sir. You're mistaken.' If she had ever despised her mother, she despised her now.

'There'll be such rejoicing as has never been known.'

Jessica was still reeling from the disclosure of Rupert's long-term relationship with her mother. She who had lain with Richard Fullwood on the night Deliverance Daniels had been killed. She who had been soaked in blood. And all the

417

time there was another — a third man whom she had lusted after since childhood.

'It will lift her spirits. She's distraught in mourning for Uncle Nehemiah.'

It brought Jessica back to the present. 'Grandfather's dead?'

'A little over a sennight ago. After much pain.'

She was sad to hear of the death of her grandfather. She had been fond of him.

'I'm sorry,' she said.

Nehemiah had not understood her but he had tried. He had not been close, but then no one had ever been allowed to come close to her. She wished now that she had seen him, just once, before he died.

'We buried him alongside Aunt Anne.'

She became aware of another man, a younger one, who came to stand behind Rupert.

'Allow me to present Simon Ashwell.'

'It's an honour and a privilege, Mrs Daniels, to make your acquaintance.'

He had used the title of married woman accorded to her as an actress. She was slightly flattered but had no intention of letting it show and merely dipped her chin by way of acknowledgement.

'I saw your performance yesterday and was most impressed by your reading of the part. I've never seen it so well played.'

She inclined her head again. She was still reeling from the revelation concerning her mother and wanted to get away.

'He's a great admirer of plays,' laughed Rupert. 'He'd be at the theatre every day, given the chance.'

'If you'll excuse me?' she said. 'I must have time to prepare.'

But there was activity all around them. The gallants began to move off to take their seats among the audience, the actors to take position upon the stage. It was already too late.

'We'll watch the performance,' said Rupert. 'Afterwards, we'll take you back to my lodgings. We must sup and get to know one another.'

'I'm sorry,' she said, 'but that's impossible.'

'Why?'

'I've rehearsals,' she lied. 'Important instructions for tomorrow's performance.'

'Then I'll speak with Killigrew and have you released.'

'No,' she floundered. She had no wish to involve Thomas Killigrew in her deception. 'I'm afraid it's impossible.'

'But I must be gone tomorrow. I'm returning to Dunscombe.'

'Oh.' It brought some measure of relief.

'And I can take you with me.'

Alarm rose again. She had no intention of returning.

'There's no need for rehearsals. I can take you back with me tomorrow — back home, where you belong.'

'I can't.' The play was about to start. Someone was dragging her by the elbow, reminding her that she must be on stage. 'I trust you'll convey greetings to my mother but I can't go.'

It was as much as she could do to spit out the pleasantries concerning her mother. She never wished to see her again.

From her position upon the stage, she watched as Rupert and the young man made their way to their seats among the audience. From the corner of her eye she continued to watch them throughout the performance, embarrassed when Rupert clapped and roared at her every entrance. The young man, although quieter, appeared to be watching her intently.

Afterwards they came backstage again. 'Magnificent! Truly magnificent,' said Rupert.

'I enjoyed the play,' said Simon Ashwell. 'I'd be pleased to have the opportunity to discuss it with you some time.'

'And you'll have changed your mind,' said Rupert. 'About supping with us? There's so much to say.'

'I'm afraid not. I trust you'll forgive me but I can't come.'

'But why? My business is finished. I must return to Dunscombe. I shan't be back for at least a month.'

She did not know what to say.

'And I can't wait to take you home, to tell your mother that I've found you. Who would have thought it? Here in London, and upon the stage. You must tell me how you came to be here.'

She tried rapidly to change the subject. 'You've business here in London, sir?'

'I come quite often. It's a pity I didn't come sooner to the theatre. It was young Simon here who enthused over your performance and mentioned your name.'

'Oh,' she said. It had never occurred to her that she should change her name.

'If you can't sup with us, we must make arrangements now about tomorrow. I'll have Simon come and collect you first thing. The coach leaves at ten.'

There was nothing for it but to stand her ground. 'I'm sorry, sir, but I've no intention of coming with you.'

'What?' He was hurt and puzzled.

'I wish to remain here in my chosen pursuit. I don't want to go home.'

'But you must.'

'No, sir, I've no intention of returning.'

'Then you'll want, at least, to visit your mother? She'll be so pleased to know you're safe.'

'I've duties here and can't be released.'

'Nonsense. I'll have a word . . .'

'No. Please.'

He stood and looked at her for several moments. 'You're quite determined,' he said. 'I can't begin to understand why.'

'I'm sorry, sir.'

'Your home is waiting, warm and welcoming. Everyone will be overjoyed to have you back.'

'I'm sorry.'

Then he smiled. 'You've more than a little of your mother's spirit. I don't understand your reasons but I'll not attempt to force you.'

'Thank you, sir.' She was greatly relieved to know that he would not use force. There was little she could have done had he chosen to.

'I can only hope that, with time, you can be persuaded. I'll be back in London in about a month. I'll look you up.'

'Yes, sir.'

'And, in the meantime, I'll give you details of my lodgings. You can get news of me there.' He outlined details of an address in Broad Street. 'Ask for Mrs Hardwick. She'll know when I'm next due to be there.'

'Yes, sir.' She took note of the instruction. It would have

420

been quite easy to locate his lodging but she had no intention of doing so.

'You'll be in need of money.' He held out a gold coin but she drew back.

'Thank you, sir, but I'm not in need.'

She had not yet repaid Bridget and was further indebted to her for the price of a new petticoat, but under no circumstances would she take the coin from Rupert.

'There must be things you need? A little extra comfort.' He twitched the coin towards her again. 'There must be something you could spend it on.'

'Thank you, sir, but I've all I need.'

He smiled. 'You've pride as well as spirit. You're certainly the daughter of my dear Margaret.'

She had no wish to be likened to her mother.

'I can't wait to tell her that I've found you.'

She lowered her eyes. She did not know how she was to cope with the pressures which lay ahead. She could not hide. Exposed here, upon the stage, she was available at any time Rupert wished to seek her out. She did not know how she could withstand his intention to take her back to Dunscombe, particularly if his patience grew thin. It would be a simple matter to take her by force.

She could abandon the stage . . . but, no, that was out of the question. She must stand firm. Whatever happened, she was certain of one thing — she had no wish to return to her mother.

He had been standing looking at her, feeling awkward, not knowing how to take his leave. 'Well, until next month, then. We'll see you then.'

'Yes.' She raised her eyes. 'I look forward to it.'

Rupert smiled at her response but Simon Ashwell knew it to be a lie. She could see it in his eyes.

She watched them go, then turned to wipe the make-up from her face. The candle beside the mirror was burning low. She realized that she was trembling.

When Margaret heard the news, she broke down and wept. Weeks, months — twenty months of uncertainty. Jessica was alive and well.

But, almost immediately, relief was overtaken by a

different emotion. She was on the stage with all its connotations of loose living and low moral standards. It was contrary to everything Margaret believed to be right and good.

And Jessica did not want to come home. All those months of worry — and Jessica was on the stage. The doubts, the fears, the self-castigation — and her daughter did not want to come home.

'I'll bring her with me next time I return,' promised Rupert.

'There's little point,' said Margaret quietly, 'if she doesn't wish to come.'

'But she'll have changed her mind. She'll have had time to think.'

'But not to change her heart. There's little to be found here for one who chooses to remain elsewhere.'

The feeling of betrayal hurt more than all the previous feelings of loss and grief.

'Then I'll take you with me when I go. You've always wanted to visit the city. I remember how, years ago, you longed to see London. I wager you've never been.'

Margaret picked up her needlework which had been lying in her lap. 'I've travelled enough. And I've duties here, amongst my household.'

'But you must see our daughter. You must see her perform upon the stage.'

'I've no wish to see her perform upon a stage.'

'You'd be proud. Oh, Margaret, you'd be so proud.'

Pride was the last thing in her mind. 'It's enough to know that she's alive,' she said. 'I've no wish to see her flaunt herself upon a stage.'

She put down the needlework and went to supervise the preparation of the family dinner. 'I shall see Jessica at such time as she chooses to come home to me.'

CHAPTER 19

It was not until 1663 that the Theatre Royal eventually opened on its site behind Drury Lane, by which time the cost to Thomas Killigrew had almost doubled from his initial estimate. The Duke's Company had been installed for almost two years in their new theatre at Lisles Tennis Court while the King's Company had grown tired of making do in cramped and unsatisfactory surroundings.

The new theatre opened in style on 7 May with a revival of *The Humorous Lieutenant*.

For a long time they had made do without scenery but the new large stage allowed painted flats to be drawn back at the close of each scene to reveal others behind. At the sides, cut-outs, slotted into grooves in the stage floor, gave added dimension. A glazed cupola let in light above the pit while, above the stage, huge candelabra lit the scene.

The audience now had a much better view of the performance, had they cared to give it their full attention. Benches in the pit were raked at an angle forming an amphitheatre — seven rows in front, another seven raked at a steeper angle. A circle of five boxes each had five rows of benches and above that was a gallery with a further eight.

The King continued to be a frequent playgoer, often in the company of his mistress, Barbara Palmer — now Lady Castlemaine and mother of his children. There was constant rumour, too, concerning other women in his entourage. The Queen, married a little over a year, showed no sign of producing an heir. Already there was talk of her being barren.

Jessica was given larger, more important parts. But she was waging a losing battle in her efforts to make the audience sit up and take notice. The few who did appreciate her skills must contend with those whose minds were centred upon other matters.

Gallants, hungover from the debauches of the previous night, had spent the morning lying with whomsoever they had found beside them; and had then got up to dine and saunter along to the theatre to survey those gathered there in the quest for further titilation.

In the course of the play they climbed over rows of benches to reach the women of their choice, or sent boys with notes to climb into the boxes. Others called back and forth across the heads of their neighbours – propositioning, rebuffing, making assignations – all interspersed with much bawdy comment from the spectators round about.

And, all the time, the prostitutes and orange sellers plied their trade, paying little regard to those trying to make themselves heard upon the stage.

Jessica frequently bemoaned her difficulties to Bridget. She was doing so one day as they sat in the tiring-room where Ben sat upon the floor, playing with a shoe.

'They'd enjoy the performance if only they'd just listen.'

'I know, luv. Only yesterday there was that Lord Rochester and all 'is cronies, drunk as the lord's what they are, standin' in the boxes pissin' on the 'eads o' the poor sods underneath. So drunk as they couldn't even aim straight.'

Jessica smiled. 'I know, but they did hit that awful Lady Maxwell.'

'And that pox-arsed Sir Percy Smythe – goin' round cursin' as what there ain't a woman left in the place what 'e ain't 'ad, blamin' ol' Killigrew f' not bringin' in a few new 'ns, and everybody else 'cause there ain't no maidens left!'

'It's quite impossible to make yourself heard above all that noise.'

'It'd be better,' commented Bridget, 'if they was made t' pay afore they comes in.'

'They've got to be given the chance to see if they like the

play. If they don't like it after the first act, then they're free to go.'

'I know, but it'd stop all that wanderin' about. All them geezers what's lookin' round t' see as who's 'ere, then wanderin' orf out again t' see as if there's anythin' better what's t' be picked up down at the Duke's.'

'Not everyone does that. Some people leave simply because they don't like the play.'

'If they was made t' pay f' the first act, then a few more of 'em might stay.'

'I doubt it. A lot of them find sport in trying to avoid paying, anyway, even at the start of the second act.'

'And that's another thing. It'd stop all that chasing about by the doormen, hollerin' at people what 'asn't paid up; and them arguing the toss as they 'as; and all them others dodgin' about tryin' t' skip bein' caught in the first place.'

Jessica sighed. 'If only they'd just sit down and listen.'

'You must be jokin', luv. I can't never see 'em doin' that.'

It was shortly after one o'clock: the doors of the theatre had been open for a little over an hour. Jessica looked out into the pit. 'It's already quite full. There aren't many spaces left.'

It was usual for patrons to sit upon the benches from the time the doors opened at mid-day until the start of the performance at three-thirty — or, more likely, to pay someone else to sit there for them.

'There's enough of 'em in 'ere,' commented Bridget, looking round at the gallants already lounging about the tiring-room. 'Pity they ain't got nothin' better t' do.'

'I must admit they do put me off when I'm trying to get ready.'

'And talkin' o' gettin' ready,' said Bridget, 'it's time you were gettin' dressed.'

Jessica had been sitting in her usual resting smock of Holland linen. 'There's plenty of time.' But she enjoyed the excitement of preparing for a performance.

'Come 'ere, I'll 'elp you with yer stays.' Bridget reached for the wooden stays and began lacing them about Jessica's waist.

A man stepped forward. 'Permit me, ladies. May I be of assistance?'

'Piss orf,' said Bridget.

'Shush, you'll get me into trouble. They pay to come in here and watch.'

'Watch, maybe, but they can keep their poxy 'ands up someone else's skirt.'

'Well, don't offend them.'

'Offend 'em! I'll kick 'em where it 'urts if they s' much as lays an 'and on you.'

Jessica smiled and took a deep breath to allow her to tighten the stays.

'You dancin' today?'

'Yes.'

'Then you'll be needin' yer drawers.' Bridget searched around for a pair of Holland drawers, at the same time finding a pair of green knitted stockings and the garters with which to secure them.

Jessica gently took her shoe from Ben. 'I must get another pair. These are nearly worn through.' She turned it in her hands. 'I'll have to stitch back the buckles, or they'll fall off one day when I'm dancing.'

'There's a raid t'night. I'll talk t' Pa.'

'Oh, I didn't mean . . .'

'Come 'ere, and let me fasten on this 'ere petticoat.'

'I can't, Bridget. So many things . . . I'll never be able to finish paying you back.'

'Will you stop yer twitterin' and let me tie this string? We'll 'ave this white petticoat, then the pink. And 'ow about the scarlet f' the bodice?'

Jessica brushed her lips across Bridget's cheek. 'I'm going to repay you somehow, you know that.'

Bridget grinned. 'Out o' what you earn? Not an 'ope. Unless, o' course, you decides t' warm the bed o' one o' them cow turds what's givin' you the eye?'

Jessica merely gave her a look without bothering to answer.

'Then you'd best marry that young fella what comes 'ere with yer pa.'

Jessica shuddered. 'Don't even think about it.'

''E's not s' bad.'

'I'd rather have one of these. Anyone would be better than a member of my father's household.'

426

'I dunno what you've got against 'im.'

'It's not him. It's just that I don't even want to think about anyone connected with my father.'

She had met Rupert on many occasions over the past two years. He spent a good deal of time in London and always came to the theatre at least once on every trip. She wanted to forget her ties with her family and wished that he would not continually remind her of them. She just wanted to be left in peace.

Rupert had never stopped trying to persuade her to return to Dunscombe but now he did it with a smile, knowing that he stood little chance of success. He appeared content merely to keep contact with her on his visits to the city and to seek her company for an evening over supper. She believed from his remarks that her mother did not want her to return home, and was glad.

He had many times offered her money but she had always refused. On one occasion only, she had accepted and had tried to give it to Bridget. But her friend, knowing the way that Jessica felt about her father, had refused it. They had given it away to the first beggar they had met in the street.

'I reckon as how you could do worse than that Simon Ashwell.' Bridget sat her down and began to arrange her hair, tying bunches of corkscrew curls above her ears and sweeping the rest back up into a bun.

'Oh, do shut up,' snapped Jessica, then she smiled an apology for her retort. Bridget, unoffended, went on twisting the curls around her finger.

Simon Ashwell was Rupert's constant companion. Jessica assumed that he was learning her father's business affairs but she was not sufficiently interested to ask. He was a pleasant enough young man who spoke knowledgeably and intelligently about the theatre. In other circumstances she would have been pleased to converse with him, but she had no wish to show interest in someone so closely linked with Rupert.

''E comes 'ere every day when 'e's in London with yer pa.'

'He enjoys the plays.'

'P'raps 'e comes t' look at you?' Bridget was teasing now.

'He does no such thing.' She reached for powder and red

427

ochre to colour her cheeks. 'And I should very quickly set him straight upon the matter if he did.'

Bridget shrugged. 'Well, I think 'e's sort o' nice.'

'Then you can have him.' She began applying eye kohl rather more liberally than she had intended.

''E wouldn't 'ave me. I ain't a lady like what you are.'

'I am not a lady,' Jessica said deliberately. 'I'm an actress.'

'I know, luv, but I can't 'elp thinkin' as 'ow yer gonna 'ave t' admit ter bein' a lady, one o' these days.'

'I do wish you'd stop going on about it.' She was genuinely annoyed now. 'How many times do I have to keep telling you? I'm nothing.'

'Course you are,' said Bridget kindly.

'I'm nothing, I tell you. Just a bastard with a mother little better than a whore.'

'But yer pa's claimed yer. 'E comes 'ere t' see you all the time.'

'So?'

'Well, it makes all the difference.'

'No, it does not. What difference could it possibly make to me? I'm still a bastard.' She was close to tears.

'You've never got over it, 'ave you, luv? Bein' a little basket.'

'It doesn't worry me in the slightest,' she said tightly. 'I'm merely stating a fact because you will keep going on about my being some great lady. I just get fed up with it.'

'Come orf it, luv.'

'I'm quite used to living with the knowledge that I wasn't meant to be born.'

Bridget put her arms about her and gave her a hug. 'But you was, luv. And you ain't made a bad job of it, for all o' bein' a basket.'

Jessica turned her head into Bridget's shoulder. 'Sorry, Bridget.'

'Get's t' you, don't it, luv, every time?'

Jessica nodded. 'After all these years I'm still ashamed.'

'Gawd knows why. 'Alf o' Wappin' don't know their pas.'

'That's an exaggeration. And anyway it was different in Dunscombe.'

428

'Yeah, it's always different bein' a lady.' Bridget thought for a moment then bent down and lifted Ben into her arms. 'P'r'aps it's as well me own poor little basket weren't born a toff.'

'Oh, Bridget.' Jessica reached out for him too. 'It's different for Ben. He's family.'

'You 'ave a family of yer own if only you'd let 'em love you.'

'No,' she said. 'I don't want anything from them.'

'Course you do. Yer just too damned cussed t' admit it.'

'Oh, Bridget, I wish I didn't hate her so.' She tried, unsuccessfully, to stifle a sob.

'You don't 'ate 'er, luv, you just thinks yer do.'

'I do,' she insisted. 'I really do.'

''Ere, don't cry.' Bridget held Ben on one arm while with the other she tilted Jessica's chin and wiped the tears from her eyes. 'Else you'll get streaks all down yer make-up.'

'Oh, Bridget, if only she had . . .' Jessica reached out in order to encompass both Bridget and Ben in her arms; but, in doing so, she knocked the comb to the floor.

Immediately, a man leapt forward to retrieve it. 'Permit me, ladies . . .'

'Piss off!' they both yelled in unison.

Margaret fingered the paper upon which Jessica's name appeared.

'You'd be so proud of her, Margaret. She looks so fine upon the stage.'

Mrs Jessica Daniels to take the part of 'Cordelia' in Mr Shakespeare's 'King Lear'.

'I've no wish to see Jessica upon the stage.'

'You're so stubborn, my dear.'

'I'm not stubborn. I've just no wish to see her on the stage.'

'You've not seen her at all.'

'No,' she said. 'Two years and still she doesn't choose to come home.'

'But neither have you been to London.'

'I've no need to go to London. I'm here amongst my own household. Why should I go to London?'

'One of you must be the first to move. Someone has to take the first step.'

'Her home is open to her,' said Margaret. 'Any time she chooses to come.' The pain of knowing that Jessica did not want to return still bit deep.

Rupert shook his head. 'I love you both. It pains me to see you standing so far apart like this.'

'No more than it pains me,' she said. 'Jessica is my daughter.'

'And mine,' he said but did not press the point.

'You say she's well?'

'Very well, and very beautiful.'

'Her looks have always been her downfall.'

'She's extremely beautiful.'

She glanced at him, irritated that he had completely missed her point. She put the paper down upon the table. 'I must go to the dairy,' she said. 'That new young dairymaid needs constant supervision.'

'You work too hard.'

'No more than I have always done.'

'Are you happy?'

He took her by surprise.

'Are you?' he asked again. 'Here with me?'

She stopped and gazed for a moment out of the window. 'This is my home.'

'But are you happy?'

'Rupert, I really haven't got time . . .'

'I do try, you know.'

She looked at him for a moment. 'Yes,' she said. 'I know you do.'

'I'd give anything to make you happy.'

She thought again of Richard and knew that Rupert could never make her happy.

'Is there anything that I can do?'

'In what way?'

'To make you more content.'

'I'm quite content.'

'But not happy.' He looked at her for a long time. 'I know you don't love me. I've given up hoping that you'll ever love me.'

She lowered her eyes.

'It was too much to ask.'

She let a moment elapse. 'I'm grateful that you've given me a home. And that my family . . .'

'I didn't for one moment intend to cheat you, you know.'

'I know you didn't.'

'It was the King's intent to return the sequestered lands to their former owners.'

'He must have changed his mind.'

'It was expedient for him to do so. It proved in his best interests to let matters stand.'

'It doesn't matter,' she said.

'But if Uncle Nehemiah had stood out for ownership, Oakbourne would have passed to Tobias.'

'It doesn't matter,' she said again. 'It was Father's decision to assign the deeds back to you.'

'I feel that I cheated him.'

'No,' she said. 'I don't believe that was your deliberate intention.'

'Thank you.'

'He said you were the rightful heir.'

'It's long been in my family. But in the circumstances . . .'

'It was his wish,' she said. 'He was a strong believer in the rightful succession from father to son.'

'And his other wish?'

'What other wish?'

'That you should marry me.'

'Oh.'

'Have you come to regret it?'

'No,' she said quietly. 'You've treated me well.'

'I've done my best, you know.'

'Yes, I know you have.'

'It was all I ever wanted.'

'I'm grateful for all that you've done for me and for the family, and it's good to see Oakbourne brought back into prosperity again.'

'Thank you, Margaret. You could have felt bitterness towards me.'

'No. I'm too tired for bitterness.'

'And will you go to see Jessica?'

'No,' she said. 'I'll not go and see her.'

He sighed and went to stand beside her. 'I do love you, you know.' He put his arm about her shoulders.

She tensed. 'I really must get down to the dairy.'

'I'm sorry.' He removed his arm. 'I mustn't delay you.'

A further two years passed. Jessica was twenty-two, well established as a member of the King's Theatre Company. Her dark hair was suited to the dramatic roles of John Dryden, presently much favoured as a fashionable playwright. She had had roles in his *Wild Gallant*, *The Rival Ladies* and, most recently, his much acclaimed *Indian Queen*.

She revelled in the demands and challenges of her work – *Othello*, *Henry IV*, *The Alchemist* – constantly learning new plays. She was often called upon to play breeches parts in which she played a maiden masquerading as a boy.

She played beside Charles Hart and Michael Mohum, with Edward Kynaston – who still on occasions played female roles – with Catherine Carey, and Beck Marshall and her sister Ann. Nell Gwynn had newly joined the company and was already showing promise in her dancing and her singing.

The licentious behaviour of those in the audience had not abated and was matched in good measure by that of members of the company. Killigrew employed a girl for the sole purpose of satisfying the sexual appetites of the players and a number of the actresses supplemented their wages in the back alleys off Drury Lane.

Others became mistresses of the gentry. There was constant rivalry and backbiting as each jostled for the attention and the favours of the rich. They laughed at Jessica and taunted her with their presents of fine clothes and jewels; but Jessica was unmoved and continued to make do on her meagre pay.

Pregnancies were inevitable. Actresses waddled the stage until the day of their lying-in, their minds more occupied upon searching the audience for possible new liaisons than upon remembering their lines. There was greater amusement at the sight of a round-bellied woman playing the part of a maiden than ever there had been at seeing a middle-aged man in the role.

Jessica no longer enjoyed Bridget's constant companionship. She had fallen in love with a sailmaker from Rotherhithe and was now happily married and settled in a small house backing on to the river. Last summer she had given birth to another boy whom they had named Robert.

Jessica missed her desperately. She also missed Ben. The little boy had been so much a part of her life, she felt that she had been parted from her own child. But she liked Will Pett and went as often as she could to stay with them at Rotherhithe.

Jessica had given up the room in Southwark: it had seemed lonely there on her own. Instead, she had taken a room in Long Acre which was much more convenient for the theatre.

For her part, Bridget came as often as she could to London to see the play and to spend an hour or two with Jessica. She was there one day in early June – a special day, as it turned out, for news was released of victory against the Dutch. There had been threat of war for the past year, with the Dutch sinking English trading vessels and the King's Fleet prepared to do battle. But it was not until 3 June that the two fleets engaged.

Prentice boys ran through the streets shouting exaggerated figures of enemy dead and vessels captured. It was difficult to know the truth of it, except that the English had won. Bonfires were hastily lit on street corners, disposing of the piles of waste matter which lay at every door, sending rats scurrying from beneath piles of rotting entrails outside the butcher's shop.

But, as the two girls walked down Drury Lane, their talk was of other matters. Three houses were shuttered and with a red cross painted upon the door. The plague was again in London.

'There's been talk of it for the past month,' said Jessica. 'We've orders from the Lord Chamberlain to close the theatre for a while.'

'You'd best come to Rother'ithe, out o' the way.'

'I can't. I've promised to help another girl to learn her part. We're going to rehearse together.'

'Bugger re'earsin',' said Bridget. 'If they've closed the theatre, yer to come on down to Rother'ithe.'

'I will if it gets bad. I expect it's just a scare because of the hot weather.'

Bridget looked doubtful. 'Well, I don't like it. If it does take 'old, there's no one as knows 'ow many it'll take.' She looked at Jessica. 'You ain't never seen it, not when it gets real bad. I still remembers, in forty-seven, when I were just a little nipper . . . it nigh on took the 'ole o' London.'

Jessica felt uneasy. 'There's no reason to think it'll be like that again.'

'You don't know as what it's like. Get took sick o' the consumption and someone'll nurse yer. Get took sick o' the plague . . .' Bridget ran her finger across her throat. 'Yer on yer own.'

Jessica shuddered.

'Nailed up in that 'ouse with no one to give a toss. No one as'll come near you. No one t' s' much as look at you, not till they comes t' bury yer. You'd do just as well to nail up yer own coffin as be nailed up in that 'ouse.'

Jessica took another look over her shoulder at the boarded houses, then shuddered again.

'You'd best go the long way round next time yer goin' 'ome,' said Bridget. 'Go by Bow Street and Covent Garden. Better than walkin' past them 'ouses again.'

That night when Jessica heard the tolling of the death-cart bell she looked out of her window and watched it trundling down the street. A little later another bell tolled – this time the watchman's: 'One of the clock, and all's well.' She closed her eyes and determined that next day she would wash down her door with vinegar and get a bottle of plague water from the apothecary.

Forty-three people were taken with the plague that week. The next, when the death toll rose by another one hundred and twelve, she thought seriously of Bridget's invitation to go to Rotherhithe. By the end of the month, when it had reached a further two hundred and sixty-seven, she packed up her few belongings and set out to take a wherry downriver.

The streets were crowded with people, coaches and wagons piled high with everything which could be carried. She saw the account books and ledgers of businessmen preparing to move their offices to safer locations. A number

434

of shops were already closed. Everyone with the means to do so was making arrangements to leave the city.

She walked down Bow Street, past the Maypole standing in the Strand, dodging between people and handcarts, wagons and coaches, each forcing their way through the milling crowds.

At the river stairs she realized that she stood little chance of hiring a wherry. Too many people stood haggling and arguing, each trying to commandeer the next available craft, calling out and begging passage on larger barges passing downstream. She decided to walk and set out down Fleet Street towards Ludgate Hill, past St Paul's and Watling Street, on towards Fish Street and London Bridge.

In Cannon Street she saw a woman lying huddled, propped in a doorway, scarce able to summon the strength to raise herself upon one elbow. Her eyes were inflamed and her swollen tongue lolled from the side of her mouth.

A small child clung to her, calling: 'Mama, Mama, please get up,' as he attempted, vainly, to drag her to her feet.

The woman looked up as Jessica passed and, with a great effort, pushed the child towards her. 'Take my child. For the love of God, please take him.'

The child screamed and threw himself upon her. 'No, Mama. Get up. You must get up.'

Jessica hesitated. She was about to go down on one knee when she changed her mind and began to walk away.

'Please,' the woman begged. 'For the love of God take him for me.'

Jessica swallowed hard and crossed the street. She could still hear the cries of the child imploring his mother to get to her feet but the woman's voice was too weak to reach her ears.

'May God forgive me,' she breathed, 'and preserve me from a similar fate.'

She did not look back until she was about to turn the corner. The child was still screaming but the woman appeared to have fallen backwards into the doorway.

By the time she reached Rotherhithe she was trembling; sweating from the heat of the weather and from the effort of carrying the heavy bundle containing her belongings.

''Ere sit down, luv.' Bridget took her by the hand and led her to a stool. 'You looks done in.'

'It's awfully hot.'

Bridget fetched her a pot of ale and ran a hand across her clammy skin. 'You got an 'eadache?'

Jessica nodded.

'Show me yer eyes. Do they 'urt when the light shines in 'em?'

'No.'

'You let me know if they starts 'urtin'. And if yer back gives you jip.'

Ben ran in from the workshop where he had been helping Will Pett. He climbed up on Jessica's knee. 'You come t' see us, Aun'y Jess?'

'Yes,' she smiled. 'I've come to stay.'

Bridget clipped him lightly on the ear. 'You get back to 'elping yer pa,' she said. 'Aun'y Jess is all done in.'

'Bridget, there was this woman in Cannon Street.'

Bridget smiled at her sympathetically, recognizing the distress upon Jessica's face.

'She wanted me to take her child.'

'You didn't touch it? You didn't do nothing as could 'ave . . .?'

'No,' said Jessica quietly. 'May God forgive me, I walked off and left her.'

Bridget placed a hand on her shoulder. 'You 'ad no choice, luv. There's no point in feelin' bad 'bout somethin' as what you couldn't do nothin' about.'

'I know, but . . .'

'I knows 'ow you feels, luv, but there ain't nothin' you can do. If you'd 'ave touched the little fella, you'd 'ave been good as dead.'

'What'll happen to him, Bridget? I can't help but keep wondering what will happen to him.'

'I know, luv. It don't bear thinkin' on.'

'And what's going to happen to us?'

'Come on,' said Bridget gently. 'Get that ale down you and stop all this chat 'bout w'at might 'appen. F' all we knows, we might get struck down by lightnin' t'morrer but there ain't no point in worrying 'bout it afore it 'appens.'

By mid-July the death toll had reached seven hundred in

436

a single week. By the end of the month a further three thousand had died.

The Lord Mayor ordered that the filth should be cleared from city streets and that all cats and dogs should be put down, but nothing was done about the rats which ran free through the empty streets and the nailed-up houses. People were asked to be indoors by nine o'clock in order that the sick might leave their homes for air.

Men, women and children, who were terrified of those lying sick, were drawn with morbid fascination to the graves of the dead. Crowds stood gazing down into the plague pits which daily increased in number.

During the last week of August more than six thousand people died.

''Ere,' said Bridget, 'this ain't no joke.'

It was a gross understatement. The girls had watched constantly for signs of the disease spreading to their own locality.

'There's an 'ole family been took in Black Street. That's the third in a week.'

'I saw that pedlar on the corner again yesterday,' said Jessica. 'He was selling potions. Perhaps we should get some.'

'Don't talk daft. Them things don't work.'

'It's worth a try.'

'Waste o' money,' said Bridget. 'Might as well chuck it in the river.'

'Well, we've got to do something. And there were an awful lot of people buying from him.'

Bridget shrugged. 'S'pose there ain't nothin' else we can do.'

'I just feel that I've got to do something.'

Bridget nodded. 'S'pose it ain't no more daft than sittin' 'ere on our arses doin' nothin'.'

'Perhaps we could try to get away.'

'Where to? There ain't nowhere left t' run.'

Jessica closed her eyes. She was more frightened than she cared to admit.

'You oughta go. There ain't nothin' to stop you. You could go t' yer folks in Dunscombe.'

'No,' she said sharply. Then, swallowing hard, she bit her

lip. 'I would go,' she said, 'but only if you'd go too.'

Bridget shook her head. 'We belongs round 'ere,' she said. Dunscombe seemed a thousand miles away to someone who had never ventured beyond London. 'We got t' stay 'ere 'side o' Will.'

'He could go too.'

Bridget half-smiled. 'Not our Will. 'E ain't never gonna leave Rother'ithe.'

Jessica knew it to be true. Nothing would persuade Will Pett to leave his home. 'Looks like we'd better try the potion.'

'W'at was 'e sellin'?'

'I'm not sure. He seemed to have quite a selection. I noticed some dried toad and something with gunpowder.'

'W'at about unicorn 'orn?'

'I wouldn't trust the unicorn horn,' said Jessica with feeling. 'I remember what sort of stuff Joseph used to pass off as unicorn horn.'

'Well, w'at d'you suggest?'

'Let's see if we can get some lily root. He had lily root with arsenic. They say arsenic's good for all sorts of things.'

Bridget shrugged. 'Sounds as good as any.'

'I'll go straight away, see if I can find him.'

Bridget busied herself in searching about the room. 'I'll find you some money.'

'Oh, Bridget.' Jessica took an inward breath.

'Now don't go startin' that again.'

'But I'm eating your food . . .'

'You can't do nothin' else when the theatre's closed,' said Bridget matter-of-factly. She was searching for any coin she could lay her hands on.

'It's over two months since I was paid and goodness knows when they're going to re-open.'

'You 'elps Will in the workshop.'

'Of course I do, but that's not enough.'

'W'at else is friends for?'

'You and Will have the children to feed. And now, with another one on the way . . .'

'You don't eat much,' said Bridget, giving a small squeal of pleasure as she discovered a coin where she had not expected one to be. She examined the collection in her hand. 'Reckon that oughta be enough.'

'One of these days . . .'

'Yeah.' Bridget grinned and poked her in the ribs. 'One o' these days them pigs is gonna sprout wings.'

Jessica smiled wanly.

'Go on, luv, go an' get us a potion. Get enough f' the five of us.'

Jessica brushed her lips across Bridget's cheek. 'Thanks again,' she said softly.

'F' what? F' 'avin' the best mate in the 'ole o' London? Where's the thanks in that?'

'You haven't got the best mate,' said Jessica. 'I have.'

She went out into the street and had little difficulty in locating the pedlar who was doing a good trade. She bought the mixture of lily root and arsenic and took it back to the family.

'Let's 'ope it tastes better than that tobacco,' commented Bridget. 'We've chewed s' many wads o' that stuff, the kids' tongues 'as turned black.'

She lined them up.

'Ben, come 'ere. You can be the first, then little Rob.'

Ben was now five years old. He came reluctantly, knowing that he was about to be fed a potion.

'Open wide, then I'll give you a drop o' gin.'

He obeyed, pulling a face even before he tasted the concoction. Bridget tipped it in and closed his jaw with a quick flick of the wrist. 'Swallow!'

He spluttered, swallowing and coughing on the unpleasant taste which refused to clear his palate.

Bridget went to thump him on the back but, at the same moment, Ben lifted his arm in a convulsive movement which knocked the remaining potion from her hand.

'You stupid little arse 'ole,' she shouted. 'You stupid little arse 'ole!'

The potion had spilled across the floor, disappearing quite irretrievably into the covering of rushes.

'Look what you've done. You've spilled it. Now w'at's the rest of us gonna do?'

'I'm sorry, Mama.'

Jessica bent and hugged him, shielding him from his

mother's wrath. He was still coughing on the unpleasant taste.

'Now w'at we gonna do?' Bridget was close to tears.

'I'll see if I can spoon some of it up,' offered Jessica.

'You ain't got an 'ope. And we ain't got no more money.'

Ben was crying. 'I'm sorry, Mama. I didn't mean it.'

'W'at 'bout Rob? W'at 'bout the rest of us?'

'I'm sorry, Mama.'

'Yer a stupid little arse 'ole,' she began again, but then took hold of herself. She went down on her knees and took him from Jessica's arms. ''Tweren't your fault,' she sobbed into his hair. 'But we only 'ad one lot. And we ain't got no more money.'

Jessica put her arms about them both. 'Don't cry,' she begged. 'We're not going to get anywhere by crying about it.'

'W'at we gonna do, Jess?'

'I don't know. My grandfather would have said to trust in God.'

Bridget wiped the palm of her hand across her eye, while the smallest hint of a smile began to return. 'We never was much o' the prayin' kind.'

Jessica smiled back. 'Perhaps we should try.'

Bridget gave a loud sniff and wiped her nose with the back of her hand. 'Oh, I dunno,' she grinned. 'Them potions don't work 'alf the time anyway.'

They both burst into laughter.

Bridget gave Ben a push on the bottom. 'Go on,' she said. 'Get orf and 'elp yer pa.'

'I'm sorry, Mama.'

'Go and 'elp yer pa,' she said. 'But come 'ere first and give yer ma a kiss.'

That night Ben was sick. Bridget cleaned him up and put him back to bed but very shortly afterwards he was sick again.

'My tummy 'urts, Mama,' he complained. 'And I'm all 'ot.'

Bridget ran a hand across his forehead. 'W'at d'you think, Jess?'

Jessica placed her hand on his brow. 'Could be just

440

something he ate,' she said, but she was aware that her voice had emerged with a high-pitched tightness.

Bridget gave her a glance but said nothing.

'Just put him back to bed and we'll keep watch.'

'Is 'is eyes 'urtin'?' asked Bridget, searching for symptoms.

'No more than you'd expect when he's feeling ill.'

Soon the vomiting was accompanied by diarrhoea.

'Best keep our eyes open f' the buboes.' Bridget could not keep still. She continually checked his armpits and his groin.

'I wouldn't recognize a bubo if I saw one,' commented Jessica.

'Oh, yes, you would. You'd know a bubo if you saw one.'

They were joined by Will who also began pacing the floor. Ben was now vomiting almost continuously, retching and heaving in a lather of distress.

'We mustn't worry,' urged Jessica, struggling to keep calm. 'It's probably nothing.'

'It's good of you t' say so, our Jess,' said Will. He was a gentle, soft-spoken man. 'But I think as you'll agree 'e's mighty sick.'

Jessica merely nodded. There could be no denying the seriousness of Ben's condition.

Bridget knelt beside him, hardly holding her panic in check as she struggled to relieve his distress. 'W'at else d'you look for?'

'I don't know,' said Jessica. 'I've never seen anyone with the Black . . .' She could not bring herself to say the final word.

'Don't make no difference. 'E's failin' any'ow.'

'No. He can't be.' Jessica dropped to her knees beside her, willing the little boy to rally.

'I can see 'im goin'.' Bridget turned forlornly to Will. 'I can see 'im goin', Will, afore me very eyes.'

Tears were glinting in Will's eyes too. 'Don't go sayin' things like that, gal, not while there's 'ope.'

''E's goin', I tell yer.' Tears were streaming down her face. 'An' I don't know what t' do.'

Jessica put her arms about her. 'Pray. For God's sake let's just pray.'

They did, each in their own way — begging Him, blaming Him, offering their own lives in return. But Ben let out a long quivering sigh and they knew that he had gone.

Control broke and all three cried, clinging to one another and sobbing convulsively.

'I shouldn't 'ave been cross with 'im. 'Tweren't 'is fault.'

'Ssh. You were upset.'

'But I shouldn't 'ave sworn at 'im when 'e dropped that potion.'

'He knew you didn't mean it.'

'And now 'e's dead.'

'Ssh.'

'W'at can we do?'

'Let's not do anything till morning.'

'It's nearly light.'

'Yes.' Jessica was surprised to see the dawn beyond the window. 'We've been up all night.'

Will knelt with his head resting upon the dead child. He had loved him as his own son. 'Ta-ta, ol' son. We'll be thinkin' of you. You were a good boy.' The sobbing made his words indistinct. 'I'll look after yer ma, an' I'll finish that little job you started f' me yesterday.'

It was not possible to organize a proper funeral. There were too many dead. They conducted their own impromptu service then handed him, reluctantly, to the man in charge of the death cart. He was thrown unceremoniously upon the heap of bodies and wheeled to the pit where he joined the thousands.

For days they wept, unable to put their minds to anything else.

A cross had been painted on the door of the house and they were forbidden to leave. Neighbours crossed the street rather than pass by, while others more compassionate left food upon the doorstep.

'We'd best watch Rob,' sobbed Bridget. 'Case 'e comes down with it, too.'

But no one else in the family developed the symptoms. A week later, while they were still grieving, none bore the physical signs of illness.

'Why little Ben?' asked Jessica. 'And he was the only one to take the potion.'

''Tweren't like no ordinary plague,' said Bridget. 'It were too quick and there weren't no buboes.'

'Poor little Ben.'

'Well, I tell you one thing,' sobbed Bridget, 'so much f' them bleedin' potions.'

In mid-September the death-toll began, at last, to slacken. There were five hundred fewer deaths than the seven thousand of the previous week. It was the first sign of relief. People began to relax, casually accepting the deaths of hundreds each day, where previously there had been a thousand.

Will and the two girls thought only of one. The memory of Ben was everywhere — at the table when they ate, in the workshop, upon his empty truckle bed.

'I miss 'im, Jess,' said Will. ''E were gettin' t' be such an 'elp t' me.'

'I know.' Jessica's throat ached every time she spoke of him. 'He loved you, Will. You took him in like he was your own boy.'

''E were my boy. Made no difference where 'e come from.'

'Yes,' she said quietly and was forced to consider her own feelings concerning Rupert.

'D'you remember, Jess,' put in Bridget, 'the way we used t' carry 'im about?'

'Yes,' she smiled. 'Sat him on the tray among the oranges.'

'Little bleeder learned t' walk in the Salisbury.'

Jessica nodded. 'Then he was into everything, once he could walk.'

''E were a good boy, though, our Ben.'

'Yes,' said Jessica softly. 'Such a good little boy.'

Bridget was now heavily pregnant. Jessica helped her in every way she could and also spent a good deal of time helping Will in the workshop.

She was there one day when Simon Ashwell came and stood at the door. She gaped in amazement.

'I looked for you in Long Acre,' he said. 'I eventually found another member of the company who told me I should find you here.'

She was too shocked for words.

Will put down the length of canvas on which he was working and rubbed his hands across the seat of his breeches. 'There ain't no need t' stand on the step, sir. Yer welcome to me 'umble 'ome.'

'Thank you.' Simon dipped his head. 'I apologize if I'm inconveniencing you.'

''Tain't no inconvenience, sir. I'll call the wife.' He turned his head. 'Bridget!'

She came running from the house.

'Cor blimey, Mr Ashwell, sir. W'at on earth you doin' 'ere?'

She began flicking the corner of her apron across a nearby surface.

'I came, Ma'am, to see Mrs Daniels, if you'll excuse the intrusion.'

'Why, course you 'ave. You must come in the 'ouse, sir. I'll get you a nice drop o' ale.'

She gave a quick jerk of the head towards Jessica, indicating that she should close her mouth.

'Jess, luv, come in the 'ouse and 'elp Mr Ashwell to a mug o' ale.'

'What? Oh, yes.' Jessica shook herself, almost visibly, and followed them into the tiny room in which the family lived and ate.

'I'll leave you to it, then.'

Jessica turned, about to beg her to stay, but Bridget had walked away.

'You'll sit down,' she said, indicating a stool.

Simon Ashwell waited for her to take another. 'I come with news of your father. He's taken with the sickness.'

Despite herself Jessica gasped.

'I thought you'd want to know.'

She considered the information for a moment, then said: 'Why is he in London? I'd have thought he'd have stayed away during the sickness.'

'He had urgent business. He waited weeks, then decided to take a chance. He was only going to attend to some papers in his lodgings. He didn't speak to a soul apart from Mrs Hardwick but two days ago he was taken very sick with a fever. I fear it's the plague.'

'Oh.'

'I begged him not to come, but he said he couldn't wait till winter.'

'I see.'

'I thought you'd want to know.'

'I'd best go to him.'

'No.' He looked at her gravely. 'I beg you, Mrs Daniels, don't even consider it.'

'I think I must.' She surprised herself as much as him.

'But why?'

'He's my father.'

She attempted to analyse her own feelings and failed completely.

'But you've rejected him.'

'I know.'

She had no idea why she needed to go.

'I beg you, think about it. I came because it was my duty, but I can't bring myself to take you back to risk the sickness.'

'I'll get my things,' she said. 'We'd best leave at once.'

Bridget had been listening at the door. 'You stupid pisspot, Jess. You must be addled. You'd be mad goin' up there.'

'I'll be all right.'

'No, you won't. You'll get took sick, then what'll we do? You dead, and all 'cause o' some toff what you can't abide.'

'He's my father.'

'You didn't take much note o' that when 'e was 'earty.'

'I know, but I've got to go.'

Bridget threw up her hands. 'Tell 'er, Mr Ashwell. Come 'ere, Will: tell this woman as what she's not t' go.'

'Please, Mrs Daniels,' said Simon. 'I wish now that I hadn't come.'

'I'm glad you did. I thank you for it.' She looked up at the sky. 'I'll fetch my cloak. It looks like rain.'

He had a boat moored down by the steps at Rotherhithe. The boatman rowed them back upstream towards the city.

It was the absence of noise which she noticed first — the lack of hammering and ringing coming from workshops along the wharfs. Where were the streetsellers crying their wares? No water sellers — 'Sweet river water; penny a bucket.' So few people. The nearer they got to the city, the

445

fewer there were. It was early evening and the mizzling rain gave an added feeling of depression to nearly deserted streets.

At Lion Quay they disembarked and took a coach. She was surprised, at first, to see the coachman working, then realized that some different kind of life still went on in the city despite the absence of so many people.

Two out of every three shops were closed. Grass grew up through the cobbles in side streets. Those people who were about walked with their faces covered, many holding onions or lemons to their noses.

Row after row of houses bore the mark of the plague — many grown faint now after months of weathering. Latterly, no one had bothered to make the mark: the numbers had been too great.

Shutters swung off their hinges, vandalized for fuel to stoke the fires which had been burned to clear the filth. And yet, more filth had gathered — the waste matter of those who continued to live and to die here; nightsoil from a thousand sickbeds tipped into the street.

They proceeded up Gracechurch Street, past the Cornhill conduit, through to Bishopsgate where they alighted.

'Your father's lodgings are a little step down here.'

He led her a short distance off London Wall to a row of houses backing onto Gresham College. They had spoken little during the course of the journey but he smiled at her now and took her arm. She was glad of his company.

Mrs Hardwick, a plump, middle-aged woman, greeted Jessica at the door.

'Welcome, dear. Come on in out of the rain.'

'Thank you. And it's good of you to care for my father.'

'Why, bless you, dear, what else could I do?' The landlady ushered her in and took her cloak, indicating a large fire by which to warm herself. 'I've looked after Sir Rupert for all of these past five years. Three rooms he's had here and laundry and a bit of dinner every day when he's in London.'

Jessica smiled her thanks as she watched Mrs Hardwick put ale to warm beside the fire. 'But in the circumstances . . .'

'In the circumstances, dear, we trust in God. There's no

446

way I could see Sir Rupert want for care.' She shivered. 'All those poor people. So many gone.'

'One in every four, I hear. A quarter of the city.'

'And the charnel houses filled beyond hope. Never a doctor nor apothecary left alive to treat the sick.' She stopped and shook her head. 'I couldn't see Sir Rupert . . .'

'It's good of you.'

'All those people nailed up in their houses. They left them free to wander in the end, you know. Too many to cope with. You never know who you might be passing in the street these days.'

'It's easing now.'

'Yes, but not in time for your father.'

'How is he?'

Mrs Hardwick made a gesture with her hand which indicated there was little hope. 'I'm sorry, dear, but there's not much I can do.'

'It's good of you . . .'

Mrs Hardwick stilled her with another gesture. 'I'll take you up.'

Rupert lay sprawled on the bed, his nightgown in disarray where he had been tugging at it in his discomfort. The exposed parts of his body were covered with sores and with red blotches caused by skin haemorrhaging. Jessica adjusted her eyes to the dim light of the room, shaded against the discomfort to his eyes. The bedding was stained with vomit and with diarrhoea.

'Sir Rupert?' The smell was almost unbearable.

He opened his eyes and smiled. 'You came.'

'I thought I should.'

'It was good of you.' It was difficult for him to talk because of the swelling of his tongue. 'But very unwise. I think you'd best go quickly before you place yourself in danger.'

'I'm here now,' she said. 'I'll not stay long.'

'Make sure you don't,' he said wearily. 'I've no wish to have you sick with the fever.'

'I'm sorry to see you feeling so ill.'

'Dying,' he said. 'Let's not deny the truth of it when it's staring us in the face.'

She was not sure how to respond.

447

He feebly raised an arm, indicating a large turgid gland beneath his armpit, glistening and inflamed. 'There's not much doubt about the cause of this, and there's another in my privies. There's only one way out of it with lumps like that.'

'We'll try to draw out the poison: a hot poultice, perhaps?' She examined the bubo in his armpit. She had never seen anything like it. 'Or perhaps it ought to be lanced.'

'It's all been done. There's nothing Mrs Hardwick hasn't tried.'

'You mustn't give up. I'll ask her for a needle. We'll see if we can discharge the venom.'

He smiled at her. 'I'm glad you care.'

She was embarrassed. She had not been conscious of her own feelings of compassion.

'It's been lanced,' he said. 'All that happened was that another grew.' He closed his eyes. 'And I'm so tired.'

'You'd like to rest?'

'No, I'd like to talk. Now that you're here, there's something I need to say.'

'Can I get you anything? A little water?'

He nodded and indicated a small bowl placed beside the bed. She scooped up some water and held it to his lips, dribbling it across his swollen tongue.

'Thank you.' He flopped his head back upon the pillow, exhausted by the effort.

She idly flicked a flea from beside his face.

'The fleas have been particularly troublesome this year,' he said feebly. 'It must have been the weather.'

She nodded and held the spoon ready to give him more water but he closed his eyes and turned away.

'I need to speak,' he said, 'about my affairs.'

She wondered why he should choose to speak to her of his affairs.

'You realize, of course, that you're my heir?'

'What!' It had never once occurred to her that she might be.

'You're my only living descendant.'

'Oh.' Then realizing that she knew so little about him: 'Am I?'

448

He smiled. 'Except, of course, for the ones I don't know of.'

'Oh,' she said again.

'You didn't know?'

'No,' she said, 'I truly didn't.'

'Then we must set the matter straight at once. You're heir to my estate and all my wealth.'

'All of it?'

'With one proviso.'

She looked at him, waiting.

'You will, of course, be required to marry Simon Ashwell.'

'What?'

'Is that so repugnant to you?'

'Yes . . . no . . . It's just . . .'

'It's what I've had planned for you; what I've been grooming Simon for.'

'I had no idea.'

'He's a good man. He'll make a good husband to you.'

She was shaking her head. 'No,' she said. 'I'm sorry but I can't.'

'Can't what?'

'I can't marry him.'

'Why not?'

She floundered for words. 'Because . . .' She struggled to bring her own scrambled thoughts into some kind of manageable order then said: 'Because I don't want to.'

He smiled at that. 'You've got my Margaret's spirit.'

'I'm nothing like my mother,' she retorted.

'Oh, yes, you are,' he smiled. 'Indeed you are.'

'Look, I don't want to,' she said. 'I'll not have anyone tell me whom I should marry.'

He sighed as though lacking the strength for lengthy persuasion. 'Supposing I should tell you,' he said, 'that in that case, you'll not receive a penny.'

She stopped and thought on it for a while. 'In that case,' she said, 'I should simply remain as I am today. Until a few moments ago I'd no idea that I was to receive anything.'

'You've that much pride?'

'It's not a matter of pride . . .' she began.

'Whatever it is,' he sighed, 'you're going to cause me great problems at this time of my dying.'

'I'm sorry.'

He closed his eyes and lay back on the pillow.

'Sir Rupert, couldn't you . . .'

'Not Sir Rupert,' he said. 'Call me Papa.'

She bit her lip.

'In the circumstances,' he said feebly, 'just once — couldn't you call me Papa?'

'Papa,' she said awkwardly.

'That's better.'

'It's not that I don't thank you for naming me as your heir,' she began again.

'Of course you're my heir.'

'I just hadn't realized.'

'And you're not married.'

'No.'

'Well, surely you understand that I can't leave my entire estate in the care of a woman?'

'No, I suppose not.'

'Well, there you are then. Marry Simon and the matter's resolved.'

'I don't want to marry him,' she said. 'I'm sorry but I won't be told whom I should marry, simply so that I can come into an inheritance.'

He opened his eyes, just long enough to give her a look of exasperation, then closed them again. 'Doesn't Oakbourne mean anything to you? It's been in our family for generations. It's imperative that we ensure it remains that way.'

'Leave it to Mother. She knows how to run the estate.'

'You're my heir,' he said. 'You must carry it down through future generations. And Margaret is sick.'

'She's sick?'

'I'll give you a year,' said Rupert.

'My mother is sick?' asked Jessica again.

'A year in which to think upon it. That's more than generous on my part. Most fathers would be far less patient.'

'I'm sorry.'

'During that time, Simon can hold the estate in trust. I only beg you . . .'

450

'Why not let him have it?' she said. 'If that's what he wants.'

He heaved another sigh of exasperation. 'You're my blood,' he said. 'How many times do I have to tell you? My flesh and blood.'

'I'm sorry.'

'And I put in so much effort on your behalf,' he said. 'Simon's a good man, like my own son, and he's skilled in handling my affairs.'

'I've no wish to cause you problems.'

He opened his eyes and smiled at her indulgently. 'I can't complain about a little spirit. After all, it's what I admired so much in my dear Margaret.'

'She's sick, you say?'

'Yes,' he said quietly. 'I'm afraid she is.'

'In what way?'

'Poor Margaret,' he said. 'It breaks my heart to see her so.'

She waited for him to continue but he closed his eyes and appeared to drift into a doze.

She sat and looked at him, still trying to assimilate the shock of the conversation which had passed between them. She had not seen Simon Ashwell since they entered the house. He had discreetly slipped away.

'Does Mr Ashwell know of this?'

'Not yet.' Rupert opened his eyes for a moment then went back to sleep.

She was glad about that. She would have felt foolish had he been aware, all the time over these past years, of the role he was expected to play. She re-ran old conversations through her mind, trying to place them into new perspective in the light of present knowledge.

Another flea hopped across the pillow and she flicked it towards the floor.

Most women would have complied with the stipulation without question. But she was not like other women. And, in any case, a new kind of woman was emerging; there was a new sense of freedom which she firmly endorsed. She would most certainly not be told whom she must marry.

She sat and looked at her father sprawled there upon the

bed. She had little contempt left for a man so obviously dying.

'Jessica . . .'

'Yes?'

'I'm so afraid of dying.'

'Oh, Father.' She took his hand.

'But if not from the plague, it was bound to come sooner or later.'

'We must all die.'

'Pox,' he said almost conversationally. 'I'm riddled with it.'

'Oh.' She knew of many people with venereal disease, but it seemed strange to think of her father suffering from syphilis.

'Burned by those damned whores in Holland and France. We all were, you know. Damned whores.'

She was not sure how to respond.

'Not much else to do but wench. All those damned years holed up in wretched foreign lands, far from home, no hope of getting back to our families and the business of living.'

'It was a long time to be exiled.'

'And all the time thinking of my Margaret. I loved her so much, you know.'

She thought again of Richard Fullwood and Deliverance Daniels.

'And she never once complained.'

'Complained about what?'

'Seven years she spent in New England, you know. Never once complained.'

'I was there.'

'And with that man.'

She wondered for a fleeting moment to which one he referred.

'I watched him, you know, during the time I was there.'

'You were in New England?' It surprised her to learn that he had been in America.

'Called himself a minister.'

She felt personally affronted. 'He was a good man.'

'More like the spawn of the Devil!'

'Papa was a good man.'

'I'm your Papa.'

452

'He was a good man,' she repeated vehemently.

'Call me "Papa".'

She looked at him.

'Please.'

'Papa,' she said tightly.

He smiled. 'You're too young to remember. He was anything but good.'

She was angry. 'I remember him well.'

'He was a liar and a hypocrite.'

'No!'

'And he had people beaten worse than I would beat my dogs.'

'No.' She was frustrated by the knowledge that she could not vent her anger against a man so obviously near his death. 'I think, sir,' she said, 'you are mistaken.'

He paused and smiled at her. 'It's strange,' he said, 'how we remember things as we'd like them to be rather than how they actually were.'

She toyed for a moment with the power of disclosing to him her memories concerning Richard Fullwood. The thought of Margaret caused the old contempt to rise again in her throat.

'You were too young to know.'

She looked at him, running through her mind the possibility of revealing to him the true character of her mother and of her infidelities. She left it so long that he lapsed back into sleep, leaving her with a deep sense of hurt and frustration.

'I waited so long,' he said eventually, making her jump. 'Waited so long to make her mine.'

She closed her eyes. There was no point in destroying his illusions. A feeling of pity outweighed her desire for revenge. 'What happened?' she said. 'Why didn't you marry her as a girl?'

'I loved her so much . . . No man ever loved a woman more than I loved my Margaret.'

'Why didn't you marry her?'

'Such a long story,' he sighed. 'So many things that I ought to have done differently.' He paused, attempting to collect his thoughts, but it was obvious that he did not have the energy to do so. The conversation had exhausted him.

453

'I'll tell you some other time,' he said. 'You'd best be leaving now; in case you catch the sickness.'

'I'll stay if you like.'

'No, it wouldn't do for you to be struck down.'

She had a sudden fleeting thought concerning a situation in which both she and Simon Ashwell were struck down with plague, but it was too dreadful to sustain.

'I'll come back later.' She shuddered, still forcing down the thought which had come to mind.

'No. I won't see you again.'

'Father . . .' She felt a need to cry.

'And remember what I've said — you have a year. After that time the estate will have to be passed over to Simon. I can only beg of you . . .'

'Father, please.'

'Don't argue,' he said feebly. 'I've never in my entire life known anyone so wilful and so headstrong. And I've neither the wit nor the energy left to deal with it.'

'I'm sorry.'

'But you're a fine woman,' he smiled. 'There's not a man in the land won't envy Simon the taking of you.'

'I'm . . .'

'You'd best be going,' he said. 'And send Mrs Hardwick to me as you leave.'

She touched his hand. She was about to bend and kiss his forehead but the smell of the bedsheets inhibited her. Instead she squeezed the hand which responded limply to her touch.

'I'm glad we talked,' he said. 'I can go in peace.'

She hesitated but he had slumped into the pillow. She could see that he was almost beyond words.

'And go to see your mother,' he got out. 'One of you has to make the first move.'

She went to fetch Mrs Hardwick and stood waiting by the fire for her return.

'He's spewing blood,' she said. 'It's a bad sign.'

'I'd better stay.'

'No, dear, you'd best be gone. It's not good for you to stay round here too long.'

'You've been so good to him.'

'It's little enough,' she said. 'He's been generous to a poor widow. I don't know what I'd have done if he hadn't taken these rooms.'

Simon Ashwell appeared from behind her. 'I'd best be taking you back to Rotherhithe, Mrs Daniels, if you're ready to go. You've already been here too long.'

She looked at him with new eyes, embarrassed by the thought of what his reaction might be when Rupert told him of his will.

'I'll get your cloak,' said Mrs Hardwick.

'Thank you.'

Jessica was too embarrassed to look at her escort. He would be pleased that he would not ultimately be required to marry her. He could have the estate — and welcome to it. She would gladly pass it over rather than be forced into a marriage which was not of her own choosing. It was difficult to make any kind of conversation in the circumstances. There was a strange power in knowing more about this young man's future than he knew himself.

'We'll take the coach back to the river.'

'No,' she said. 'I'm not going back to Rotherhithe.'

He looked at her questioningly.

'I'll not risk carrying the sickness with me.' She tried to keep her voice calm but realized the tremor had not gone unnoticed. 'I'll go to my room in Long Acre.'

'Yes,' he said gravely, 'perhaps it would be best.'

CHAPTER 20

Margaret had been ill for some time and was deteriorating noticeably, sometimes speedily, sometimes with periods of remission.

She had been aware of it for a long time. Not in the early stages when she had been troubled by fevers – she had had fevers before – but gradually, as weakening muscles robbed her first of speed, then of mobility. Gradually, insidiously, the everyday movement of life became an effort, until one day, she had fallen on the stairs. Now, she spent most of her time in a seat beside the window, gazing out across the hills.

Also, there was the problem of her mind. It was not of great import to Margaret but it seemed to cause a great deal of concern among the household and to the members of her family. It seemed that she was forgetting things.

Sometimes it irritated her but for the most part she could not understand why it should be the cause of such consternation.

She spent a lot of time wandering the hills, the soft dip and sway of a pack pony beneath her, deep in conversation with her father, who would, without fuss or warning, suddenly become Richard. The conversation would continue without so much as a ripple disturbing its fluency. It was wonderful that, at last, after all these years, Richard was here.

She spent hours inspecting the sheep, face upturned to the sun and the wind of the high places, or dropping at will to the sheltered seclusion of hidden coombs or to the moist coolness of woodland, with the scents of primrose, parsley, bruised dandelion and garlic all wafting and combining, irrespective of place or season.

Then she would find herself in a field of maize – tall, broad-leaved maize, with fat cobs of yellow kernels. They would be making love – she and Richard – the glorious, flowing freedom of love. There would be the sound of Native children playing, women talking, papooses on their backs.

Then someone would speak; and it would be Abigail, come to bring her dinner.

She wondered sometimes if the people of the household were aware that Richard was here. In her more lucid moments she wondered if she had called out his name: but she knew that she had not. She had spent seventeen years learning to keep him hidden.

In lucid times, too, she was well aware of the continued deterioration of her health. She was in no doubt as to where it would lead. But it did not matter now. She was released from the burdens of responsibility: there was no one totally dependent upon her. She was free to wander the hills, to talk with Richard. Her father would take care of her. It did not matter that her bodily functions were failing: her mind had a freedom of its own.

It irked her sometimes that Mrs Leach had come to take over the duties of the household. There had been no reason for Rupert to bring her in. The woman did not perform her duties adequately. She did not carry them out as Margaret would have had them done. And she would not be told. Margaret had given instructions, time and again, yet still Mrs Leach ran the household in her own contrary manner.

But, then again, there were other times when it was good to sit here and to know that she need not bother, that she could ignore the need to hurry down into the dairy to supervise the making of the cheeses, that she could leave until next week the inspection of the gathered fruit. Somehow, the conserves would all be made, wines would appear on the table.

It was all such an effort. It was so much easier to sit here and to gaze out across the hills.

Simon had told her of Rupert's death. She had wept a

458

little, her feelings mixed. Her duty was done. She had known him since childhood. It seemed such a long time since she was a child.

She remembered her father taking her to collect the yarn. Fourpence halfpenny a pound and a chat at the cottage doors with the spinsters.

'They were good days, you know.'

Simon smiled. 'Sir Rupert's last words were of his love for you.'

'Rupert?'

'Yes, before he passed into death. His last words were of his love.'

'That's nice. How did he die?'

'Of the fever, Lady Mainwaring. You'll remember, I told you. I regret it was the plague.'

'Oh, how dreadful. Did he suffer much?'

'No,' he lied. 'He went in peace.'

'That's good. I wouldn't have wanted him to suffer.' She sat in thought for a long time. 'My own father, you know . . . he was in such pain.'

'I know, Lady Mainwaring,' he said gently. 'If you remember, I was here.'

'Oh, yes. I remember you were.'

'I must tell you of Sir Rupert's instructions.'

'How long have you been with us?'

'Five years, Lady Mainwaring. Since Sir Rupert returned.'

'Oh, yes, you came with him.'

'He brought me with him when he returned from Holland, after my father died.'

'Oh yes, of course. They were great friends.'

'Comrades throughout the war and during their exile in Holland.'

'Are you here to stay?'

'Yes, Lady Mainwaring. That's what I wanted to speak of.'

'Were you also in Holland?'

'Yes. You'll remember I told you that my father sent for me after my mother died.'

'Oh yes,' she said. 'Of course he did.'

He let some time elapse. 'Sir Rupert's instructions, Lady Mainwaring, about the estate . . .'

'I'm very sorry to know he's dead.'

He was not sure if she referred to his father or to Rupert. 'We must consider the future of Oakbourne.'

Suddenly she became agitated. 'I must get up.' She struggled to rise from the chair and he went hurriedly to assist her, steadying her with an arm as she attempted to gain some control over her feet.

'Please don't distress yourself. There's no need for alarm.'

'Oakbourne,' she said. 'There's no one now to run Oakbourne.'

'I have it in hand,' he said gently. 'Please don't distress yourself.'

'I must go down . . . '

'Shall I call Abigail? She's in the yard.'

'No, she has work to do.'

'She'll come at once if I call.'

'No. I can manage alone.' Even as she said it she slumped backwards into the chair, muttering over her inability to control the use of her legs. She knocked him away in irritation and he took a step to the side, watching her as she struggled to manoeuvre herself into an upright position.

A tear trickled down her cheek. 'I think I'm losing the ability to walk.'

'No,' he said gently. 'You're merely tired.'

She sighed and put a hand to her face. 'I'll go down later when I've had a rest.'

'Yes,' he said. 'You can go down then.'

They sat for some time in silence, she with her face in her hand, he sitting quietly looking at her.

'You're good to me, Simon,' she said.

'Really?' He smiled.

'You're like my own son.'

It pleased him greatly. He reached out and gently touched her arm. 'You've given me a home.'

'Have you come to stay?'

'Yes,' he said. 'I'm here to stay.'

'Are there others with the plague?'

'Many, I'm afraid. Many, many more.'

'Oh dear, we must be prepared.'

'It hasn't reached Dunscombe,' he reassured her. 'But there are many other places stricken.'

'And Rupert's dead?'

'Yes,' he said. 'I'm afraid he's gone.'

Another tear trickled down her cheek. 'When Richard died . . . '

'Richard?'

The discipline of years took hold and bade her be cautious. 'How silly,' she said. 'I get confused.'

'Your daughter,' he said. 'Sir Rupert has named her his heir.'

'Abigail? Abigail is Rupert's heir?'

'No,' he said. 'Mrs Daniels.'

'Of course it's Jessica.' She looked at him as though it were he who was being obtuse. 'Of course she's his heir.'

'Indeed,' he smiled patiently.

'His children died, you know.'

'Yes, I know.'

'And poor Isobel. He was unkind to that poor woman.'

'He told me of her. He did try but his love for you was very great.'

'I never met her, you know. My father met her once, a very long time ago. I seem to remember it was during the war.'

'On his way to London, before he joined the Redcoats. You've told me of it many times. I expect it's slipped your memory.'

'Yes,' she said wearily. 'I seem to forget a lot of things these days.'

'Mrs Daniels . . . ' he began again.

'She's his heir, you say?'

'Yes,' he said. 'He wanted Mrs Daniels to have Oakbourne.'

'She won't come back, you know.' Margaret turned and stared hard at him though her sight was failing and she could see little. 'She won't come back.'

'I trust she will.'

'No,' she said sadly. 'She won't come home.'

'Sir Rupert asked her. She hadn't known that she was his heir.'

Margaret became agitated again. 'I must get up.'

'Please stay where you are.'

'There's no one, no one left. Who's to run Oakbourne?'

'I have it in hand. He made it clear.'

'You know what to do?'

'Yes,' he said gently, 'I've worked five years upon the estate and about his business.'

'Yes,' she said. 'How silly of me. Of course you have.'

'Oakbourne is in my hands until such time . . .'

'She won't come back, you know. She won't come back.'

'Lady Mainwaring.' He let a moment elapse and coughed uncomfortably. 'There was something else.'

'Such a long time, and she's never come back.'

'I hardly know . . . Sir Rupert instructed that she was to marry me.'

That caught her attention. She seemed to struggle with the idea for some time. 'Marry?'

'Yes. Sir Rupert instructed that I should marry Mrs Daniels.'

'I'd like that.'

'Would you?'

'She won't come back, though. She'll never come back.'

'That's what I fear.'

She sat and looked at him. He knew that she could not really see him.

'And what of you?' she asked.

'Of me?'

'Do you want her as a wife?'

'She's a very fine woman, Lady Mainwaring, and extremely beautiful.'

'Yes,' she said blankly. 'That was always a problem.'

'I've long admired her.'

The short period of lucidity dissipated and she went off again into the depths of her own thoughts. 'We searched everywhere, you know. She was just a child. I suppose she must be a woman now.'

'A very fine woman.'

'The tinker took her, you know. I didn't know it at the time but Rupert told me. The tinker took her.'

'So I believe.'

'We tried to find her, but she'd gone without trace.'

'Yes,' he said gently. 'It must have been a terrible time.'

'And you say you're to marry her?'

'I fear she won't have me.'

'We looked everywhere. They say the tinker took her.'

'I'd have asked her long ago but I knew that she'd never consider me.'

'No,' she said, appearing to return again to the conversation. 'She's never done as she was told.'

'I'd want her to want me; but I fear she has a very poor opinion of me.'

'You're a good man,' said Margaret. 'I love you as my own son.'

'Thank you, Lady Mainwaring. But I fear that Mrs Daniels has other opinions.'

'She won't come home, you know,' she began again.

'He has given her a year.'

'She won't come home.'

'She has a year in which to consider her inheritance. I'm afraid it's tied up with marrying me.'

'We should have found that tinker. We should have brought her home.'

'It's very embarrassing,' he said. 'I could never deprive her of her inheritance.'

'But we did search, you know. William went first; then Tobias and the men of the estate. We looked everywhere for her.'

'She has no wish to marry me. And Sir Rupert had it all tied up. She can't have Oakbourne unless she agrees.'

'Did Rupert know?' she asked, suddenly lucid again.

'About what?'

'Your wish to marry her.'

'I think he did, though it was never spoken.'

'She should do as she's told,' she said. 'She's always been wayward.'

He smiled at her. 'I'd only take her if she truly wanted me.'

'It never used to be like that,' she said wearily. 'How times have changed.'

He smiled again. 'There are many things which are altered.'

'I don't think I can cope with change. I think I must be getting old.'

'No,' he said gently. 'You're just very tired.'

She was forty-one. She had aged greatly in the past few years.

'She has a year in which to consider the matter.'

'I hear she's on the stage, you know. No good will come of her being on the stage.'

'Meanwhile I hold it in trust.'

'I'm glad you're here. Father would be glad you're here.'

'I'll do my best.'

'He's dead, you know.'

'Yes, I fear so.'

'And now Rupert's gone. Did I hear you say he's dead?'

'Yes, Lady Mainwaring. Sir Rupert's dead.'

'Well, never mind. I'm glad you're here.'

'Yes,' he said gently. 'I'll take very good care of you.'

Jessica did not weaken in her resolve. She had no intention of marrying Simon Ashwell. They had met on occasions and, while each had been polite to the other, they had been equally embarrassed. As the deadline approached, she assumed that he would take up the inheritance and that nothing more need be said.

He had spoken, tentatively, on one occasion.

'I've no wish to deprive you of your rightful inheritance.'

'It wasn't your doing. It was my father's instruction.'

'It seems he had it all planned.'

'So I understand.'

'I didn't know, believe me. I hadn't realized what he was grooming me for.'

'I know,' she said. 'He told me that you didn't.'

'It wasn't until a few hours before his death . . . '

'He seemed to think that we'd just do as he asked without question.' It was highly embarrassing. She kept her face averted, finding it impossible to look him in the eye.

'I'm sorry that you found it such a disagreeable proviso.'

'It was totally unacceptable,' she said uncomfortably. 'There was no way that I could agree to such a condition.'

'No,' he said. 'I can understand that it might be unacceptable to you.'

She was almost totally overcome with embarrassment. She had no wish to offend him but it was, after all, in his own

464

best interests that she should refuse. 'In the circumstances,' she said, 'it seems best that you should just take Oakbourne and we'll say no more about it. There's no way that I could agree to my father's proviso, and he made it quite clear that in that case you should have it.'

'But you can't just turn down Sir Rupert's entire fortune.'

'I can, if he sets provisos I can't fulfil.'

He sighed as though not knowing what to say. 'Then I must make provision for you. Perhaps you'll allow me to provide a house and an income to suit your needs?'

'No. I've no wish for charity.'

He looked hurt. 'It isn't charity. It's your right.'

'I'm sorry,' she said. 'I didn't mean to offend you but I've got no rights. I've agreed to forego them.'

'You've refused to obey your father's instructions,' he said. 'That doesn't mean that I should deny you what is rightfully yours.'

'Oh, just take it,' she retorted. It was even more embarrassing when he was kind to her.

'I'm sorry,' he said. 'Now I've offended you.'

'No, I'm not offended. But surely you must realize that it would be totally wrong. I've refused his demands so I've no claim on the inheritance, and I've no wish to be obligated by your charity.'

'I apologize,' he said. 'I must have expressed myself very badly.'

She felt sorry, angry, embarrassed, all at the same time. 'Just go back to Dunscombe,' she said quietly. 'You'll make a good master and I wish you well. But, please, just go away and leave me alone.'

He took his leave and she regretted that she had so obviously offended him. She did not see him for several months and when she did eventually meet him in the street one day, their conversation was polite but distant.

Bridget thought that she was mad. ''E's so good 'earted,' she said. 'All you got t' do is marry 'im. And you'd 'ave that big 'ouse and all them servants.'

'There aren't many servants. At least, there weren't in my grandfather's day.'

'Just one 'd be good enough f' me.'

'Oh, Bridget.' Jessica placed an arm about her shoulders.

'If I did have Oakbourne, I could repay you for all the things you've done for me.'

'Don't talk daft. You does as you thinks fit, and that's an end of it.'

'I could take you back to Dunscombe. You could have everything you always wanted.'

Bridget laughed. 'Not much call f' a sailmaker in the 'eart o' the country.'

'No, I suppose not, but we could find something for Will to do.'

'No, luv. Will was born 'ere and raised 'ere. 'E wouldn't take t' bein' in the country.'

Jessica nodded. 'Then I could provide you with a few luxuries, here in Rotherhithe.'

'It's good of you, luv, but we can manage. There's no call f' you goin' orf and marryin' some toff just so's you can buy us cake. I'd rather 'ave you 'appy 'n' smilin'.'

Jessica gave her a hug. 'Oh, you're good to me, Bridget. What did I ever do to have a friend like you?'

'Dunno,' grinned Bridget. 'You can be a damned cussed pisspot, when you puts yer mind to it.'

'Sorry,' she grinned, and gave her another hug.

The theatres had still not re-opened. Life had returned to normal on the city streets but there was still evidence of plague in nearby towns and villages. Fifty people had died last week in Deptford. There was great fear of a resurgence and places of entertainment had been ordered to remain closed. The Theatre Royal was not to re-open until November, some eighteen months after it was first closed.

Jessica had been without income for most of this time. She had kept inside her room in Long Acre until she was sure she had not contracted the plague, and had then returned to the greater safety of Rotherhithe. She had remained there for the best part of six months but had felt unable to justify her keep. A new baby had been born to Will and Bridget, this time a girl. She had helped Bridget with the baby but eventually had returned to her lodgings in Long Acre and approached a family of good standing with an offer to teach their children to read. It earned her sufficient for food, and to pay for her room, but, as always, she was short of money.

Simon Ashwell came to her lodgings on 2 September, two weeks before the deadline. It was a Sunday and Jessica was preparing to go downriver to spend the day with Bridget and Will.

'I've come at an inconvenient time,' he said.

'No. I'm about to take a wherry to Rotherhithe but I can delay my departure for a little while.'

'I shan't keep you long.'

They stood looking at one another. She wondered why he was here.

'I've come,' he said, 'to make one last appeal to you to marry me.'

'What?'

'I know that I'm distasteful to you.'

'No, it's not that.'

'I know you don't like me, but I feel you don't know me well enough.'

He had embarrassed her again. 'No, it really isn't like that.'

'I've hopes that if you really knew me, you might look upon me just a little less unfavourably.'

'I'm sorry . . . '

'I realize that you've reason to dislike me.'

'I don't dislike you,' she said. 'I've never disliked you.'

'But I thought . . . '

She stood looking at her hands, her face turned scarlet. 'I told you of my feelings, right from the start. I made it quite clear.'

'You said . . . '

'I said I couldn't marry you. I didn't say I didn't like you.'

'Isn't it the same?'

'No, it isn't. I simply said that under no circumstances would I be *told* whom I must marry.'

'Oh,' he said.

They stood in an uncomfortable silence, each staring at opposite walls.

'I don't understand,' she said at last. 'It's to your advantage that I don't marry you.'

''It would be to my greatest advantage if you did.'

'But why? Without me, you can take everything.'

'Without you, I've got nothing.'

She still did not understand.

'It's nothing to do with the inheritance,' he said.

'Then what?'

'Mrs Daniels, I've long admired you.'

'What?'

'From the moment I first saw you.'

'Oh.' She thought he referred to her acting.

'You're the most beautiful woman I have ever met.'

'Really?'

'But, more than that, you're quite unlike any other that I've ever known.'

'I'm very ordinary,' she said, half turning towards him.

He smiled at that. 'There's nothing ordinary, Mrs Daniels, about you.'

She turned again, a little further this time, until she was almost facing him.

'You've a spirit of fire. You stand up for what you think is right and you refuse to be conquered.'

'I'm sorry.' She knew that this was not always considered seemly in a woman.

'No,' he said. 'I can't help but admire it.'

She blushed.

'You've stood alone, and you've become a great actoress. Yet, at the same time, your character has remained without blemish.'

She thought of her early days in London and prayed that she would never be questioned too closely upon them.

'You would do me the greatest honour if you would agree to become my wife.'

She went to sit down. 'I can't,' she said shakily.

'May I ask why?'

'I don't know . . . I just can't.'

He showed his disappointment.

'I couldn't marry you anyway,' she said after some time. 'I'm an actoress.'

'That's part of what I admire.'

'I want to remain here in London, on the stage.'

'There's no reason why you shouldn't.'

'I couldn't do both.'

'I don't see why not. We could buy a house here; engage servants. You're only required to work thirty weeks a year in the theatre. For the remaining twenty we could return to Oakbourne.'

'You can't be serious.'

'Perfectly so.'

'You'd be the laughing stock of all society — a gentleman of quality with a wife upon the stage.'

'I don't much care about the opinions of society,' he said. 'I'd be the proudest man in all of London — in all of England, for that matter.'

'You haven't thought this through,' she said. 'You can't possibly know what it is that you're suggesting.'

'I've thought about little else since the day I met you. But I thought you couldn't abide me.'

'Gentlemen have mistresses upon the stage,' she said. 'They don't have wives.'

He came and took her hand. 'It would give me the greatest pleasure, Mrs Daniels, to have you as my wife.'

She had half risen from the chair but now sat down again. She looked at him steadily for a long time. 'You'd really be prepared to go against all convention? To be ridiculed by society?'

'Yes,' he said.

'You really *do* care for me.'

'I love you,' he said simply.

Still she sat looking at him.

'Please say that you'll marry me.'

'I'll think about it,' was all she managed to say.

He took her hand and brought it briefly to his lips. 'That's all I ask. I've no wish to harass or offend you.'

'I'm not offended.'

'I'm glad we've had this talk,' he smiled. 'I think we've both been under a misunderstanding.'

'I must get you something,' she said, looking about her. 'I've been less than hospitable. A glass of wine, perhaps?'

'No, you were about to leave. I mustn't delay you.'

She had forgotten about her trip to Rotherhithe. 'I was about to take a wherry, but it doesn't matter.'

'To the contrary. If you'll allow me to escort you perhaps we can travel together? I've business in Fenchurch Street.'

She nodded and went to collect a pair of lace mittens and a purse.

'I trust you didn't mind my calling upon you?'

'No,' she said shakily. 'It was fortunate that you found me in.'

She closed the door of her room and they went downstairs into the street. Although it was September, the weather was very warm. There had been a drought and as they set out along Long Acre a strong southerly wind blew dry refuse and dust into the air, swirling it about them.

He took her arm. 'Is there anything I may do for you?' he asked. 'Is there anything you need?'

She thought on it for a time. 'There is just one thing.'

'Yes?'

She hesitated.

'You've only to name it.'

'A house,' she said. 'Not too big. She wouldn't want it too big. But nice. And with a decent workshop. Somewhere in Rotherhithe.'

'You'd like me to secure you a house in Rotherhithe?'

'Not me. Bridget.'

'Oh,' he said. 'Mrs Pett.'

'Yes. Something really nice where Will could work and the children could grow up.'

He smiled. 'Consider it done.'

'I owe it to her, you see. She's been such a good friend.'

'You were always together.'

'I want just this one thing to pay her back.'

A carriage came close and he drew her to the side, pressed against a wall as it passed.

'And surely there's something I can do for you?'

'You have, if you buy the house for Bridget.' She paused for a moment. 'It's not asking too much?'

'It's your inheritance,' he said. 'I'm only administering it on your behalf.'

She blushed and felt uncomfortable, wishing she had not asked.

'And may I ask one thing of you?' he asked.

She was not prepared for that.

He took her arm and they crossed into Bow Street. The strong wind, as they turned right, blew the dust into their faces.

She still had not replied. He waited a while then went on:

470

'Whether or not you return to Oakbourne as my bride . . .'

She tripped and he steadied her with the pressure of his hand.

'Whatever you decide, I would ask that you go back just once — to make your peace with your mother.'

'No,' she said sharply.

'Why not?'

'I couldn't do that. You don't understand.'

'I think I do.'

She doubted it. 'I'd rather not, if you don't mind.'

'All right,' he said gently. 'If that's the way you feel.'

He allowed a long time to elapse during which they dodged from side to side, avoiding people and traffic.

'It's very busy today.'

'Yes,' he said. 'It's even more busy than usual.'

He held her a little more tightly as he steered her round a cart piled with the possessions from someone's house.

'She loves you, you know. It would mean so much to her to see you again.'

Involuntarily, she pulled her arm away from him. He glanced at her briefly and released her without resistance.

'She wouldn't admit it, of course, any more than you. You've both got pride.'

She did more than glance in return. He smiled at the look she gave him.

'Her heart would be eased if you'd come back just once, to visit her.'

'I'd rather not.' She walked on, staring at the cobblestones until he caught hold of her and guided her out of the path of another carriage.

'I've come to know her well during the time I've lived at Oakbourne. I'm immensely fond of her.'

It had never occurred to her that Simon could be fond of her mother.

'She's told me about her days in New England; about the ways in which she and your grandfather struggled to keep Oakbourne going before Sir Rupert returned. She's a most remarkable woman. She's told me so many interesting things about herself.'

'Not everything, I'll wager,' she muttered to herself.

He raised an eyebrow but did not pursue it.

She was embarrassed again. She had spoken out of turn. 'How long have you lived at Oakbourne?'

'Six years. Sir Rupert brought me back with him from Holland.'

'Oh.'

'He and Lady Mainwaring gave me a home. Without them I'd have been destitute.'

'And now you have the estate.'

He glanced at her quickly.

She smiled, realizing that she had been misunderstood. 'You'll make a good master,' she said. 'I wish you well.'

'Only if you'll agree to be my wife.'

She went quiet again.

'Sorry. I didn't mean to press you.'

They walked in silence. They were approaching the river stairs and became aware of great activity.

'What's going on? It seems the whole of London is on the river.'

He searched for an available wherry and signalled for it to collect them. The wherryman manoeuvred into position to allow them to board.

'Will you come with me to see your mother?' he asked again. He took her hand and helped her into the small boat which rocked in the wake of so many passing craft. 'While there's still time.'

'Time?'

'You know she's sick?'

'Yes, my father told me.'

'There's not much time.'

'In what way is she sick?'

'It's difficult to say.'

She clung to the sides of the wherry as it rocked its way out into midstream. She had not thought that her mother's life was in danger. 'Why? Is she about to die?'

'Not die, perhaps, not yet. It's just . . . ' He looked uncomfortable and searched for words. 'The disease has caused a distemper of the brain.'

The fear of insanity was far more disturbing than death. 'She's crazed?'

'Not crazed, exactly, but there are times . . . ' He paused.

'Yes?'

'There are times when she imagines things to be different from what they are.'

'I see,' she said, not seeing at all.

'It's important that you come soon, while she's still able to know you and to make her peace.'

'I hadn't realized.'

'It's very important,' he said gently. 'I don't mean to distress you but I think you should know the seriousness of her condition.'

She stared at the river water and at the many craft coming from the opposite direction, crowded and jostling. Many were laden down with possessions. It reminded her of the great escape at the time of the Plague. She wondered what was going on.

'Sir Rupert didn't explain.'

'Then you'll come?'

'I don't know,' she said. 'You don't understand.'

He looked at her for a while. 'You made peace with your father,' he said gently. 'Is it so much more difficult to speak with your mother?'

'Yes.'

'I see.'

'No, you don't.' But she had no intention of explaining. She resumed staring at the passing craft.

'Well, I'll leave you to think about it for a while. But I can only beg you not to leave it too long.'

'I can't imagine why there are so many people,' she said, as much to distract her own thoughts as to deter him.

'There are a great many about,' he agreed. He turned to the man pulling on the oars. 'What ails the people, wherryman?'

'It's the fire, sir, down by the bridge.'

'What fire?'

''Aven't you 'eard, sir? Durst big fire, biggest I ever saw.'

'Good heavens!'

'Been burnin' since two o'clock this mornin'. Close on three 'undred 'ouses gone, and still burnin' strong.'

'What a dreadful thing.'

'Started somewhere down Puddin' Lane, sir. Now it's reached the bridge and 'alf o' Fish Street.'

473

'God's blood,' said Simon. 'I was hoping to alight at Old Swan.'

'You'll not get off at Old Swan, sir. 'Tis all aflame up this way as far as Old Swan.'

'What about the other direction?'

'Down t' St Magnus Church in that direction, sir. All burned down.'

'The church has been burned?'

'All gone, sir. Saw the roof come cavin' in with me own eyes.'

By this time they could smell the smoke and it was not long before they saw the glow − a shimmering red heat haze sending showers of sparks into the sky with an explosive crackling roar.

River craft crowded in both directions, some escaping, others wanting to watch and to get as close as possible to the fearsome sight.

The wherry nosed its way slowly, finding gaps in the traffic, and keeping to the south bank away from the heat and sparks. They passed the Bear Garden and the church of St Mary Overie and came to the bridge, still sound on the southern end but, to the north, buildings were blazing.

'Do you want t' walk round the bridge, sir?' It was usual for passengers to alight on one side of the bridge then to walk downstream to re-board the wherry on the other side. The turbulence of the water constricted beneath its many arches made the crossing uncomfortable.

'No, I think we'd best stay aboard.'

'Right you are, sir, but you'd best 'old tight.'

Simon nodded to Jessica who reached out and gripped the side of the wherry. At the same time he placed his arm across her back.

With a great rocking motion they swept through the nearest arch.

'Hold tight!' But his voice was drowned by the noise of the foaming torrent. Spray shot up around them and descended like rain, leaving them damp and temporarily blinded.

'Sorry about that,' Simon apologized on the other side. 'But in this crowd it seemed unwise to disembark.'

On the north bank great orange tongues of flame were

474

licking the sky. Buildings were tinder dry following the drought and the narrow, closely packed streets acted as funnels, drawing the flames at speed. The strong southerly wind was blowing the fire away from the river, into the heart of the city. Warehouses along the waterfront, stocked with pitch, tar, oil and brandy, were exploding with ferocity, sending showers of sparks to ignite others from the sky.

No one was taking action to stop the fire, only to escape from it. Poor people, unable to command a craft, were throwing their possessions into the water, running from one flight of steps to the next as the fire threatened to overtake them. Carts and coaches, hastily laden with furniture and cash boxes, clocks and silver plate, were making for the haven of churches, or to the homes of friends away from the path of the fire. Sick people, unable to walk, were being carried on truckle beds.

Some small attempt had been made to pull down houses but to little effect. The flames moved faster than people's ability to form a firebreak.

'I'll set you down 'ere, sir.' Once beyond the reach of the fire, the wherryman rowed the boat cross-stream towards Custom House Steps. 'You can walk up Water Lane and Mark Lane t' Fenchurch Street. But be careful of yer step.'

'Thank you.'

'You'd best not go,' said Jessica who was thoroughly shaken by the sight she had just witnessed.

He smiled. 'Don't worry, I'll stay well clear of the fire. Will you be all right?'

'Yes,' she said. 'They're expecting me at Rotherhithe.'

He took her hand and brought it briefly to his lips. 'Take care,' he said. 'They should have it under control by the time you return. If not, it might be wise to spend the night in Rotherhithe.'

She nodded. 'Don't worry. I'll be all right.'

He jumped on to the steps. 'And you'll come with me to Dunscombe?'

'I don't know . . . '

'I'll come for you on Thursday,' he called. 'The coach leaves at ten.'

She began to protest but the wherryman cast off and began to row away downstream.

'Till Thursday,' he called, and watched as she was rowed away from him.

In the evening, when she returned, the fire was still raging. Dusk was gathering and the flames lit up the darkening sky, spreading across the hill above the river in an orange arc. The smell and the noise were almost more frightening than the sight of it.

The water was littered with the pathetic remains of furniture thrown into the river. A dead cat floated by, bloated and soggy; a child's toy bobbed and swirled amid the jetsam.

Simon called on her next day to check that she was unharmed. The fire was still burning.

'You didn't stay in Rotherhithe?'

'No, I needed to return. I'm employed to teach a young family to read.'

He raised a kind but admonishing eyebrow at her. 'Well, at least you're quite safe now,' he said. 'The fire's a long way from here.'

'But what about all those poor people living in its path?'

'I don't know. There seems to be no stopping it. It's hellbent on taking all before it.'

She hesitated. 'You'd best take care of yourself.'

'I'll be all right. But I must attend to matters of business, and help Mrs Hardwick. The fire's coming towards her house. I must help her pack.'

'I'll come, too,' she said. 'I can be of help.'

'No. You're safer here.'

He had rushed away before she could insist but all night she thought of Mrs Hardwick. She was a good woman who had been kind to her and had cared for her father. She did not like to think of Mrs Hardwick's home being overtaken by fire.

Next morning she got up early and after gaining leave of her employer went to see for herself. She chose not to go by wherry for, with the north bank burning, she was not at all sure she would be able to alight. Instead, she began by walking down Drury Lane and Wych Street but as she neared Fleet Street she could see that the fire was burning at its far end. She turned left into Fetter Lane, hoping to go round it.

People were pouring out of the city, each making their escape as the fire spread towards them. Coaches and carriages were filled with all manner of possessions, horses labouring beneath the weight, skittish with the acrid smell of smoke in their nostrils. Women and children pushed handcarts, old men struggled, bent double beneath loads carried on their backs. Jessica, carrying nothing, felt a need to help them but they were all going in the opposite direction.

On a street corner a woman sat with three small children amid a pile of bundles. She was crying.

Jessica had a sudden mental image of Bridget and went down on one knee beside the woman. 'May I be of help?'

The woman looked at her, surprised. There were few people willing to help: all were too engrossed in saving their own possessions. 'That's very kind.' She wiped her dirt-smudged face with a tired hand. 'Three times,' she said. 'Three times I've moved my possessions to the homes of friends. And each time the fire has overtaken us. Now we must move again.'

'How dreadful,' said Jessica. 'Where must you go?'

'I've a sister in the village of Chelsea.'

'That's a very long walk.'

'I know. But I've got to get the children out of the path of the fire.' She used the same hand to drag back the hair which had fallen into her eyes. It was a slim, well-cared-for hand. 'This time I must get them far away.'

'I'd like to help.' Jessica was going in the opposite direction.

'Since my husband died . . .'

'Look,' she said, 'I've a room in Long Acre. Take the children there and rest. Stay as long as you like until you feel fit enough for the walk to Chelsea.'

The woman turned her face towards her. It bore the unmistakable look of refinement. 'That's most kind,' she breathed. 'But why would you do this for a stranger?'

'I don't know,' said Jessica. 'When I saw you with the children it reminded me of a friend.' She touched the boy on the head. 'And a little boy named Ben.'

'My name's John,' he said.

'Hello, John.'

The woman had taken new heart. She got up and began redistributing the bundles amongst the children. 'Are you quite sure?'

'I'm on my way to help some people I know,' said Jessica. 'Rest in the room for as long as you need. There's food there to give to the children.'

'May God bless you.' She took both Jessica's hands in her own and kissed her. 'I shall never forget your kindness.'

'You're welcome. It eases my conscience a little.'

Jessica remembered the woman she had left lying in the doorway, dying of the plague. She gave instructions for locating the room and they parted company.

'Take care,' the woman called. 'You're going towards the path of the fire.'

'I shall be all right. Safe journey to Chelsea.'

She continued up Fetter Lane into Holborn, over the Fleet River. The site of the fire was to her right. Parts of Shoe Lane were burning and she realized, with dismay, that the Salisbury Court Theatre must have gone. Old Bailey, too, was in flames but the most awesome sight of all was St Paul's. Above the roof tops the great building towered over all others, sending huge tongues of orange roaring into the smoke-filled sky. The sight of it made her catch her breath and she stood watching as sections of the vaulted roof collapsed with explosions of noise into the blazing interior.

She thought of all the soothsayers who had been giving warnings concerning the significance of the number 666. In this year of 1666, could it really be the end of the world?

At Aldersgate, she had to turn further north. The swathe of the fire was even wider at this point. She went up along London Wall until she reached Bishopsgate and was able at last to go a little southerly, down towards her destination beyond Gresham College.

The street was still intact but flames could be seen in the distance above the rooftops. She knocked at the door, not realizing until this moment the nervous tension she had endured. Her hand was shaking.

'Good heavens, my dear.' Mrs Hardwick took hold of her and brought her inside. 'What on earth could have brought you here? Come on in and I'll get you something.'

'Thank you, Mrs Hardwick.'

The area inside the door was piled high with furniture and boxes.

'Excuse the confusion, dear. As you'll see, we're getting prepared.'

'I came to help.'

'Why, Mrs Daniels!' Simon almost ran down the stairs. He sounded angry but she recognized it as concern. 'You've no right to be here. Didn't I tell you to remain where it was safe?'

'I came to help.'

'To help?' he exploded. 'What help will you be when you're overcome by the fire?'

She stammered a reply but Mrs Hardwick put in: 'It was very good of her, Mr Ashwell, sir. I'm sure she meant well.'

He overcame his shock and apologized. 'I'm sorry,' he said. 'Of course it's very good of you but you've put yourself in danger.'

'No more than you.'

'It's rather different . . . ' he began but decided not to go on with it.

'What can I do?'

'I'll get you some refreshment,' said Mrs Hardwick.

'No, I came to help. Please tell me what I must do.'

Simon looked at her and sighed. 'We're bringing down everything which can be carried,' he said. 'I've a wagon outside. It won't take everything but we'll pile in as much as it will carry.'

'Do we load it now?'

'No,' he said. 'With God's grace the fire might be halted before it reaches us. We must pray that it won't be necessary.'

'I saw the fire above the roof tops. It's not far away.'

'I know. But they're pulling down houses to halt the spread. The trouble is that the flames keep vaulting the firebreak.'

Suddenly, there was a great explosion somewhere in the distance.

'God's blood ! What on earth was that?' Simon rushed out into the street.

'They're using gunpowder!' someone shouted. 'Down near the Tower. They're blowing up the houses.'

'At least that should clear a path.'

They worked all day. The anti-climax came when there was nothing left to do. They sat amid the piled-up possessions waiting for the time when they would be forced to load them into the wagon and abandon the house.

'This is the third day,' said Jessica. 'When will this fire ever end?'

'I don't know. There are all sorts of rumours abounding. Some say it's a plot by the French; others say it's the Dutch.'

'And is it?'

'Who knows? But there are fresh fires breaking out everywhere.'

'Perhaps it's the end of the world.'

'No,' he smiled gently. 'It's not the end of the world.'

He reached out to brush a cobweb from her hair. It seemed a most intimate gesture. They both blushed.

'It was good of you to come,' he said to hide his confusion.

'I felt helpless, knowing Mrs Hardwick was in danger.'

'I'm glad you came.'

She studiously examined her fingertips, uncomfortable under his scrutiny.

'And may I ask if you've come to any decision?'

'About what?'

'About my proposal.'

'No,' she stammered. 'I can't. I've really not given it a lot of thought.'

'I'd hoped you would.'

'I'm an actoress,' she said firmly, considering it sufficient to terminate the subject. 'There's no way I can marry you.'

It was his turn to study his hands. The disappointment showed on his face. 'Then you will, at least, come with me to Oakbourne?'

'I can't.'

'Please,' he said. 'It would mean so much to her.'

'I doubt that very much.'

'Can't you take my word?'

'No,' she said. 'You don't understand.'

'I understand far more than you realize,' he said. 'I understand how two people can love one another and neither wants to be the first to speak.'

'I don't love her.'

'I can't believe that.' He reached out and took her hand. 'When this is over, we'll take the coach and travel down there together.'

She made to protest but he reached out a finger and touched her lips. 'Please,' he said, 'if you won't do it for Lady Mainwaring, and you won't do it for yourself, then will you please do it for me?'

She hesitated.

'If you have the smallest feeling for me, I'm asking you to do this for me.'

'I . . .' she floundered. 'That's most unfair. You've been kind to me. I'm obligated . . . '

'Not obligated,' he said. 'Let's just say that it would please me enormously.'

She glanced sideways at him. 'You drive a hard bargain,' she said. 'I don't sit comfortably taking orders from men.'

He smiled at that. 'Perhaps,' he said, 'I might be making a little progress.'

'I'll think about it,' she said. 'I'll do no more than think about it.'

He smiled again. 'I suppose I must be content with that.'

They sat up all night. Mrs Hardwick made a pot of broth with the few remaining provisions and they sat eating it, perched on stools which they had retrieved from the piles stacked in the yard. No one knew what to say. Each half-hour they went outside to survey the progress of the fire. There was no darkness that night, the approaching flames acting as a giant smoke-laden nightlight.

At last, at three o'clock they abandoned hope and loaded the wagon, piling in everything they could but leaving much scattered upon the ground. Mrs Hardwick was weeping. Neighbours on all sides were taking like action and the night was filled with shouting and activity.

When the last possible item was placed upon the wagon Simon set the horse moving and the vehicle creaked away with the two women following behind on foot. There was no room for them to ride.

They went out to Clerkenwell where Mrs Hardwick had a cousin who would take her in.

'I'll come to see you in a week or two,' said Simon. 'We'll talk about your future.'

'Thank you, Mr Ashwell, sir.' She was weeping again. 'Between you and Sir Rupert, no woman ever had finer benefactors.'

'I'm grateful, Mrs Hardwick, for your care. Rest now, and when this is all over you'll look after me again.'

It took a further time for Simon and Jessica to make the journey to her room in Long Acre. It was Wednesday morning, the fourth day of the fire.

The woman and her children had gone but a lace handkerchief had been left as a clear mark of thanks.

Simon saw Jessica to the door. 'I feel,' he said, 'that perhaps we know each other a little better than we did before.'

She smiled. 'It's not the way I'd choose to learn more about my friends.'

'It's been quite a day.'

'And night. It's already mid-morning.'

'And tomorrow's Thursday. The coach departs at ten.'

She looked away.

'Take a rest,' he said gently. 'I'll call for you tomorrow in good time for us both to be on it.'

That same day the fire was at last halted. But by that time Fenchurch Street and Gracechurch Street were gone; Cornhill and Threadneedle Street lay in ruins; the Royal Exchange was a smouldering heap, its pillars and statues buried beneath charred debris. The Poultry, Cheapside, Paternoster Row, all burned up as far as the Holborn conduit. The Fleet River had done nothing to halt the blaze; the fire had leapt it and swept on as far as the Temple, just short of Chancery Lane. Downriver, the Tower stood sentinel at the charred edge, standing firm and erect overlooking the desolation.

In all, nearly four hundred acres lay in ruin, together with more than thirteen thousand homes and eighty-seven parish churches.

The fire had stopped a mere few streets beyond Mrs Hardwick's house. Just another two hundred yards and it would have been saved.

For several more days isolated fires broke out but the main blaze had been extinguished. All that remained were thousands of men, women and children without a home, camping out on the outskirts, waiting for the ashes to cool in order that they might troop back and attempt to find their few charred sticks.

CHAPTER 21

On Thursday morning Simon called for Jessica and they took the coach as far as Stow-on-the-Wold where he hired horses on which to ride to Dunscombe.

As they approached the village Jessica felt her stomach tighten. It seemed strange, returning to familiar places. Nothing had changed — except herself. They rode down the village street, through the wood, and out towards Oakbourne House.

There were workers in the fields who raised their hands as they passed. She thought they were saluting Simon until someone called out: 'Welcome home, Miss Jessica. 'Tis good to see you.' It gave her a warm feeling which she had not expected.

The door of the house was open and Simon ushered her through. The servants were there — most with familiar faces. She was greeted with warmth.

'I've your old room ready, Miss Jessica. It's good to have you home.'

'Thank you, Jane. You're looking well.'

'Married now, Miss. And a little one on the way.'

She realized again that it was seven years since she had left home.

An older woman whom she did not recognize came forward.

'How is she, Mrs Leach?'

'She's well, sir, in her way.'

Jessica understood, with a shock, that the woman had replaced her mother. Margaret would never have employed

485

the services of a housekeeper. It did more to emphasize the seriousness of her condition than all Simon's warnings.

'I'll take you to her,' the housekeeper said to Jessica. 'She'll be waiting in her room.'

'It's all right, Mrs Leach. I'll take her up.'

Simon led her up the wide oak staircase to a room in the south wing overlooking the garden. It was large, and filled with sunlight. Margaret was seated in the window, a book in her lap, gazing out towards the distant hills. She turned her head as they entered. It was obvious from the look in her eyes that she could not see.

'Her sight's failing,' he whispered. 'You'll have to go nearer.'

It occurred to Jessica that her mother could not see the distant hills towards which she had been gazing.

'Hello, Mother.'

She was shocked by the change in her. She was older — but it was more than that. There was a slackening of the muscle tone throughout her entire body and Jessica could see, as her mother moved, that she did not have complete control over her legs. Her hair was grey, and because of failing sight there was a blankness and lack of expression about her face.

'You've come home,' Margaret said flatly.

'Yes, Mother, I'm home.'

They faced one another, a few feet apart — each wanting to reach out a hand towards the other but neither able to do so, each believing that the other did not want it.

'You're looking well, Mother,' lied Jessica.

'I can't see you. The light in here is very poor.'

She took another step forward, but still not close enough to touch.

'You're wearing green,' said Margaret. 'It suits you.'

'Thank you, Mother.'

'Have you come to stay?'

'No, just to visit.'

'Oh, I see.'

'I must get back to London, ready for when the theatre re-opens.'

486

Despite the flaccid nature of Margaret's jaw, it tightened visibly. 'You're still on the stage?'

'Yes, Mother, I am.'

'Then you'll be wanting to get away.' She turned back to gaze out of the window as though she had lost interest.

A few moments elapsed. Jessica felt uncomfortable. 'The garden's looking well,' she said, attempting to make conversation. 'And the fields are in good order.'

Margaret did not respond.

Abigail stood up from her seat beside the fireplace. 'Hello, Jessica.'

She had been aware of her sister's presence but her mind had been centred upon her mother. 'Hello, Abigail, you've grown.'

'I'm seventeen.'

'You're quite grown up.'

'It's good to have you home.'

'Thank you.'

There was another awkward silence.

'You're very beautiful,' said Abigail. 'And your clothes . . . they're so grand.'

It occurred to Jessica that her clothes must appear fashionable compared to those worn in Dunscombe. And it amused her to think that, despite her struggle to survive financially, she could still be considered grand. She decided to give Abigail something of her choosing before she returned to London.

'You'll be thinking of marriage,' Jessica said. 'Are you betrothed?'

'No.' She hesitated. 'I must stay with Mama.'

'Oh, I see.'

'Abigail is your mother's constant companion,' put in Simon. 'I don't know what we would have done without her.'

Margaret appeared to regain interest. 'Why are you standing here, child?' she directed at Abigail. 'There must be work that you can do.'

'It's all right, Mama. I'll stay here with you.'

'There's no point in standing idle when there's work to be done.'

'I'll help you to bed shortly: it's almost time to rest.'

'I'm quite capable of getting myself to bed,' said Margaret tetchily. 'I'll call you if I'm in need.'

'Yes, Mama.'

'And, anyway,' she continued, 'I shan't be resting today. I'm not tired. I may go down and supervise the kitchen.'

It seemed unlikely to Jessica that she would be able to make the stairs. As if to confirm the thought, Margaret chose this moment to rise from her seat beside the window and, in doing so, stumbled, her legs giving way beneath her. Both Simon and Abigail rushed forward to assist her.

Margaret shrugged them off as soon as she was seated again. 'The wood of these floors is becoming very slippery,' she said. 'I must get it attended to.'

'Yes, Mama.'

She turned again to gaze out of the window.

'Is there anything I can get for you, Mama?'

Margaret appeared to have dismissed them all. The three stood uncomfortably, none of them knowing what to say to the other.

'You're tired from your journey,' Simon said at last. 'I'll get Mrs Leach to take you to your room.'

Jessica looked at her mother, wanting to reach out and touch her. Margaret had her back towards her. She hovered, uncertain, then turned and walked out of the room.

Margaret continued to sit and gaze out across the distant hills. It did not matter that she could not see them: she thought that she could. Life had gradually become more comfortable over this past year. The physical infirmities were a nuisance but the edges of emotional pain had become blurred.

She sat now and thought of Jessica. She wondered why she had come. Whatever had caused her to make the journey back from London, it would not keep her here. But it did not matter any more.

Abigail got up from her seat beside the fireplace. She picked up the book which had fallen from Margaret's lap and replaced it, without words, gently touching her mother's hand before she moved away.

Margaret looked up at her and smiled. She was so like Richard. She could not see to read the book but she always

488

held it there upon her lap, the pages open. 'Thank you,' she said. 'I may read a little later on.'

The deterioration in her eyes had been slow. She had been impatient at first because she could not see the eye of a needle, then later because she could not see the thread. Now she could barely see the cloth, except for its colour.

She had a moment of fear. Where would it all lead? But her father was calling: 'Margaret, we're late with the cloth.' Matthew Crawshaw would have the pack ponies ready at the gate. She jumped to her feet and ran downstairs to take the cloth to the fulling mill.

Jessica had intended to remain for only a few days in Dunscombe. Instead, she found herself making excuses to delay her return. She was surprised to discover how different it all seemed now that she was no longer tied to it, nor oppressed into subservience.

She spent time with Simon, conversing with him concerning the theatre. They argued over their differences of opinion and laughed at their ability to do so.

He took her to the library where he showed her bound volumes of plays – *Macbeth*, *Henry V*, *The Scornful Lady*, Ben Jonson's *Cateline*, the opera *The Siege of Rhodes*. She took each from the shelves and saw that they were well read.

'I've been acquiring them for some time,' he said. 'It's an interest of mine.'

She went often to sit with her mother, but she was disheartened by Margaret's apparent lack of response. The void between them had grown wider, rather than closing.

It distressed her to see her mother staring for hours out of the window. She tried to distract her attention by talking to her, raising her voice when Margaret appeared to ignore her. She wondered if she were growing deaf as well as blind.

But Margaret would turn and say: 'Aren't you gone yet?'

'I'm here for a few more days yet, Mother.'

'Why haven't you returned to London? It's where you want to be.'

Then she would return to staring out of the window. Jessica would squeeze back the tears. It was obvious that her mother did not want her here.

Margaret would look out towards the hills, acutely aware

of Jessica still sitting just a few feet away, listening to the rustling of her dress and to the sound of her breathing. She wondered why she continued to stay when it was so obvious that she had no real desire to be home.

Eventually Jessica would get up and leave the room. Margaret would let go her breath, feeling the release of tension, yet wanting to cry.

Abigail would come quietly to place an arm about her mother's shoulders and Margaret would reach up and squeeze her hand, thinking it to be Richard.

Jessica had been at Oakbourne for a little over a week when Simon asked her again to be his bride.

'I can't,' she said, but this time the tone of her voice was different to the previous occasions on which she had refused.

'You seem happy here.'

'I am.' She looked about her. 'It's strange, I'd never have believed that it could be so, but it feels different now.'

'Then marry me, and stay here as my wife.'

'I can't,' she said. 'It wouldn't be right.'

'It would be more than right.'

She shook her head. 'I'd cause you to become a laughing stock throughout London and the whole of Gloucestershire.'

'I've already told you that I care nothing for the sneers of society.'

She smiled at him. 'That's what you say now. In time, you'd feel differently.'

'I doubt it.'

'At first you'd say you didn't care; then it would all get too much to cope with. Eventually you'd ask me to leave the stage. And I'd refuse.'

'Why can't you trust me?'

'Gentlemen have mistresses upon the stage,' she insisted. 'Not wives.'

'So you've said before.'

'And you know it's true.'

'I'll grant our case is unusual, but we could find some way of dealing with the sneers of society.' He took her hand. 'And what do we care about such people? They don't matter to us, anyway.'

490

'They would. In time, they would. It would matter that you were not made welcome to sit at your neighbour's table.'

'Then I'd sit at my own and gaze at my wife.'

She smiled at that. 'Why can't you take the matter seriously?'

'I can. Seriously enough to know that I can't live without you.'

She shook her head. 'You'll have to, Simon. I can't agree to something which is so obviously filled with enormous difficulties for you.'

'These past days . . .' he said. 'These days we've spent together here at Oakbourne have only made me more certain of the way I feel. I love you, Jessica. I want you to be my wife.'

'I'd be nothing but trouble to you.'

He threw back his head and laughed. 'Of that, I've no doubt.' But then he smiled at her with deep tenderness. 'But you'd also be a great joy to my heart.'

She turned away from him and went to examine the last of the summer roses still blooming in her mother's garden.

'Could you really put up with me?'

He came and stood behind her, his hands on her shoulders. 'Yes, my dearest girl.'

A light breeze wafted the scent of the roses.

'You've never once asked me to return your love.'

He turned her round to face him. 'Give it time,' he said tenderly. 'I think in time you could surprise yourself.'

'I think I'm afraid to.'

'I know,' he said, and took her in his arms.

In the cool of the evening Jessica went into Margaret's room. 'Mother?'

Margaret looked up from her seat beside the window. 'You're feeling well?'

'I'm well. Why should I not be?'

'I just wondered . . .'

'I'm perfectly well. I must be getting up. I need to go downstairs.' She began to move her feet, preparatory to making some effort to rise.

Jessica went hurriedly to sit near her in the hope that she would settle. 'Mother?'

491

'Yes?' Margaret looked at her though she could see nothing but the deep saffron colour of her dress.

'I'm going to marry Simon.'

'Oh?' For the first time she appeared to take a real interest.

'He asked me again and I said yes.'

'Asked you what?'

'Asked me to marry him.'

'Oh, yes, how silly of me. You must forgive me.'

Jessica sat and looked at her, not sure what to say next.

'Does that mean you'll stay?'

'No, Mother, I must get back to the theatre.'

'Oh.' She turned away.

'But I shall come often. I'll come back during the times when I'm not needed at the theatre.'

Margaret appeared to ignore her.

'You realize, Mother, that Oakbourne will belong to me. Sir Rupert . . .'

Margaret turned. 'Where is Rupert?' She searched her mind. She could not remember having seen him for some time.

'Sir Rupert's dead, Mother. He died last year.'

'Oh, yes.'

Almost immediately she became agitated.

'What's the matter, Mother?'

'Oakbourne,' she said. 'Who's to run Oakbourne?'

'Simon is.'

Margaret was looking about her, making abrupt twitching movements and picking at the tips of her fingers.

'Is anything wrong?'

'I thought that Simon . . . ' She was struggling in the depths of her mind, struggling to remember. She grasped at strands, piecing them together, but they were too fragmentary. Rupert was dead. Had there been a will?

'Can I get you something, Mother?' Jessica reached out and took her hand. It was the first time she had touched her.

'Child?' The response was immediate.

'There's something wrong, Mother?'

'No, child. I just sometimes get confused.'

Jessica did not release the hand but moved a little closer and sat holding it.

'I'm becoming very foolish in my old age.'

'No, Mother, you're merely sick.'

'I forget things, you know.'

'Don't worry about it, Mother. Everything's going to be all right.'

They sat for a long time without speaking, Jessica holding her hand.

'So you're going to marry Simon,' she said at last.

'Yes, Mother.'

'I'm glad.'

'I only hope that I'm doing the right thing.'

'Right thing, child? What is it that you're going to do?'

'Marry Simon, Mother.'

'He's a good man, you know. I love him as my own son.'

'He loves you, too.'

'Jessica?'

'Yes, Mother?'

'Why did you leave?'

It took her by surprise. She sucked in her breath. 'The tinker . . .' she said after a long pause.

'We looked for her, you know. We looked everywhere for her but she was never found.'

'The tinker, Mother. He took me away.'

'We never found her.'

'I'm here, Mother.'

'Oh, yes, child. Of course you are. Why didn't you come back?'

Jessica bit on her lip, chewing it until it became painful, fighting back tears which threatened to escape.

'Did he hurt you, child?'

Jessica hung her head, unable to speak.

'Did he prevent you from coming home?'

'At first,' she got out. 'At first he did.'

'We searched, you know. The tinker had her.'

'After what he did . . .' She stopped and fought the tears. 'I knew I couldn't come home after what he did.'

Margaret turned and looked at her with the greatest compassion that Jessica could imagine. 'Oh, child, if only you knew.'

'Knew what, Mother?'

'How much I understand.'

493

'You couldn't understand, Mother. You've no idea . . . until it happens.'

'I can imagine,' said her mother. 'I can well imagine how it feels.'

'He forced himself upon me, Mother, and I felt ashamed.'

'I know, child, I know how it feels.'

'How could you?' she began but it sounded like impudence.

Margaret went off again into her own thoughts. 'We looked for her, you know. William first, then Tobias, but she'd gone without trace.'

'I'm here now, Mother. It doesn't matter any more.'

'Later,' said Margaret suddenly, 'when you were upon the stage, and Rupert found you — you didn't come home.'

It was difficult for Jessica to keep track of the conversation. 'No, Mother.' She looked at the woman sitting beside her, pitiable in her infirmity. How could she speak of bitterness and of hatred, of Deliverance Daniels and of Richard Fullwood?

'Didn't you want to come home?'

'Do you remember Papa?'

'He's dead, you know. I believe it was the plague.'

'No. Papa in New England.'

It was many years since Margaret had thought of Deliverance Daniels.

'He was a good man, Mother.'

Margaret began to wander confusedly through old wounds long left undisturbed.

'Sir Rupert . . . ' Jessica left her for a while then began again. 'Sir Rupert said harsh things about him. They weren't true.'

Margaret forced her way back to the present. 'You remember him, child?'

'Yes, Mother, I remember him well.'

'And you've fond memories of him?'

'Yes, Mother. He was a good man.'

Margaret had sufficient command of her mind to know that she had no wish to spoil the delusion. 'He lived his life according to the Scriptures.'

'And he was a good father to me.'

'Yes,' she lied. 'He was a good man.'

'Then why . . . ?' But she could not go on. She looked at her mother sitting beside her. She knew that she was about to hurt her by raising the subject of Richard Fullwood, and there no longer seemed much point.

It was the longest conversation Margaret had held for a long time. It was visibly tiring her.

'I love you, Mother.'

'Do you, child?' Margaret turned and smiled at her. 'I love you, too.'

'I'm sorry I caused you pain.'

'My dear child, I'm a proud and foolish woman.'

'I should have come home.'

Margaret used what little strength she had to increase the pressure of her hand. 'You're home now, child, and that's all that matters.'

Jessica placed a cushion behind her head and settled her more comfortably in the window seat. 'Just sleep, Mother.' Jessica kissed her lightly upon the cheek. 'I'll come back later when you're rested.'

She met Abigail outside the door.

'I'm just going in to check on Mother.'

'She's sleeping,' said Jessica. 'I've just settled her into her seat.'

'I'd better just go and see if she's all right.'

'There's no need. She's gone to sleep.'

The two girls stood facing one another.

'Abigail, can we be friends?'

'I thought we were.'

'I know, but . . . friends.'

'Of course. I'm glad you're here. You're going to marry Simon.'

'I'll be here at Oakbourne a good deal more often.'

'Yes. It'll be nice to have you home.'

Jessica wondered why Abigail always made her feel so uncomfortable. 'It will free you,' she said. 'To make a marriage of your own.'

'Oh.' Her sister looked surprised. 'I thank you, but I must stay here with Mama.'

'There's no need. She'll be well cared for.'

'Thank you, but I'd rather stay.'

Abigail opened the door and went inside. Jessica walked

495

away down the corridor. She wished that her mother could love her as she loved her sister.

The marriage took place in the parish church of Dunscombe. Margaret sat at her window and listened to the bells. Then her father came and told her that he was taking her to marry Richard.

As Jessica stood and took her vows she could see, upon the wall of the church, a tablet which had been placed there in memorial to her father. Simon had brought him home to be buried in the centre aisle.

Near this stone lieth the mortal remains
of Sir Rupert Mainwaring

Jessica had the strangest feeling that he was seated in the congregation, smiling. She had done as he had required of her.

Her Uncle Tobias was there with Aunt Lucy and their family, as were her Aunts Sarah and Rachael with their children, and young Uncle William, more like a brother than an uncle. But not Abigail: she was at home, sitting with their mother.

Simon took Jessica by the hand and led her out into the autumn sunshine.

'You've made me the happiest man in the whole of England.'

She smiled uncertainly. 'I'll try,' she said, 'but there'll be difficult times ahead.'

Margaret lived for another year. She cared little about the pain but sat at her window and slipped slowly, inexorably, towards her death. It was only in the very last days that they removed her from the window seat and confined her to her bed.

But it did not matter: her mind was free. At her very last breath, she was seen to smile.

They took her and laid her in the centre aisle, beside Rupert. No one thought to take her across the hills to the churchyard in which lay her parents, with Samuel and the children.

Jessica instructed the stonemason to add an inscription to Rupert's stone.

. . . and his beloved wife, Margaret. Born 1624. Departed this life 17 October 1667

The apples had all been gathered in. The wine had been made.

Jessica stood with Simon before the stone.

'She was a wonderful woman,' he said. 'We shall miss her greatly.'

Jessica used one fingertip to wipe away the tear which trickled from her eye. 'Yes,' she said. 'I only wish that I had understood her more.'

GLOSSARY OF NATIVE AMERICAN NAMES

Mawnauoi	(mau.NOW.oy)	'Very Strong'
Gettonahenan	(get.to.NAH.he.nan)	'Great Turkey'
Sasketupe	(SAS.ke.toop)	'Great Man'
Niccone	(Nik.KONE)	'Blackbird'
Ketottug	(ke.TOT.tug)	'Whetstone'
Seaseap	(SEE.seep)	'Duck'
Pausochu	(POW.so.chu)	'Little Journey'
Bequoquowes	(be.QUO.quo.wees)	'Little Head'